Rick was used  e.
"Explain."

The Robo-scie_____ ne
monitor with a _____ It
has vanished, admiral—the Protoculture.
Disappeared."

Rick's dark brows beetled. He reached out to
reactivate the screen but Lang's powerful
hand restrained him.

"Take my word for it, admiral, the Protoculture
has vanished." It would have been senseless to
talk about the shadowy presence of the black-
robed wraiths Rem had taught him to
recognize. "Yes, exactly as it disappeared from
the SDF-1," he added, discerning Rick's
thoughts.

"But how?" Rick began. "Why—"

"To teach us a lesson, I think."

Rick shook his head. "A lesson?" He swept his
arm through an all-encompassing gesture.
"Listen to me, Lang. Reinhardt and the rest of
the fleet are out there waiting for us. Do you
understand what that means?"

The scientist gave him a pitying look. "I assure
you, Admiral, the fleet is not out *there*."

"Then where the hell are we?" Rick said, at the
end of his rope. "And don't tell me 'no where'."

Lang folded his arms and met the intensity of
Rick's gaze. "All right. It's possible that we're
still in hyperspace, although there is no
evidence to support the hypothesis. Or that
we have somehow jumped to a void in
intergalactic space—perhaps jumped beyond
the expansion wave of the Big Bang itself."

Rick went wide-eyed. "You mean we've jumped
outside the galaxy?!"

Published by Ballantine Books:

THE ROBOTECH™ SERIES

THE SENTINELS™ SERIES

ROBOTECH™:
THE END OF THE CIRCLE

Jack McKinney

A Del Rey Book
BALLANTINE BOOKS • NEW YORK

FOR RISA KESSLER—AGAIN
—AT THE END OF THE
CIRCLE.

A Del Rey Book
Published by Ballantine Books

Library of Congress Catalog Card Number: 89-91799

ISBN 0-345-36311-6

Manufactured in the United States of America

First Edition: January 1990

FOREWORD

The publication of *The End of the Circle*, the eighteenth book of the series, concludes the Robotech saga. The story now spans five decades, from 1990 to 2040 or thereabouts, save for a period of "lost years," covering the rise of Monument City and the Army of the Southern Cross, an account of which may yet see the light of day. Some of this material is in fact already being covered by other sources.

With nearly one million words of print in the Ballantine/Del Rey series alone, eighty-five episodes of powerful animation, an equal number of comic book adaptations, numerous art and role-playing books, and supplemental source material—including several college theses—it should be clear that Robotech has traveled a great distance since "HAL," Haruhiko Mikimoto, sat down at his desk one day and inked the first sketch of raven-haired songbird, Lynn-Minmei.

As most readers of Robotech are aware, the eighty-five "continuous" animated episodes (which still show up in U.S. television markets) were actually a complete reworking—in terms of music, dialogue, and storylines—of three separate *anime* series that appeared in Japan over the course of several years: *Macross*, *Southern Cross*, and *Mospeda*. Credit for this unique accomplishment goes to Carl Macek, as well as Harmony Gold U.S.A. Inc. Together with a talented team of writers, voice-over artists, and production personnel, Robotech Master Macek found an overall grand visual theme in the Japanese series and redefined both Robotechnology and Protoculture.

It is a source of continuing disappointment that the project, as envisioned by Mr. Macek, was never brought to completion. The result would have been an additional sixty-five episodes of animation detailing the exploits of the *Sentinels*, and who knows how many more devoted to the material covered in this final book, presented here for the first time.

But perhaps Robotech's most important contributors have been the fans themselves, who have kept this project vital for five years running. More than seventy thousand strong have been aided and abetted in their efforts by the following, to whom the author wishes to express his heartfelt gratitude: Comico Comics, especially Markalan Joplin, who died shortly before completion of the illustrated series; Eternity Comics, which has inherited the mantle and is currently publishing twice-monthly issues of the *Sentinels*; Kevin Siembieda and the staff at Palladium Books for their role-playing games; Kay Reynolds and Ardith Carlton, creators of the Starblaze Robotech Art Books; Kevin Seymour of Books Nippan; and a special thanks to Claude Pelletier, Michel Gareau, Alain Dubreuil, and the staff at *Protoculture Addicts*, the official Robotech fanzine.

We should all do it again sometime.

PART I
WHEEL
IN SPACE

CHAPTER
ONE

"Beware the skies, for the cerulean raiments of that sweet-scented realm mask a darkness and evil that know no bounds. And do not look to heaven for peace, for there resides hell. And beware all who descend from those skies, for they are the harbingers of death and destruction."

Dogma of the Church of Recurrent Tragedy
as quoted in Weverka T'su's
*Aftermath: Geopolitical and Religious
Movements in the Southlands*

THE STARSHIP *ARK ANGEL* HUNG IN GEOSYNCH, 36,000 kilometers above Brazilas in the Southlands. Recently returned from a distant campaign, it alone had been spared the wrath of the Invid's transubstantiating departure, one ship among scores in that moment of victorious defeat.

Scott Bernard had yet to decide whether its survival constituted a curse or a blessing.

He could just make out the warship's underbelly through a small oblong viewport set high up in the curved hull of the chemical shuttle's passenger cabin. A soft-soled boot, free-floating, drew his attention forward, and he watched it for a moment, thinking: *Weightless.* Hugged to the padded contours of an acceleration couch by web belts and Velcro straps, as if on some nostalgia-steeped theme park ride.

Although *restrained* might have been a better word to describe his present circumstance, as in temporarily prevented from doing harm to himself or others. Not that he would. But there were half a dozen G2 analysts planetside who thought differently.

Scott sniggered aloud, unperturbed by the curious glances his self-amusement had elicited. He returned the looks with interest until one by one each of his fellow passengers in the cramped cabinspace turned away.

Oh, he had it, all right: what Rand had once called *the look of the lost*.

Scott inclined his head to one side to get a better angle on the ship, her dark symmetry obscuring a narrow sweep of stars. Built and christened on the other side of the Quadrant, she was the very ship Colonel Wolff had pirated from Tirol orbit years before. The ship that had become the Sentinels' own.

Running lights illuminated an array of weapons and sensor ports dimpling her underside—retrofitted sometime during the three years since Scott had last seen her—along with a swath of heavily blistered alloy, where angry tendrils loosed from the Invid's mindstuff phoenix had brushed her just three months before. She rested alone in gravity anchor, save for the countless metal fragments that drifted above and below her: the lingering debris clouds of Dolza's fleet; of *Little Luna*, the Zentraedi factory satellite; of the hapless, goose-necked ships of Mars, Venus, and Jupiter Divisions; of the Robotech Expeditionary Force's tri-thrusters and Karbarran-manufactured boilerlike monstrosities.

Earth was in fact haloed by death and destruction. But liberated—or so it seemed.

A Tiresian-accented voice cautiously interrupted Scott's painful reverie.

"Colonel Bernard," the woman repeated as Scott turned from the view. She stood wavering in the narrow aisle, Velcroed in place, strands of auburn hair wafting out from under a pearl-gray shuttle bonnet. The smile, too, seemed fastened there, detachable with the slightest tug.

"What is it?" Scott asked, masking his thoughts.

"Sir, General Grant wishes you to be informed that he'll be on hand to meet the shuttle. Mrs. Grant and Senators Huxley and Penn are with him, sir."

Scott nodded and put on a pleasant face, certain it read as a twisted malicious grin. But the woman only broadened her smile in response and asked if there was anything he needed before docking. He told her he was fine and leaned over to watch her space-step down the aisle, a child learning to walk.

So much to relearn, he told himself. So much to forget.

The chemical shuttle itself was symbolic of the change. Launched from a twenty-five-year-old reconstructed base in Venezuela Nueva, the ferry and a handful of others like it were humankind's only existing links with near space. There was the *Angel*, of course, but she had remained in geosynch ever since the disastrous finale to the assault on Reflex Point, the Invid queen's hivelike stronghold on the North American continent. Word had it that a small portion of the REF's mecha—Alphas and Shadow fighters, principally—was still functioning, but most of the older generation Cyclones and Veritechs had simply given up the ghost.

No one knew what to make of the events that had occurred at Reflex Point. In the wake of the Invid departure all sorts of reports had reached Scott and his team of freedom fighters. The REF fleet had been destroyed; it had survived. The Invid had exited the solar system; the Regis had relocated her horde in the Southlands. The SDF-3 had been destroyed; it had manifested from fold and been swallowed up by the Invid phoenix; it had failed to appear at all . . . Eventually, Scott learned that the fleet had indeed been vaporized and that the flagship had failed to emerge from hyperspace. He had not bothered to wait around for verification. With an assist from Lunk and Rand, he had managed to commandeer and make serviceable an anni-disc-ravaged Beta, only to find that the VT was not much good outside the envelope and that the *Ark Angel* had removed herself to stationary orbit over the Southlands.

It had begun to make sense after the initial anger and disappointment had washed through him. Much of the northern hemisphere was devastated, and where else would reconstruction commence but in the south, where several cities had actually flourished during the occupation. Norristown, once the site of a Protoculture storage facility, was fast emerging as the leader of the pack, and it was there that Scott had ultimately set down. Like a fly on lacquered paper. Mired in red tape for close to two months before Provisional Command had okayed his request to be among those shuttled up to the starship.

The question he had heard most often those two months had been: "Scott who?"

It seemed that Mars and Jupiter Divisions were filed away in Command's mainframe as having gone down with all hands, and so the person claiming to be Lieutenant Scott Bernard of the 21st Squadron, Mars Division, had to be a ghost, a zone loonie, or an ambulatory case of what the neurometrics were calling Post-Engagement Synaptic Trauma— PEST, for short.

Ask Dr. Lang about Scott Bernard, he had pressed. *I'm his godson, for chrissake!*

Only to hear: "We're sorry, er, Lieutenant *Bernard*, but Doctor Lang is not available at this time."

Later, Scott would learn that his godfather and mentor had been aboard the ill-fated SDF-3 when it had jumped from Tirol. But in the meantime he suggested that Captain Harrington might be able to vouch for him. Harrington had commanded the first wave of Cyclone ground teams the REF had directed against Reflex Point.

After all, it wasn't like he was asking for medals, Scott had assured the analysts. But the least Command could do was acknowledge what he had achieved on the yearlong road to Reflex Point or applaud his one-on-one with the Invid Corg in the seasonally shifting skies above the hive cluster. Why, some of Harrington's team had even seen the Invid simulagent's flame cloud, had even seen Scott go *into the central dome*!

He was sorry he said it even before the words had left his lips.

"Now, uh, what was that you were saying about *talking* to the Regis, Lieutenant?" the boys from G2 had asked. "You did say something about her being, let me see here, 'a bald-headed column of light twenty feet high.' "

And so he had played the PEST for them, steering clear of any mention of Marlene or Sera or any of the mind-boggling time-space displacements he'd experienced inside the hive chambers.

In retrospect, he had to ask himself whether pulling out all the stops would have brought the med teams' debriefing reports to Jean Grant's attention any sooner, but they had reached her on their own momentum in any case, and Scott had finally been granted permission to come aboard.

And issued a battlefield commission to full bird, to boot.

For Scott it was something else to snigger at: a promotion, in an armed force without ships or soldiers, defenders and liberators of a world that wanted little part of them even now.

The shuttle docked in one of *Ark Angel*'s starboard bays just as Sol was flooding the eastern coast of the Southlands with morning light. Scott drank in the view that had been denied him when Mars Division had approached a year earlier: Earth's characteristic clouds and swirling weather fronts, its deep-blue water oceans and healing landscape. And for the first time in years he found himself thinking about Base Gloval, his father's forefinger thrust upward into the Martian night, pinpointing a homeworld. Huddled afterward in the prewarmed comfort of his sleep compartment, he would grapple with the notion—that faint light, a *home*. But even after his family had been transferred to the factory satellite to work on the SDF-3, Scott could not regard Earth as such. And he had so few memories of those years that he called Tirol home now and perhaps always would.

Only a week ago he had learned that his parents were still there.

The memories surrendered to more recent recollections as Scott and the rest of the shuttle's privileged boarded a transfer vehicle that ferried them into the ship proper, *Ark Angel*'s artificial gravity settling on him like oppression itself. Nearly every component of the ship was different from what he remembered, from the illumination grids that checkered the holds to the persistent foot-tingling basso of the dreadnought's internal systemry.

He soon caught sight of Vince Grant, towering walnut-brown and square-shouldered over a small gathering of civilians and military personnel bottlenecked at the arrival hold's security gate. There were hands in the air, salutes, a welter of voices that brought to mind vid-scenes of turn-of-the-century airport arrivals, and it was obvious to Scott all at once that the REF was as altered as the *Angel* herself. He sensed something cool but determined in the ship's slightly sour air, a single-mindedness at work he had not experienced since Tiresia.

A male aide appeared out of the crowd to escort him

through security, and a moment later he stood facing the Grants and the two Plenipotentiary Council senators.

"Colonel Bernard, reporting as ordered," Scott said with a crisp salute. "Permission to come aboard, sir?"

"Granted," Vince returned, working the muscles of his massive jaw into a tight-lipped smile. "Welcome home, Scott."

"Oh, Scott," Jean said, rushing forward to embrace him. "God, let me look at you."

He took a step back to allow for just that, extending a hand at the same time to Justine Huxley, then Dr. Penn. Vince and Jean were outfitted in modified REF uniforms, collarless now but with flared shoulders and simleather torso harnesses retained. The senators wore loose-fitting jumpsuits of a design that had originated on Garuda.

"Good to see you, my boy," Penn said with paternal sincerity. "I only wish Emil and Karen could be here with us."

There was no mention of Karen's lover, Jack Baker; certainly there was no love lost between Dr. Penn and Baker, in any case. Karen, like Bowie Grant, had elected to ship out aboard the SDF-3. *Let them all have better luck than Marlene and I had,* Scott thought. *Even if that means dying together.*

The scientist's words had thrown a curtain of silence around the five of them, a spot of stasis amid the bustling activity in the hold. "Is there any word?" Scott asked, hoping to break the spell.

Jean shook her head, her dark honey complexion paled by the exchange. Her hair was pulled back into a tight chignon, imparting a touch of severity to what was normally the warmest of faces. "We've received some garbled subtrans from Tirol. The ship folded soon after Rheinhardt and the others were away. There's been no word from the SDF-3 since."

"I think we should have this discussion elsewhere," Vince said with a hint of suggestion in his voice. "We all have a lot of catching up to do."

"Colonel," Huxley said before everyone set off, "I do want to apologize for this somewhat subdued welcome." She gestured around the hold with a quivering, aged hand. "As you can well imagine, we've all been trying to adjust to the loss of our friends and compatriots."

Scott could see that she was referring to the destruction of the fleet rather than the presumed loss of the SDF-3. "I understand, Senator," he told her. "No need for apologies."

"Besides, Colonel," Huxley continued after a deep breath, "what with the Council trying to set up summits with our planetside counterparts and Jean's medical teams doing what they can . . . Well, I'm certain you do understand, Colonel Bernard."

Scott did not envy either group but thought it might be particularly rough going for the Council itself. To the last they had been respected members of the United Earth Government. But that was before the ascendancy of the Army of the Southern Cross, the arrival of the Robotech Masters and the Invid, and the factionalism and isolationism that had thrived during the occupation. Those would-be leaders below barely trusted their neighbors, let alone a council of lawmakers and theoreticians absent for fifteen years. Scott was not sure whether Huxley, Penn, and the rest had grasped the fact that Earth was a changed world.

Scott found Vince Grant studying him when he looked up.

"I know the promotion might not seem like much, Scott, but we haven't gotten around to honoring individual effort just yet."

Scott was taken aback. "Excuse me, sir, but if you're talking about medals or citations—"

"You've certainly earned them, Scott," Jean said hurriedly, glancing up at Vince before showing Scott an uncomfortable look. "We just want you to know—"

Scott held up his hands to stop her from saying anything further. It was a sham, and everyone knew it—or at least they should have. There were no heroes this go-round, Scott said to himself, as he had so often the past three months. No matter who had done what at Reflex Point or anywhere on either side of the envelope.

There were only *survivors*.

CHAPTER
TWO

There isn't a man or woman aboard the [Ark Angel] that wasn't thinking about the SDF-1 when Dr. Penn announced our intention to make a trial jump to the moon. But do we have a choice? Doesn't it make more sense to strand the ship a safe distance from Earth rather than strand her in Martian orbit as some have suggested out of sheer superstitious fear of repeated misfortune? All this, of course, presupposes that the fold generators will fail, which I am inclined to believe will not be the case. As for our inadvertently ending up near Pluto or some such celestial locale, I can only pray that doesn't occur. Should it, however, I might as well state now that I have always regretted missing the jump that landed Claudia and the rest at the frozen edge of our home system. Perhaps I'm bound by destiny to follow her now.

> General Vincent Grant, ship's log of the *Ark Angel*

See you on the dark side of the moon.

> Late twentieth-century song lyric

JEAN GRANT PURPOSELY FELL OUT OF STEP WITH VINCE and the two senators so that she might observe Scott without setting him off as she had almost done in the arrival hold. Her sentiments had been sincere if awkwardly expressed. She was not unaware of the meaninglessness of promotions and medals at this stage of things—she had always held that battles were better forgotten than immortalized by ribbons, in any case—but gestures were important for morale, even of the salute and handshake variety favored by armies the Quadrant over. And God knew morale was in short supply just now.

She took note of the slight limp in Scott's long-legged stride as Vince led everyone to his personal quarters aft of the *Ark Angel*'s bridge. Up close, when she had felt Scott stiffen in her short-lived embrace, she had seen the scars on his still youthful face and graceful hands. Nineteen now—or twenty-six in Earth-relative years (a system she readily dismissed because of the havoc it wreaked on her own age)—he was growing to resemble his father more and more. But from beneath the broad forehead and slick black hair peered the dreamy eyes of his mother. He had her prominent ears as well, but the limp and the stoop in his formerly erect carriage were gifts of a war that refused to go away.

REF staffers and administrative officers stared openly as they hurried through the ship's corridors, trying no doubt to puzzle out the identity of the stranger who had been admitted into their midst, the undernourished apparition in rust-red knee boots and tattered mauve and purple flightsuit adorned with Mars Division unit patches. The scarred warrior wearing an archaic Badger on his hip.

Jean listened closely to Scott's words as everyone settled themselves behind drinks in Vince's quarters. And she heard the strange accent he had acquired during his time on Earth, the bitterness in his breaking voice when he recounted the Mars Division's assault against Invid-occupied Earth—how the ships had literally come apart in space, defeated long before the Regis's Shock Troopers and Pincers had moved in to loose their hyphenstorms, their fiery coup de grace.

Scott told them about the long road to Reflex Point, a journey that seemed to have become something of a personal odyssey to despair and disillusionment. Of the rogues, traitors, and cowards who populated that war-torn landscape. Of his encounters with Jonathan Wolff (Scott's template for cynicism, Jean thought), with the geriatric star-struck mechamorphs who had returned with Major Carpenter; and with Sue Graham of the Jupiter Division's 36th. Jean remembered the photojournalist well and the agony, real or imagined, she had put Lisa Hayes Hunter through.

Her ears pricked up when Scott mentioned Reflex Point itself and spoke of some of the things he had described to neurometric analysts planetside. She saw no reason to doubt the veracity of Scott's claims—that he had actually conversed with the Invid hivequeen—but she also sensed that Scott was leaving something unsaid. G2 had tried to put a trace on the freedom fighters Scott claimed had accompanied him inside the complex, but a search had proved impossible among the population displacements and shifting conditions below.

In turn, Vince caught Scott up on the incredible events that had transpired on Optera shortly after Mars Division had folded for home space. Scott was attentive, but it was apparent that he had already heard most of it from REF mecha pilots. Nevertheless, he had questions about Dana Sterling's nearly miraculous appearance and the so-called Nichols drive that powered the Shadow fighters and retrofitted *Ark Angel*.

Jean waited for a lull in the shop talk before attempting to return the conversation to personal concerns. She had risen from her chair to gaze out the viewport, mesmerized by the scintillating dance of Earth's orbiting debris. Of late, every viewport in the ship seemed to be a window into her private torment. She could not regard Earth or stars without recalling the phoenix vision she had beheld when the *Tokugawa* had met its terrible end above Optera or the real-time manifestation of that phoenix as it had scorched its way through the expeditionary fleet.

Nor could she help thinking of Gardner and Ackerman and Gunther Rheinhardt, all dead. And Rolf Emerson—dear Rolf, who had died in Bowie's arms. The news of his death had seemed unreal on Tirol, but now, so close . . .

"We were so sorry to hear about Marlene, Scott," she said at last.

By sheer reflex, Scott's hand went to his breast to feel for the heart-shaped holo-locket he wore under his flightsuit.

"Her parents are onboard," Jean added.

Scott nodded grimly. "And I'm sorry to hear about Bowie," he said, meeting her eyes.

Jean saw concern and hatred in those eyes—hatred for Musica, the Tiresian clone Bowie was in love with. Jean saw little purpose in going into it now that Scott was exhibiting signs of outright xenophobia. She wondered whether Dana, too, would fall prey to his distrust. Dana, who had remained with her parents on Haydon IV.

"We'll find them," Scott said suddenly, watching as meaningful glances were exchanged. Then: "All right, what aren't you people telling me? You said you received transmissions from Tirol.''

"From Cabell,'' Vince answered, setting aside his drink. "But it's only what we've told you, Scott. The SDF-3 executed its fold shortly after Rheinhardt's Neptune and Saturn groups were away. Rheinhardt's final communiqué with Admiral Hunter—''

"Rick,'' Jean thought to point out.

"—involved decisions on deployment of the Cyclones and Shadow fighters.'' Vince paused. "And the use of the neutron 'S' missiles if all else failed.''

Scott's eyes widened. Then the rumors were true: Rheinhardt had been prepared to render the planet uninhabitable rather than surrender it to the Invid. "Madness,'' he said through clenched teeth.

Vince looked to his wife and let out a long breath.

"It wasn't an easy decision to arrive at, Colonel,'' Senator Huxley said. "There was a high probability that most of the southern hemisphere would survive the saturation.''

Scott stared at her, then ran his hands down his face. "So where the hell's the ship if they completed their fold? It's been three months now!''

"Easy, Scott,'' Vince said, straightening in his chair. "We're doing all we can.''

Scott glared at him. "By sitting here? No, I don't think so. Hasn't anybody thought of returning to Tirol? There has to be some trace of them.''

Dr. Penn cleared his throat. "The truth is, son, we're not sure we *can* return. We are, however, planning to execute a trial jump to lay all doubts to rest.''

Scott nodded in comprehension. "The Protoculture. The same thing that's plaguing most of the mecha downside. The reason I had to ride a damn *chemical* shuttle up here. Nothing's working, is that it?''

"Yes and no,'' Penn said quickly. "Some of the Veritechs are functional and fully capable of mechamorphosis. Others have limited capacity for flight or combat maneuvering. Not that this last is something I find disturbing.''

Scott glanced at Vince before responding; if the general was willing to let Penn's comment slide, so would he. "I heard some talk: there's something different about the Flowers you harvested from Optera.''

"New Praxis," Justine Huxley amended.

"New Praxis, then. But why would the older models suddenly shut down now?''

At the viewport, Jean folded her arms. "We were hoping you might be able to tell us, Scott.''

Scott touched his fingertips to his chest. "Me? What could I—'' Then it occurred to him. "The Regis," he snorted.

"We've read your debriefing reports, Colonel," Huxley said. "You claim you were inside the central hive just before the end, that you actually spoke with the Regis.''

Scott swallowed and found his voice. "Yeah, it's true, but come on, it's not like she *explained* herself to me.''

"Then what did she say?" Jean asked.

Scott smoothed back an undisciplined comma of hair. "What did she say?" He laughed nervously. "I'm still not sure what I heard and what I imagined. But I think we were, well, *arguing*.''

"Arguing?" Huxley said dubiously.

"Yeah. About . . . ethics. About whether the Invid had a right to Earth after what the Masters had done to Optera.'' Scott searched the faces appraising him. "It sounds crazy, I know, but she was just raving about what warlike beings we are, about how the universe would be better off without us.''

No one said anything for a moment.

"Anyway, I still don't see what all this has to do with the SDF-3. The Invid are history, aren't they?''

Jean turned to the viewport and thought of the phoenix once more, the transubstantiation of an entire race. "Maybe the ship went where she went," she suggested softly. Vince sent her a questioning look as she swung around. "The Regis, I mean.''

Penn made a knowing sound. "It's a pity there are no Invid left to quiz as to just where she might have gone.''

Scott put a hand over his mouth as though to bite back his words. Somewhere below, in one of the burgeoning cities of the Southlands or wandering the waste of the Northlands, were two of the three children the Regis had conjugated in human form. Sera and Marlene—clone-close in appearance to the Marlene lost to him over a year ago.

Could he face them again? he asked himself. Could he enlist the enemy's help in finding his friends?

"What is it, Scott?" Jean said, watching him.

Scott clamped his jaws shut, then relented. "Not all the Invid have left," he told them at last.

Above them rose crystal palaces and translucent spires, mansions of white-frost gingerbread and platforms of smoky blue glass, elfin halls and minarets, stately columns, onion domes, and ethereal towers.

Above them were alloy plains three hundred miles wide and burnished smooth as a looking glass, idyllic landscapes dotted with sea-green lakes, and skies of gold filled with cone fliers, hovercraft, and outsize magical carpets. A dreamy world of perfect days and tranquil nights, of exotic biota and gliding beings in high-collared robes whose silent speech was a gentle thought carried on the wind.

And below them . . . below them was that which had given shape to the illusion above: the ultratech complexities of a planet-sized artifact, birthed in the mind of an alien genius who had left his mark on half the far-flung worlds of the Fourth Quadrant. A genius met in lore and legend or encountered in towering shrines that masked the being himself.

He had perhaps imparted his name to the artifact or left that for others to do, but that his very essence was there reflected—in those spires and domes and artificial lakes—was not to be denied.

And suspended between—in the boundless chamber that contained them—was this place of instrumentality nodes and info-networks, the material interface with the Awareness Haydon had set in place to mind his clever works. So this place was neither one nor the other but a middle ground from which to know creator and created, sacrosanct, then, truly suspended. For from where else could one take the proper measure of things?

Exedore ceased his mystical musings even before he sensed the soft intrusion of Veidt's sendings. This was what mingling with humans and Garudans had wrought, he told himself, a penchant for the metaphysical. Questions commencing with why.

How far he had come from the directed, purposeful nature

of the Imperative! he would catch himself thinking. Feeling as remote from that now as his recontoured physical self was from the genetic vats that had conceived him. Normalized in both size and aspect and drained of the conquering urge, the compulsion to obey without question. Given to metaphysical ponderings. *How un-Zentraedi, indeed!* And how Great Breetai would have mocked him!

"A moment more and the requested correlations will be available," Veidt sent from the data column.

Exedore swiveled in his chair to regard the limbless Haydonite—his partner these past years. A response formed on the tip of his tongue, though there was little need of it. An old habit, difficult to break. "I, um . . ."

Veidt hovered through a quarter turn to face him with what nearly approximated a smile.

"I am well aware that my workings please you, Lord Exedore. Your words are an echo, you understand—an unnecessary redundancy."

Exedore favored him with a genuine grin, as difficult to suppress as the habit itself. This was as close as they came to jesting or arguing, he still was not sure which. Veidt's face had already resumed its normal configuration, which was to say, blank. *As featureless as an unfinished mannequin's,* a tech aboard the SDF-3 had once commented in Exedore's presence.

"Featureless, yes," Veidt sent, "but hardly unfinished, Exedore."

Early on Exedore had found it somewhat unnerving to have his thoughts scanned on a moment-to-moment basis, but he was long past concern or misgiving. It was logical, in fact, that he open his mind to Veidt, if only to expedite the unraveling of the cosmic puzzles someone had seen fit to send their way.

And "baffling" only began to describe them.

The SDF-3 was missing, not merely disappeared into hyperspace but vanished from the Quadrant. The ship had not emerged from fold anywhere in known space, nor was it trapped in the netherscape of the hyperdomain. Haydon IV's Awareness had told them that much already. But what the artificial sentience could not tell them was where the ship *was* or whether it existed at all. The SDF-3 had simply ceased to be, and yet there were no indications that it had met with any of the thousand ills matter was heir to.

That the dematerialization had coincided with a reawakening of a myriad slumbering computer components, Exedore initially read as a sign that the artifact planet had been in some sense *responsible* for the event. Subsequent investigation, however, had led him to the conclusion that the Awareness had not been responding to the SDF-3's plight, after all, but to a concurrent phenomenon that had taken place clear across the Quadrant.

Along a spacetime curve that led to Earth.

Something originating there had sent an energy pulse through the fabric of the continuum, whose destination seemed to be the distant collapsed giant the Tiresians knew as Ranaath's Star.

Haydon—he has returned to our world! Veidt had sent at the time, and—novice astrophysicist that he was—Exedore had taken him literally. But literalness was not something the Haydonites practiced with regularity, and the expression—for that was what it was—was best translated by the Terran self-condemning phrase *Well, I'll be damned!*

The very one Exedore had used sometime later when he had learned of the Invid's departure—months ago, Earth-relative, after a series of mostly interrupted exchanges between Earth and Tirol and between Tirol and Haydon IV. Since then, the Awareness had been spewing out a steady stream of mathematical calculations and puzzling data readouts, conversing with itself on an information level the likes of which Exedore had never encountered. Veidt had been successful in eavesdropping on the Awareness's inner dialogue and enticing it to display some of its findings—in holographics, projecbeam, and the occasional verbalization (which, remarkably enough, issued forth in fluent Tiresian lingua franca). But little of it made any sense to Exedore, on whose shoulders the search for the missing flagship had fallen.

The Zentraedi could almost smile, recalling Zor's original fortress, the SDF-1. He had been successful in tracing that one, but that hardly qualified him as an expert in the field.

Cabell had promised to tear himself away from Tiresia to join in plying the Awareness with questions, but Exedore thought the coded outpourings might outdistance even the master himself.

They needed Emil Lang or the Zor-clone, Rem, who had contributed so much to the facsimile matrix fashioned by the REF to empower its fleet. They needed the combined intellect of the SDF-3's Robotechnicians.

Better still, they needed Haydon.

"My thought exactly, Lord Exedore."

Exedore chuckled to himself. "Yes, Veidt. The Earthers have a saying, I believe. 'Great minds think—' "

The chamber had begun to vibrate. That in itself was nothing unusual. In fact, during the five years Exedore had been on-world he had known instances where the vibrations were strong enough to rattle the alloy walls and rumble data discs out of their holders. But the sudden tremor was more intense than any he had experienced.

"Another atmospheric cleansing?" the Zentraedi asked in a quavering voice. "A seasonal change? An internal overhaul, the upwelling of a new lake or the damming of a stream—send something, will you!"

Veidt had glided back to his station by the central data pillar, his high-collared cape a screen for projecbeam schematics, a dizzying light show of flashing alphanumeric analogues and equational abstracts.

"An intruder, perhaps," Exedore continued, his stubby hands spread atop leaping sheets of hard copy like some Ouija board reader. "An unannounced ship—"

"I heard you," Veidt sent with a sting. "It is none of those things. Something novel, unprecedented."

Exedore ceased his futile efforts to steady his work and with some difficulty swiveled to regard the strobing databanks of the Awareness, data scrolls and cards tattooing to the floor at his feet. The information traffic displayed was enough to render the Invid leave-taking a minor itch.

"What is it, Veidt?" Exedore pressed, a note of alarm in his voice. A deep-space view of Haydon IV advanced through the 3-D field of a projecbeam, a variegated ball in time-lapse motion. "Veidt," he repeated.

"Primary activation sequences have commenced," the Haydonite sent with curious detachment. "Atmospheric integrity is constant for the moment. Surface damage is projected to be well within accepted parameters. Casualties among offworlders are not expected to exceed a thousand.''

"Casualties?" Exedore said, up on shaky legs, bulging eyes darting between Veidt and the projecbeam field.

Veidt rotated to face him, a lavender brightness pulsating from the center of his smooth forehead. "The crossing is achieved. The Event is occurred. Praise Haydon.''

Careful not to be too literal, Exedore reminded himself. *Praise Haydon* could mean almost anything. "The Event?" he asked cautiously.

Veidt nodded. "Haydon IV is leaving orbit. Shortly, we will depart the Briz'dziki system entirely.''

Exedore's mouth fell open. "Haydon," he muttered. "He has returned to our world.''

CHAPTER THREE

The motion to leave Earth irradiated rather than leave it to the Invid Regis was carried by a narrow margin. Balloting was kept secret, and there has yet to be discovered a person-by-person breakdown of the vote. Of the ten members of the [Plenipotentiary] Council, there are believed to have been two abstentions— from Stinson and Longchamps. Obstat, Huxley, and others have elsewhere indicated the basis of their individual decisions. Of the participating members of the REF command staff, seven voted in favor of using the Neutron-S missiles, five against. It is altogether ironic that the decision to irradiate Earth was arrived at in Tiresia, where, centuries before, the Robotech Masters had sentenced Optera to suffer a similar fate.

Ahmed Rashona, *That Pass in the Night:
The SDF-3 and the Mission to Tirol*

LISA DREAMED A TUNNEL IN THE SKY, A RADIANT COR-
ridor stretching timeless across the heavens. Warm to her
hands and bare feet, secure and enfolding, redolent with aromas of spring and summer. At one end her father waved
good-bye, a smashing figure in his United Earth Government
tunic with its breast salad of ribbons and braid; at the other
end was a patch of scudded sky that could have belonged
only to once-upon-a-time Earth.

It occurred to her that she could not have been more than
seventeen, returning to Macross Island after her first real
leave. Was this carpeting below her, then? The warm glow
the lights of some airport concourse or jetway?

But where were the flight attendants, then; where were her
guides? And how could she hope to find her seat without a
boarding pass?

She slapped the pockets of her long coat as she walked, panic gaining on her. The light ahead was almost too intense to behold, like the sun itself on a cloudless south Pacific afternoon when there was not a breeze in the world.

The hot sand was making her hurry along, but it was the voice she was responding to now. The panic evaporated, trailing behind her ghostly and diffuse, and the warmth returned. Her mother's voice, her arthritic hand waving in the light at the end of the corridor. Her guide, to be sure, a smile broadening as Lisa outran the years; the deaths and disappearances that ruined her garden. A child as she approached the light, Earth too remote to touch . . .

I'm dead! she thought—

—as noise filled her up and air swelled her lungs, bringing renewed life to her pounding heart. A dream, she told herself, the recurrent one her mind reserved for hyperspace folds.

Everyone had them, those nightmares and visions, brief excursions to private heavens or hells. *Space lace*, some of the crew called it. With an ever-present out-of-body component, an after-life accompaniment.

Only this time she *had* died, and that had never happened before. Grief coursed through her, a profound sense of loss, a kind of terminal nostalgia. Had it been stirred by the dream? Or did it emanate from the nurturing other she had discovered within herself?

Roy was suddenly on her mind, her bright center in the universe, her barely five-year-old hero. The thought of having to open her eyes filled her with fear. But open them she would.

And the grief propagated.

The SDF-3 bridge was as dark and silent as a tomb. Sweat burst from her palms like splinters of ice.

"Lieutenant Toler," she said. "Mister Hakawa?"

"Here, sir," someone answered from a duty station behind the command chair. She called to the rest—Williamson, Price, Martino—and one by one they responded, reborn from dreams. Lisa flathanded the com-line stud built into the arm of the chair and called for Dr. Lang in engineering.

"All systems are down, sir," said a voice in the darkness—Price, Lisa ventured correctly. "No response from any of the backups. It's like we're unplugged."

"Nonsense," Lisa returned. "We're obviously not weight-less, Mister Price. And unless we've somehow defolded on Earth's surface, I'd hazard a guess *some* systems are operational."

"Yes, sir."

"Doesn't anyone keep a damn flashlight up here?" she said, cautiously feeling her way out of the chair. Off to her right she heard a pneumatic hiss, a tear of Velcro. "Everyone stay put," she called toward the sound. "We're still on full alert, gentlemen. Besides, I don't want anyone walking into a bulkhead." She directed her voice starboard, toward Toler's station beneath the threat board. "Mister Toler, you're the youngest among us. How's your vision?"

"Better than perfect, sir," Toler told her, a crack in his voice on the last word.

"Do you think you can make your way to the hatch and engage the override?"

"With my eyes closed, sir."

Everyone laughed, and the tension eased somewhat. "Yes, well, you can keep your eyes open, Lieutenant. This isn't a test of your agility. I just want to know if the whole ship's in this fix."

"I understand, sir."

Lisa heard Toler's chair swivel. A few moments later came the low thud of retracting bolts. The air stirred as the hatch slid open and the sound of half a dozen voices drifted in from the operations room. Toler and someone else made startled sounds.

"What happened?" Lisa asked.

A man's voice growled: "Who is that?"

"Lieutenant Toler. Who's that?"

"Commander Forsythe, Lieutenant. Stand aside."

"Sir!" Toler snapped.

Lisa heard a hollow meeting of flesh and bone and a follow-up wince of pain. "Damn, boy," her bald-headed exec said, "you don't have to salute me!"

Just then the emergency lights came up, banks at a time, red and somber throughout the bridge. A slight shudder swept through the ship, and Klaxons wailed midnote, signaling battle stations.

"That's more like it," Lisa enthused. "Showing up crippled would send one hell of a message to the Regis."

Forsythe stepped through the hatch, throwing Toler a hard look before joining Price at one of the forward heads-up display screens.

"We're still dead in space, sir," Hakawa updated. "Auxiliary power forward and to all priority stations, but all scanning, ECM, and defense systems are nonop."

"Can we determine our position?" Forsythe asked.

"Negative, sir. Guidance, telemetry, and astrogation are still down."

Lisa traded frowns with Forsythe and glanced over her shoulder at the watch officer. "Well, we can at least take a look outside, can't we?"

"Yes, sir."

"Raise the forward cowl, Mister Hakawa," Forsythe said impatiently.

Lisa could barely contain herself. It was almost as though she could dismiss this latest snafu the way a cyclist might shrug off a punctured tire after a thousand-mile journey. *Earth*, after close to fifteen years. With nothing unforeseen in store for them this time: no accidental jumps to Pluto, no fold hitchhikers to rescue, no surprise attacks by alien cruisers. The REF knew who and what they had come for: the Regis and the world they had lost to her. They knew, too, the Shock Troopers and Pincers they would be facing, and they knew how to engage them.

And best of all, they knew they would succeed.

Six years of effort had gone into this one day, and the fleet that was the result of that labor would be spread out before them, weapons arrays and combat mecha targeted for Reflex Point. *Earth*, Lisa said to herself again as the forward viewport shields retracted. *Earth!*

Light of a sort began to filter onto the bridge, only it was neither the welcome warmth of Sol nor the reflected brilliance of their blue-white homeworld.

It was the alien light at the end of Lisa's tunnel in the sky. It was death light.

On the command balcony of the fortress's cavernous Tactical Information Center, Rick Hunter stared uncomprehendingly at the monitors affixed to the portside bulkhead.

"I'm sorry, sir," an enlisted-rating tech stationed at a nearby console repeated, "but the opticals *are* on-line. This *is* the external view. Sir."

In the phasing, satanic illumination of the emergency lights the room could have been a corner of hell. Rick would have taken odds that it was just that: the hell of his space lace given shape during the fold. But unlike Lisa's recurrent tunnel, Rick's nightmare vision did not require a jump to ignite it. The set, the setting, the thousand separate elements that composed it could all be traced back to the Genesis Pits on Optera. Walk away from it you might, but turn around and the fear would be there, waiting for you, beckoning you back into its sinister embrace.

An intercom buzzed insistently at Rick's back. "Command One," he heard his adjutant say at last. "Doctor Lang, Admiral," the colonel continued, conveying the mobile over to him.

"What the hell's going on?" Rick shouted into the mouthpiece. "Where are we?" He glanced at the monitors once more before proceeding. "It looks like fog out there, Lang. Is that possible?"

"I would like to humor you, Admiral," Lang said, *"but, unfortunately, there is little humor in the situation. And if it is indeed a 'fog,' as you suggest, it is of the quantum sort. We have life support, but little else, as I'm sure you're aware."*

Rick's boot continued to tap the floor long after Lang had finished. The two men had grown distant from each other on Tirol, Lang like some Prometheus with his facsimile Protoculture matrix, and Rick busy with Roy more often than not. The wizard of Robotechnology kept getting stranger while Rick just kept getting grayer.

"How long before you can return power to the drives?" Rick demanded.

It was to be the REF's final battle, he thought, the one that was to decide their fate, return to them their homeworld or send them back to Tirol, an irradiated Earth in their wake.

Lang launched his patented maniacal laugh through the earpiece. *"Perhaps you should abandon your post for a moment and come below, Admiral. There's something I'd like you to see."*

"I don't have time for this, Lang," Rick told him. "Just tell me where we are." He heard the urgency in his voice and noted that his adjutant was fixing him with a concerned look.

Lang's laugh trailed off as he cleared his throat. *"You may not like the answer, Admiral."*

Rick's hold on the phone became viselike. "You let me be the judge of that."

Lang was quiet a moment, then said: *"Nowhere."*

In whispered voices behind cupped hands it was often suggested that Dr. Emil Lang ran the ship. Not that he had much to do with command decisions or actual hands-on astrogation, but that he ran the ship in the sense of *driving* the ship, fueling it. Word was passed in those same engineering huddles that the Reflex furnaces and Protoculture drives were nothing but pretense—mock-ups constructed to put the uninitiated at ease—when in fact Lang himself *was* the drives. Lang folded space; Lang jumped the fortress from realm to realm.

Lang was aware of all the rumors but did little to discourage them. Myths concerning his powers and prowess had been in the making since the first day he had set foot inside the grounded SDF-1. No one had seen him take the Protoculture mindboost that had altered the direction of his life, but they had read the change in his reshaped eyes. And had his eyes not betrayed him, even had he not taken the boost, they would have invented it for the myth, witnessed that he alone among Earthers was destined to see deeper and clearer than the rest, that the Protoculture had a natural affinity for him.

But that was just the sort of thinking that pointed out how great a distance he had yet to travel. The ship's drive, he sniggered to himself. Hardly. The ship's *driven*, perhaps; the SDF-3's preconscious libidinal urge . . .

Lang lifted his eyes to regard the displays once more. Onscreen were remote views into the heart of the fortress's power plant, safely rendered for a mortal's eyes, for one did not look long into the naked eye of God and live to describe it. But there was no burning bush now, no ten thousand stars or golden heavens, simply the absence of those things. What

Lang saw instead was a reflection of his own pride, the hubris that had dominated him for the past five years. He and Cabell and the Zor-clone, Rem, havesting the Flower of Life from Optera's regrown fields, coaxing the secret of the Shapings from its trifoliate core, creating a matrix of their own design.

And now this.

Lang saw his face in the display screen and laughed out loud. The Shapings were teaching him a lesson.

He was still laughing when Rick Hunter rushed in, threading his way through the chaos, techs and their bewildered assistants moving frantically from station to station.

"What'd you get me down here for, Lang?" Rick barked, pacing behind Lang's chair and glaring down at him.

Lang's upturned look was unreadable as he indicated the displays. His humanity as well as his age seemed to have been arrested by continual contact with the Protoculture.

"See for yourself, Admiral."

Rick spread his hands atop the console and leaned toward an on-screen computer-enhanced translation of the engines' subatomic fire. He held the pose for a moment, then glanced at Lang in annoyance. "I don't see anything wrong, Doctor."

Lang snorted. "No, of course you wouldn't, Admiral."

Rick was used to the condescending tone. "Explain."

The Roboscientist sighed and blanked the monitor with a tap of a crooked forefinger. "It has vanished, Admiral—the Protoculture. Disappeared."

Rick's dark brows beetled. He reached out to reactivate the screen, but Lang's powerful hand restrained him.

"Take my word for it, Admiral, the Protoculture has vanished." It would have been senseless to talk about the shadowy presence of the black-robed wraiths Rem had taught him to recognize. "Yes, exactly as it disappeared from the SDF-1," he added, discerning Rick's thoughts.

"But how?" Rick began. "Why?"

"To teach us a lesson, I think."

Rick shook his head. "A lesson?" He swept his arm through an all-encompassing gesture. "Listen to me, Lang. Rheinhardt and the rest of the fleet are out there waiting for us. Do you understand what that means?"

The scientist gave him a pitying look. "I assure you, Admiral, the fleet is not out *there*."

"Then where the hell are we?" Rick said, at the end of his rope. "And don't tell me nowhere."

Lang folded his arms and met the intensity of Rick's gaze. "All right. It's possible that we're still in hyperspace, although there is no evidence to support the hypothesis. It's also possible that we have died, as some of the ship's personnel are suggesting. Or that we have somehow jumped to a void in intergalactic space, perhaps jumped beyond the expansion wave of the big bang itself."

Rick went wide-eyed. "You mean we've jumped *outside the galaxy*?"

Lang shrugged. "It's simply one theory among many. A jump beyond time could perhaps explain how and why the Protoculture vanished, although our own continued existence would seem to contraindicate it."

Rick staggered backward into a chair adjacent to Lang's. "But—but there has to be *something* out there."

Lang shook his head. "Not according to our instruments. We are no*where*, Admiral. Not even a *when* that I can determine. I'm sorry, but there's no other way to put it."

Rick turned to face him. "Then get us somewhere, Doctor."

Lang rubbed his chin. "What would you have me do, fashion a world for you out of nothingness?"

Rick forced out his breath. "Yes, damn it. Fashion us a world if you have to."

CHAPTER
FOUR

> *"It's absolutely true. Mom really did have a look, a different grimace for every occasion. But I'll tell you something I've never told anyone before: The strangest of all Mom's looks was the one she reserved for any mention of Scott Bernard. Seriously. For the longest time I was convinced that they'd had an affair or something. But then one day Mom told me about the time he stopped by looking for Marlene. There was that look again, the whole time she told the story. And I suddenly realized that I wasn't seeing one of those what-might-have-been looks but one that was saying* what-never-should-have-been.

Maria Bartley-Rand, quoted in
Xandu Reem's *A Stranger at Home:
A Biography of Scott Bernard*

SCOTT BREATHED A SIGH OF RELIEF AS HE FELT THE craft settle down, rubber tires chirping against the tarmac of a smooth but long disused stretch of Southlands highway. Mission priorities and the usual red tape had made it impossible for him to procure an old VTOL, much less an Alpha, so Scott was stuck with a forty-year-old air breather, a civilian five-passenger *jet* some group in G4 must have liberated from a pre-Wars museum. They'd blown the dust off the thing and fitted it with new rubber, but the cockpit had seen far better days, and the instruments were ancient. Scott's biggest problem was refraining from trying to *think* the aircraft through mechamorph maneuvers. A lot of good that would have done, anyway; the thing wasn't even equipped with a neural interface thinking cap!

Priorities aside, though, there were good reasons for flying civilian and denying any military affiliation just then. Earth's surface, the Southlands especially, had become a sorry place for soldiers. With the so-called fall of Reflex Point and the Invid abandonment of their hives, Flower of Life orchards, and POW camps, humankind was once more on the move. People were quite literally crawling out of the holes they had buried themselves in when the Invid had landed. Tens of thousands, many of whom had spent the past year or more in internment centers in what had once been called Canada, were migrating south from the ruined Northlands, lured to Brazilas by rumors of massive reconstruction efforts and the promise of a United Earth Government rising from the ashes of the Southern Cross apparat. At the same time thousands more had taken to the cracked and rutted roadways of the thrice-invaded world in search of lost friends and loved ones, while others busied themselves by exacting vengeance on spies, sympathizers, and any who had profited during the occupation.

Soldiers of any army, private or otherwise, were often at the receiving end of the general wrath and blood lust, especially those unfortunates who had fancied themselves insurgents or freedom fighters. It was an accepted fact that insurgency had done more damage than good—Invid reprisals having far outweighed the dubious worth of destroying a handful of Shock Troopers or Pincer ships—and that the Regis had not really been defeated but had willingly abandoned the planet in search of richer hunting grounds. The returning REF consequently was not looked upon as some beneficent force of liberators but as yet another conquering army, a gang of thugs looking to resume control after a fifteen-year absence.

Under the circumstances, Scott's small jet was less a product of choice than of sheer necessity. And the same held true for his civilian attire.

Mention of the Invid sister simulagents had dropped him right back into the lap of the REF's intel people for two more weeks of memory probes and debriefings. Ultimately, however, Scott's inquisitors had come to accept that Marlene's present whereabouts were unknown and that Scott himself stood the best chance of finding her. That he had agreed to do, under the condition that he be given an opportunity to undertake the search alone and in his own fashion.

G2 had acquiesced, figuring that it would prove a simple matter to assign a team of agents to the colonel, but Vince Grant had received word of the operation and vetoed it before a single operative had been assigned. Back on the surface, meanwhile, Scott had been quizzing migrants, bribing local officials, and bartering with foragers for a line on any one of his six former teammates—counting one for Lancer, and Marlene among them. He had concentrated on Rand, who months ago at Yellow Dancer's final concert had said something about heading for the outskirts of Norristown, where he planned to write his memoirs.

A downside week had gone by before Scott locked onto what seemed a worthy lead, and that lead had now brought him and the toy jet to Xochil, a pueblo not far off the route the team had taken through Trenchtown, in the heart of the Southlands.

A tatterdemalion crowd of vacant-eyed townspeople and rough-trade foragers was gathered around the craft by the time Scott raised the canopy and climbed out. He answered a few questions about the state of things on the north coast in exchange for information on Rand and, for five hundred New Scrip (with a promise of that much again when he returned from town), enlisted the services of a couple of locals sporting turn-of-the-century military-issue projectile rifles to keep an eye on the jet.

Twenty minutes later he was negotiating a narrow alley off Xochil's earthen main street, zeroing in on the throaty revvings of what he took to be a fossil-fueled motorcycle engine.

Rook Bartley was standing alongside the chopped machine, twisting the handlebar throttle with her right hand while her left ponytailed her long strawberry-blond hair. Seeing her, Scott smiled genuinely for the first time in weeks.

She was dressed in mechanic's coveralls, back and rolled-up sleeves emblazoned with motorcycle brand-name patches. She was also quite a few pounds heavier than when they had exchanged good-byes, her hands and one cheek smeared with grease and grime. Scott waited for the bike's growling sounds to die down before he called her name.

Someone's metal-rock rendition of "Look Up" was blasting from stereo speakers. The song had become something of an anthem in the Southlands, much as Lynn-Minmei's "We Will Win" had captured the spirit of the First Robotech War.

Rook turned, startled, and regarded him quizzically for a good ten seconds before a smile split her freckled face. "Well, now maybe all this exhaust is getting to me, but I'd swear that's Scott Bernard standing in the doorway."

"Hello, Rook," he told her over the music and the rumbling sound of the idling machine.

She shook her head in disbelief, wiped her hands on a scrap of towel, and sauntered over to embrace him, kissing him lightly on the mouth and then jabbing a fist into his upper arm.

"I thought you were off looking for your friends, soldier boy. Figured you'd be halfway to Tirol by now." Rook's blue eyes gave him a quick once-over. "And look at you—what'd the REF boot you back into real life or something?"

"You look great," he said, beaming.

Rook took a step back and pinched out the coveralls' pants legs as though she were wearing a skirt. "You think so, huh?"

Scott nodded. "Guess you're eating better now."

Rook laughed. "Figures you'd notice, Scott. Fact is, I'm pregnant."

"Pregnant? Jeez, I thought there was something different, but—"

"Six months," she said. "She's going to be a Virgo if I've computed it right. But then I figure it's about time they changed the signs of the zodiac, don't you?"

"She?" Scott said.

Rook smiled broadly. "Call it woman's intuition. Rand's skeptical, but I've even got her name picked out—Maria. Maria Bartley. What d' you think?"

Scott ran it through and nodded. "I like the sound of it. So this place is yours?" he asked after a pause. In the naked glare of generator-fed incandescents sat a score of partly restored bikes. There were perhaps a dozen engines resting on blocks, spoked wheels hanging from the rafters, rusted frames and spare parts piled in corners or littering the top of thick wooden worktables. The air reeked of solvents and exhaust fumes.

"Will be someday," Rook said, looking around. "Right

now I'm only helping out." She caressed her stomach. "Gotta keep the family fed."

"Why here, of all places?"

Rook tugged at her lower lip. "Trenchtown, mostly."

Scott recalled something about rival motorcycle gangs in Rook's past, the Blue Angels and the Red Snakes. "You've got family there, don't you?"

"Mom and a sister. Guess I'm thinking about mending fences one of these days."

Scott grinned. "What about Rand?"

Rook screwed up her face. "The Great Commentator, you mean?" She jerked a thumb over her shoulder. "We found a place a couple clicks west of town. All he does is write—morning, noon, and night. Like there's going to be an audience for his book or something."

"Have you read any of it?"

"Yeah, I have," she said, moving back to the cycle she had been working on. "And it's actually not bad. 'Course I have to straighten him out on a lot of the facts. To hear him tell it, you'd think he won the war single-handed." Rook was quiet for a moment. "So what brings you around, Scott? I don't figure you just happened to be in the neighborhood."

"I'm not," Scott confessed. "I'm looking for Marlene, Rook."

Rook appraised him silently. "Talk about mending fences . . . That oughta be some reunion, partner. You plan on selling tickets, or what?"

Scott worked his jaw. "Have you heard from her, Rook?"

Rook goosed the throttle, and the bike sent up a cloud of white smoke. "Think you better talk to Rand, soldier boy. I don't want to get in the middle of this one."

Scott recognized examples of Rand's handiwork in the dilapidated wooden cabin he and Rook called home. It was not much to look at on the outside, but the two main rooms were comfortable if Spartan and reflected Rand's utilitarian nature. Scott also recognized the small notebooks stacked atop the writing desk, the ones Rand had guarded with his life during the journey to Reflex Point.

"Here you go," Rand said, handing over a tall mug of

home-brewed beer and pulling a stool opposite Scott's chair. "I bottled it when we first moved in."

Rand had already explained how Rook had enticed an REF Alpha pilot to fly them down to Norristown after Scott had taken off for the skies.

"What's weird is that I was just thinking about you," Rand resumed. "I was reading in my notes about the day you and I met. The time I saved your ass from three blues."

Scott almost spewed his beer across the room. "*You* saved my—" He wiped his mouth on his sleeve, deciding it didn't merit an argument. "Right, I remember now."

"Yeah, those were the days," Rand mused, shaking his shaggy mop of red hair. "Foraging, surviving on the road . . ." He looked up at Scott. "I'm going to call the book *Notes on the Run*."

"Your baby, is that it?"

Rand's thick eyebrows bobbed. "So Rook told you. She also give you that intuition crap about her being sure it's a girl?"

"Maria, I think she said."

"Yeah, well, don't put scrip on it." Rand sipped his grog. "Either way it goes, though, I'm going to make sure the kid is raised to appreciate books and movies and learning in general." He gestured to the writing desk. "Maybe she'll even end up a writer like her old man."

"You said 'she,' Rand," Scott pointed out.

They both laughed, but it was not long before an uncomfortable pause crept into their conversation. When Scott mentioned Marlene, Rand's smile collapsed entirely.

"What do want from her, Scott?" Rand asked.

"I just need to talk to her. That's all I can tell you right now."

"And I don't suppose you can tell me anything about why most of the Cyclones have stopped working, either. Lot of unemployed 'Culture hounds wandering around out there all of a sudden, amigo."

"Sorry, Rand," Scott told him. "We're all in the same dark."

Rand smirked. "Same ole soldier. What is it—your REF people want to debrief her?"

Scott shot to his feet. "Hey, you think this is easy for me?

You think I want it? I look at her and I see the Marlene I loved. I look at her and I think about what the Invid did to us.''

Rand rolled his eyes. "Oh, for chrissakes."

"The Regis planned to exterminate us, Rand," Scott snarled. "You don't remember that? The Flowers had hit their goddamned trigger point. If the fleet hadn't returned, we'd all be dead."

Rand stood up. "Yeah, and if the Regis hadn't decided to leave when she did, your precious fleet—" He pointed toward the ceiling. "—your precious fleet would have irradiated the lot of us!"

"You'd rather let the Invid have this planet?"

"I'd rather *none* of this happened, Scott. But I don't see how dragging Marlene back into it's going to serve any purpose now. She's living a normal life, Scott. Let her be."

"Where is she, Rand?" Scott pressed. "It's possible she knows where my friends are."

Rand regarded him. "The SDF-3? How do you figure?"

Scott forced out his breath. "The ship didn't emerge from hyperspace. Relatively speaking, it vanished at the same moment the Invid left Earth."

"So you figure what?"

"That they may have ended up in the same place." Scott held Rand's gaze. "It's possible Marlene is still in rapport with the Regis. That's why I need to talk to her, Rand."

The smaller man shook his head. "You're putting me between the proverbial rock and the hard place, *mano*."

"Just tell me where she is, Rand."

Rand took a long pull from his mug. "She's with Lunk and Annie. They're in Roca Negra."

Scott tried to place it.

"Remember the book Lunk tried to deliver to Alfred Nader?"

"Of course," Scott said in sudden realization.

"That's where you'll find them."

"Thanks, Rand."

Reluctantly, Rand accepted the proffered hand. "One thing, Scott," he said when they were seated again. "Lunk's not going to be as easy on you as I was."

CHAPTER
FIVE

TO: NILES OBSTAT
EYES ONLY
FROM: SCIENCE AND TECHNOLOGY DIRECTORATE
RE: PROJECT STARCHILD

DNA ANALYSIS OF BLOOD AND TISSUE SAMPLES TAKEN FROM INVID
SIMULAGENT (A.K.A "MARLENE," "ARIEL") PROVE UNEQUIVO-
CAL MATCH TO ON-FILE DNA PROFILES OF MARS DIVISION E.R.
TECH MARLENE RUSH (SEE APPENDED NOTES). SUGGEST THAT RE-
GIS EXTRACTED RUSH TISSUE FROM WRECKAGE OF MARS GROUP
AND USED FIND AS TEMPLATE FOR HER HUMANOID CREATIONS.
IT IS YET TO BE LEARNED WHETHER USE OF RUSH TEMPLATE WAS
DELIBERATE OR COINCIDENTAL. QUERY: IS COLONEL BERNARD TO
BE INFORMED? SUGGESTION: WITHHOLD ALL KNOWLEDGE OF
CLONING UNTIL FULL DISCLOSURE IS WARRANTED OR DEEMED
ADVISABLE.

G2 dispatch, quoted in,
Sara Lemole's *Improper Council:
An Analysis of the Plenipotentiary Council*

"She's got the right dynamic for the New Frontier."

Twentieth-century song lyric

UNDER REFLEX POWER, THE *ARK ANGEL* LEFT GEO-
synch and inserted itself into orbit where the Robotech factory satellite had once played the role of Earth's inner moon.
The departure point for the trial jump to Luna's far side was
the very same spatial coordinates the SDF-3 had used in its
fold to Fantomaspace.

Vince had been elsewhere when the SDF-1 had jumped
from Macross, but he was well acquainted with the accounts

of that fateful day logged by Henry Gloval, Emil Lang, and countless others. The far side had been targeted for the position jump, but the fortress had missed the mark by what amounted to the radius of the solar system. Gloval had given the command, but Lang had borne the burden of the blame. Inexperience, pilot error . . . An official inquiry was never performed. Years later, though, while Breetai's ship was undergoing its face-lift in the factory satellite's null-g core, the then-micronized Zentraedi commander had shown Lang where he had gone wrong. Yet in spite of that, the feeling remained that Lang was innocent of any technical oversight or wrongdoing. Human control was considered a moot point where Protoculture was involved.

So, cinched into the *Ark Angel*'s command chair—a well-padded motorized affair similar to the one he had had designed for the GRU a lifetime ago—Vince Grant had to ask himself just what Protoculture might have in mind for the day's fold.

Seated at duty stations to the left and right of him, techs and bridge officers were running through a final series of system checks as the ship counted down from double digits. Jean, steadfast in her refusal to remain planetside for the test, was with her med group elsewhere in the ship. Vince was on file as insisting on a skeleton crew for the test, but he was secretly thankful that the Plenipotentiary Council members had overruled him. When it came right down to it, no one wanted to be left behind.

Even if the Protoculture had a surprise destination already picked out.

In truth, the *Ark Angel*'s drives were Sekiton-fueled—a peat derived from Karbarra's abundant Ur-Flower crop. Vince supposed the distinction was a minor one, but that belief was not shared by the half dozen Karbarrans who headed up the ship's engineering section. Protoculture, the ursinoids were fond of pointing out, could be handled by almost anyone, but Sekiton responded to Karbarrans *only*, a condition Haydon the Enigmatic had been responsible for, or so Vince had been given to understand.

"Ten seconds and counting, General Grant," a young female tech reported.

Vince's hand elongated the noble features of his broad

brown face. He considered the recent transmission the ship had received from Cabell.

"Seven . . . six . . ."

Exedore, still on Haydon IV, was of the opinion that the Awareness held some key to the SDF-3's disappearance.

"Five . . . four . . ."

Dr. Penn, Jean, and several others were of the same mind.

"Three . . . two . . ."

Now if the *Ark Angel* could only get there.

"One. Fold generators engaged."

Vince sent a silent prayer to the ship's drives and their Karbarran overseers.

A lunar crescent suddenly filled the forward viewport.

The bridge crew applauded wildly. Exuberant cheers filtered in from distant quarters of the ship.

"Yirrbisst has blessed on us this day, Commander," one of the ursinoids gutturally announced over the com-line, invoking the name of his homeworld's primary. *"Praise Haydon."*

Vince thanked everyone for a job well done. Two or three Council members had suggested a second trial jump, to Mars perhaps, if the first succeeded, but Vince had renewed confidence in the ship and saw no need for further tests.

Earth ascended into view as the *Ark Angel*'s attitude thrusters repositioned the ship for the return jump.

Vince turned to his communications officer. "Inform Cabell that we'll soon be folding for Haydon IV."

Lunk was standing in the center of a small patch of cleared ground a kilometer east of Roca Negra proper, attacking a stump of hardwood with a heavy ax. He was shirtless in the morning heat, long black hair tied back, brutish features determined, barrel-chested torso glistening with sweat. He checked his swing momentarily to monitor Scott's approach—ax handle resting on his shoulder and a hand to his brow—then resumed his work, putting increased effort into each blow.

"Good to see you, Lunk," Scott said, keeping what he determined to be a safe distance.

The former Southern Cross soldier stopped only to mop his face with a Paisley bandanna. "I guessed it was you when

I saw the jet come down," Lunk grunted after the blade bit wood. "The way I read it, you must be on leave or undercover. You land on the old highway?"

"Just."

Lunk took another swing. "A Lear, isn't it?"

Scott's boot tip drew a shallow trench in the tilled ground. "I suppose so. Pre-Wars. But I almost lost it this time."

"Yeah, well you'll be lucky if the thing's still there when you get back."

"It's being looked after, Lunk," Scott assured him.

The big man went back to chopping. "So how'd you find us, Lieutenant?"

Scott squatted, waving insects away from his face. "I found Rand. But I think I'm supposed to mention that he wasn't exactly eager to tell me."

"Sure," Lunk said.

"So you're homesteading, huh?"

Lunk turned to face him. "The townspeople gave us a place to live and a bit of land to work. The Invid came down hard on everyone after we passed through last year, but the town's rebuilding. They're good folk, Lieutenant. What's past is past. We're all making new lives for ourselves."

Scott caught the warning in Lunk's baritone voice and decided not to mention the promotion. "I can see that," he said, glancing about. Well-tended fields of grain stretched emerald to distant hills. On nearby terraces, men and women were harvesting and threshing golden stalks of rice. "Annie around?" he asked after a moment.

Lunk threw the ax into the wood and gave a twist to the blade. "She left right after we got here. The idea of settling down didn't suit her too well. Went off to find that guy Magruder. The kid's still got stars in her eyes."

Scott smiled to himself, picturing Annie in her "E.T." cap and faded green jumpsuit.

"What d' ya say we skip the small talk and come to the point, Lieutenant," Lunk said suddenly.

Scott contemplated the line his boot had drawn, then raised his eyes. "All right, Lunk. The fact is, I'm looking for Marlene."

Lunk spit. "I thought so. What happened, Lieutenant— got lonely for you up there?" He motioned with his chin to the cloudless sky. "Figured maybe you'd passed on a good thing down here, a girl that was only trying to love you the best she knew how?"

That from the guy who had called Marlene a traitor that day in Reflex Point, Scott thought, getting to his feet. "It's nothing like that, Lunk."

"Think you can just fly in here with your little jet and pick up where you left off, huh?" Lunk held the ax like a hatchet and shook it in Scott's face. "Lemme tell you, you're way off the mark, Lieutenant. Marlene's had a rough time of it, but I've been helping her. She's kinda come to rely on me, and I think your showing up is just gonna gum up the works, understand me?"

"Look, Lunk, I just want to talk to her."

"I'm tellin' ya how it is, Lieutenant."

Scott left a brief empty space in the exchange, waiting for Lunk to cool down. "Back at Command everyone's still scratching their heads about what happened at Reflex Point," he commenced on a casual note. "There's a possibility the SDF-3 got itself caught up in the Regis's exit." He looked at Lunk. "I think Marlene can help out."

Lunk glared at him, then threw the ax down into the stump and left it there. "Come on," he said, storming off across the field in the direction of Roca Negra.

Scott fell in behind him for a silent walk that delivered them fifteen minutes later to two spacious freestanding tents erected side by side on a small parcel of land dotted with olive trees. Lunk's battered APC was parked off to one side.

"Marlene," Lunk bellowed, rustling the mosquito-netting front flap of the larger tent.

"Lunk?" Marlene responded from somewhere inside. "You're back early."

Scott's heart broke at the sound of her voice; save for a hint of Southlands Forager accent, it might as well have been that of Marlene Rush.

As the Invid simulagent stepped into the sunlight, luxurious red hair shorn to her shoulders and skin as pale as a Tiresian's, Scott thought: *She is Marlene!*

The Regis's daughter took a moment to absorb the scene before she collapsed into Scott's slapdash embrace, sighing. "I knew you'd return for me, Scott, I knew you'd return."

Lunk quickly turned his back to the two of them, afraid they would see his tears.

Scott immediately realized that Marlene had undergone a profound change since they had last embraced. Marlene then had been alive and vital to his confused thoughts and anxious hands, a woman of human lusts and needs, nothing like the insubstantial being he cradled in his arms now. It was something he could not articulate, but it was obvious to all who dared to look deep enough into her eyes.

Scott led her into the shade, to a canvas-backed chair at the head of a split-log longtable. Lunk positioned himself behind the chair, his large callused hands resting on Marlene's frail shoulders. "I told ya she was having a rough time of it, Lieutenant. Ya never shoulda come back."

Marlene patted Lunk's hand and gazed up at him fondly. "I'm all right, Lunk. Really."

Scott felt her eyes return to him and swallowed hard as he perched himself on the edge of the table. "Marlene," he began, "how much do you remember about those last few days at Reflex Point?"

"Only some of it, Scott. I remember when we were all inside the central chamber together. With Sera and Corg and the Queen-Mother."

"What made the horde—er, the Queen-Mother leave, Marlene? I mean, I'm sure she realized the fleet had plans to irradiate the area, but it seemed like she'd decided to leave before the neutron missiles were launched."

Marlene nodded and reached across the table for a water bottle. "It's true, Scott. And something vital left me when she departed." She took a long pull from the bottle. "I know you sensed it when you held me. I feel as though I'm only half-here, as though if I breathe too deeply I'll fade from sight. But I have a knowledge of things, Scott, a knowledge that seems undreamed of by any race."

"Don't worry," Lunk said, "I'm not about to let you fade away."

Marlene squeezed his hand. "You see, Scott, the Queen-Mother finally understood the reasons for all that had happened on Optera, Tirol, and Earth, and that knowledge liberated her."

"But what was it she understood?" Scott asked.

Marlene quivered. "I can't tell you, Scott."

"Please, Marlene," Scott snapped.

Lunk stepped out from behind the chair. "I'm warning you, Lieutenant."

Marlene put a hand on his balled-up fist. "No, Lunk, Scott doesn't understand. It's not that I'm *keeping* something from you, Scott. I only mean that you're asking the wrong person."

"Sera," Scott said after a moment's reflection.

"Yes. She was more closely bound to the Regis than I was. But I fear that bond has affected her more than it has me."

"Do you know where she is?"

Marlene closed her eyes and took a shuddering breath. "I can sense where she is. Sometimes I can almost see through her eyes and feel her suffering."

Scott edged closer to her. "Where, Marlene?"

"The city of tall towers in the Northlands. The one Sera and Corg were to rule."

Scott and Lunk exchanged looks and simultaneously said: "Mannatan."

"Yes. She is with Lancer."

Scott was already on his feet. "Will you come with me, Marlene? You, too, Lunk," he was quick to add. "Just until we locate her."

"Forget it, Lieutenant," Lunk said. "Marlene's not going anywhere."

Marlene stood up and gently swung Lunk around to face her. "But I am, Lunk. Don't you see that I have to go?"

Lunk's face fell. "No, Marlene, no. You can just stay here and let me take care of you. You said yourself you were all right. I could just—"

"No, Lunk, it's no good this way," she cut him off. "Remember who and what I am."

Lunk stiffened. "You're Marlene, that's it."

Marlene shook her head. "I am Invid, Lunk." She reached up to stroke his face. "But that doesn't mean I haven't loved you."

Lunk steeled himself, holding back his anger and grief. "You'll come back to me?" he asked softly.

"Nothing can take away these past few months, Lunk."

It was Scott's turn to avert his gaze.

He swore to himself he would never love again.

With Marlene in the copilot's seat, Scott returned the jet to the REF's provisional planetside base on the Venezuelan coast and apprised Vince Grant of his plans to continue on to the Northlands. The general informed him of the successful position jump undertaken by the *Ark Angel* and the rapidly approaching launch window for the fold to Haydon IV. To speed Scott and Marlene on their way, Grant ordered that they be escorted to and from the Northlands city in one of the ship's few remaining reconfigurable Veritechs.

From what Scott could gather, Mannatan—recently returned to its original name of New York—was fast becoming a population center once again. The narrow island city had miraculously escaped saturation by Dolza's deathbolts, only to suffer disastrously some twenty years later at the hands of the Regis's power-mad "son," Corg. But by then the city had already fallen into the hands of street crazies 'who had somehow survived a radiation pall that had hung over the city for more than fifteen years' and roving gangs of Foragers and rough-trade Southern Cross deserters. A scarcity of food and arable land had kept the population numbers low, but now that New York had become a kind of raw-materials depot for developing towns to the south and west, a barter system for foodstuffs had been implemented.

The Veritech put down west of the Hudson River, leaving Scott and Marlene to negotiate the rest of the journey on foot, along with hundreds of other migrants who were talking or buying passage through checkpoints on the single bridge that linked city and mainland. Scott saw the end result of Corg's fiery campaign to bring the city to its knees: huge leveled tracts where tall brick and stone buildings had once stood, gridded by the scorched remains of asphalt and concrete roadways.

Marlene acted as guide, drawing on her recently enhanced psychic talents to close on her sister simulagent's whereabouts. In a certain sense she seemed more the Terran than Scott. But Scott refused to be fooled by the human guise the Invid Queen-Mother had fashioned for her, and so their conversations were strictly of the pragmatic sort. Scott, after all, was on a military mission.

Marlene led them ultimately to a refurbished theater in the city's midtown district, where a young Hispanic named Jorge greeted them at the door and affirmed that Lancer was in fact part of a troupe of actors, singers, and musicians.

After the less than warm reunions with Rand and Lunk, Scott was expecting more of the same from Lancer, but the former stage gender-bender surprised him by running up the broad aisle after Jorge's announcement and embracing the two of them like family.

"Scott, I can't believe it!" Lancer said, gripping him by the arms. "God, it's great to see you again." He had equal enthusiasm for Marlene, along with a bear hug that went on for well over a minute.

Lancer looked lean and limber in tight-fitting trousers and a sleeveless shirt, but Scott noted dark circles under the singer's eyes and a somberness beneath the cheeriness of the moment. The natural color of Lancer's hair was growing in. Scott thought briefly of Yellow Dancer and wondered whether she was gone for good.

"You don't know how I need you guys right now," Lancer continued, taking hold of their hands.

"What is it, Lancer?" Marlene asked.

"Your sister," he said, favoring Marlene's hand. "I'm afraid she's dying."

Sera was bedridden in Lancer's backstage room, a tight, cluttered space that apparently served as living quarters and dressing room. A man named Simon was ministering to her, but he exited as Lancer entered, stopping only to introduce himself to Scott and Marlene in an affected, slightly effeminate manner.

Fetally curled beneath the bed's threadbare blankets, Sera seemed hardly more than a specter. "I've been waiting for you to come, Ariel," she said as Marlene kneeled beside the bed and laid a comforting hand on her heaving breast.

"Sister—"

Sera pressed a finger against Marlene's lips to quiet her. "Do not weep for me, Ariel. I am to rejoin the Queen-Mother."

"Then I'll return with you, sister."

Sera shook her head. "No, Ariel, your destiny lies along a different path. And what a wonderful one it is."

Marlene leaned closer to her sister, her eyes brimming with tears. "Tell me, Sera."

"You need know only this, Ariel: that the world can be remade. The Queen-Mother learned this when she mated with the Protoculture—the goal of the Great Work, the transmutation of our race."

"The Protoculture!"

"Yes, Scott," Sera said, looking at him. "Your people will understand what to make of this."

"Stay, sister," Marlene pleaded with her. "Love has the power to keep you here."

Sera smiled. "No, Ariel. Love has the power to release me . . ."

With that, the Invid simulagent shut her eyes and surrendered her all too brief life.

Scott watched horrified but transfixed as Sera grew subtle and translucent, then slowly faded from sight. An eerie breeze caressed his cheek as the blankets dropped empty and silent to the foam mattress.

Lancer clutched desperately for what was no longer there.

"This is my fate also," Marlene said, turning to Scott with tears coursing down her cheeks. "You were right to promise you would never love again!"

CHAPTER SIX

Of course I understand how you feel, you big jerk. You think I want to break up the team? But look at things from my side, will you, Bowie? First, I've got Max and Miriya riding my tail about shipping back on the fortress, and now I find out that Rem's going along for the ride. I can't handle it just yet, that's the long and short. I look at him, and I see Zor Prime. Ask yourself what it would have been like if Musica had died instead of Octavia—god forbid. I mean, how could you look at her without thinking about Musica? So maybe Haydon IV's going to work out for me. Maybe I'll even get to know Aurora a little better. Anyway, from what I hear, at least it'll be a change for the quiet.

Dana Sterling in a letter to Bowie Grant, quoted in
Altaira Heimel, *Butterflies in Winter:
Human Relations and the Robotech Wars*

DANA STERLING TIGHTENED HER GRIP ON THE BALcony railing and launched phrases of gratitude into Haydon IV's amber skies. In the plaza twenty stories below her, pedestrians were scurrying for cover as Glike rumbled and shook. Like bare trees caught in the hurricaning mass of a storm front, the city's tapering glasslike spires swayed and snapped, falling in a prismatic rain of deadly gems. Skyways danced loose their walls and roofs of transparent sheathing and sent them crashing to heaving, buckling streets and garden-lined thoroughfares. Onion domes and entablatures fissured; ornate facades and friezes peeled away from buildings and archways; water surged from canals and drained from lakes into the planetoid's ruptured seams.

" 'Bout time there was action around the place!'' Dana yelled to no one in particular.

She leapt back from the railing to flatten herself against the building's exterior wall as a plummeting guillotine blade of permaplas struck the balcony edge and splintered into hundreds of angry fragments. At the same time the entire city seemed to tilt radically to one side, the normally clear skies tainted with smoglike roilings of clouds. Where she could see the horizon, Glike's backdrop of photo-perfect mountains wavered, as though dazzled by atmospheric heat.

We're finally seeing Haydon IV's other face, Dana thought.

She had heard all about the battle that had been fought there years before between the Sentinels and the Invid Regent, but that might as well have been a campfire tale. Glike had been fully rebuilt by the time she had arrived, and it had been nothing less than paradise since.

Hopelessly boring.

But something had finally happened to shake things up. It did not seem possible that Haydon IV could be subject to tectonic shifts, but who could tell? Well, Exedore maybe, or his free-floating good buddy Veidt. Some internal malfunction, then, some glitch in the unfathomable technology that kept the world turning. An actual *invasion* was too much to hope for—a chance to see for herself those well-concealed planetary defenses everyone talked about. The ones said to react to the mere *suggestion* of aggression, the ones that forced everyone on-world to hang up their hip howitzers when they rode into town.

But even if it turned out to be nothing more than a quake, it was certainly more excitement than she had seen since Exedore had burst into the Sterling's high-rise quarters three months ago, raving that the planetoid's so-called Awareness had gotten itself all fired up about something or other.

The collapse of a structure down below sent a swirling cloud of debris up the face of the building. Dana heard panicked cries in several offworld tongues.

"Dana!" her parents shouted from inside their living quarters.

She turned and passed through the balcony's field portal in a long-legged rush, blond hair in wild disarray. Her father was by the lift-tube door, a few obviously irreplaceable items clutched to his chest. Her mother had Aurora, Dana's eight-year-old sister, by the wrist. Dark-eyed and otherworldly, she was nearly five feet tall already and a regular pain in the ass. It was hard for Dana to believe they had had the same father, but that was a thought she kept to herself. Veidt claimed that Aurora's rapid development and psychic gifts had come about as the result of Miriya's experiences on Garuda, but Dana ventured that it had more to do with something the Haydonites were putting in the food.

Aurora was not calling Dana's name. The child spoke so infrequently that when she did, everyone stopped to listen. But even though she was mouse-quiet, one always knew when she was around.

"Hurry, Dana!" Miriya said, joining her husband at the lift. She, too, had a few things in hand. Dana glanced around the room and quickly decided that there was nothing she needed to keep.

Let it all come down, she thought.

Llan and Anad, their two Haydonite advocates, were already in the tube. It was the only place planetside where everyone got to hover together, except on the city's Arabianlike flying carpets. Dana often wondered just whose bright idea those things had been. Some planet-hopping culture hero named Haydon was credited with *building* the world; Dana had him figured for some kind of kidder.

The tube field was as calm as the eye of a storm.

"What do you think, Max," she said excitedly, "an attack?" She rarely called him "Dad." Somehow it didn't feel right to her after their thirteen-year separation. Not that she didn't love him and Miriya both; it was simply that they had *changed* so much.

"I hope not, Dana," Max told her, adjusting his glasses so that they sat where they were supposed to. "For the sake of whoever'd be foolish enough to try."

So gentle-voiced, Dana thought. It was a continual source of amazement, especially when she tried to picture her parents mixing it up inside the SDF-1 with knives or battle mecha. And Max—*cripes*! Max had been gobbling Malcontents for breakfast when Dana was a toddler!

"Upon exiting the lift tube, you must proceed across the plaza and descend the elevators to level four," Llan sent, as if he were giving orders all of a sudden. But only Dana seemed disturbed by the tone.

"Level four, my ass, Llan. I think we better shuttle up to one of the trade ships. I'd rather ride this out up there—whatever this is. Wouldn't you, Max? Miriya?" Dana noticed that Aurora was giving her one of those funny looks.

"No, Dana," Miriya answered. "I think it's best that we follow Llan's advice for the time being."

"Your mother is correct," Llan sent with emphasis.

Dana folded her arms across the sequined bib of her jump-suit and faced off with the taller of the two Haydonites. "Yeah? Then tell us what's going on."

"A slight readjustment," Anad answered.

"Slight?"

"We are arrived," Llan interrupted as the tube field opened onto the plaza.

Things were even worse close up, Dana realized. On the far side of the plaza, the entire colonnade of a Tiresian-style commercial hall had crumbled, burying dozens of Karbarran traders and visitors under tons of debris. The ursinoid beings, who had been enjoying great prosperity among the Local Group worlds since the fall of the Regent, constituted the majority of Haydon IV's alien population, but Dana could see quite a few injured Praxians emerging from the ruined building. Elsewhere, a couple of dazed Spherisians were wandering aimlessly through the pandemonium. The Hay-donites themselves, however, were unhurt; it was as though they had known beforehand which areas to avoid.

"Move quickly and orderly if you wish to avoid injury," Llan sent to the Sterlings, attempting to hurry them along by hovering at their backs a yard off the plaza's adamantine-smooth surface.

"They need help," Dana said, indicating a small group of Karbarrans who, heedless of the dangers overhead, were attempting to dig out their trapped companions.

"*Move!*" Anad sent sharply in response.

Max could not fail to notice the change in Anad and Llan and was about to protest, when a series of blindingly blue energy bolts tore up into the sky from the outlying sectors of the city. From somewhere deep outside Glike's obscuring haze came scattered reports of explosive light that reached the surface like heated thunder.

"It *is* an invasion!" Dana exclaimed.

But even as she said it, she noted something inexplicable going on around her: Individual Haydonites had begun to employ some sort of energy weapon to herd the plaza's off-worlders toward the subwaylike entrances to the city's sub-surface maze of transport corridors and multilevel shelters. On closer inspection, Dana saw that the light-prods were emanating from the Haydonites' foreheads, from the cabochon-like organs centered there, which Veidt had once called *dzentile*. The English term that came closest was *governor*, but Dana suddenly understood that those regulators could be made to serve a double-edged function.

She took a quick head count, calculating just how many Haydonites she would have to take down to clear a path out of the plaza. Beginning with Llan, who was still hovering at her back, although he had yet to demonstrate any light-prod capability. Answering to Anad's telepathic insistence, Max, Miriya, and Aurora were already halfway across the square.

"Move!" Llan sent with sufficient force to make Dana's eyes cross.

Oh, you're gonna get yours, she promised herself, mentally forging her spin kick. But no sooner had she commenced her turn than Max grabbed her around the shoulders and swung her off her feet. "Dana, we don't have a chance," he told her.

Dana watched a nascent glow center itself above Llan's expressionless visage. "Well, we certainly don't now," she said, shrugging out of Max's restraining hold.

Llan and Anad were more vigilant after that, making certain to keep the entire family between them for the rest of the dash across the plaza, relaxing their guard only after the Sterlings were well inside the accessway, dwarfed by several dozen Karbarrans who had been funneled in from the collapsed commercial center.

"That was a foolish thing to do," Max said in a lecturing tone, loud enough to be heard above the ursinoids' unnerving growls and grumblings.

"Maybe it was," Dana conceded, "but I don't like it when somebody says they're concerned for my safety and then aims a weapon at me."

The incident only pointed up the differences between them. Dana had had reservations about returning to Haydon IV with her parents as early as those first few weeks in Tiresia, but it had meant so much to them that she get to know Aurora and give peace a chance. And then, when she had learned that Rem had assigned himself to the SDF-3, she saw no alternative but to give Haydon IV a try. Oh, she supposed she could have signed aboard the *Ark Angel* or any one of the ships of the fleet, but she saw little purpose to it.

It had come as quite a shock to find yet another Zor-clone waiting on Tirol after she had just finished her brief go-round with one on Earth. Rem and Zor Prime were more like twins separated at birth than clones, but there were enough underlying similarities to make her feel as though she were dealing with the same person. She thought the original Zor must have been one mixed-up character, another trickster in a galaxy full of them.

She still couldn't explain just what it was about the slender, elfin-featured clones that drew her to them. But it seemed obvious that the attraction arose from the Zentraedi, biogenetically engineered side of her personality.

Those thoughts were with her for the duration of the short descent to Llan's "level four," where, she imagined, luxuriously appointed shelters awaited them. She had even begun to feel guilty about her perhaps misguided outburst in the plaza and was about to apologize to Max, when from up ahead in the corridor—the recycled air thick with the musky smell of Karbarran fur and fear—came cries of protest in trader's tongue.

"You limbless mechanoids!" one Karbarran yelled. "May Haydon curse the lot of you!"

Dana went up on tiptoe in an attempt to discern what all the commotion was about, but all she could see was the backs of massive shoulders and knob-horned heads. It was not until the group reached the terminus of the corridor, where it opened into a vast, domed chamber lit by an unseen source, that she glimpsed the reason for the Karbarrans' distress: A police force of black-cloaked Haydonites a meter taller than the norm were using their enabled light-prods to segregate the confused crowd into planetary types, shepherding each into separate rooms similar to ones Dana knew had been used by the Invid Regis to contain the Sisters of the Praxian diaspora.

"Comport yourselves in a manner befitting the intelligence of your race and no harm will come to you," the police line sent to everyone in frightening telepathic discord. "Your nutritional and medical needs will be attended to. Haydon IV will strive to make you as comfortable as possible in your containment."

"Imprisonment, I'd say," said an all-too-familiar voice off to the left of the Sterling family. Dana caught sight of Exedore peeking out from behind the high-collared cloak of one of the hovering jailers.

"Yes," he added, folding his arms and glancing around. "I suggest that we consider ourselves under arrest."

As expected, their individual cells were splendidly designed affairs with all the necessary conveniences and furnishings, all the more sinister in their homeyness. Exedore and the Sterlings found themselves lodged with the four Praxians whose very size dictated that they be given the largest of the four rooms. Their section of the jail was flanked by Karbarran and Spherisian quarters but was effectively sealed off from them, with access to the central portion of the domed chamber barred by laser fence. Thoughts of escape were not only difficult to entertain but periodically discouraged by squads of the now obsequious jailers who glided through sweeps of the area.

Dana, however, had not yet given up on the idea and sat timing the patrols while Exedore filled everyone in on the details of his own arrest.

"One moment Veidt and I were interpreting the results of our latest calculations, and the next I was being hurried out of the data room by two of these black-cloaked fellows, with Veidt warning me to obey their every command."

"Our advocates acted the same way," Max said. "Turned on us without warning."

"Oh, I don't think it safe to assume they were *acting* at all," Exedore cautioned. "It's my belief that the Awareness sent a command to each and every Haydonite—a telepathic stirring, if you will, analogous to that which prompted the planet to reorient itself in space."

"Then we are . . . moving?" Miriya asked.

Exedore nodded. "Most definitely moving."

"But we saw a salvo of energy bolts, Exedore," Dana interjected. "The planet's probably moving because it's under attack."

Exedore shook his head. "There's been no attack, although what you witnessed was certainly defensive fire. It seems that the commander of one of the Karbarran cargo ships armed his weapons array when planetary realignment commenced. The Awareness registered this and responded as programmed. I'm afraid several ships were destroyed in the process. This much I was able to learn from Veidt."

"Then our lives are in danger," Miriya said, hugging Aurora to her.

"No, child. Haydon IV is not only abandoning its orbit around this system's primary but shedding its atmosphere as it accelerates. That's precisely why we've all been brought down here.

"For all this sudden militant posturing, they do seem to have our safety in mind. Haydon knows they require no true atmosphere for themselves, nor any need of Glike, for that matter." The Zentraedi snorted. "A surface paradise, indeed, for that's all that it was—a veneer, to borrow a Terran word.

"It only confirms what I've been saying all along: that Haydon IV is not a planet transformed by ultratech wonders but a *ship*. Its very name suggests as much. Haydon *IV*, and yet it occupies the third place in the Briz'dziki system." Exedore adopted a puzzled frown. "No. It has come to be known as Haydon IV because it was Haydon's *fourth*."

"Haydon's fourth what?" Max wanted to know.

Exedore threw up his hands. "Any answer I give you would be pure speculation. Much as my guess as to exactly where it is that we're headed."

"We'll know when we get there, is that it?" Dana said.

"Well put."

Max looked from Exedore to Dana and back again. "But what about these calculations of yours? You still think this has something to do with the SDF-3?"

"I'm certain of it," Exedore affirmed. "And with the Invid departure as well. A pulse of novel energy has been sent into the known universe. Our calculations prove beyond a shadow of a doubt that the focus of this outpouring is the dead star we Zentraedi know as Ranaath's.''

Miriya sucked in her breath. ''Exedore!''

''Yes, Miriya, I'm afraid so. But there's more: This pulse has also caused subtle but potentially dangerous quantum and gravitational shifts throughout the continuum. All standard measurements seem to have been infinitesimally affected.''

''Meaning what?'' Max said.

''Meaning that something unprecedented has occurred, Max. It's as though everything is suddenly drawing closer and closer together.''

CHAPTER
SEVEN

> *Eventually, Rem saw the logic of the REF's arguments [that a Protoculture matrix was essential to ensure certain victory against the Invid Regis]—or at least he gave Lang every impression of being convinced. Just as Zor had once given sway to the Robotech Masters' conviction that knowledge went hand in hand with power and that all real power sprang from the conquest of life itself . . . This tendency to submit, this plasticity, was a character flaw inherited by both clones—Rem and Zor Prime— and taken advantage of by yet new generations of masters. "Zor, the reshaped," as Lang himself once thought to describe Rem in his notes. Who else could have enticed Protoculture from the secret places of the Flower but one of equal lability?*
>
> Adrian Mizner, *Rakes and Rogues: The True Story of the SDF-3 Mission*

EVEN WITH THE KNOWLEDGE THEY HAD BEEN ABLE TO amass during the voyages of the SDFs-1 and -3 and with what little they had been able to beg, borrow, and steal from the Sentinels, the fortress's chief astrogators still considered themselves among the Quadrant's least experienced travelers. So while the void they had been folded into presented a novel challenge, there was no sure way of ascertaining whether this "newspace"—as it had been termed—was not just some commonplace occurrence among the more well traveled. To this end, interviews with those Sentinels aboard—Kami, Learna, Lron, Crysta, Baldan, Gnea, and others—had thus far proved unenlightening, a not entirely unexpected development given that the original crew of the starship *Farrago* had never been top-notch spacefarers to begin with.

Lang nevertheless had gone about his investigation of the

ship's environment with unflagging confidence and textbook determination. The results of Jack Baker's brief extravehicular recon were in. Exterior background temperatures and the velocity of light had been measured and found to be constant; the fortress chronometers were still functioning. Physical laws inside the ship—and within a radius of a half million kilometers from it—were in fact operating much as they should have. It was simply that the stars—indeed, space itself—had disappeared.

The SDF-3's reflex engines were functioning, but there was still no*where* for the fortress to go.

"I'm inclined to favor the hyperspace hypothesis," Lang was saying, eyes glued to an immense tabletop display screen in his office. Rem stood behind him, just off to one side, the handsome features of his pale face highlighted by the screen's intermittent flashings. "We've somehow become trapped in the fold corridor itself."

Rem grunted noncommittally. "You're dismissing the popular notion, then—the one circulating through the ship?"

"What, that we're all actually *dead*? I certainly am."

No one knew just how the rumor got started, but it seemed that the results of a survey taken of some two hundred crewpersons had revealed remarkable similarities in their fold, space lace experiences. These included feelings of tranquillity, out-of-body experience, the encountering of a presence or a deceased relative in a dark tunnel, a sudden urge to review one's life, a warm and accepting light at the end of the tunnel, and a brief merging with that light prior to an immediate return to physicality.

"If we were all dead," Lang continued, "we probably wouldn't have returned at all."

"And how to prove it in any case?" Rem said, smiling. "Against *what* can we measure nonexistence?"

Lang turned to regard the Tiresian, pleased that he had finally succeeded in spiriting him away from Minmei, if only for a short while. One would have thought the strangeness of the ship's predicament alone would have been enough to pique Rem's interest, but the Zor-clone had agreed to a conference only after Lang had made mention of the vanished Protoculture.

Lang had reminded himself later that he should have known

better; Protoculture was the only thing that ever brought Rem around. But Rem did not share Lang's enthusiasm for Protoculture's application to mechamorphosis or astrogation. In fact, the REF had had to coerce him into lending his brilliant talents to the creation of the facsimile matrix by painting lurid scenarios of what was bound to occur throughout the Quadrant should the Invid Regis have her way with Earth. How long, they asked him to consider, before the Queen-Mother would decide to spread her vengeful horde across the stars as her husband had done? How long before her armies would return to the Local Group for what they had been forced to surrender—Optera itself? And what of the Praxians, then, who had made that tortured world their own? And what of Tirol and Spheris and the rest, so recently liberated from the claw hold of that very race?

Rem could be infuriating at times, but how Lang enjoyed the few discourses they had shared! How *thrilling* it was to converse with an intellect as powerful as his own. What they might be able to achieve together, he often thought, were it not for Rem's preoccupation with the biotransmutational aspects of Protoculture or his inexplicable attachment to Lynn-Minmei.

Lang swung back to the tablescreen. "Oh, I'll admit there's something to this afterlife speculation that's worth pursuing," he said abruptly, "but for the present there are more tangible enigmas to grapple with." He motioned to the displays. "These are the latest readouts."

Rem leaned over the table.

"Either this void has yet to decide which set of physical laws it plans to subscribe to, or our scanners are in over their artificial heads." The Terran scientist's voice was a mixture of apprehension and excitement. "I haven't seen anything like it since my supercollider days thirty years ago. But at least I knew then that our accelerators were *manufacturing* all those weakly interacting massive particles. Here, there's no rhyme or reason to it. One could almost believe we've entered a kind of dark-matter universe."

"I doubt we could exist in such a place, Lang."

"Precisely my point. The findings are more consistent with fold anomalies than anything else."

Rem nodded. "Then the real question we should be asking

ourselves is whether the ship is still on its way *to* somewhere or whether it has in fact arrived.''

Lang threw him a skeptical look. "I don't see how we can possibly be on our way to something without the fold drives.''

Rem made a dismissive motion with his hand. "The Protoculture is only essential for *initiating* a fold, Lang; it has little to do with destination.''

"But how are we to emerge, then?''

Rem's gaze grew unfocused. "You fail to see the potential, Doctor.''

"Perhaps I do, Rem, but—''

"When all you need do is think back to your experiences inside the ship you called SDF-1 when it crash-landed on Earth.''

Lang's face went blank.

"Your own notes state that you were at a loss to explain the time deplacement you and your team experienced inside the ship.''

"Yes . . .''

"And so you postulated that some 'quantum'—your word, Doctor—some quantum of hyperspace had adhered to the ship.''

"And the team was actually walking through a kind of hyperspace dimension,'' Lang finished in a rush. "Yes, of course, I remember now.''

Rem laughed. "Ah, what tricks the overmind plays with us!'' He offered Lang a tight-lipped smile. "Listen to your words, Doctor: 'I remember now.' That's what the SDF-3 is doing. Zor's ship captured a quantum of hyperspace and conveyed it into the world of time. Our ship has captured a quantum of time and carried it into hyperspace.''

Lang glanced at the mathematical constructs assembling themselves on the tablescreen as if to confirm something.

"I don't know why the Protoculture chose this particular moment to abandon us,'' Rem resumed, "or just what Shapings are to be inferred from it. But I do know that the SDF-3 is remembering now—*now*, Lang.'' He gestured toward the exterior bulkheads. "And what I think we're seeing out there is a universe in the making.''

* * *

"Remember when he was just learning to walk?" Rick asked, regarding his five-year-old raven-haired son from the transparent side of the nursery's one-way mirror. "It was like he wanted to start off running. Always in a hurry to get somewhere.".

Lisa's eyes narrowed somewhat. "No thanks to you. Walking must have seemed awfully tame after all the aerial acrobatics you put him through."

Rick laughed. "Guilty as charged. But I didn't have anything to do with turning him into a whiz kid. That's gotta be your doing."

Lisa patted the bun of gray-streaked hair at the back of her head and laughed with him.

In meeting at the nursery, the two proud parents had agreed to call a moratorium on discussing the fortress's present circumstance, at least until Lang and Rem could sort out whether they had punched themselves into some misty uncharted corner of hyperspace or were simply on line in limbo, waiting for judgment. Morale was low in all sections, and so Lisa had ordered most of the ship to secure from battle stations.

She returned her eyes to Roy and to the transformable puzzle block one of the ship's child-care specialists had handed him. Silently, as she watched Roy rotate the alloy block in his tiny hand, she applauded his analytical powers: the way he seemed to size it up before making a move, the way the expression on his sweet face mirrored his intense concentration. At the same time she marveled at the dexterity he demonstrated as he began to expose one after another of the block's hidden forms, nimble fingers prying open doors, separating sections, twisting others, extending telescoping parts.

And just as silently she worried.

Up until a few months ago Roy had seemed just an ordinary child to her, perhaps *too* ordinary, if anything. For all her efforts at keeping him as far from the SDF-3 as she could manage, at seeking to raise him as someone other than the son of two career officers, Roy had been going through the same action/adventure stages as his peers aboard the fortress. One could take the child away from Earth, but one apparently could not take Earth away from the child. Airplanes, action figures, toy guns . . . even an invisible friend who still showed up every so often.

But things had changed once she and Rick had completed their transfer to the SDF-3. Suddenly it was puzzles that fascinated him, both manual and computer-generated. And then there was *the look* he would give her sometimes, as if to say: *I know exactly what you're thinking.* To hear Kazianna tell it, her son Drannin and some of the other Zentraedi children were behaving likewise, and there had been occasions when Lisa had had to drag Roy screaming from his outsize "playmates." She still didn't know whether to feel comforted by all the youthful bonding or even more worried than she already was. More than anything she wished Miriya were there to tell her what it was like to nurture a genius, what the Praxians sometimes called a *Wyrdling*.

And how much of it, Lisa wondered, could be traced to the ship itself?

She felt Rick's arm go around her shoulder, and she rested her head against his.

"We've had some good days, haven't we?" Rick said softly. "Especially these past few years."

She knew what he meant: how good it had been to absent themselves from the endless tasks they had overseen during Reconstruction and again after the destruction of New Macross.

Rick turned to face her. "I've been missing them lately. Really feeling at a loss."

Lisa recalled her postfold malaise and shot him a look. "You, too, Rick? Like you've lost something important?"

He nodded. "First I thought it was just leaving Tirol, but it's more than that. Lately I've been thinking about Pop's air circus, Macross Island, even the *Mockingbird*."

"But it's pervasive, isn't it?" Lisa said. "Like you can't pin it down."

Rick bit his lower lip. "I think I know what it is now," he began with a nervous laugh. "I'm willing to lay odds it's the Proto—"

"Begging your pardon, sirs," Rick's adjutant interrupted, stepping through the observation room hatch. "Tactical Center requests the admiral's immediate presence."

"What is it?" Lisa asked, hurrying to the room's intercom.

"We've got a screenful of bogies, sir."

"Signatures?" Rick said.

"Not yet, sir. Radar's silent. The ship's bio-sensors made the call."

Rick and Lisa traded looks. "Bio-sensors?"

"TIC patched the system into IFF, sir, but couldn't raise a signature or profile."

"Invid?" Lisa said, cocking her head to one side. "Some self-mutated form?"

Rick met his adjutant at the hatch. "Maybe someone's shown up to lead us home," he suggested, and was gone.

Belowdecks in one of the fortress's mecha bays, Captain Jack Baker gave a downward tug to his flight jacket as he paced back and forth in front of his small audience of veteran pilots and mechamorph aces.

And not one of them had soared where he had now.

"You may think the background stuff's unimportant, Captain Phillips," Jack was continuing after a bothersome interruption, "but what I'm trying to do is give you a sense of the experience."

Sean Phillips threw an imploring look to the high ceiling. "No offense, Baker, but I think we've all heard about what happened when you piloted the VT down to Haydon IV. I just don't see the relevance."

Jack's innocent face reddened. With so many heavy hitters to choose from, he still could not figure out why the admiral had singled him out for the void recon. He hoped, of course, that Hunter's finger had simply gone right to the top of the list, but then, he supposed that list could have been alphabetical. Jack nevertheless was determined to make the most of the distinction while it lasted.

"I'm talking about the *unknown*, Captain," he told Sean. "The importance of state of mind."

"Like going against the Robotech Masters was a given?" Sean asked.

Jack grew flustered. "I'm not saying that. I'm just saying that what Haydon IV threw at us was totally unlike anything we'd faced."

"Did we ever tell you about the spade fortress that put down just outside of Monument City?" Sergeant Angelo Dante asked in a conversational tone, the only one of the group who had refused to accept a commission. He swung around to face everyone, elbows flared, large hands on wide-spread knees. "The Fifteenth ATAC was ordered to recon the ship, see. So we tank out there and—"

"Now who's being irrelevant?" Jack cut in. "I mean, why don't we just invite some of the Karbarrans in here to entertain us with *their* war stories? Or how 'bout getting Gnea in here to talk about hand-to-hand."

"Yeah, I'll bet you'd enjoy that, Jack," Marie Crystal laughed, affectionately nudging Karen Penn with an elbow. Black Lion leader during the Second Robotech War, she was just another officer here. Sean, who had been her fiancé three times over the past year, was being his usual arrogant self, and while she rarely approved of his teasing sarcasm, Baker was so easy to put off balance. "What d' you think, Karen? Shall we call the Praxians in?" she contributed.

Karen smiled and regarded Jack from her seat. Lithesome and honey-blond, she appeared to be every bit Marie's opposite, but in fact the two had grown to be close friends. "That's up to Captain Baker," she said. "It's his show."

"Jeez," Jack muttered, brushing back a recently styled silver-tinted pompadour, *"et tu?"* He spread his hands in a conciliatory gesture. "All right, for cryin' out loud, I'll get on with it."

The pilots applauded wildly as Jack called up memories of his brief EVA.

"It's like flying through a cloud," he began on a serious note. "Only there's no vapor around you, no droplets streaking your canopy. Other times it's like moving toward a cloud you can't seem to reach. I had a hard time looking forward, because everything started to go solid on me. But watching your displays doesn't help, because there's absolutely nothing happening on-screen. I kept feeling like I was close to punching through it, but it just went on and on. And it never changed, no matter which heading I took. The SDF-3 is your whole world, the only game in town."

He blew out his breath and shook his head. "I don't know what more to tell you, really. The VT performed well, no glitches in any of the systems. I thought it through a couple of reconfigurations, and there were no problems. Weapons systems seemed to be fully operational, but I was under orders not to enable. Dr. Lang's thinking is that missile propulsion isn't affected.''

"When do we get a crack at it?" Sean said, rising to his feet for added effect.

As soon as Admiral Hunter figures you're ready, Jack was about to tell him, when hooters drowned out the thought. The ship was returning to full-alert status. A female voice boomed from the flight bay's overhead speakers:

"We have uncorrelated targets closing on the fortress in all sectors. Captains Baker, Phillips, Penn, and Crystal report with your teams to assigned launch bays immediately. Substations November, Romeo, Tango, Zebra, prepare for . . ."

Jack let the rest of it pass right through him. Phillips and his 15th cohorts were already up and hurrying toward their VTs, pale-faced but eager wingmen—combat virgins the lot of them—falling in behind.

Jack stepped down from the missile pallet that had been his temporary stage, Karen was waiting for him, a grin forming.

"Cheer up, flyboy," she said, linking arms with him as he approached. "For what it's worth, you'll still go on file as being the first out."

Jack snorted sullenly. "Fame's a damned fleeting thing these days."

CHAPTER
EIGHT

The elderly spokesperson for what remained of the planetside contingent of the Army of the Southern Cross introduced herself to me as 'Regina Newhope.' The woman's associate—as facially scarred and ghoulish-looking a creature as I have ever encountered—went simply by the name 'Farnham.' I recall thinking at the time that there was something strangely familiar about the pair of them, something I wanted to connect to the deceased Lazlo Zand. Then, when I subsequently learned that Newhope's real name—her pre-Invid name—was Millicent Edgewick, I realized that the Zand connection was a sound one. And even now I'm certain that 'Farnham' was none other than the First Robotech War's most wanted political criminal, Senator Alfonse Napoleon Russo.

Dr. Harold Penn, quoted in
Justine Huxley's *I've Been to a Marvellous Party*

THE REF PILOTS WHO HAD ESCORTED SCOTT BERNARD to New York were ordered to return the colonel and his alien charge directly to Norristown rather than to the launch pad in Venezuela. The Southlands city—where tech crews ferried down from the orbiting *Ark Angel* had been working overtime to clear a landing zone for the soon-to-be-arriving dignitaries—had been selected as the temporary site of the reunited Earth governments.

No sooner had the VT set down than Marlene was whisked away to the REF's planetside HQ by three sinister-looking men from G2 dressed in dark suits and opaque glasses. Scott, too, was hurried off to yet another debriefing, but this time at the hands of the intel directorate chief himself, former Plenipotentiary Councilman Niles Obstat, the balding and stoop-shouldered old-guard ally of Emil Lang. Unlike the neurometric specialists whose job it had been to evaluate Scott's psychological state, Obstat was interested in learning all he could about the political climate of the Southlands. Which towns had impressed Scott most? Who seemed to be in charge? Who controlled the wealth, the distribution of goods, the private armies and fringe groups? Who had been partisans, and who had been sympathizers? And who headed up the quasi-religious movements like the Church of Recurrent Tragedy or the so-called Interstellar Retributionists?

Scott answered as best as he could, covering much of the same ground he had covered months earlier. Obstat pursued oblique lines of questioning, ever on the alert for nuance, personal impressions, the recollection of some seemingly trivial episode.

The sessions continued for two days. Scott was asked to thumb-print oaths and papers and was instructed not to discuss anything about the SDF-3 or the returning REF with "downsiders," which he understood to mean planet-bound Terrans of all varieties.

Afterward he was left pretty much to himself, and more than a week slipped by. Marlene was kept incommunicado; as far as anyone in G2 was concerned, the Invid simulagent was military property. Besides, as someone had suggested to Scott, she was a lot better off than she would have been on the streets, where if word of her background got out she wouldn't have lasted a day.

He didn't fully understand the reasons for all the secrecy about the missing flagship and the sudden inactivation of much of Earth's Protoculture-driven mecha until Vince Grant invited him to attend an introductory summit held in Norristown's city hall, a castlelike affair that had served as an Invid Protoculture storage facility during the occupation.

The REF was represented by the Plenipotentiary senators Penn, Huxley, Stinson, and Longchamps. The latter two, still in some sense allied with the old Southern Cross apparat, were a faction in their own right, hoping to reconnect with whoever was currently representing the interests of the demolished government of Wyatt "Patty" Moran, General Anatole Leonard, and Dr. Lazlo Zand. And while all three men had died during the final days of the Second Robotech War, a small group recently released from an Invid internment camp did step forward to speak on their behalf.

Planetside Earth had numerous secondary spokespersons as well, several of whom Scott recognized by sight and a few of whom he knew by reputation. Donald and Carla Maxwell, for example, from Deguello; and Terri Woods, one of Lancer's contacts in the resistance, who now headed up a diverse but vocal contingent of REF supporters. Then there were the two women Obstat had told Scott to keep an eye out for: ex-GMP lieutenant Nova Satori, the charismatic leader of the Homunculi Movement, and Jan Morris, Corporeal Fundamentalist, whose large following advocated a return to agrarian and religious primitivism.

Loyalists, separatists, cultists . . . each group took its turn at the podium, and each stirred argument, debate, in some cases violence among the gathered crowds. Scott could see that Huxley was bent on reaching accommodations with one and all, even though her patience was wearing thin. The Council's principal aim was the restabilization of humankind's understandably paranoid mind-set in the hope that Earth could avoid a return to the feudal mentality that had prevailed during the Masters War and the occupation. It was obvious that the REF figured to achieve that with the promise of advanced technologies in exchange for a large piece of the planet's geopolitical pie.

No mention was made of the missing SDF-3, nor was any attempt made to explain mecha failure or Earth's sudden energy crisis. The Council not only acted as though the situation were easily reversible but suggested that *they had even had a hand in bringing it about*!

No decisions had been reached by the time Scott was shuttled up to the *Ark Angel* to attend a prelaunch briefing. Justine Huxley, Longchamps, and the rest, backed by several squadrons of functioning mecha, remained on-world to press the REF's case. A select few were apprised of the fact that the *Ark Angel* would soon be leaving Earthspace.

The briefing was held in a dungeonlike cabinspace located on the starship's engineering level that had come to be called the Sentinels Bay, for it was there that campaign strategies had been hammered out. Scott arrived in the company of the

Grants' adjutants and aides; Vince and Jean were already positioned at the compartment's horseshoe-shaped table, along with Dr. Penn, Niles Obstat, and a dozen or so of the ship's command and intel officers. But the briefing did not get under way until the table's remaining seats were occupied by five of the most bizarre-looking civilians Scott had encountered in quite some time. Dressed alike in tight-fitting black jumpsuits studded with what looked like chrome stars, the five sported round mirror-lensed goggles and hairstyles that made the outlandish razor cuts and permtints of the century's first decade seem tame by comparison.

"Professor, I believe you're acquainted with everyone here," Harry Penn said by way of welcome. "With the possible exception of Colonel Bernard." Turning to Scott, he added: "Colonel Bernard, Professor Nichols, and his team from Cyber-Research, Doctors Stirson, Gibley, Strucker, and Shi-Ling."

The five Penn had addressed as doctors nodded in unison; they might have been clones or biogenetically engineered quadruplets. Of their apparent leader, a short, lantern-jawed man with an enormous pompadour of henna-colored hair, Scott asked, "Nichols, as in *Louie* Nichols, creator of the Syncron drive?"

"*Adapter* of the Syncron device, Colonel," the professor said, adjusting his glasses as if to sharpen their focus. "But yes, one and the same."

"I'm honored, sir," Scott said in obvious awe. The Nichols drive, as it was sometimes called, had been responsible for assuring the nearly instantaneous return of the REF fleet from Tirol. "Your reputation has reached clear across the Quadrant."

Nichols smiled tolerantly. "And we've heard about you, too, Colonel."

Scott's face flushed; Nichols's tone of voice left it unclear whether he had been complimented or insulted. His assistants, meanwhile, had begun to set up some sort of computer station off to one side of the table. Scott had never seen decks or consoles quite like the ones they were unpacking.

"Dr. Penn informs me you have some news for us, Professor," Vince was saying.

"Yes," Nichols said after a moment, "thanks to the colonel's capture of the simulagent."

Vince appraised Scott with a quick look. " 'Capture' might be too strong a word, Professor. As I understand it, the Invid, er, operative voluntarily turned herself over to REF custody."

Nichols made a dismissive gesture. "File it where you want, General. The important thing is that the simulagent gave us the go-to we needed on the Protoculture. Based on what we managed to access from it—"

"*It* has a name, Professor," Scott cut in angrily. "We called her . . . Marlene."

Nichols stared at him from behind the mirrored goggles. "Sorry about that, Colonel. I screened it but misfiled it somehow. Well, this *Marlene*, then, gave us a solid return on our investments. The Regis did in fact *wed* her race to all existing Protoculture at the moment of transubstantiation— the incident that gave rise to the 'phoenix vision' some of your own ship's crew have confessed to experiencing, Doctor."

Penn leaned back in his chair, stroking his chin as muttered questions and exclamations were exchanged around the table. "But Professor," he queried at last, "you said *all* existing Protoculture. And yet dozens of mecha remain fully functional, to say nothing of the *Ark Angel* herself."

Nichols traded amused looks with his associates. Scott noticed that the four had linked their terminals together, employing cables of peculiar design. From each console dangled equally strange-looking umbilical jacks.

"A valid prompt, Doctor, but you don't need a simul— er, a Marlene to run it. What I should have said was all the *first-generation* Protoculture—the pure strain that came from Zor's original matrix, along with the home brew the Regis was concocting from the orchards here."

"As distinct from what?" Penn asked.

Nichols let out an exasperated sigh. "As distinct, Doctor, from the Flower stuff the REF cooked down in this facsimile matrix Lang and the Tiresian—what's his name?"

"Rem," Gibley said.

"Rem. What Lang and Rem cobbled together on Tirol."

Penn and the REF staffers mulled it over for a noisy moment.

"That would account for the fact that certain mecha are still functioning," Vince offered. "But of course we'd have to do a complete craft-by-craft accounting. As far as the *Ark Angel* is concerned—"

"It is Sekiton-fueled," Nichols completed.

Penn's ruddy face registered astonishment. "My God. You're saying that the SDF-3 . . ."

Nichols nodded encouragement. "The fold generators of the SDF-3 were taken from Breetai's flagship and the Robotech factory satellite, both of which were fueled with first-generation Protoculture."

"And that Protoculture," Penn said, "was caught up in the Invid transformation that occurred here, on Earth."

"You've got it," Nichols told him, "If we can learn where the Invid went, we'll find the SDF-3."

"But how can we do that?" Jean Grant asked.

"Folding for Haydon IV is a good way to start," Nichols said. "The more I hear about Haydon and this 'Awareness,' the more I'm convinced there's a lead there. Second, we can take the Invid . . . woman along. Some part of her is still on-line with the Invid group-mind, wherever it is, in this dimension or some other."

Some other dimension? Scott wanted to ask him. Wrinkled foreheads and bobbing Adam's apples suggested that he was not alone in his concern. Nichols's group, however, seemed to be taking the revelations in stride. Scott watched the one named Gibley. He had one of the umbilicals in hand and seemed to be applying some sort of spray lubricant to the jack.

" 'We,' Professor," Vince said. "Can I take that to mean that you and your associates have agreed to accompany us?"

Nichols nodded. "But not for the reasons you probably imagine, General," he was quick to add. "Like most of you, we have friends on that ship who are important to us. But as for viewing Protoculture as a necessity in shaping Earth's future, we couldn't disagree with you more."

Scott's mouth dropped open as he saw Gibley part his long tail of bleached hair and insert the multipronged jack *directly into the base of his skull.*

Nichols caught Scott's expression. "They're called cyber-ports," he told Scott, fingering aside the hair on the right side of his cranium to reveal a similar alloy receptacle.

Jean Grant blanched as the rest of Nichols's team began to follow Gibley's lead.

"And we call this headlocking," Nichols explained, regarding the table for a moment. "You see, despite what you may think, Protoculture's reign is finished. Robotechnology is dead.

"It worked its final shapings in the Quadrant when it merged with the Invid. I suspect, in fact, that that was its raison d'être all along—to be both mate and propellant for the Invid transformation.

"But I repeat: It has no place in the world it reshaped in the process." Nichols shook his head, his eyes a mystery behind mirrors. "No. From this point on it will be up to *us* to shape our destiny as a race, and we will have to look to superintelligences to help us define and design our course."

He motioned to his headlocked associates, their activated consoles and rapt expressions. " 'Machine mind' holds the answers. Through it we will accomplish all that we have failed to accomplish in the past. Through it we will achieve where we have failed. Through it we will journey where we have never been."

The table waited in silence.

"Not out among the stars, either," Louie said with a grin. "But in a reality we will create. Using the power of our own enhanced intellects and the immortal machine bodies we will someday soon fashion for ourselves."

CHAPTER
NINE

*During the cruel reign of the Robotech Masters, Karbarra had
exported its revolution (along with tens of thousands of its pneumatic projectile rifles) to several Local Group worlds, including
Garuda, Praxis, and Spheris. During the Invid occupation, Karbarra had seen its very future (i.e., the Karbarran childcubs)
held hostage. The origin of the planet's subsequent turn to dreams
of empire is most often traced to its solid defeat over the (T. R.)
Edwards-controlled Invid on Optera (see La Paz, Mizner, Lon-
don, et al.). But who if not Haydon himself [sic] was Karbarra
rising up against—Haydon and the curse of his [sic] Ur-Flower.*

Noki Rammas, *Karbarra*

DANA WAS READY TO JUMP THE FIRST HAYDONITE
that glided across the laser-barred threshold to the Sterlings'
plush level-four lockup. But when that visitor turned out to
be Veidt, all she could do was quietly lay aside the Praxian
hardwood war club she had fashioned from a table leg, try
to ease unnoticed from her place of concealment behind the
couch, and join her parents and Exedore in questioning the
being who had been like family to all of them in their time
on-world.

She was encouraged to hear Veidt address everyone as "my
friends."

Exedore made his relief known with a slow exhalation of
breath. "What *is* going on, Veidt?" he asked, staring up into
the hovering figure's bilaterally symmetrical suggestion of fa-
cial features. "I certainly can't tell anything from your expression."

"Would that you *had* learned to discern our nuances,"
Veidt sent to everyone. "You would have undoubtedly no-

ticed alterations in my countenance since the initial stirrings of the Awareness some months ago. Our inner states are as much on display as your own, you know.''

"Tell us what's happening to you," Exedore said.

A dull, pulsating glow lit Veidt's *dzentile*. "Thoughts come not without great difficulty now, Lord Exedore.''

"Try, Veidt," Miriya said, "please.''

Veidt's hairless head rolled briefly within the high collar of the robe. "One might compare it to the Compulsion the Robotech Masters used to extract unfailing allegiance from the Zentraedi." The Haydonite regarded Max. "I have found nothing in Terran history that invites comparison, although my intuition tells me otherwise.

"We Haydonites nevertheless have as a world been forced to respond to a type of behavioral programming that up until recently has lain dormant within us. But it appears that those of us who have had continued contact with offworlders can exercise intermittent control over the programming.''

Exedore and the Sterlings could sense Veidt's musings. Alone among his planetary companions, Veidt had shed tears on the occasion of the death of Sarna, his mate in captivity, whose body had been delivered into the cupped hands of Haydon IV's towering shrine to its creator.

"The process is somewhat analogous to the defenses your bodies utilize in the resisting of biological contamination or infection," Veidt continued.

"I guess Anad and Llan haven't got the hang of it yet," Dana said.

Veidt rotated to face her. "They were probably more helpful than you realize, child.''

Exedore spoke up before Dana could respond. "But what brought this about, Veidt? Surely it has something to do with the Invid's departure. Only a believer in coincidence would fail to see the connection.''

Veidt's sendings ceased for a moment. "The Event has occurred, Lord Exedore. I can offer little more data than that. From the deepest center of my being arises an understanding that this world itself has been waiting and preparing for the Event for countless millennia, and yet I cannot speak of it. I know only that the waiting is complete.''

"You're telling us you've no idea what you've been waiting *for*?" Dana said.

"I am. Nor do I know what to expect."

"Why have we been arrested, Veidt?" Max demanded.

The Haydonite glided to the center of the room and back. "Arrest is not the appropriate term. You've done nothing illegal, nothing to warrant imprisonment."

Dana pointed to the laser-barred threshold. "In case you haven't noticed, Veidt, we're not exactly free to come and go as we choose."

"Protective custody is the term I would use," Veidt offered, as though he had been scrolling through a phrase file. "As I'm certain Lord Exedore has already informed you, Haydon IV has left orbit and is accelerating even now. Surely you accept the fact that you never would have been able to survive on the surface."

"Granted, Veidt," Miriya said. "We were brought down here for our own good; we've accepted that much. But does that mean we'll be released when we reach wherever it is we're going?"

Veidt's forehead pulsed with subdued light. "Not exactly. You see, it is important that you not be permitted to interfere with the successful completion of the secondary and tertiary stages. Therefore, you are to remain in protective custody until all post-Event phases have been carried out."

"But how long are we talking about?" Dana managed.

"As long as the operation requires," Veidt sent.

Max and Miriya stared at each other aghast. Exedore and Aurora assimilated the disclosure silently. Dana considered lunging for the hardwood war club she had stashed behind the couch.

"Violence should not be considered an option," the Haydonite said without facing anyone directly. "I should add that I have sought audience with Vowad."

Father of a sort to Sarna, Vowad was a high-ranking member of Haydon IV's Elite.

"And?" Exedore asked.

"He can do nothing. Offworlder contact has mitigated the impact of the Compulsion on Vowad as an entity, but he is still obliged to answer to the Elite, who have thus far remained fully responsive to the programming."

Dana felt her anger rising again.

"Perhaps I should remind you that one incident of violence has already been answered in kind," Veidt sent in her direction.

"The Karbarran vessel," Exedore said.

"*Vessels*, unfortunately. One Spherisian ship did, however, escape the acceleration unscathed."

"Has Karbarra been informed of the incident?" Max asked out of genuine concern.

"Yes, by the Spherisians themselves," Veidt sent. "In fact, there is some reason to believe that a Karbarran battle group is en route to Haydon IV at this very moment."

Max shot to his feet. "But you just said that interference couldn't be permitted! You've got to see that they're warned away."

Veidt grew quiet, as though accessing some remote mainframe. "I'm sorry, all of you. But it is apparently too late for that now."

At Admiral-Elect Lron's urgings, the Karbarran dreadnought had been named *N'trpriz* in honor of some Terran ship of primitive design. And while Commander K'rrk had not been against the idea at the time, he would have preferred a different vessel to call his own, a Sekiton-powered ship-of-the-line with a proper Karbarran name. The *Tracialle*, if he had had a choice or, failing that, the battlewagon *Yirrbisst*.

K'rrk sat in the command chair of the *N'trpriz*, shaking out the lingering effects of spacefold as his bridge crew fed him updates on the ship's position and readiness.

"Haydon IV coming into view, Commander," Mav reported from one of the forward duty stations. "All cruisers accounted for. Establishing matching velocity with the planet in three point seven units, sir."

"Thank you, Mav," K'rrk said from the helm chair. "Let's have a look at it."

The artificial planet resolved on the bridge's forward screen, variegated, rotating, but atmosphereless. A celestial wanderer no longer, but more the starship it was. Parsecs distant from that which it had called its home star for a time, and still accelerating.

K'rrk cupped a paw around his muzzle in a contemplative

gesture. Off to one side of the helm chair stood an enormous wooden wheel, a vestigial adornment overruled by Tiresian-made astrogational computers buried deep in the ship's heart but left in place out of respect for the Sentinels' "steamship," *Farrago*.

K'rrk turned to regard his science officer. "Could they be preparing to fold, Lorek?"

"A distinct possibility, Commander."

"What do scanners show?"

"Areas of extensive surface damage," Lorek responded after a moment. By Karbarran standards, he was tall and lean, with mottled fur and a curious cant to the diminutive, mushroom-shaped horns set between his ears. "Glike appears to be completely deserted, sir, although bio-indicators are registering life signs in several subsurface chambers."

"Do we have a fix on whatever's powering the thing?" K'rrk asked.

"Affirmative. All drive systems are controlled from a central AI nexus concealed under what used to be a system of reservoirs and interlinked canals. It has apparently been given the name Awareness, Commander."

"Defenses, Lorek. Shields? Antiparticle fields?"

"None that scanners can discern, Commander."

K'rrk growled with pleasure as he turned to the ship's communications officer. "Reeza, inform all battle group commanders to hold their positions."

"Done, Commander," she responded almost immediately.

K'rrk made an approving sound. "Open up a hailing frequency, Lieutenant."

"Frequency opened to all traffic," Reeza told him.

K'rrk cleared his throat and slapped a paw down on the chair's translator stud. "This is the Karbarran starship *N'trpriz*. We wish to make contact with whomever is presently in control of Haydon IV." He repeated the request twice more.

"Incoming, sir," Reeza said as a synthesized voice speaking formal Karbarran began to issue from the bridge's communication ports.

"*Attention*, N'trpriz," the voice began. "*Your vessel is*

being scanned. Do not, repeat, do not attempt to arm or deploy any weapons.''

K'rrk flashed his weapons officer a paw signal for restraint and patience. "Understood, Haydon IV," he directed toward overhead audio pickups. "With whom are we speaking?"

"You are in communication with Haydon IV's Awareness. State your purpose, N'trpriz.''

K'rrk glanced at his crew, then said, "We must be permitted to establish a docking orbit around Haydon IV for the purpose of extracting our citizens."

Ursine eyes fixed on the forward screen and speakers.

"That cannot be permitted,'' the Awareness replied at last. *"Your citizens are in no danger. Do not, repeat, do not attempt an approach or your vessel will have to be destroyed.''*

K'rrk bared his fangs in a twisted smile. If the normally dour Karbarrans had learned anything from the Sentinels' victorious campaigns, it was that fate, *destiny*, could be grasped as one would a prize piece of fruit. And just now Haydon IV was that prize, a conquest that would consolidate Karbarra's power among the worlds of the Local Group and reward a certain commander with the dreadnought of his choosing for all subsequent sorties.

"Nonsense," K'rrk told the Awareness with a gurgling snarl. "Release your prisoners at once or suffer the consequences." He hit the com-interrupt stud and swung to Lorek. "Do we still have a fix on the nerve center?"

"Affirmative, Commander."

K'rrk struck the arm of the command chair with a huge fist, nonretractable claws finding their usual grooves. "Activate all electronic countermeasures and prepare for evasive action. Mav, prepare to secure us a counterrotational orbit at my command. Cano: target primary torpedoes ground zero on nerve center coordinates."

"We're being warned away, sir," Reeza said.

"Engineering," K'rrk growled across the com-line as the *N'trpriz* began to close on the accelerating sphere that was Haydon IV.

"Engineering here, Commander,'' a thickly accented Highlander's voice returned.

"We're going to try a hit-and-run, Rash. Will your engines back us up?"

"By Yirrbisst, you know they will, Commander."

K'rrk grinned. "All right, Cano, on my—"

A blare of two-note warning horns overpowered his words.

"Commander," Lorek reported in an astonished voice. "Ship's auto-destruct has been armed and is counting down!"

K'rrk rose halfway out of the helm chair. *"What?"*

"Auto-destruct set for thirty units, sir."

K'rrk spit a curse at Haydon IV's on-screen image. "Toy with us, you will not! Mav, plot a course directly for the surface. I want us in this ship sitting right over the Awareness!"

"Twenty units, sir."

K'rrk slammed a paw down on the chair's control panel. "Ship's computer," he said, catching a whiff of his own muskiness. "Abort auto-destruct sequence. Priority override, K'rrk-two-K'rrk-one, cancel."

Lorek entered a similar verbal code, and the warning horns were silenced. "Auto-destruct sequence aborted," Lorek updated.

K'rrk grinned knowingly. "All engines full reverse, Mav."

The navigator tapped a flurry of commands into his console, then threw a wide-eyed look over his shoulder. "Sir, the ship isn't responding!"

"Rash!" K'rrk barked over the com-line. "Get your engines on-line!"

The chief engineer's reply was panicked. *"By the Ur-Flower, we're trying, sir!"*

K'rrk heard Lorek's sharp intake of breath under the blare of reactivated warning horns. "Auto-destruct reinitiated, Commander. Counting down from thirty units."

"Haydon!" K'rrk bellowed. "Mav: Return to previous course heading, all ahead full!"

"Twenty units, Commander."

"We've got full reverse, sir," Rash said proudly from engineering.

K'rrk's muzzle fell open at the sight of Haydon IV dwindling on-screen. "Full ahead! Full ahead!"

"No response, sir!" Mav said.

"Ten units, Commander."

"Ship's computer," K'rrk sputtered. "Abort auto-destruct sequence. K'rrk-two-K'rrk-one."

"You forget to say 'priority override'!" every officer on the bridge cried at the same time.

"Five units, Commander."

"Ship's computer," K'rrk started again. "Priority override— No! I mean Abort K'rrk-two— No, I—"

"Four units, Commander!"

"Ship's K'rrk! Computer sequence—"

Mav and Cano had abandoned their duty stations and were approaching him with murder in their eyes.

"Abort, K'rrk! Abort—"

"Three units."

"Cancel priority—"

"Two units."

Even Reeza had joined the mutiny, the claws of her hands poised over the helm chair.

"Arrrggggg!"

"One unit."

K'rrk was still butchering commands when the *N'trpriz* added its brief fireball to the heavenly sweep.

CHAPTER
TEN

> *One of the things I liked about having [Sean] Phillips around
> was that his relationship with Marie Crystal was even more con-
> fused than mine was with Karen [Penn]. But we were competitors
> from almost the first moment he set foot on Tirol. I had it figured
> then that the 15th thought they'd done the job the REF had been
> sent to do—cut the Robotech Masters down to size. After all,
> none of us [in the REF] had dealings with the Masters. As far
> as the Invid were concerned, the 15th had left Earth before their
> arrival and docked on Tirol after the Invid had already left. So
> of course I made a thing about talking up the Sentinels and what
> we'd been through on Praxis and the rest. But who could blame
> me when the 15th had gotten a bigger reception in Tiresia than
> the Sentinels had gotten when we'd returned victorious from Op-
> tera.*

> Jack Baker, *Upwardly Mobile*

JACK WAS FIRST OUT OF THE LAUNCH BAY, NINE VERI-
techs formed up on his tail. Newspace veteran Jack in his
scarlet Alpha, out into the fog that was not.

That was the real kicker, he told himself. That newspace,
as Lang's Robotechs were calling it, felt more like a state of
mind than a state of matter. Extravehicular, immersed in va-
porless white light, you got the feeling you were not so much
"out there" as you were, well, *inside something*.

Against the black star-strewn backdrop everyone was used
to, you were occasionally overcome by the magnitude of it
all. You could sense just how insignificant you were in the
grand scheme, and it made for easy combat when one figured
your single ship didn't amount to squat. (But jeez, how it

could bring on the night terrors afterward! That amoebalike sense of immersion, the loss of self . . .)

That was where newspace was something else. Because *in there*—he might not say it, but he could not help but think it—one started to feel just *too* significant, as though every action one took set into motion a chain of immutable reactions.

The "fireflies" found by the fortress's bio-sensors were on-screen and closing on all sides. They winked light just like the real things, here one moment, gone the next, vaguely blue against the colorless, ambient glow of newspace.

"Command to Red Team leader. Do you copy, Red leader? Repeat, do you copy?"

The SDF-3 was a black slash at nine o'clock, the mecha constituting Red and Blue Teams circumferentially deployed like widely scattered paint flecks chipped from the ship's hull.

Jack chinned into the command frequency, opening a line to the Tactical Information Center. "Red One receiving you loud and clear, Command. What have you got for us?"

A video image of Colonel Vallenskiy's head and shoulders appeared on one of the Alpha heads-up display screens, strobing harsh light into the cockpit. "Nothing yet, Captain. Bio-scanners are still showing hot signatures but no profiles."

"Copy and confirm, Command," Baker said. "Sorry to disappoint, Colonel, but our view doesn't seem to be any better than yours."

"Roger that, Red leader. TIC requests you maintain present position. Let's see if they're willing to come into the playground."

Terrific, Jack thought. *Just hang us out here like fresh meat.* "This is Baker," he directed into the tactical net helmet pickup. "Maintain position. Lights alive at two thousand meters, all points and closing."

He could see them overhead, given false color and solidity by the cockpit canopy's polarized tint. Only now he saw that the bogies were not spherical at all but the rounded, light-emitting tips of tendrillike forms. He flashed on the Sentinels' encounter with Haydon IV's antibody defenses, thinking: *But no . . . No one at the briefing had been interested in hearing about* that *episode*.

"They're onto me," one of Marie Crystal's wingmen blurted. *"It's like I'm looking at tentacles. B—but they're not attached to anything!"*

"Hold your position," Jack heard Marie tell the pilot.

"Christ, Captain, they're practically all over me!"

"Blue Six, you are not to engage unless provoked," Vallenskiy ordered over the com net. *"Maintain position."*

Jack felt something graze the Alpha's radome and cockpit and realized that the VT was being probed and explored. Reflexively, he crouched down in his seat, suddenly feeling as though he were about to enter an old-fashioned car wash. But what would have been brush tips were flickering lights.

Blue Six gave a panicked cry. *"Holy shit, they passed right through me, Captain! The things just shot right through me!"*

Jack shuddered, chilled to his center, as one of the light tips pierced the hull and thudded wormlike against his "thinking cap." It was incredible: The tendrils were not puncturing the hull but simply *penetrating* it! Some tore right through it, while others were whizzing lightning-quick recons around the cockpit. A few seemed to enter his body and course up and down his arms and legs; one even took a fast tour of his mind, leaving him dizzy and momentarily nauseated.

The tac net was filled with the sound of gasps and near exultation as the lights penetrated one Veritech after another. No one was capable of responding to Command's urgent requests for updates.

Jack braced himself for the lights' return the way one tightened up at the crest of a roller coaster drop. But at the last instant the tendrils that were headed for the Alpha divided and joined separate groups closing on Jack's two wingmen. This time, however, they did not pierce the VTs but danced around them, forming dazzling nimbi of light. Then, almost simultaneously, the two fighters winked out of existence.

Jack could not get his voice to work. When he did, he had difficulty reporting what he had just witnessed. Command, however, had apparently seen the two Veritechs disappear from the threat board.

"Red and Blue leaders, we show two, make that four, missing spacecraft," Vallenskiy said. *"Can you confirm? Repeat, can you confirm?"*

"They're gone!" Jack managed. "Atomized, dematerialized, disintegrated . . . I don't know what. The lights surrounded them, then took them out."

"That's affirmative," Marie said, answering for the Blue Team.

"Did you engage? Any of you?"

"Negative," Jack said, counting follow-up denials on the net: Dante, Crystal, Penn, Phillips . . .

"Can you verify present UCT positions, Red leader?"

Jack glanced at his displays and screens, tipping the Alpha starboard with a brief firing of the VT's attitude jets. The lights had lost interest in the squadron. Beneath him, the tendrils were like spears gone ballistic, the SDF-3 soon to be pincushioned or worse.

Jack said, "You're the center of attention, Command."

"Then you are to engage, full teams," Vallenskiy returned. *"Stop those things from reaching the ship!"*

Rick stood on the TIC's command balcony, listening to Vallenskiy relay commands to the mecha recon teams. Unless his eyes or the fortress's exterior cams were lying, he had just seen four VTs dematerialized by an *enemy light.* And now he had ordered the squadron to counterattack. With the hope of accomplishing what? he asked himself. Punishing the light for its omnipotence? According to the available data, it was not even light they were facing but some animated form of electrical energy.

Something like the synaptic firing of a neuron, Lang had explained.

"Fortress defensive shields raised," a tech announced from the command console. "Red and Blue Teams falling in to engage, sir."

Rick swung around to the monitors in time to see the Blue Team pilots imaging their VTs over to Battloid mode. Captains Baker and Penn and what remained of the Red Team were configured as Fighters or Guardians.

Rick briefly considered what he would do if he was out there. He pictured himself strapped into the cockpit seat, one hand clasped on the Hotas, face bathed in display light, scalp tingling from contact with the helmet's neural sensors, the smell of fuel and heated circuitry. *No good to use heat-seekers,* he thought. *Go right to lasers.*

"Lasers fired, sir," the same tech reported.

Rick squinted at the monitor screens.

And what he saw blinded him for the next ten seconds and left him with a dull ache in the back of his head he knew he would feel for a week.

His eyes opened to the sight of men and women throughout the TIC bent over their consoles in postures of anguish.

The lasers had only fed strength to the light.

Succeeded in angering it.

Sirens wailed: *Brace for impact!*

Kami deliberately placed himself in the path of the first light tendril to penetrate the hold. It shook him with all the force of a baleful premonition, a minatory sending from the *hin*.

And how like the *hin* it seemed—the source of this light!

Garudan, Kami had an intimate knowledge of such nonordinary states of mind—that which Terrans considered *nonordinary* was the norm on Garuda. Credit Haydon or blame him, but his tamperings had resulted in a planet that was hell for those offworlders who chanced to breathe its rarefied atmosphere, a heaven for those fortunate enough to have been born into it. No, hell for the lupine Garudans was to be deprived of their homeworld's atmosphere. And it was thanks only to treatments received on Haydon IV that Kami could function aboard the SDF-3 without the transpirator he had worn through the Sentinels' perilous campaign.

Credit Haydon again. Or blame him.

Kami saw that Learna, his mate and partner those long years of war and tenuous peace, had discerned his intent and was also about to position herself under the full force of the teeming rain of crazed light. Her sendings were strong as she ventured forth from useless cover, the *hin* both guide and umbrella.

From across the hold came shouts of concern from their Terran shipmates and Local Group brothers and sisters in arms. Gnea said something in Praxian neither Kami nor Learna could comprehend. Baldan, Lron, Crysta, and several other Karbarrans were nearby. There was barely a corner the light had overlooked by then, save for what some called "the Pit," where Kazianna Hesh and a dozen or so Zentraedi were suiting up in power armor.

And it was not until the tendrils found the warrior giants that the Garudans' allies in the *hin* opened a portal to the truth.

Kami realized at once that the SDF-3 was not dealing with some blindly malicious Luciferian strike force but the scouts and emissaries of a powerful but childlike superintelligence. His encounter was brief by necessity, for he could barely maintain his individual self in the suffocating intoxication of the experience. The portal had been opened into a realm unlike any he had ever visited in the *hin*, opened into a soul unlike anything met there. The call of life's beyond, a siren song of such warmth and transcendence that Kami was tempted to surrender himself and be absorbed.

It was only Learna's presence that saved him, Learna, anchored firmly in the nonordinary and beckoning him back with her love.

The light in the fortress's belly was retreating, dazzling eye and mind with its speed and brilliance. It had discovered something in the Zentraedi that filled it with fear, a fear that sent it screaming through the rest of the ship, as though desperate to find a route to its own safety.

"Please, Rem, hurry," Minmei said, tugging at the flared sleeve of the Tiresian's tunic. "I don't like this; I'm frightened of it!"

Rem was standing in the center of the cabin, arms akimbo and face uplifted to the ceiling. He looked like a dreamy-eyed teen in love with the idea of being caught out in a spring shower.

"You're a child sometimes," he told her with a laugh. "Something wondrous seeks us out, and you'd have me hide under the bed. What frightens you?"

Minmei opened her mouth to speak but realized she had no response in mind. The truth was that she could not articulate what it was about the lights that frightened her, but all her instincts told her that Rem was in danger.

That he was not listening to her came as no surprise, really, for who was she to tell Lord Protoculture anything? Oh, once he would have listened, when she was still the voice that had won the Robotech War, but it had been years since that voice had sung, and it was Rem's star that had been on the ascendant since. Playing Johnny Appleseed on New Praxis with the Flowers of Life, conjuring Protoculture from them, fabricating the matrix Lang and the REF command worshiped like some sacrosanct icon.

Rem suddenly took hold of her narrow wrist and pulled her close, encircling her shoulders with his right arm. "Let it find us together," he said, still eyeing the ceiling expectantly. "Open your mind to it."

She tried not to quiver so in his embrace, but dread was sluicing through her veins like ice water. She wanted nothing more than to dig a deep dark hole for the two of them to hide in.

The first lights passed through the cabinspace with scarcely a moment's hesitation, piercing the room obliquely from ceiling to floor. A second group followed from the opposite direction. But the third and fourth entered through the starboard bulkhead and instead of exiting along their line of flight began to dart around the perimeter of the cabin, as if to fence the couple in.

Rem took a bold step forward and immersed a hand into the flow. The light raced up the length of his arm and outlined his body, as it was doing to other objects in the room. Minmei instantly became part of the tableau, her thoughts sent reeling by the tendrils' inquisitive caress. And suddenly there was more longing in her heart than her mind could process, more light in the cabin than her eyes could absorb.

Rem bellowed the most mournful sound she had ever heard and collapsed in a heap on the floor.

CHAPTER ELEVEN

With the confusion of the Great Transition behind them, the Zentraedi Imperative in place, and the Compulsion implemented, the Robotech Masters went about systematically expunging Zor's name from all records of the technovoyages of the starship Azstraph. They sought nothing less than to rewrite history in such a way that credit for the discovery of the Protoculture would go to the Elders themselves. However, Zor's own accounts of those voyages survived in secret for some time, until destroyed by the young scientist himself as he began what has been termed his quiet rebellion—save for a precious few jottings preserved by Cabell. All details of Zor's early investigations and experiments vanished with the destruction of these notebooks and journals. And it is likely that we will never know more than we do now about the Azstraph's first sighting of Optera.

From Emil Lang's introduction to Cabell's
Zor and the Great Transition

REM'S CELLS REMEMBERED.

So many worlds to explore, countless even within the limited zone defined by the ship's reflex superluminals. So many alien landscapes to wander across with devices in hand, hillsides to climb, forests to penetrate, skies to soar. So many lifeforms to contact, cultures to experience—more than a mortal man should be allowed to glimpse, let alone contemplate, more than an understanding god would have created . . . They were there but to tempt, those climes of eruptive heat or frozen waste, those worlds of nascent sentience or eons-old evolutionary struggle. But was there any greater rapture than to journey from one to the next? To watch worlds turn through the cycles of their lives? To gaze from a ship's deck upon the sweep of time itself? . . . If there was, it was surely beyond the scope of his intellect to imagine, and even had that gift of imagining been his, would he choose to deprive himself of this joy? He supposed not . . .

Always those thoughts upon awakening from the essential sleep, Zor told himself. *The artificial extension of life, while the* Azstraph *thrust itself from star to star. Man's little game played with time. A bit of existential trickery . . .*

He regarded the sleep chamber now—the nutrient drips that sustained the body, the contact studs that stimulated muscle and bone, the headband that helped to nourish dreams—and laughed away his musings, chest aching from disuse, unaccustomed to the sudden return of those chaotic, nay, inspired, rhythms.

Vard was watching him from afar—able servant and faithful friend—the rest of them already hobbling away from their opened cocoons like aged ministers hurrying off to meetings and conferences. A spectacle ill befitting the courageous crew they were—scientists to the last, sworn to exploration and the search for truth. Zor breathed deep, congratulating himself on the choices he had made, the paths that had turned him away from government service and carried him offworld at last, clear of Tirol's crowded skies. If only Vard could feel the same—content with the quest itself—instead of continually focusing on the goal.

But Zor was too astute, too used to their calculated designs, not to feel in Vard's promptings the hand of his Elders in the Academy. The hungry members of the Grand Chair; perhaps even Cabell himself, mentor and father in his own curious fashion. No, the data he transmitted were never enough for them: the trade arrangements and scientific exchanges too profitless to sate their appetites for progress.

We must have worlds to use as way stations for our glorious expansion, *they would tell him, as though it were* conquest *they had in mind.* We must have discoveries that will further the glory of our race, *as though it were immortality they were striving for.*

Oh, Vard, he thought, filling his lungs with the ship's sweetened air, *perhaps this next world will be the one your real masters would have me find. One with wondrous things to offer, the miraculous things they feel certain are out here for the taking.*

He stood up and stretched, as though reaching for the very stars beyond the reflective sheen of the viewport overhead. "Out among you somewhere," he said to the fixed lights. "Out among you is the world I'm destined to discover. By Valivarre's will, may the cause of peace profit above all."

Karen Penn tried one final time to inflict some damage on the lights, to extract a toll for whatever it was they had done to her Red teammates. With disciplined hand and quieted mind she reconfigured the Alpha to Fighter mode and burned for the fortress's stern, where the lights had clustered on and around the reflex drive exhaust ports. Jack was in plain view at three o'clock, his burn through the eerie glow of newspace complete, a Veritech pas de deux as they fell toward the ship.

The Blue team mecha, Battloid-configured, were hitting hard at the SDF-3's bow from just below the midline, head lasers emitting a deadly light of their own.

Karen planned on depleting her undercarriage lasers this time, taking no quarter, routing the light or luring it away, making it cry uncle or roll over and die.

She was shifting her weight in the padded seat, composing herself for the kill, willing the VT in, when all at once the fog of newspace lifted.

Her eyes were so fixed on the reticle of the Alpha's targeting screen that it took a moment for the change to register. Then, suddenly, there was darkness where there had been glow, and the lights were gone.

"Sonuvabitch," she heard Jack exclaim. *"We're home, gang—we're home!"*

But Karen was not buying it. Though they seemed to be drifting through the inky blackness of home space, something vital was missing.

"If we're home, Jack," she asked over the net, "where the hell are the *stars*?"

On the fortress bridge, Lisa mimicked Lang's on-screen head-scratching pose. She did not understand it, either: One minute the lights were *digesting* critical portions of the ship, and the next they were gone. Had the SDF-3 punched or been punched out of the hyperdomain? she wondered. And was that actually the *real world* outside the viewports or yet another black tunnel in the sky?

"Stations shipwide report all clear, Admiral," Forsythe said from across the bridge. "The lights are gone."

Lisa ran a palsied hand through her undone hair. "Damage assessment, Mister Price. Immediate. All decks."

"Aye, aye, sir."

Lisa returned her attention to the com-line monitor. "Well, what about it, Lang? Are we home?"

Lang looked at something off-screen and shook his head. "No, Lisa, nothing has changed."

"Maybe you'd better have a look outside, Doctor."

Lang's puzzled expression remained in place. "I have looked, Admiral, I assure you. But present readings are identical to those previously assembled." He snorted. "We're still a long way from home."

Lisa felt her heart race.

"We've lost a good deal of our reflex drive systemry," Lang continued as though to himself, pupilless eyes glazed over. "I'm beginning to believe that the reason the Veritechs were assimilated had nothing to do with defense against intrusion. No, whatever was directing the lights had need of specimens. Perhaps it has yet to make up its mind about us."

Lisa swallowed hard. "You make it sound like our pilots were appetizers, Doctor."

"In effect, they were just that," he told her, more animated suddenly. "By the time the lights reached the ship, they knew exactly what they were after."

"We're crippled, then. Is that what you're telling me?"

The scientist shook his head. "Oh, no, we have some drive capacity left to us, although nowhere near what we'd require to go superluminal. In fact, as things stand we would be as stranded in our own space as we are here."

Lisa let out her breath. "You're full of good news, aren't you?"

Lang shrugged. "I'm sorry if I can't tell you what you'd undoubtedly like to hear."

Lisa waved a hand at the screen. "I'm the one who's sorry, Doctor. But you've got to give me something to go on. I mean, do we sit here and wait for those . . . *things* to come back and nibble away at more of our systemry?''

"As opposed to what, Admiral?" Lang wanted to know.

"Christ, I don't know. Move. Somewhere."

Lang smiled, recalling Rem's real-time bubble theory. "Your husband suggested that I fashion us a world."

Lisa regarded him tight-lipped. "Then do it," she said after a moment.

Minmei cradled Rem's head in her arms. She pushed his hair back from his face and leaned an ear close to his parted lips. She was certain he had ceased breathing for a time, but that heart-stopping moment was past, his exhalation ruffling the strands of hair she had hooked behind her ear. Her breath was coming in shallow gasps as she pressed his head to her bosom, praying that he would regain consciousness soon.

Holding him like that, staring down at his beautiful face, she found herself walking through an ancient memory. Tiresia, on the night of the SDF-3's New Year's celebration. The Sentinels' ship, *Farrago*, had yet to arrive in Fantomaspace, and there she was with eyes only for Jonathan Wolff. But she remembered watching Rem that night while Wolff told her all the things he must have assumed she wanted to hear. And she remembered gazing at him the way she had often observed others gazing at her, with a look people reserved for screen idols and heroes. What might have happened if Rem had remained in Tiresia instead of joining the Sentinels? she wondered. Would his presence have altered events, given her the strength to steer clear of Edwards and his grandiose plans?

It was Rem who had rushed to her side after she had killed Edwards's horrible minion on Optera. Her voice had awarded her a personal victory, a fitting end, she had decided. But on that same day Janice had walked out of her life forever. And Lynn–Kyle so soon before that . . . It had been difficult for her to go on when the memories of the sacrifices made in her behalf were so vivid. When she had been so undeserving. So evil.

But Rem had continued to stick by her in Tiresia, during the months she had languished under doctors' care, the months and years when she had so little will to survive. And looking at him now, imagining the two of them walking Tiresia's Romelike streets together, she was not sure she was envisioning a past that almost was or a future that could be. A kind of alternative present, she told herself. One they could fashion together to erase the mistakes both Zor *and* Minmei had made.

She ran a hand across her belly and sighed. At the same time a soft groan escaped Rem's lips, and he moved his head against her.

"Rem," she said. "Oh, please, darling . . ."

And his eyelids fluttered and opened.

Jack knuckled his eyes with gloved hands, wondering what could have given him such a shot to the head that he was seeing stars. It was not exactly unheard of for the "thinking caps" to malfunction and send a jolt of current through one's system—to bite the head that fed them, as the saying went—but that usually left one with twitching limbs or feeling like someone had unzipped one's backbone and poured hot lead down one's spine. Not seeing stars. And he didn't think he had sustained a hit from one of those lights, either, because he had seen them retreat into the black curtain newspace had unexpectedly lowered.

Hadn't he?

Jack forced his eyes wide open.

And kept seeing stars.

It was as though the retreating light tendrils had simply decided to hang themselves out there for his benefit.

"Uh, this is Red One," he said slowly. "Is anybody seeing what I'm seeing? I mean, is anybody, uh . . ."

Karen's face resolved on the tactical screen, but she didn't speak. She seemed to be staring off into space, and Jack had to call her several times before she responded.

"Jack, did you see it?" she said.

He exhaled in a relieved way. "I'm seeing stars if that's what you're talking about."

"But the way they got there, Jack . . . It was like they just assembled themselves into constellations."

"Yeah, well, it's like Lang said. We were trapped in hyperspace, and now we're not." Jack gestured to the blackness outside the Alpha's cockpit. "That's real space out there, and those are stars. We're home, kid. Get used to the idea."

She looked directly at him. "You don't seriously believe that, do you?"

Jack fell silent for a moment. "No, I suppose I don't," he conceded, contemplating the view. "But I guess I'll take it over the alternative any day."

PART II
COHERENT
LIGHT

CHAPTER
TWELVE

The question of Professor Nichols's whereabouts during the years following the end of the Second Robotech War, including that period now referred to as the Occupation, remains a source of controversy. While it has been elsewhere demonstrated that he remained with Jonathan Wolff through March of 2033 (see Tasner's Sheep in Wolves' Clothing), *his subsequent alliances are more the product of conjecture than hard-earned investigative proof. However, based on evidence that links Nichols's associates (Gibley, Shi-Ling, Stirson, et al.) to the Yakuza organization that inherited the remains of Lang's Tokyo complex (see Makita and others), the author is of the opinion that Nichols somehow prevailed upon Wolff to furnish him with safe passage to Japan, where he, we know, was eventually located by intelligence operatives assigned to his case by the REF G2 chief, Niles Obstat.*

From Ronstaad Irk's preface to the fourth edition of Nichols's
Tripping the Light Fantastic

"I'M SORRY I EVER HAD TO DRAG YOU INTO THIS . . . Ariel,'' Scott said, finally working up the courage to meet her gaze.

"Please don't make things worse," Marlene told him weakly. "And don't refer to me by that name, Scott. I'm Marlene. I have been since the day you found me."

Scott's nostrils flared. "You're not Marlene, damn it!" he yelled, turning away from her. He stormed three steps toward the cabin's security door before swinging around. "You're Ariel, and the sooner you understand that, the better." He gestured offhandedly about the shipboard cell G2 had fashioned for her. "Why do you think you're locked up in here? This isn't some free ride. Intel's convinced you know where the Regis is. So put yourself in touch with your real self, Ariel. Tell them what they want, for your own sake.''

Marlene hung her head, waves of red hair falling forward to conceal hollow cheeks and colorless lips. ''Don't you think I'm trying, Scott?'' She lifted her face to him. ''Look at me. Can't you see what this is doing to me?''

He didn't want to look, but when he did, he could not stop himself from hurrying to her and encircling her frail form with his arms. She was so pale, so thin. And he kept recalling Sera, wasting away in Lancer's bed. ''Marlene,'' he whispered, rocking her gently back and forth. ''Marlene . . .''

He had already been through the same argument just hours earlier, shortly before the *Ark Angel* had folded from Earth-space. Some numbnuts from G2 had given permission for Kurt and Lana Rush—the *real* Marlene's parents—to observe, by remote, one of Obstat's brain probe sessions with Ariel. The Rushes had sought Scott out immediately afterward, understandably upset, visibly distressed and angered.

''How could you do this to us, Scott?'' Lana had sobbed from the safety and comfort of her husband's thick arms. ''Even if Marlene *was* captured and conditioned by the Regis. Why couldn't you have left her alone? How could you let her be put through this hell?''

Scott had been dumbstruck. ''But that's not your daughter,'' he had managed to reply. ''That . . . creature in there has *green blood* in its veins!''

He remembered Marlene's father taking a menacing step forward, fists balled up. ''Damn you for that, Bernard!'' Rush had seethed. ''I don't care what color they turned her blood and hair. I know my own daughter. That's Marlene your intel freaks are torturing with their devices. And *you* put her there!''

There had been no convincing them and, in the end, no way of convincing himself, either. Each day saw more and more of Marlene emerge in the simulagent, more and more of what had been Ariel submerge. And each day seemed to bring both personalities closer and closer to death.

Scott huddled with her on the cool floor of the cell, railing silently at the thought of *losing her a second time*.

''I'm going to try harder, Scott,'' Marlene said, full of false hope. ''I know how much your friends mean to you, and I desperately want to help you find them. You know I'd give up my life—''

''Don't,'' Scott said, stopping her. ''I don't want to find them only to lose you in return. I'll help you. Maybe together . . .''

She showed him a wan smile.

''We'll be on Haydon IV soon,'' he went on. ''Exedore will have some answers for us, I'm sure of it. We've made a start, Marlene, that's what's important. We'll find the Regis. Even if we have to go back in time to do it.''

In a spacious cabin aft of the *Ark Angel*'s astrogation section, Louie Nichols locked his hands behind his head and leaned away from a screenful of hyperspace position grids and spacetime calculations. ''Well, I think it's a righteous intro to interstellar travel,'' he told Harry Penn and Vince Grant. ''I mean, I've heard of missing the hoverbus, but missing an entire *planet* . . . This is one for the record files.''

Gibley and Strucker, two of the mohawked members of Nichols's team, laughed from their seats at the far end of the table, where they were headlocked into an interactive video comic book pulled up from the ship's entertainment mainframe. Gleaming interface plugs studded their cranial cyber-ports.

Penn, a curl to his upper lip, eyed the two with disdain, their tattoos, tight clothes, bad skin, and bad hair. Now that he had gotten to know Louie's team a little, he had decided they were as unappealing a lot as he had ever encountered. Video fiends and substance abusers, they related only to things they could plug themselves into. Despite all their raving about artificial intellect and ''machine mind,'' it was almost a pre-Protoculture, electronic age fascination that animated them.

The portly scientist cleared a low growl from his throat. ''And I'm telling you we're exactly where we're supposed to be, Professor Nichols. If anything's *missing*, it's Haydon IV.''

Nichols, grinning, put a hand to his round-lensed goggles as he peered over his shoulder at Penn. ''Some wrinkle in the Newtonian universe, Doctor? A planet gets it in mind to leave orbit, and off it goes?''

Penn scratched at his beard. ''Need I remind you of some of the wonders we've experienced these past thirty years, Professor? Besides, with that world anything's possible.''

Nichols smirked. "Relax, Harry. I'm sure your aim was true." His forefinger called up data on the touchscreen. "What we have here are indications of gravitational perturbations throughout this star system. So I believe it's safe to assume the planet has in fact vanished."

"But Cabell had been in communication with Exedore," Vince thought to point out. "There was nothing in his transmissions about . . . *this*."

"Then it's likely the event occurred recently," Nichols said. "Obviously within the past Earth-standard month."

"I concur," Penn said.

The bridge com-line tone sounded, and Vince leaned forward to respond.

"Receiving an urgent distress call," his exec began. *"Survivors from the Karbarran ship* N'trpriz.*"*

"Survivors? What happened?"

The line was quiet for a moment. *"Sir, the* N'trpriz *was ordered to Haydon IV on an extraction op. Seems that several hundred Karbarran traders were taken prisoner during the rebellion."*

Vince and Penn traded astonished looks. "What rebellion?" Penn demanded.

"It's unclear, Doctor. Apparently the Haydonites have risen up against the Awareness. Offworlders caught up in the rebellion have been transferred to subsurface confinement areas below what remains of Glike."

"This is madness," Vince said. "Ask them if the *N'trpriz* attempted to engage the planet."

"Affirmative, sir. N'trpriz *was in communication with the surface when the planetary Awareness succeeded in arming the ship's auto-destruct systems."* Grant's first officer paused momentarily. *"The survivors claim to have jumped ship in an escape vehicle prior to detonation. They claim that the ships of their own battle group deserted them."*

Vince tightened his lips. "Tell them we're on our way to their position. But ask if they can give the approximate present location of Haydon IV."

"Negative, sir. They say no can do."

"Why in heaven's name not?" Penn said.

"Response, sir: "'Because Haydon IV executed a fold.'"

* * *

After rescuing the Karbarran survivors, the *Ark Angel* executed a jump of its own not, however, for the ursinoids' homeworld but for Fantoma's third moon, Tirol.

Scott had to call in most of the favors owed him to get himself included among the small landing party that was shuttled down to Tiresia. But the hassle was well worth it, if only for the quick ride through the city's streets to the Royal Hall, which still towered argent and pyramidal over the cityscape like a holy mountain.

Otherwise, the place had changed dramatically in the three years since the Mars Group's departure. Scott had not been here for the return of Jonathan Wolff's starship, and with it the arrival of the 15th ATAC and the Tiresian clones they were conveying home. Nor had he been around for the first Flower of Life harvest on New Praxis or the development of Lang's facsimile Protoculture matrix, which had been left in Tiresia for safekeeping. That alone had returned enormous wealth and prosperity to Tirol, what with liberated worlds throughout the Local Group hungry anew for interstellar transports and inexpensive but efficient sources of energy to assist in the mammoth task of reconstruction. Most of the actual manufacturing of ships and machines had been farmed out to Karbarra, but it was Tirol that had reaped the rewards. The moon had become a kind of cultural crossroads, almost on a par with Haydon IV in the trafficking of information and construction techniques.

Thus, Tiresia's public buildings and housing structures sparkled like gems in an emerald setting. Under REF supervision, the clones and indigs had irrigated and terraformed the city's once-denuded outskirts, and while a Rome-analogue look had been preserved in places, reconfigurable stadiums and ultratech high rises dominated the skyline.

Scott's parents, both of whom were engineers largely responsible for the rebuilding of Mars Sara Base, were among a group of Terran settlers and exiled Ghost Squadron pilots who had elected to remain on Tirol. He was eager to see them again, plans for a meet having already been firmed up during a short ship-to-surface conversation earlier on.

Cabell—the bald and bearded wizard who had seemed such a sinister figure to an eleven-year-old Scott Bernard—was on hand to welcome the landing party and escort them, in a caravan of surface-effect vehicles, to that part of the Royal Hall given over to Local Group affairs. There, Vince and Jean Grant, Harry Penn, and the rest were greeted by planetary envoys from Karbarra, New Praxis, Spheris, Garuda, Peryton, and several emerging worlds once dominated by the Robotech Masters and Invid that had never been visited by the Sentinels.

The Haydonite foreign minister and the whole of the ambassadorial legation had been placed in custody.

"They haven't revealed so much as a thought since their arrest," Scott heard Cabell inform Vince while a Karbarran representative had the chamber's floor. "And of course we know of no way to *force* them to send. I'm certain they've fallen victim to the same programming that has set their homeworld in motion."

"First the Invid, then the SDF-3, now Haydon IV," Jean whispered back.

Cabell nodded, flaring white eyebrows bobbing. "And these disappearances are only the beginning."

"How so?" Vince asked.

The Tiresian voiced a note of frustration. "The very fabric of the continuum has been affected in some way. It would require a complex array of instruments and measuring devices to demonstrate my findings. But I will say this much: Our universe appears to be *shrinking*."

Penn blanched. "But—"

"Wait." Cabell cut him off, holding up a graceful hand. "Hear this one out."

There was commotion on the floor. Scott saw that the Karbarran who had been growling demands at everyone had been issued a message of some sort and was pacing before the amphitheater seats, waving the crumpled thing overhead in a clenched paw-hand.

"Let it be known to all members of the Local Group that Karbarra is fully prepared to go to war unless reparations are made for the capture of our citizens and the destruction of three of our vessels."

The audience of diplomats and staffers muttered among themselves.

"And how many more ships will you have to lose before you see the error of interference?" a Spherisian shouted from the hall's upper tier.

"The next time it won't be a single ship but a fleet we commit," the Karbarran snapped.

"Fleets have been destroyed in the past, Nal," a Praxian said.

"Legends," Nal scoffed. "Karbarra has outgrown such things."

"And Karbarra would like nothing better than to see Haydon IV added to its growing list of indentured worlds," sneered someone from the Perytonian contingent. "You try the patience of the committee, Nal."

Nal gestured with a paw-hand. "Such accusations from the chief debtor world in the Local Group. Peryton tries *our* patience, Minister Marak."

"Silence! All of you," Cabell said loudly enough to quiet a score of separate arguments that had broken out. He looked to Nal. "Talk of reprisals and reparations is not only premature but pointless, given the fact that Haydon IV has managed to elude us. I strongly suggest—"

"No longer, Tiresian!" Nal waved the message sheet in Cabell's direction. "Our recon forces report that Haydon IV has emerged from fold and inserted itself in orbit around Ranaath's Star."

"*Ranaath?!*" Cabell said, struggling to his feet. "Are you certain of this?"

"Our reconnaissance forces pride themselves on their accuracy," Nal told him.

"But Ranaath is a . . . black hole system," Cabell said for the benefit of the Terran contingent. He had yet to tell Penn or Grant about Exedore's determination that Ranaath had been at the receiving end of the energy pulse that had accompanied the Invid departure. "Why would the Haydonites willingly place themselves in such a godforsaken place?"

Nal folded powerful-looking arms across his massive chest. "We'll be sure to ask them," he said, hurling the message to the floor and storming from the room.

CHAPTER
THIRTEEN

At 66:18:740, Commander in Chief Dolza committed the last of the Golthano Fleet ships to the dark maw of Ranaath's Star, and once more the ships were torn asunder by (translator's insert: tidal forces encountered at the event horizon). Losses to this date number 670 ships, 42,000 Zentraedi lives. It would appear that the Zentraedi ships are of insufficient durability to negotiate penetration of the (horizon) or the (realm jump) that is a suggested probability should such a penetration be effected. Be aware that Commander Khyron of the Botoru Battalion is fully prepared to undertake the next attempt. He would have it made known to you that he in fact requests to be afforded the honor.

Exedore, in a communiqué to the Robotech Masters,
as quoted by Rawlins in his *Zentraedi Triumvirate:
Dolza, Breetai, Khyron*

MAX STERLING WATCHED EXEDORE PLAY THE CONsole Veidt had delivered to their cell, stubby fingers pecking away at command keys. To offset any suspicion that the furtive delivery might have aroused among level four's cadre of humorless, hovering overseers, the terminal had been designed to include an archaic touchpad. The armless Haydonites had no call for such a tedious approach, and in truth neither did Exedore, who had grown accustomed to the Awareness data lab's neural headbands. The console consequently resembled nothing so much as a child's learning aid, which was exactly what the jailers were meant to make of it. To buoy the ploy, Aurora was seated alongside Exedore, ostensibly under the Zentraedi's tutelage, issuing appropriate sounds of excitement and discovery as the screen displayed responses to Exedore's prompts.

Miriya and Dana were in the Praxians' quarters, trying to reassure the four Amazons that Veidt's sudden turnaround was genuine.

Well, Miriya was, Max thought. Dana was probably encouraging everyone to tunnel beneath the walls.

The former Skull Squadron ace found himself thinking about twentieth-century prison escapes as he cast a wary eye at the cell's laser-barred threshold. It had been pastry surprises back then, files and hacksaw blades concealed in cakes and long loaves of bread. But breakouts now required *break-ins* of a sort, direct data links to the security system's keymaster—in this instance, Haydon IV's artificial sentience, the Awareness.

Exedore voiced a plosive sound of frustration. "Another mistake. My fingers have forgotten just who it is that does the thinking for them. They seem convinced they have a mind of their own."

"Take your time," Max advised under his breath. "Remember, you're supposed to be a teacher, not some interloper."

"Teachers have been known to lose patience," Exedore retorted. "In any event, keeping watch on the front door—such as it is—does little more than draw attention to us. I suggest to you that the Haydonites would have filled these rooms with monitoring devices if they for one moment suspected we'd be foolish enough to attempt an escape."

Max glanced at the alloy partitions and ceilings. Veidt had been responsible, too, for the holo-views that adorned the long, rear walls—vistas of rolling hills crisscrossed with hedgerows and low stone walls. A sun shone in the false sky, rising and setting in breathtaking colors; if nothing else, it had at least returned the captives to a semblance of circadian normalcy. Max sometimes felt as though he were back in the SDF-1, carousing after a mission with Rick and Ben in downtown Macross under EVE's projected cloudscape.

And there he was, the only full-blooded Terran in the room.

"I'm certain of one thing," Exedore resumed. "Haydon IV has defolded."

"I guessed as much," Max told him, gratified that he could still rely on his own senses to differentiate between real time and hyperspace. "Can you find out where we are?"

"I have already established that. Although I'll confess I should have suspected it all along."

Max laid a protective hand on Aurora's shoulder; the doe-eyed child looked up at him and smiled as Exedore took a deep breath.

"We are inserted in orbit around a small, carbonaceous moon that circles this system's sixth planet—an equally desolate place, I might add. The Zentraedi knew the system's dying primary as Qalliph, a word approximated by the Panglish term *dread*."

Max raised an eyebrow. "Go on."

"Actually, it isn't so much the star itself that inspired the name but the phenomenon to which it in turn pays gravitational obeisance. The Masters named it Raanath's Star, after an especially barbaric warlord from Tirol's pre-Transition past. Your own astrophysicists have labeled such phenomena black holes."

Max whistled lightly. "I've always wanted to get a look at one of those things."

Exedore frowned at him. "Yes, I recall from my delvings into Terran literature that your race has endowed these black holes with near-mystical importance. This was especially true among your so-called science fiction writers, I believe. A blend of romantic fascination and morbid curiosity. But I can assure you, as one who has seen an entire battle group swallowed by these sinister portals, that even the most ghoulish of your imaginings doesn't come close to detailing the horrors of the experience."

"So what are we doing here?" Max asked after a moment of nightmare reflection.

Exedore did input at the console, then studied the displayed results in silence. "The reason is twofold. First, I believe that we—Haydon IV, that is—are in pursuit of the energy pulse that originated in Earthspace with the Invid defeat. Based on the results of my previous investigations, I posited that Ranaath's Star was the terminus of that pulse.

"Second, Haydon IV is apparently making use of radiation bleeding from the collapsed star, but to what purpose I cannot fathom. The Awareness has also issued a series of commands to the planetary drives, which will soon bring us dangerously close to the cratered satellite we have been orbiting." Exedore regarded Aurora but continued to address Max. "An external view would be most helpful, but I have yet to determine whether visual data are available. The Awareness had been operating in a purely abstract mode."

Max was just beginning to reply when Dana burst upon the scene.

"You can put away the toy," she directed to Exedore. "Unless you can use it to find out whether the Awareness believes in an afterlife."

Exedore cocked an eyebrow.

Miriya was only a few steps behind, wearing the worried look she reserved for her eldest child.

"The Praxians have worked out a wall-tapping commo code with the Karbarrans next door," Dana explained. "Seems one of the jailers let it slip that a Karbarran recon vessel homed in on our new address and radioed a burst transmission to Karbarra. Since then, a fleet of Local Group battleships has folded from Tirol. They're due any hour now."

Max searched his wife's face.

"It's true, Max," Miriya said. "At least that's what they told us. The Karbarran prisoners claim to have discovered some way to override the threshold confinement lasers as well. They're prepared to ready a full-scale revolt as soon as the battle group arrives and the attack commences."

"But they've already lost three ships," Exedore reminded everyone. Beside him, Aurora had reached a hand over to enter a command into the console.

"They'll never learn," Max said absently, monitoring Aurora's movements peripherally.

"Yeah, well, a *fleet* can do a lot more damage than a single ship," Dana argued, hands on her hips. "I say we throw in with the Karbarrans. Anything's better than being cooped up in here."

"An uprising would prove a terrible mistake," Aurora interjected quietly.

It was as though an oracle had spoken. Exedore swiveled in his seat, but something on the display screen caught his attention and brought him up short.

"Figures you'd say that," Dana replied uncertainly.

"You must tell them to be patient, sister," Aurora added in the same assured tone. "The Karbarrans must wait until the Awareness is preoccupied."

"Preoccupied how?" Dana wanted to know.

"Here!" Exedore said, an unsteady index finger aimed at the monitor.

Max narrowed his eyes as a series of complex schematics flashed on-screen.

Dana got a grip on the Zentraedi's shoulder. "Don't go mute on us now, Exedore, or I'll—"

"It's changing," he said before she could complete the threat. "The entire planet. Haydon IV is *reconfiguring*!"

"The second star to the right?" Rick asked, wondering when he had heard the phrase before. "Why that one?"

Lang's broad shoulders heaved. "It's the closest. It *appears* to be, I should say. Light seems to enjoy playing games with itself in this place. One moment the star lies directly along our course, the next it doesn't. One moment it's effectively beyond reach, the next at our bow." The scientist gestured to the engineering room's tablescreen. "You see! There it changes again. As if it were compensating for the deficiency of our drive system or trying to decide just where to locate itself." He shook his head. "What's the sense of trying to discover the essential mechanics of this realm where there is nothing immutable to measure against?"

Several theories had been advanced when the fog of newspace had lifted and distant stars had appeared, all of which had since been quickly overruled by updated findings: The SDF-3 had not been returned to hyperspace, nor had it manifested from fold somewhere in the intergalactic void.

According to some, however, the present darkness was but the afterlife tunnel itself, and next would come encounters with deceased relatives and shadowy presences.

Many, in fact, had already begun to review their lives.

Screen-weary, Rick was massaging his eyes with his fingertips. Here was a universe to behold from the viewports, but to hear Lang tell it, the stars might as well have been insubstantial.

Rem was standing behind the two of them, silently brooding.

Lang said, "We train our scopes on the farthest reaches, millions of parsecs distant, and what do we find?"

Rick waited, then realized that he was supposed to answer. "Uh, I don't know. What do we get?"

"Stars literally *winking* into existence." Lang punched a

scancorder's playback bar. Eyes on the monitor again, Rick felt as though he were soaring over the crest of an invisible hill to watch stars appear on the horizon.

"Maybe we're inside some sort of torus," he ventured. "Our motion's a continuous curve instead of the straight line we perceive."

Lang's upper teeth were bared when he turned Rick an over-the-shoulder look.

Rick felt skewered. "It was only a suggestion."

"Of course," Lang said with unconcealed condescension.

All at once Rick was aware of Rem's breath on the back of his neck. "Are you just going to stand there?" he asked, adopting Lang's curdled expression as he swung around.

"I have nothing to add," Rem told him.

Rick inclined his head to one side. "Rumor has it you blacked out when the lights hit us."

Lang twisted around in his chair. "I heard nothing of this."

The Tiresian regarded them coolly. "Minmei exaggerates. We unfortunately found ourselves at a nexus point. The experience was somewhat overwhelming. I may have lost consciousness, but only for a moment."

Lang traded looks with Rick. "Why didn't you report this?" Rick pressed.

Rem shrugged. "There was nothing to report. A slight feeling of dissociation, not altogether unpleasant."

Rick regarded him for a long moment. "The next time you find yourself at the center of something, Rem, you come to tell us about it. That's an order."

Jack gave the Alpha's thinking cap an angry toss as he climbed from the cockpit. The sensitive helmet struck the forward seat with an audible thud and drew the attention of a burly flight mechanic who was standing nearby.

"You wanna watch that, sir," the man said as Jack dropped to the deck. "Next time your bird's not answerin', you know why, right?"

Jack considered making an issue of it but in the end apologized. "I'll watch it."

"That'd be smart, Cap'ain."

Everybody's a goddamn expert, Jack thought, striding away. *Command when they order you not to engage, mechies when they're telling you how to care for your gear. And Sean and the rest of the 15th jockeys when they're telling you how to pilot your craft.*

Captain Phillips was approaching from across the hangar bay, Dante and Marie Crystal on either side. Jack looked around for Karen, but she was nowhere in sight. *So I'll go it alone.*

"That was some soarin' there, hotshot," Sean began. "Where'd you think you were, in an air circus?"

"And I suppose *you* had the whole thing sussed, is that it, Phillips?"

"At least we knew enough to go to Battloid, Jack," Marie interjected.

Jack glared at her. "*Enough* to go to Battloid? That was the most asinine thing I've ever seen. Even a VT cadet knows better than to go upright when going to lasers. It's not only a waste of fuel but a wasted thought. I don't know if that kind of stunt flying cut it against the Masters—personally, I doubt it—but this is null-g, folks. I mean, you Troopers better get your exo shit together if you're gonna stay with the program."

The three ex-tankers exchanged wide-eyed looks.

"Can you *believe* this guy?" Sean said. "He goes in teats-up, belly lasers engaged—full *retro*, mind you—and he's got the nerve to rag us about stunt flying?"

Jack fumed. It was the same argument they had been having for two years. Of course there had been no missions to fly all that time, so the competition had to be saved for practice runs with green cadets outside Tirol's envelope or the occasional deep-space prototype op off the *Ark Angel*. Then there were the nights on leave when things got roughneck and rowdy downside in some Tiresian canteen. But what else could you expect from mechamorphs who had suddenly been plucked from combat and practically returned to school when they were not drawing watch assignments in ordnance factories or on some Karbarran-manufactured peat-cruisers?

"I'm gonna have to trim your course some, Phillips," Jack said menacingly.

Sean motioned his teammates back and set himself in a bent-knee stance. He curled his fingers at Jack. "Come on, then, Jack. Make your move."

Jack really had not expected things to go that far but clearly realized there was no backing down. "Suit yourself, Sean," he said, about to raise his fists.

"That'll be quite enough of that," a voice said loudly enough to bring everyone around. Jack thought for a moment that Karen was coming to his six, but one look at her face told him he was flying blind.

"This is positively the most *pathetic* excuse for a debriefing I've ever witnessed."

"We weren't exactly debriefing, sir," Dante started to say.

"That's right," Sean said with a glowering glance at Jack. "It was more in the way of comparing styles."

Marie said, "Look, Karen, we were just—"

"Maybe you've forgotten that we lost several good pilots out there, is that it?" She shook her head in disapproval. "Real heroes, all of you."

"Jeez, Karen," Jack said with a hangdog look.

"Save it," she told him.

"How are they being listed, sir?" Angelo Dante asked softly as Karen was about to walk away.

She turned to face him. "A new classification to suit our new situation, Sergeant Dante. Neither killed in action nor missing and presumed dead."

"How then, sir?"

"Presumed missing," she told him.

Elsewhere in the superdimensional fortress, retired 15th ATAC corporal Bowie Grant was making music.

The return of the stars, the lightstuff of real space, had proved something of an inspiration for Bowie and his female lead singers, Musica and Allegra—two of the clone population Jonathan Wolff's starship had returned to Tirol—and they were trying out their gifts on a new composition when Minmei's quiet entrance into the music room startled them into silence.

"I—I didn't mean to disturb you," she said.

Bowie was speechless.

"I just wanted to listen for a moment."

"C—come in, *please*," Bowie stammered. The two clones, poised like museum statuary on either side of his rack of keyboards, regarded him with bemused expressions.

Octavia, their sister in the triumvirate, had died on Earth, where Musica's mystical rapport with the Cosmic Harp—an instrument whose melodies had once given shape and effect to the telepathic power of the Robotech Masters—had died too. But Musica's voice was more alive than ever, as was Allegra's, and together their harmonies came close to recalling for Bowie the magic of his first taste of that ethereal sound.

He had been a keyboard artist then, masquerading as a tanker, just another artist caught up in the war. But he had been lucky enough to emerge from it with his creative impulses intact, and love to boot. Love for Musica: his pale and slender green-haired muse, his vocal accompaniment, his very life. Even limboed in newspace, they had each other, the separate world created and sustained by their music.

For years Bowie had tried with synthesizers and samplers to play the part of their missing third. But a rendering, an *interpretation* was the best that had been achieved. Oh, the harmonies might sound pleasing to an audience of untrained ears, but for those lucky enough to have experienced the triumvirate songs, the reconstructions were as far from the pure as Lang's facsimile matrix was from Zor's original creation.

Missing in both cases was some immeasurable emotional component, the true conjurer's magical touch. Lang lacked it, and Rem as well. And Bowie, for all the love that went into his work, simply could not push the compositions over the top. In the end what the trio had had to settle for was virtuosity, when the goal had been transcendence.

What they lacked was a voice: powerful, heartfelt, sublime. Minmei was possessed of the gift, and countless times the past two years Bowie had wished that she might sing again. Now, suddenly, there she was standing in the music room's curved hatchway.

"You really want to *listen*?" Bowie asked as the hatch hissed closed.

Minmei approached the keyboards tentatively, as though afraid of them somehow. "Well, more than listen, really." She pressed a finger down on a black key. "Is it true you've learned to play some of Octavia's vocal parts?"

Bowie looked up at her. "Yeah, I have. Sort of. I mean, I sampled her voice before she . . . died." He gestured to one of the keyboards. "Electronics do most of the real work. But we can't get the harmonics Octavia's voice used to create."

Minmei paused to consider that, then smiled lightly at the

sister clones. "Do the three of you ever . . . well, do you ever sing any of the ancient Tiresian psalms?"

"The Clonemasters' songs?" Musica asked.

Minmei bit her lower lip and shook her head. "No. I was thinking of the psalms from the early days, before the Great Transition."

Allegra looked surprised. "You know something of our ancient culture, Minmei?"

"Some," she confessed. "I read quite a bit when I was in Tiresia." *In the hospital,* she left unsaid. "And of course Rem talks about those times."

The sister clones eyed one another.

"So, you'd like us to sing one of the old psalms?" Bowie said uncertainly into the silence.

Minmei fingered a minor chord. "Actually, Bowie, I was wondering if you could teach me some of Octavia's parts."

Lisa hurried through the ship's corridors, returning salutes when she was forced to but primarily attempting to avoid everyone's gaze. Not that she heard so much as a giggle from the crew, but she knew what they were all thinking.

She huffed to herself as she exited the lift on the med deck. One did not have to be a telepath to read the expressions of concealed amusement, to take note of the near smiles.

She came through the hatch to the nursery's observation room with fire in her eyes, the anger palpable enough to be felt clear across the room by the on-duty pediatric nurse and child-care staff.

"Sir?" the nurse asked cautiously after springing to attention.

Lisa threw everyone a cold, appraising look. "Which one of you made the PA announcement?"

A small hand went up, and a corporal stepped sideways into view from the rear of the group. "I did, sir?" the young male staffer said in a tone that modulated to falsetto.

Lisa coughed into her hand, suppressing a smile. "Now hear this, mister. When my presence is required or requested, you can send a courier or you can key into my command channel. But I don't ever—repeat: *ever*—want to hear a call like that over the PA again. Is that understood?"

"Yes, sir," the corporal returned crisply.

" 'Admiral wanted in the nursery' " Lisa muttered to herself. "Remember, all of you, we have to at least *pretend* that I'm running this ship. That I'm not just some working mom fitting a job around child rearing."

"Sir!" said several voices in unison.

Lisa adopted a theatrically firm expression. "Good. Now what's all this about?"

"The children, Admiral," the nurse said, indicating the nursery's one-way observation window.

Lisa stepped over to have a look, a puzzled frown contorting her features. Roy and a couple of human toddlers, along with Drannin and the rest of the Zentraedi children, were assembled in what was called the "creative crafts area," where a sphere a good fifteen feet around had been fashioned out of extruded plastifoam. Lisa could see that some sort of hinges were inset along the equator of the sphere.

"They didn't do all that by *themselves*, did they?" she asked in alarm.

The corporal shook his head. "No, sir. They asked for our help with the . . . globe or whatever it is. But they told us exactly what they wanted."

"I take it it opens somehow."

The head nurse chuckled. "It does indeed, Admiral."

Lisa regarded the two of them. "What's inside?"

"The most amazing thing," the nurse said, enunciating each word. "They've been working on it all day long, everyone pitching in. The Zentraedi doing the heavy work, Roy directing the other kids in the fine work. But with barely a word exchanged among them. It's like they knew from the start what they were after."

Lisa felt a chill run through her. "And what is it?"

The nurse looked to the corporal, who drew a breath. "Their own version of a puzzle block or a transformable toy. Made entirely out of what they could salvage from other toys, except for a few items they asked us to procure: springs, cams, lubricants, that sort of thing."

"Lubricants?! You should be in there supervising them."

"We tried that, Admiral," the nurse said. "But they stop playing whenever anyone enters the nursery. Frankly, sir, I find it a little, well, *unnerving*. That's why I asked you down."

Lisa folded her arms, considering. "I think it's time we found out just what they're up to." She spun on her heel and stepped to the nursery door. "I'm going inside," she told the staff, one hand already on the knob.

In a silent and deserted corridor on the recreation deck, Rem pressed an ear against the hatch to Bowie's music room. He had promised Minmei he would wait until conditions were right before attempting to reachieve the altered state of mind that had gripped him when the lights had penetrated the fortress, but walking past the music room had proved too great a temptation.

Rem understood that the nucleic memories awakened by those probing lights were not his own but Zor's—Zor's to a degree he had never experienced. Not at the insistence of the Regent and Haydon IV's mind-bending devices, not with Cabell's guidance, not under the influence of dried Flowers from Optera's regrown gardens. The lights—and whatever intellect animated them—had accomplished something perilously wonderful by unveiling the sensate content of his progenitor's experiences. And though the lights had vanished, perhaps never to reappear, they had left open a frequency to his other self.

He ventured that he needed only attune himself to that uncommon freq and the flood of psychoid stuff would recommence. And with it, answers to just where the fortress was and for what purpose it had been brought there.

Reluctantly, Minmei had agreed to assist him. *The clones' songs will provide the prompt I require,* he had told her.

But how much greater the effect if the triumvirate's harmonies could be reinstated! For Minmei it would mean coming out of voluntary retirement, facing fear, relocating the voice that had worked miracles.

And Rem could hear that voice now, muted by distance and inch-thick alloy. Bowie's synthesizer was teaching her a vocal line, a measured, seemingly impossible leap of octaves. Minmei sang and Rem grinned: *Yes, yes!*

"All right," Bowie said. "Let's see what happens."

The three singers joined voices.

And a spike of pure light pierced Rem's mind.

CHAPTER
FOURTEEN

I must admit that even I am somewhat stunned by the sudden reappearance of this comforting darkness and these distant stars, because I cannot help but recall what I said to Hunter that day in engineering: What would you have me do—fashion you a galaxy? Words to that effect, at any rate. Hunter, as usual, didn't know how to take the remark. But could it be that I have actually succeeded in doing just that? Has the Protoculture finally endowed me with the ability to Shape, *as Zand always maintained it would? And what, then, becomes my next move? Do I impose my will on the laws of this domain or simply think into being a world for us to orbit?*

Dr. Emil Lang, *The New Testament*

SCANNERS INDICATE A PROFUSION OF LIFE-FORMS, m'lord, *Vard had told him.* Perhaps this one will prove our treasure trove, eh?

Zor could not recall his reply now—a glance, a glower, some noncommittal sound. It was true that treasures were sometimes found or discovered, but most often they were the end result of greed, plunder, willful extraction . . . "Which is it that you hold in store for us?" he asked an arc of reflected light outside the viewport. "A discovery that will reward us with wealth and fame, the accolades of our distant fathers? Or a world that will bring out the worst in us, a world for the taking?"

The planet was the fifth of this star the charts called Tzuptum, a lush wanderer with a single oblate moon to light its night skies. Zor had a preference for such celestial partnerships and shivered thinking of Tirol's long night, Fantoma's oppressive proximity. It was not fitting for sentient creatures to be so overruled, rotated in the shadow of something monstrously huge. Thought and contemplation required a more subtle interplay of forces: of winds and tides and natural rhythms. In the absence of that grew an urge to dominate, to absorb the power of that larger other, to extend influence in the basest of manners, to conquer all that would threaten to overshadow . . .

He brought his face close to the hull's transparency, as though his eyes could tell him something the scanners could not. *But what was there to discern from up here?* he asked himself. Hailings had gone unanswered, and yet there was, as Vard had indicated, abundant life of a complex sort. So the planet's life-forms were either pretechnological or atechnological. *Primitive* was the operative classification used by the ship's cyber-networks, but Zor knew better than to accept that as in any way descriptive.

Maybe they are *right* not to respond to us, he thought. *Their way of saying they want no part of whatever it is we are offering . . . But something told him there was more to it than that. From somewhere within him arose a belief that the dominant life-forms on this world were simply too self-involved to answer. That deep in the dense forests below, an experiment of grand design was taking shape. And perhaps even now those beings were cursing their misfortune, decrying the fact that in this vast universe someone had found them—had found them* out!

The dropships were standing by, Vard was telling him from the hatchway. With hailings still unacknowledged, ship's General Command was recommending accompaniment by surface-effect drones and a full complement of armed Troopers. What General Command called standard operating procedures.

The method had been utilized on dozens of worlds to no lasting ill effect, but Zor could not suppress a feeling that such techniques might prove calamitous here. He could argue the point, of course, but Command would ultimately have its way.

He turned to give the planet one final look before following Vard out into the corridor. In place of the anticipation he normally felt prior to a drop came apprehension.

"You are from this day forward changed," he said aloud,

uncertain whether his words were directed to the planet or to himself . . .

Rem had been found lying unconscious in a rec-level corridor.

And Dr. Wenslow, astrogation's wide-scope expert, had detected a planet orbiting Lang's indecisive second star from the right.

The two messages had arrived simultaneously in Lang's lower deck study, where Rick and the scientist were still poring over star charts and indices. While Rick attended to the former, Lang linked systems with Wenslow to see for himself just what was out there.

"We've got him down in med lab, sir," a female lieutenant named Clay reported over the intercom.

"Any idea what caused it?" Rick asked.

"Not yet, sir. He was found outside the music room."

Rick checked a half-formed expletive. *Music room,* he thought. This was the "emergency" he had excused himself for a little over an hour ago?

"He was alone? No one else around?"

The lieutenant cleared her throat. *"Mister Grant and Miss Minmei were inside the room, sir. But they apparently had no knowledge of Rem's presence."*

"Minmei?" Rick said. "She was there?"

"Yes, sir. Singing, sir."

Rick's mouth fell open. "You must have gotten that part of it wrong, Lieutenant."

"I don't think so, sir. She was singing with Mister Grant and the two Tiresian women."

Rick pushed a hand through his long hair. What the hell was happening to his ship? he wondered. What had this place—those lights—done to everyone? He exhaled slowly and brought out his command voice. "Lieutenant, I want you to find some excuse for keeping Rem under close medical observation for the next, let's say, two hours." Rick glanced at his watch. "He is not to be released until 1900 hours."

"Yes, sir."

Rick patched himself through to security next and instructed the chief of station there that Rem's whereabouts were to be discreetly monitored at all times until further notice.

"And have someone keep an eye on Minmei as well," he added as an afterthought.

That much accomplished, he turned to Lang, who favored him with an enigmatic smile.

"We've actually got ourselves a planet?" Rick said.

Lang shrugged. "It would appear so." He activated a screen on his desk and beckoned Rick over. "Polar caps, mountain ranges, a verdant equatorial belt, Earthlike atmospheric conditions . . . Custom-made for us, wouldn't you agree?"

Rick raised an eyebrow, one hand flat on the intercom control panel again. "Yeah, a little *too* custom-made," he started to say as the bridge responded.

"Bridge, Commander Forsythe."

"Raul, Hunter. Put me through to Lisa, would you?"

"Sorry, Rick. She's not here. You might check the nursery."

Rick felt his face flush. Another "emergency," no doubt, like Rem's need for a stroll around the ship and Minmei's sudden urge to sing. "Raul, what the hell is going on around here? Is everybody going space-happy? Who's running this ship, anyway?"

Forsythe was quiet for a moment. *"Which question do you want me to respond to first, Rick?"*

Rick let out an exasperated sigh. "Skip it, Raul. Just stand by for new course headings. And when the admiral returns, tell her I want to see her in the briefing room, ASAP."

Forsythe signed off, and Rick swung back to Lang. "Suggestions, Doctor?"

"I suppose it could be a trap of some sort, an attempt to lure us in," Lang began. "But I don't see that we have much choice. If the planet is inhabited in addition to being hospitable, we stand a chance of learning a bit about this place, perhaps even a way out of it. Certainly more than we'll learn from these stars something has seen fit to provide."

Rick studied Lang's expression. "You're serious about that, aren't you?"

Lang nodded.

"All right. Instruct astrogation to plot us a course in."

While reflex drives were carrying the SDF-3 toward a planet that had seemingly leapt into existence only moments before, the *Ark Angel*, recently reemerged in normal space, was bearing down on a world that had traveled hundreds of thousands of parsecs to settle itself on the dark edge of annihilation.

The Terran legation had tried to convince Karbarra to stay its warlike hand, if only until Haydon IV had a chance to respond to the charges brought against it. In this, the *Ark Angel* promised to act as intermediary and arbiter. But it had been plain that Karbarra was out for more than blood vengeance. The ursinoids had agreed not to obstruct Earth's representatives from communicating with the Haydonites but had assured everyone that a flotilla of Karbarran ships would be folding at the *Ark Angel*'s stern and that any hostility Haydon IV directed against them would be met in kind.

Vince, Jean, Harry Penn, Scott, Cabell, and Nichols and his interface addict associates had passed most of the journey from Tirol gathered in the starship's situation room, discussing strategic options and speculating on the SDF-3's present whereabouts.

Scott, his body hot-wired on an assortment of liquid stimulants, thought he might simply spontaneously combust before the session ended. The brief reunion with his parents had only aggravated the concern he felt for his missing friends, and to top that off he had finally taken his tortuous relationship with Marlene to its predictable conclusion.

Back on the *Angel* after the nearly disastrous summit in Tiresia, he had gone to her cell—against his better judgment—where one thing had led to another, and had ultimately found the two of them pressed against a spot of bulkhead inaccessible to the prying eyes of the security cams, making love with animal intensity. Green blood or no, Marlene was a woman of human needs and passions. And while Scott was still deliciously dazed from their sensual intertwining, the encounter had left him more confused than ever.

"I'm sorry to make it sound like this, Cabell," Vince was saying, "but we didn't make the jump from Earth to get ourselves entangled in Local Group affairs. We came back for the SDF-3, not to assist Karbarra in its push for control of the spaceways."

Cabell's clear eyes narrowed. "Perhaps not, Commander,

but I suggest the time has arrived for Earth to consider itself part of the Local Group. After all, it was at the insistence of your Plenipotentiary Council that this war machine was built to begin with.''

The Terrans waited.

''I would point out to you that the SDF-3 had the capacity to fold to Earth shortly after the end of the Sentinels' campaign. You could have returned then, with the Local Group's blessings and thanks, instead of anchoring yourself in Tirol-space for an additional three years.''

Vince snorted. ''Embark on a five-year voyage to find our homeworld occupied by the Invid Regis?''

''So you chose to defeat her in a war,'' Cabell said in a casual way. ''The result is the same. You perhaps succeeded in chasing her off, but at what cost? The fleet you labored to construct is gone, atomized. Your planet is devastated. And your philosophy of answering might with might has had a telling effect on the Local Group worlds.'' The Tiresian raised an accusatory finger. ''You knew full well when you left Tirol what you had set in motion on Karbarra.''

Scott was grateful for the momentary silence that followed Cabell's remarks. On the voyage out from Earth, Vince had brought him up to date on Local Group grudges, but Scott had not expected the once morose Karbarrans to be so radically affected by their recent economic windfalls. And aside from problems of a localized sort, there were, to hear Cabell and Nichols tell it, problems in the grand scheme of things as well. Scott could not follow half the mathematical proofs the scientists had offered up as evidence, but something had apparently worked a bit of underhanded universal micro/macro magic, tugging matter in both realms just that much closer together. Cabell had even said something about pulsar stars *disappearing* entirely a ''Big Crunch'' in the working.

''I don't see what Karbarra *or* Haydon IV's got to do with us,'' Scott interjected. ''General Grant's already said it, Cabell: It's the Regis we're after.''

Scott noticed Nichols and Cabell trade looks.

''We were hoping you could update us on that score, Colonel,'' Nichols said at last.

''Me? How so?''

''Well, you've been having intimate . . . discussions with

her agent, haven't you?'' Nichols asked. "We thought maybe Marlene had told you something in confidence."

Scott's face went crimson. He might have known it was not that easy to get around the security cams in Marlene's cell. "She hasn't told me anything," Scott muttered, eyes averted from the table.

Nichols made a dismissive motion. "All the more reason for communicating with Haydon IV, then."

"If we only knew more about the descendants of Haydon," Jean said.

Cabell looked at her. "Descendants of Haydon? Surely you don't mean Veidt's brethren?"

The expression on Jean's brown face flattened. "Well, yes, I did."

"The beings we call Haydonites," Cabell said, "bear no more relation to Haydon than do Karbarrans, Praxians, or any other Local Group race." He caught sight of Jean's puzzled look and added, "Perhaps I should explain."

Vince said, "Perhaps you should."

Cabell rubbed the side of his nose. "The one we call Haydon is thought to have been a member of an ancient, highly evolved spacefaring group, whose collective name—if indeed they possessed one—has not been passed down to us. Nor, for that matter, can we be certain that 'Haydon' was the name applied to a single entity or the group itself.

"Jean, Vince, Scott, you have all seen some of the shrines erected to Haydon, and certainly you recall how dissimilar they are to one another, save for their age and gargantuan size. But not one is believed to represent Haydon as a living being."

"But there has to be some record of him, or them," Jean said. "Instruments, tools, artifacts, that sort of thing."

Cabell chuckled to himself. "You're familiar with Garudans, Praxians, Karbarrans, and such, are you not?"

Jean nodded.

"Well, Haydon's handiwork is these very races." Cabell adjusted the high collar of his cloak. "You see, each planetary race was in a sense 'altered' by Haydon. And each perpetuated Haydon in a form appropriate to their own world view. So one hears Spherisians speak of 'the Great Shaper' or Karbarrans mention 'the Great Augury,' when in effect they are all talking about the same entity or group.''

Cabell shook his head in a self-amused way. "Where that group came from we cannot begin to guess. But from myths, legends, and fanciful historical accounts that have been handed down to us emerge—'through a glass darkly,' if I may borrow a Terran phrase—two versions of the final days of Haydon's race. In one we are told that they were on the threshold of an incredible turning point in self-generated evolution when they were destroyed in some catastrophe their own tamperings may inadvertently have brought about.''

"And the second?'' Nichols asked.

Cabell let out his breath. "In the light of recent developments, this version is by far the more interesting. For it suggests that the race did not vanish—though we are so led to believe—but placed itself in a state of what I once heard Dr. Lang refer to as suspended animation.''

"We're all familiar with the term, Cabell,'' Vince assured him. "But what are these . . . geniuses supposed to be waiting for?''

"An event,'' Cabell said with a faraway look. "A cosmic event that would alter the fabric of spacetime.''

Nichols gaped at the Tiresian from across the table. "The Invid,'' he said, gazing at everyone. "Don't you get it? Their mating with the Protoculture, their transubstantiation. That's what Haydon's race was waiting for.''

He threw his head back and laughed. "They're getting ready to wake up. They're figuring on hooking onto the Invid phoenix and following it right off the map!''

CHAPTER
FIFTEEN

Of course, we had a sizing chamber aboard [the SDF-3], but Cabell's suggestion that micronization of Drannin or the other Zentraedi children could result in developmental problems had naturally filled Kazianna with a newfound fear of the device. I still believe the suggestion was totally unfounded, but because it was taken as gospel at the time, it meant that those Zentraedi who had elected to ship with us had done so full-size—not to mention what it meant for the work crews who now had to construct the nursery to accommodate children of vastly different sizes. Anyway, the experience of that day I walked into the nursery to check on the children's creation left me convinced that I'd placed too much importance on all this child bonding and that maybe it hadn't been such a good idea, after all. In retrospect I think I should have insisted that [the Zentraedi ship] Valivarre fold with the rest of the fleet instead of remaining in Tirolspace with its skeleton crew.

Lisa Hayes, in Resh N'tar's
Interviews with Admirals

"SEVEN WORLDS," EXEDORE SAID TO HIMSELF, hands clasped behind his back as he paced the alloy floor of his confinement area quarters. Max, Miriya, Dana, and the Praxians were off somewhere exchanging wall tappings with the Karbarrans. Aurora was in the front room, glued to the display screen of their monitor unit as though it were one of Earth's old-fashioned television sets.

Seven worlds, Exedore repeated in thought, head down, eyes on the floor.

The past dozen hours had been punctuated by deep rumblings from Haydon IV's artificial core, the sound of powerful machines being reactivated after who knew how long a slumber. On-screen schematics flashed by Veidt's device told him little, but it was easy enough to imagine modules being hoisted and repositioned by robotic arms, gigantic plates retracting, a change in the very sphericity of the world.

Exedore awaited some word from Veidt. Haydon IV was surely reconfiguring, but reconfiguring into *what*? An unassailable battle station, as the more nervous of the Karbarran captives were suggesting? A world turned inside out? A factory of some sort? The Awareness still had not made any external visuals available; positional data, however, indicated that the artifact was well within three hundred thousand kilometers of the small carbonaceous moon that remained the focal point of its eccentric orbit. Almost close enough to touch.

A deafening movement from seemingly underfoot rocked level four and nearly sent Exedore sprawling. There had been several jarring moments already, but no one had been hurt. No power failures, split seams, broken seals. Buried in the Awareness's neural programming were command codes that apparently ensured the safety of Haydon IV's passengers and guests.

As there were command codes that safeguarded Haydon IV from the threat of attack.

But just what had the historical Haydon—as individual or race—gone to such lengths to protect: the world's passengers or the world itself?

The Zentraedi perched himself on the edge of the bed, unconsciously adopting a thinker's pose. *Seven worlds*, he thought.

He had surmised from investigations undertaken during the Sentinels' campaign that the Awareness had had dealings with Zor in the early stages of his self-styled rebellion against the Robotech Masters. Later, the Tiresian—Protoculture's midwife—had for some unknown reason duplicated the route Haydon had taken through the Quadrant millennia before, using Haydon's chosen worlds as the objects of his seeding attempts.

Had Zor been attempting to pick up where Haydon had left off?

He had already visited Optera, where, assuredly, Haydon had brought Invid and Flower together.

But then he had gone to seed Peryton, for which Haydon had devised a thought-propelled instrument capable of altering the rotational axis of that dying world.

And gone on to seed Karbarra, which Haydon had gifted with the ursine-responsive Ur-Flower.

And Garuda, where Haydon had restructured the biosphere to facilitate a true planetary consciousness.

And Spheris, where Haydon had experimented with the evolution of crystalline life-forms.

And Praxis, where biological parenting had become a single-gender affair.

And—by way of the deliberately crash-landed SDF-1—Zor had seeded Earth, where according to Dana's accounts the Flower had taken root with perplexing tenacity.

Which suggested that Haydon had used Earth for some purpose.

But a larger question remained: What had Haydon hoped to accomplish on his namesake world? What was Haydon IV that it should at all costs be spared the injustices visited upon the rest?

"Exedore," Aurora called from the front room.

That she had said it just loud enough to be heard did not keep Exedore from jumping out of his skin. Miriya's youngest had that effect.

He entered the room a shaky step or so ahead of Max and Miriya, who had also come running. Aurora was seated in front of the monitor screen, one finger raised to it.

"It's the reconfiguration pattern," Exedore said excitedly after a moment's study of the displays. "We'll be able to see—"

Miriya gasped.

Haydon IV's northern and southern hemispheres were separating. The artifact world was about to open up like a hinged ball!

In newspace, Lisa edged quietly through the doorway to the nursery. She told herself that in addition to being a naturally inquisitive mom, she was being considerate just now, mindful not to disturb the children's play. At the same time she realized that her inner voice was not urging caution but *demanding* it; the feeling was similar to the fight-or-flight hormonal responses that were triggered every time she had to give the order to deploy the fortress's defensive shields.

The kids, human and Zentraedi, were still grouped around the enormous sphere they had constructed, completely ab-

THE END OF THE CIRCLE

sorbed in their work. The toe of Lisa's heelless boot touched down on a squeaky toy, and a dozen pair of eyes were suddenly trained on her.

"Hi, kids," she said, pinning a smile on it.

Roy glanced at his peers, rose out of his cross-legged pose on the deck, and walked over to meet her halfway. Lisa squatted down to his eye level and mussed his black hair. "Hey, that's some globe you guys made," she began. "What is it, some kind of space base?"

Roy took a quick look over his shoulder at Drannin. "It's secret, Mommie. You have to leave."

Lisa adopted a wide-eyed expression. "It's so secret you can't even let your mom have one quick peek?"

"No."

"Oh, sweetie, *please*."

Roy shook his head, adamant. Behind him, the human children had formed a guarded line in front of the sphere. Lisa straightened up to her full height. "Just one peek, Roy, and I'll leave you guys alone," she said more firmly.

Roy's eyes and faltering tone of voice betrayed his ambivalence. "You can't, Mom. We're doing something secret."

Stern-faced, Lisa folded her arms across her chest. "Now listen to me, young man, I'm still the commander of this ship. Just show me what you've built and I'll—"

Abruptly, Roy turned on his heel and rejoined the group, leaving Lisa standing in the center of the room. She shook her head in disbelief at the mirrored side of the observation window and was about take a forward step when Drannin and the other Zentraedi children suddenly positioned themselves between her and the sphere. It was like facing a fifteen-foot-high wall of muscle and bone.

Lisa tried to contain her unease. She had not had to face off with a Zentraedi in almost longer than she could recall, but some part of her remembered and pumped fear into her blood.

"Drannin," she said in a scolding voice, "I don't approve of this behavior. And Kazianna won't, either." She could see Roy peering from behind Drannin's knee. "Do you want me to go get her, or are you going to show me what you've built? I promise I'll keep the secret," she thought to add.

"It's almost finished," Drannin answered in English. "We can show you after, not before."

Lisa softened her expression somewhat. "So it's not really a secret, then."

Drannin spent a moment considering that, almost as though monitoring something just out of earshot. "No, it isn't really a secret," he said at last. "It's more like a surprise."

Angelo Dante was the one who had discovered Rem slumped unconscious in the rec-deck corridor and had carried him over his shoulder, like a fireman, down to the med lab. The experience had been more troubling than the recent EVA and had cost the sergeant the few hours of after-mission rest he had coming to him.

"The guy's bad news," he was telling Sean, Marie, and Jack. They were picking at meals in the ship's commissary/mess, Karen's harsh reprimands having worked a temporary truce among them. "I've been through this before, so help me. Once I caught him hanging around outside of Major Emerson's office. Then I found him snooping around Fokker Base."

"Wait a minute, wait a minute," Jack cut in, gesturing with both hands. "You caught Rem *where*?"

Dante showed him an impatient look. "Not Rem—Zor Prime."

Jack scratched his head. "You mean the Masters' clone, the one Southern Cross command stuck with the Fifteenth?"

Dante nodded.

"So what's Zor Prime got to do with Rem?" Jack persisted.

Dante growled. "That's what I'm trying to tell you, Captain. They're the same guy!"

Jack looked to Sean, then to Marie for support.

"What the sergeant's saying is that both Rem and Zor Prime were cut from the same cloth," Sean explained. "They're both clones of the same donor. It's like they're *identical*."

"On the nose," Dante said.

Jack tried to dredge up what little he knew about theories of nature and nurture. "Biologically, maybe," he argued. "But Rem was raised on Tirol, for cryin' out loud. Zor Prime grew up on one of those space fortresses, didn't he?"

Dante waved a muscular hand. "Splitting hairs. You find Rem lurking around, you know something's going on."

"Like what?" Jack started to say, when the sergeant suddenly shot to his feet and began beckoning someone over to the table. Jack turned and saw the keyboard man, Bowie Grant, headed their way, meal tray in hand.

"Just the person I was looking for," Dante said as Bowie was sliding into one of the molded chairs. "You heard what happened outside the music room, right?"

Bowie nodded uncertainly. "Rem passed out or something."

Dante returned to his seat and fixed Bowie with a gimlet stare. "I want to know what was going on inside, Bowie."

Puzzled but wary, Bowie tucked in his chin. "We were running down some old songs."

"Who was?" the sergeant demanded.

"Me, Musica, Allegra, Minmei. Why? What's this have to do with anything, Angelo?"

"Minmei?" Jack asked, surprised.

"Some of those old *Masters'* songs, I'll bet," Dante said. "Some of that clone music."

"Easy does it, Sergeant," Marie cautioned.

Bowie pushed his tray aside angrily. "Let's not start this again, Angelo."

"Minmei singing with you, Rem outside listening . . . Doesn't that mean anything to you, Bowie?"

Bowie glanced around the table. "Zor Prime," he said in sudden realization, then laughed. "Look, Angelo, Rem is *not* Zor Prime."

"We just had this discussion," Marie offered in a weary voice.

"Yeah, well, I'm not convinced," Dante said, rising again. "And besides, even if he isn't Zor Prime, he's a clone of the original. And look what *that* guy dumped in our laps."

In the SDF-3's briefing room, Rick checked his watch and muttered to himself. "Damn it, what's keeping her?"

Lang regarded him from the hull viewport. "Why don't you just have a seat, Admiral. I'm sure she'll be here any moment now."

Rick stiffened, then resigned himself to it, forcing out his breath as he joined Lang at the permaplas window.

"Beautiful, isn't it?" the scientist said.

Rick had to agree. Any planet at all would have been a welcome sight just then, but the one they had found—or the one that had found them—was nothing less than extraordinary. Crystalline skies like those on Spheris, verdant forests like those on old Praxis, seas to rival Garuda's own . . . And yet unlike any of those worlds.

"It makes me think of Earth," Rick said after a moment.

"Earth before the first war," Lang amended. "But yes, looking at it summons up the same feelings in me. After Tirol, Karbarra, Optera, how easy it is to forget how affecting the sight of rampant life can be." He cleared his throat. "Now, Admiral, as to a scouting party."

A hatch hissed open behind them, and Lisa stepped into the room, an unreadable look in her eyes. Rick thought it was anger but could have believed it was fear.

"Rick," she began, "you better get down to the nursery and have a talk with your son. When I tell you what he did—"

"We can save that for later," Rick interrupted. He jerked a thumb at the viewport. "Maybe you haven't noticed."

Lisa glanced at the planet. "Of course I've noticed. Raul's kept me apprised of everything. But we can't save this matter until later, Rick. Roy and Drannin—"

"Lisa," Rick snapped. "I said I didn't want to hear it. We can discipline the kids later on. Right now we've got more pressing matters to address."

Lisa's mouth tightened. "If you'd kindly let me finish," she grated.

Rick was about to interrupt again when the intercom sounded. He punched the talk-stud and barked, "Admiral Hunter!"

"This is security, Admiral," a deep base voice answered. *"Colonel Xien."*

"Go ahead, Colonel."

"It concerns, Rem, sir. He's been released from med lab and is now on his way back to rec deck."

"And Minmei?"

"The same, sir. She's with the two Tiresian women."

Rick rubbed the stubble on his jaw. "All right, Colonel.

Maintain surveillance and notify me immediately if there are any new developments."

Lisa was staring at him when he signed off. "What's this about Minmei and Rem? Did you order surveillance on them?"

Rick snorted. "I thought you were being kept apprised of things, Lisa. Maybe if you hadn't been spending your time in the nursery—"

"Rick!" Lisa said. "What right do you have to question my actions?"

"*Every* right, when you disappear from the bridge to attend to some . . . child-care problem!"

"*Child care?* If that's what you think—"

"Please, please," Lang said, stepping between them with hands raised. "We're wasting valuable time."

Rick and Lisa glared at each other over Lang's shoulder.

"Carry on, Doctor," Lisa said through clenched teeth.

Lang bowed his head. "About the scouting party, Admiral. You were about to say—"

"Pass the order to ready a party at once," Rick replied before Lang could finish. "And inform them that I will be accompanying them."

He was holding Lisa's gaze as he said it.

Minmei recalled how she had sung for her parents as a child, recalled Yokohama and trips to Kyle's house, where she would invariably be asked to perform, to entertain. It had been years later on Macross Island that singing had grown to mean something else to her. She still lived then for the chance to perform, lived for the response, the adulation, but singing had come to represent a kind of power game. More than the power to inch herself closer to wealth and popularity, though; singing was power over people: a means to move, stir, control.

To conquer.

The problem was, there were people who sought to make that power their own. To twist it this way and that to suit their own purposes. Gloval and the SDF-1 command had used her; Kyle had tried to remake her; T. R. Edwards had tried to possess her.

And now Rem needed the voice—not Minmei but *the voice*.

Only he was not out to conquer audience or enemy or to

build an empire founded on his own lust and greed. He needed the voice to position himself on a road to self-discovery. A road to redemption for a father/self he was just beginning to understand.

So she had been willing to help him, even willing to let him go on believing that by so doing he was helping her. To confront her fear, he had told her. To give full reign to her vocal prowess.

How she had been tempted to confront *him* on that one! To embrace him, really, and confess that she would sing simply because he needed her to sing, nothing more. But that could wait until Rem's inner quest was concluded. And then she would confess, and thank him, too. Oh, yes, thank him for allowing her to reexperience how wonderful it felt to liberate that voice within. For what had she been but self-contained the past five years, imprisoned, like matrixed Flowers of Life? Her voice: the Protoculture denied . . .

Musica and Allegra had played no small part in that sense of rebirth. For with them she harmonized with equals. She had come closest to such transcendent purity with Janice Em, human-made, but at the time neither she nor Janice was possessed of the songs themselves.

Ancient psalms that predated Tirol's Grand Transition and the coming to power of the Robotech Masters.

Minmei was in the company of the sister clones now, preparing her voice for the difficult parts Bowie's keyboards had taught her. Musica and Allegra had seemed pleased with her contributions thus far, to say nothing of Bowie, who was beside himself. *A dream come true*, he kept telling her, *a dream come true*.

She kept to herself that she was wearing a transmitting device, that Rem had *wired* her for sound, to use an old Earth phrase. In some sense it made her feel as though Rem were present in the music room, pressed close to her warm breast like the device itself.

Her hand brushed it through the soft weave of her tunic, then went to her belly, where it lingered a moment longer.

And she began to sing.

Not far away, Rem would be listening.

CHAPTER
SIXTEEN

Certain parallels are suggested by the fact that both the Masters' clone (Zor Prime) and the Invid Regis's simulagent (Ariel, aka "Marlene") were corrupted by their contact with Terran humankind. Those commentators who advance the view usually offer the Zentraedi as further proof to bolster their claim. Corruption, then, is equated with emotion, for it was human passion above all else that turned the tide time and time again during the Robotech Wars. Terran humankind has been singled out and in some sense denigrated. But were the pre-Robotech Tiresians any more in control of their passions? One need only look to Zor and the corruption his actions worked on the Invid Queen-Mother. Was this not in fact the original corruption?

Gitta Hopkins, *Queen Bee:
A Biography of the Invid Regis*

UTSIDE THE *ARK ANGEL*'S VIEWPORT SPUN A DARK maelstrom of stolen matter, a grave whirlpool of cosmic stuff, black as evil in its singular heart.

"My God," Vince said in utter astonishment.

"Let us hope not," Cabell offered, turning his back to the view and helping himself to food recently delivered to the situation room.

"Stellar Transylvania," one of Louie Nichols's data junkies said without bothering to explain. "Give me two pints of protons," he added, affecting some sort of middle-European accent.

In the foreground between starship and black hole floated what Vince had first taken for a dumbbell-like structure captured by the system's nearly lightless sun, the host upon which the hole had fed for countless eons. It was only after the ship's onboard AI had served up a graphic breakdown of the object that he had begun to comprehend it. One end of the dumbbell was in fact a small rouge moon, yanked from orbit by what constituted the dumbbell's twin-cupped opposite end: a radically reconfigured Haydon IV.

The cylindrically shaped bridge that joined moon and artifact world were made up of two massive conduits, which had apparently telescoped out of each of Haydon IV's now separated northern and southern hemispheres.

Vince ran a hand down his face and left it covering his mouth, as though fearful of what sounds might emerge. Just in view far off the *Ark Angel*'s port side were the ships of the Karbarran battle group, a school of predatory fish awaiting the scent of blood.

"Evaluation," Vince said, turning to find Louie Nichols headlocked to the room's comp console. Data-expedient or not, the sight of the wizard's cranial ports still left him distressed.

With an audible *pop*, Louis jacked the umbilicus out of the skull. "No doubt about it, they're mining the moon for metals. Haydon IV's turned itself into a working factory."

Vince gestured to the viewport. "You mean those, those *tubes* are mine shafts?"

"In a manner of speaking," Louie told him. "See, instead of parking yourself in orbit and shuttling payloads of raw materials up the gravity well, you construct transfer corridors ship-to-surface and suck up what you need. A variation on the old space elevator or orbital tower concept."

"But what the hell are they manufacturing?"

Dr. Penn and Cabell approached the console to hear Louie's response.

"Ships would be my guess," Nichols said, only to receive skeptical looks from the three of them.

"Assume for a moment our theories about Haydon are on the money, then put yourself in his boots." Louie stood up to make his point. "Here are Haydon and his crew wandering the spaceways for tens of thousands of years, jumping system to system, world to world. And frankly, the whole thing's becoming a yawn. They've conquered war, hunger, pestilence, disease, death . . . I mean, what's left to do?

"So all at once they begin asking themselves some serious

questions. Like maybe if there isn't more to life than galli-
vanting around the galaxy playing deity to groups of awed
primitives. They start focusing on ontological and teleologi-
cal questions about purpose and god and what's supposed to
come after you punch exit and wave good-bye to your biological parts. Of course they've been asking themselves these
questions since they crawled up out of the gene pool, but all
of a sudden there's an *urgency* attached to it. It's a kind of—
what'd they used to call it?—a midlife crisis thing.''

Louie took a breath and adjusted his opaque goggles.
''Thing is, for all their investigations into existential meta-
physics and such, for all their experiments with religion, sensory dep, mind-altering substances, and cyber-interface, they
just can't seem to break through to any of the ethereal di-
mensions they figure must be out there or in there or *somewhere*. After all, the math works, so where's the experiential
side to the equation?

''So Haydon gets the notion that maybe his or her or their
race just isn't *meant* for transcendence—I mean, they're just
not built for it. They're psychically deficient or constitution-
ally deprived or something. But that doesn't necessarily rule
out the *existence* of these other realms or the possibility that
some other race is capable of getting there.'' Louie looked
at Vince. ''You following me so far, General?''

Vince deliberated, then nodded.

Louis rubbed his hands together. ''Okay. So what they
decide to do is see if they can't speed things along by scouting the galaxy for likely candidates and lending a helping
hand wherever they can.'' Louis motioned to Cabell. ''They
hit Karbarra, Praxis, Peryton—all the worlds you mentioned—adding something here, deleting something there.
Then they sit back to see what happens.

''But—'' Louie raised an index finger. ''—we're talking
millennia again. So rather than risk a second yawn they decide to build themselves a world—that world,'' Louie said,
gesturing out the viewport, ''to do the monitoring work for
them. And they equip the AI they've set up to run the place
with instructions to call them when one of their experiments
in racial transmutation bears fruit.''

Cabell saw where Nichols was headed and smiled knowingly.

Louie returned the grin. "Yeah, you see it. The Karbarrans aren't cutting it, and neither are the Garudans or the Spherisians, but hey, what's going on over here in Optera's corner of the Fourth Quadrant? Why, we got some kind of war going on here between the Invid and the Robotech Masters over those Flowers Haydon left behind."

Louie snorted a laugh. "Well, one thing leads to another, and the Invid arrive on Earth, mate with *the Protoculture* Zor conjured from their blessed Flowers, and bing, bang boom!—transcendence. They soar clear off this mortal coil, and an alarm clock goes off on Haydon IV. The Awareness says, 'All right, all you slumbering spacefarers, it's rise and shine. A trail's been blazed, and it's time to start settin' out for the new frontier.' "

Vince and Harry Penn were hanging on his every word. Gibley and the rest of Louie's teammates had gone back to playing video games. Louie glanced at them and aimed a laugh at the ceiling. "So, I forget, where was I headed?"

"Ships," Penn reminded him breathlessly.

"Oh, right, ships. Well, that's the obvious part, isn't it? The Protoculture sure isn't going to get Haydon into the other domain. Besides, there's none of the pure stuff left. So what they need now is ships."

Cabell's forehead and bald pate wrinkled. "But if what you're saying is correct—if Haydon actually plans to follow in *ships*—the Invid's departure would have to have resulted in a detectible *physical* rend in the continuum."

"That's true," Louie said. "And I'm betting the Awareness will be programming the location of that rend into the ships Haydon IV's going to start spitting out."

Vince slapped a hand down on the table. "So all we need to do is hang around until Haydon shows up to claim the ships and tag along behind."

Louie nodded. "I don't think they'd mind a coupla hitchhikers, do you?"

"But we don't have any idea how long this process will take," Penn protested. "Ships, slumbering spacefarers . . . The idea is absurd. But even if all this is true, suppose Haydon *does* mind. Suppose they don't want to share the discovery with outsiders. What then?"

Louie pondered that for a moment. "We've still got one

other lead—the Invid simulagent. We continue to put the squeeze on her until she talks. Once we have the location, we can get a jump on Haydon's ships, beat 'em to the pass.''

"My God," Vince repeated. "What have we gotten ourselves into?"

"That's unimportant," Penn said. "The question should be phrased, What are we *getting* ourselves into?"

Cabell tapped a finger against his lips and turned to the viewport. "There's one point Doctor Nichols still hasn't addressed. Here is Haydon IV, joined to the mineral-rich moon of a dying system orbiting a gravitationally collapsed star." He swung around to the room. "Inside which are Haydon and his race hiding?"

Scott was not surprised when Obstat so willingly acceded to his request that Marlene be released in his custody. Intel had made it clear what they were after, and Scott had in some sense become their field agent.

They were in his quarters, side by side on the narrow bed, exhausted from stress and the fleeting sense of relief lovemaking had provided. Try as he might, Scott could not push the image of Sera from his thoughts. Marlene was so frail in his arms as to be intangible, and once more he had begun to fear for her life. And he kept thinking about what Cabell had said about stars disappearing, the very fabric of the universe strained. Was it that cosmic tightening that had finally brought him to his senses? Had it required nothing less than gravitational collapse to bring Marlene to his arms? She was almost asleep, but he felt the need to talk, as though spoken words might forestall the inevitable.

"These last few days have made me wish things had been different on Earth," he told her in a whisper. "I wish I hadn't been so stupid and blind. I wish we hadn't waited for this . . ."

Marlene raised her eyes to his, her long lashes fluttering against his bare chest. "Do you mean that, Scott?"

He nodded and kissed her forehead.

"And how would things have worked out, Scott? Your love for me would have kept you from leaving? You would have launched in your fighter only to return immediately to my arms?"

"Yes."

"And we would have traveled together to the Southlands and pitched in to farm and restore the planet while you left it up to your friends to search for the SDF-3."

Scott's throat seemed to dry up. To hear his wishes presented like that only undermined the sentiment and filled him with misgiving. But he answered yes to all of it.

Marlene raised herself on one elbow to study his face. "Remember Sera, Scott. You would have ended up alone."

He worked his jaw. "It wouldn't have mattered. We would have had each other."

"Like you had the Marlene Rush you can't forget?"

"Change it, then, goddammit!" he seethed. "Find the Regis and make it right for both of us! Maybe your queen can have it end differently for you. Then maybe we can have the dream you just laid out."

Marlene curled against him and took a deep, shuddering breath. "You're not making it easy for me to remember who and what I am," she said softly.

His chest where the holo-locket used to rest was damp with her tears. He squeezed her to him. "Tell me what I have to do, Marlene."

"You have to stop loving me, Scott. You have to stop treating me so *human*."

Elsewhere in the *Ark Angel* Minmei and the sister clones sang:

> *Little Protoculture leaf,*
> *Waiting for our palates,*
> *Where will you take us?*
> *Flower of Life!*
> *Treat us well!*

What had happened on this world? *Zor recalled having asked himself only a few days before. What enchanted hand or conspiracy of sky and soil had shaped that grand experiment in life?*

For as far as the eye could see there had been nothing but this: a living landscape under skies tinged with aquamarine. Life pure and unadulterated, which here had chosen but two forms *of expression*. The one, vegetal but without question sentient; the other, more the animal stuff of his own being but seemingly free of the gross entanglements so often given rise to by bone and sinew. The one, a flower, fruit, and tree, pulsating with occult power; the other, feeding from that power but returning everything to it, tranquil and self-sufficient, with no need to look outside itself to answer the questions that burned in Zor's soul. It was symbiosis of the most perfect sort, true synthesis, two life-forms nourishing each other in every possible way and altering in the process of that joining the physical structure of their environment. Nothing there seemed fixed or constant, neither natural law, nor dictated shape, nor evolutionary design. All was potential . . .

He recalled Vard calling out to him. Vard and several of the ship's crew on the trail below, the one that switchbacked down from that bit of high ground the creature had guided them to. An eagerness in Vard's voice Zor had rarely heard before, excitement prompted by the thrill of discovery. Zor, come! Hurry! He had ignored the young man's direction, still too mesmerized by sky and landscape to tear himself away . . .

Weeks before, the dropship had put down in a boundless field of the tri-petaled flowers. Triumvirate in their groupings, they were of a coral color, with elongated teardrop-shaped buds and long trailing stamens. And oddly enough they cast forth both pollen and seeds.

The landing party had made its way into a forest of spherically canopied fruit-bearing trees—impossibly tall, some of them—with rainbow-colored fluids coursing through translucent trunks. Zor remembered: Tzuptum's rays warming limbs still stiff from space sleep: the spongy ground cover wondrously welcome to feet too long accustomed to deckplates of cool and unyielding alloy. The air thick and redolent, almost too perfumed to inhale unfiltered. And in fact two members of the party had succumbed to a kind of delusional psychosis and had had to be returned to the ship. But for Zor those first weeks had been magical. He and his science team had run scans and collected botanical samples while other teams charted distances and topography and probed the surface for useful metals.

It was shortly after he had determined the inherent same-ness of flower, shrub, and tree that the landing party had had its initial encounter with the planet's indigenous beings.

Limbless, amorphous, asexual creatures—vaguely mushroom-shaped when Zor first saw them—they lived communally in conical, hivelike structures from which they made daily forays into the surrounding countryside for the purpose of hover-gathering fruits and flowers of the planet's singular plant life. After several days of observing the creatures in their routines and rituals—all of which centered on the flowers and trees—Zor came to understand that the beings made use of the plant for physical as well as spiritual nutrition. Seemingly oblivious to the presence of offworlders, they ingested the flower petals and fruits of the mature crop and often sipped the sap of the seedlings, which Zor had discovered possessed strong psychoactive ingredients.

Ultimately he had approached what he took to be the hive leader and had learned that the creatures were capable of telepathic communication. He realized, too, that they had the capacity to alter their physical being to suit their circumstances. While Zor and the hive leader had conversed, the creature had actually assumed a semblance of sexually differentiated humanoid form. It was that one who had identified the race by the name Invid *and first used the term "Flower of Life." This one who led the landing party to the overlook and told Zor about the Queen-Mother they called* Regis.

Zor! Are you coming, Zor? *Vard had shouted once more, and, reluctantly, Zor had begun to follow him down the steep slope, along a path strewn with velvety Flower of Life petals.*

And so had commenced a marvelous journey of two Tzuptum days through Flower-crowned hills and bustling hive settlements that welcomed them with silent chant and delivered them finally to the lair of the Queen-Mother . . .

Zor stood gazing at her now, eyes next to closing from the soporific warmth of the hive's central chamber. She had conjugated herself in an approximation of humanoid female form in his honor.

In his honor. *The phrase she had sent to him.*

"We have anticipated your return to Optera for so long, Bringer of Life. Forgive me if I am not yet adept at fully mimicking your present form."

You anticipated our coming? Zor had asked her, confused.

"The memory is ancient but deep within me. The Flowers were your gift to us."

Zor realized that he was being mistaken for someone who had visited Optera in the dim past and was about to correct the Regis when a sudden paralysis gripped his thoughts. The flowers of this world contained a form of novel bio-energy. They endowed life—indeed, nature and matter itself—with the power to shift and reshape, to wrestle from the gods themselves the ability to control the course of evolution.

Then consider, Zor found himself thinking, what the result might be if the plant's bio-energy could be harnessed and directed.

Would the power to light a thousand worlds seem too much to ask? The power to drive a thousand ships across the sweep of stars? The power to shape and reconfigure the very continuum itself? The extension of life . . .

And yet the secret of communicating with the Flower and harnessing that energy lay with the unknown being that had brought it to Optera. And with this Invid shape changer who had fallen heir to the Flower's fortunes.

Zor was intrigued. He realized that the Regis was the key to unlocking Optera's mysteries, and in an instant of mad inspiration he decided to set himself the goal of possessing that key—if he had to seduce this queen to make that happen!

"Yes, your highness," *Zor said to her at last.* "I have finally returned."

CHAPTER
SEVENTEEN

I knew Lisa was serious the moment she stepped out of the vanity, dressed—barely!—in that revealing black camisole Karen Penn gave her for her thirty-ninth birthday. I was surprised, even though I shouldn't have been. I mean, I remembered the look in Lisa's eye when she saw Kaziana with Drannin that first time, and, after all, we had talked over the idea some . . . Well, Lisa must have caught the look on my face [that night on the Ark Angel], because she laughed and started to accuse me of backing out. But I told her no way. And, well, let's just say I put my whole heart into what naturally followed.

The Collected Journals of Admiral Rick Hunter

THERE WAS A GIRL IN RICK'S PAST, A GAMINE, HONEY-blond California free spirit named Jessica Fisher, the eldest daughter of Alice Fisher, an old friend of Pop's. Rick had met her shortly after Pop had taken the flying circus to Sacramento in search of spectators with a bit of extra wartime scrip in their pockets.

Rick had just turned nine, and he and Jessica were introduced to one another as cousins. It had not taken long, however, to understand that there was no actual blood bond between them, especially after Pop and Alice had decided to bring their own romance out from behind closed doors. Rick, in fact, had been there when things had gotten started between his aging dad and the independent Alice, the night the four of them had gone into San Francisco and "the Visitor"—the SDF-1—had made its grand appearance. Of course, very few people realized they had seen *a ship* in the skies that night, and Russo's government had managed to keep the Macross project under wraps for the next five years. But Pop and Alice seemed to have been touched by *something* in the air, because their relationship had changed from that night on. Rick, too, had been transfigured by the event. Youthful flying ace that he was fast becoming, he had liked to think of the sky as *his* property—even though Neasian and other military pilots might have argued the claim—and suddenly *in that same sky* he had glimpsed a power that surpassed all. The impact on his young mind was as devastating as it was liberating, for while Pop had done his best to keep his only son sheltered from the disputes that had plagued Earth at the time, "the Visitor" had made it clear there would be no hiding from war's long reach.

Jessica, ironically, had guessed the truth about what they had witnessed. *I'll bet it was an alien spaceship,* she had told Rick. *And it's come down to show everybody on Earth that war isn't the only way that things get changed, that there're all kinds of powers in the universe we'll never understand if we keep thinking war's the answer.*

She was almost three years older than Rick and a lot more learned about such things. And after Pop decided to remain in California instead of taking the circus elsewhere, Rick would often sit at Jessica's feet for hours, listening carefully to what she had to say about hatred and injustice and greed, and he would pay close attention to the things she read aloud from novels and texts and some of Alice's books on philosophy and religion. Outside the year of high school he had attended in Sonoma, the time with Jessica came as close to a standard education as Rick had received; by the time he had turned fourteen, he was completely infatuated with her.

That she was *still* almost three years older than he made things extremely complicated, because by then older boys had begun to show up at the Sacramento farmhouse, guys who would stop by to visit with Jessica and fill her head with a lot of talk about what they were going to do when they joined the war.

Rick had already tried on countless occasions to express his feelings—he had even gone as far as writing her a *poem*— but the words just couldn't make it past his lips. At the same time he had tried unsuccessfully to corner her into confessing her undying love for him. There had been a bit of hand holding and a few quick kisses but nothing that approximated the passion Rick had decided the two of them were meant to share. So, invariably, when any of Jessie's prospective boyfriends were on hand, Rick could be found retreating to his room, where he would sulk for an hour or two or stare at all the trophies and medals his flying skills had earned him and wonder why they were not doing the trick. But he certainly was not about to sit out there on the porch and spew a lot of nonsense about how many enemy planes *he* planned to down when his turn came. And what was Jessie doing listening to all the lies those characters were feeding her, anyway?

The truth, as it would unfold, was that she had not been listening. One night she had followed Rick back to his room to tell him just that, and damned if she hadn't been aware of Rick's feelings all along! *But how could you even think for a minute I'd be impressed by all that war talk?* she had asked him. *I don't want* that *kind of hero in my life, Rick. I want to fall in love with someone who isn't afraid to look for different answers. Someone like you.*

Over the next six months Jessica had led him slowly into the joys of love and sexual discovery, but by the time winter had rolled around it was plain they were not meant to be lovers, that it was more important that their friendship survive than anything else. So Jessie had moved on to the sensitive hero of her dreams, and Rick had thrown himself into stunt flying with renewed fervor. But lord, how his hormones had raged for those six too-brief months! Not even Minmei or Lisa would inflame him the way Jessie had.

And oddly enough, it was Jessie he was thinking about now, laser-cutting a path through the verdant foliage of a new world, staring at Marie Crystal's shapely, jumpsuited derriere.

What the hell's coming over me? Rick asked himself, tearing his eyes away. He had not felt quite so *lustful* since Sue Graham had tried to seduce him one afternoon in the *Ark Angel*'s situation room.

Rick stopped short on the narrow trail, only to have Karen Penn bump up against his back.

"Excuse me, sir," she said. "I didn't see you give a signal to halt."

"I, er, that is," Rick began. "Listen, Captain, why don't you go on ahead for a while."

"Certainly, sir," she said, brushing past him, face to face. *Cripes!* he thought. Two women to leer at now.

Angelo Dante had the point, the rest of the human and XT scouting party spread out behind in a trailing wedge. The four Alpha/Beta VTs were Battloid-reconfigured on a flat spot of high ground where they had left them only moments before. The land was an undulating temperate zone forest of analogue firs, raucous with the calls of black birds that confined themselves to the upper reaches of the canopy. The sun was intense where it shone through; the air was aromatic, rich with the smell of life. Scans initiated from the SDF-3 had indicated the presence of an intense bio-energy nexus in the region, but several low-level passes had revealed little to add to what had already been gleaned from the ship's data readouts, and so Rick had ordered the Veritechs down.

He was not sure just what had made him think of Jessie after all those years. It was true that the argument with Lisa had touched off a cascade of angry thoughts, but no sooner had he lowered the VT's canopy in the launch bay than they had been cleared from his mind. And Marie Crystal's butt had not been responsible, either, no matter how pleasing a sight it was. Because for all the lust, Rick was experiencing strong waves of nostalgia as well. A yearning for simpler times or alternative presents.

He felt certain that something in the air had brought it on, or perhaps it was the trees themselves and the memories of northern California redwoods and home fires that their piney aroma elicited.

Memories of Earth before the wars.

Jack Baker appeared from the underbrush a few steps behind Rick, waved, and came up alongside. Rick not only saw a bit of himself in the younger man but noticed the same wistful look in Baker's green eyes. He tracked Baker's gaze to Karen's backside.

"What's on your mind, Captain?"

Baker was red-faced when he turned around. "Begging the admiral's pardon, sir. I guess I was just daydreaming."

"Daydreaming, Baker?"

"Well, fantasizing, actually, sir." He made a circular motion with his hand. "It's this place, Admiral. It reminds me so much of where I was brought up. North Carolina, sir— before Dolza, I mean.''

"You're wondering what it would have been like if things had gone differently for Earth.''

Jack looked at him searchingly. "That's it, sir. I keep thinking this planet's trying to remind us of what we lost.''

In a dark corner of the galaxy lost to the SDF-3, silhouetted against the swirling, malevolent backdrop of Ranaath's Star, floated the first nearly completed products of Haydon's IV's mining and manufacturing efforts: ships— massively proportioned—with featureless spherical hulls, attended and ministered to by hundreds of labor drones.

Inside the *Ark Angel*, Vince, Cabell, Penn, and the Nichols team were fortifying themselves with strong caffie when an unexpected transmission was received from Haydon IV.

"Veidt, is that you?'' Vince asked in a rush, eyes riveted to the situation room's commo screen. They had spent part of the Sentinels campaign together, but Vince had not seen the Haydonite in years. Even so, save for the color of his forehead sensor, a certain warmth to his sendings, and a definite swagger to his glide, Veidt was nearly identical to countless other "male'' beings on Haydon IV.

A synthesized voice answered for Veidt. "Yes, Commander. It's good to see you again.''

"And you, too,'' Vince said. "I only wish it could be under different circumstances.''

Beneath the static of the signal, Veidt's expression conveyed a wry smile. "You discern my very thoughts.''

For hours the *Ark Angel* had been hailing the Awareness without response. The flagship of the Karbarran flotilla had been attempting the same and had finally issued the reconfigured artifact world with an ultimatum: Release all Karbarran prisoners by 1200 standard hours or suffer the consequences of a full assault. Cabell had appealed to the Karbarran legation to rethink their position, but the threat stood as delivered.

"You know about the ultimatum?'' Vince asked.

"I have only just learned about it, yes. But you must convince the Karbarrans to rescind.''

Cabell leaned toward the camera. "You leave them no alternative, Veidt."

"I will endeavor to explain," the Haydonite said after a moment. "Be advised, however, that Vowad and I have undertaken communication with you at great personal risk. Should my visage abruptly vanish from the screen, you will understand why."

"Then save your thoughts," Vince said. "We think we've got a fair idea of what's been going on." Quickly, he summarized the scenario Louie and Cabell had arrived at. Veidt listened in silence. "We just need to learn where these ships you're manufacturing are headed," Vince concluded. "You have our word we won't interfere with the Awareness in any way. We only want permission to tag along, if that's possible."

Veidt shook his head. "That is quite impossible, Commander. Your ship is inadequate for such a journey."

Vince glowered at the screen. "Try to understand our side of it, Veidt. This may be our only shot at locating the SDF-3. Think about Rick and Lisa and the crew. They're your friends, Veidt, and they're in trouble."

Veidt's features betrayed little. "I might also ask that you appraise things from our vantage, Commander. To comprehend after thousands of years that your sole purpose had been to function as caretakers for a race who, if they did not create you, then surely redirected you from your evolutionary course." The Haydonite paused. "And now, even in the face of this realization, to be helpless."

Vince turned away from the camera to glance at Cabell and Penn. "We're sorry, Veidt. But all this doesn't mean we can stand by and do nothing."

The Haydonite's shoulders seemed to shrug under his robe. "The Awareness must be persuaded to release all offworlders—immediately."

"The Awareness is no longer responding to us, Commander," Veidt sent with a touch of impatience. "*We* are responding to *it*. In any case, all offworlders will be released in due course. In the meantime, everyone is being well cared for. Exedore and the Sterlings are in good health. I have even seen to it that they have been equipped with a monitoring device linked to the Awareness itself."

Louie put a hand down on the communication console's interrupt stud and turned his back to the optical pickup. "Ask him if he can put us on-line with Exedore."

Vince studied Louie's face for a moment, then reactivated the system's audio feed. "Listen, Veidt, can't you at least allow us to get in touch with Exedore and Max, just so we know they're all right?"

Veidt computed the feasibility. "I can so arrange," he said at last.

His back still turned to the screen, Louie smiled. "That may be all we need," he whispered.

Exedore, Max, Miriya, and the Sterling daughters listened attentively while Cabell brought them up to date on current events and the speculative history of Haydon IV. The five of them were huddled around the monitor, hands gripping one another's arms in contained excitement.

"Yes, yes, it all fits precisely with the facts," Exedore was telling the old sage. "The experiment shaped by Haydon has finally succeeded. The Invid have exited the continuum and opened a breach to a new realm. And the SDF-3 is trapped there." He shook his head in astonishment. "This could account for all the irregularities, Cabell—this *tightening* of the cosmic fabric."

"We think so," Cabell said. "The creation of that breach, as you call it, has possibly doomed the world we know to ultimate collapse. It is as though Haydon's 'success' has rendered all evolving life in this Quadrant obsolete. Only one was needed to achieve that passage." The Tiresian shook his head. "For the rest of us, a pat on the back and an accelerated heat death."

"Jeez, you guys," Dana cut in, "try not to sound so *cheery* about it, huh."

"Tough break, but they're right about it, Lieutenant," Louie said, his goggled, smiling face on-screen all at once.

"Louie!" Dana yelled.

"Hey, Dana. Told you you'd see me again before long."

Dana recalled the send-off party Louie's gang had thrown for the 15th aboard Wolff's ship. The memory stirred thoughts of Jonathan and their last night together. "So where'd you spend the occupation, mechie?" she asked.

Louie grinned. "No time to go into that now, Dana." He looked to Exedore. "We need to know whether the device Veidt gave you can access the Awareness."

The Zentraedi scratched at his thatch of barn-red hair. "Only in the most limited of capacities."

"But you can get in?" Louie pressed.

"Yes, but I don't see—"

"We're going to find out where Haydon's headed by hook or by crook, Exedore. The Karbarrans, God help them, are finalizing their plans. But their attack is going to provide us with the diversion we need."

"Well, we're all set down here," Dana enthused.

Catching sight of Max and Miriya's concern, Vince said, "Now look, Dana, don't try anything rash. Veidt's already told us you'll be released."

"Sorry, Commander," Dana countered with a dismissive wave at the screen, "but we're all out of trust down here. Besides, there's no harm in creating a second diversionary front while you're running your op, is there? Who knows, we might even be able to place a coupla monkey wrenches of our own."

"Dana," Max and Louie said at the same time. Max motioned for Nichols to continue.

"There's one more thing we're gonna try first, Dana," Louie told her. "We've got someone on board who might be able to tell us where the Regis went."

Dana flashed him a dubious look. "Yeah? What'd you do, Louie, bring an Invid along for the ride?"

Louie stroked his cleft chin. "Never was any fooling you, Lieutenant."

CHAPTER
EIGHTEEN

Come let me show you our common bond,
it's the reason that we live.
Flower, let me hold you.
We depend upon the Power that you give.

We should protect the seed, or we could all fade away;
Flower of Life, Flower of Life, Flower . . .

Tiresian chant of the Cult of the Three-in-One

FOR ONCE EVEN VARD WAS CONCERNED. ARE YOU CER-tain of what you're accomplishing here? *he would ask at least once a day.* And Zor could answer only with that maniacal grin that had become his ever-present look on Optera: *Of course he was certain. And wasn't this exactly what their elders in Tiresia expected of them: to return from these tech-novoyages with something extraordinary? And if that wasn't enough, who were these Invid that they should have these incredible flowers to themselves? That they alone should pos-sess the ability to reshape the world about them? No, this was for all worlds, Zor had suggested to Vard—for the galaxy in all its wondrous variety!*

Mad, in those times; possessed, though he would not rec-ognize it in himself . . .

But to achieve it, thus, *Vard would point out. To achieve it by deceiving the hive queen of the race—this Regis. To lay claim to royalty by pretending to be the long-expected one returned, the Bringer of the Flower. And to resort to seducing the secrets from this naive being . . .*

This was central to Vard's concern—the fact that Zor had

done nothing less than make love to this creature. *In her approximation of human guise and human-made raiments. In her very chambers and in her very bed . . . For such was the only way that the secrets could be revealed. The process, dear Vard, required a complete joining—mind-to-mind, body-to-body—and passion to accompany it. Or, in Zor's case, an* approximation *of passion, a semblance of love.*

Oh, in a sense he did love *her, he supposed. He certainly envied her, lusted after the knowledge the Flower of Life had imparted to her. But as to all this mindspeech about remaining on Optera, about actually relinquishing some of his physical form so that they might remain mates here . . . Well, that was arrant nonsense. He could no more live here—even with the secret shared and revealed—than he could abandon the quest for enlightenment that had already taken him to scores of star systems and hundreds of planets.*

Furthermore, there was a husband *to consider.*

Nothing like the Regis, this creature that called himself the Regent. And Zor had barely given him a second thought when it had come down to formulating his plan for seduction and conquest. But there was something about the Regent that rendered him more human *than the Regis could ever be, for all her recently evolved anatomic curves, erogenous zones, and self-shaping talents. And it was just this mysterious humanness that Zor made use of to ensure that the Regent was absent from the hive for long periods at a stretch.*

The Regent, it seemed, had a curiosity for Zor and his kind that rivaled Zor's curiosity for the Regis. Only the Regent was less interested in the physical and psychological differences that separated them than he was in the very artifacts the technovoyagers used in their everyday lives and travels. It was as though the creature wished only to fill his world with such things—instruments and devices and ships. So it had been easy enough to arrange for the Regent to be taken on a tour through this or that part of the ship or flown to distant places on his own Optera when the need arose.

And that need had arisen often these past months . . .

Zor smiled to himself, lying with the Regis now, his arms wrapped around her. He recognized that the transference was almost complete, the language of the Flower almost his. But he recognized, too, that there were rules governing the use of this language and, quite possibly, that he had been made aware of something misunderstood by the Queen-Mother herself. The Flower of Life apparently held a secret of its own, one that had yet to be seduced from it.

A secret Zor would one day call Protoculture.

Scott Bernard sat stiffly in his chair as the two majors led Marlene into the *Ark Angel's* briefing room. Cabell, the Grants, Louie Nichols, and several intelligence officers from G2 were seated at the long table. Bulkhead displays flashed color-enhanced visual close-ups of Haydon IV, an updated count of production vessels, an alphanumeric Karbarran attack countdown. The ship had turned slightly to port to keep the reconfigured artifact centered in the exterior viewports. The accretion disc of Ranaath's Star pinwheeled in the background, a sinister wheel of fortune.

Marlene, red hair pulled back behind her ears, looked ill.

"Take a seat," Vince began, sounding like a physician about to deliver bad news.

With a nervous glance at Scott, Marlene lowered herself into one of the plastic chairs. He held her gaze for a moment and looked away, tight-lipped.

Niles Obstat cleared his throat. "I think you know why we've asked you here."

"I'm—I'm not sure," Marlene told the intel chief.

Vince grimaced and blew out his breath. "We've tried to give you time to think through your position, er, Marlene. But I'm afraid time has run out for all of us. We have reason to believe you can tell us where the Regis is, and we need that answer now."

Marlene swallowed and found her voice. "I've been trying—"

"Don't give us any of that," Obstat said, cutting her off. "You're Invid, and what one of you knows, you all know. Just tell us where we can find the Regis, and we'll put an end to this. It's for your own good, too," he added. "How else are you planning to get home if we don't take you there?"

Scott was tempted to tell Obstat how Sera had gone home but held his tongue. Marlene was staring at the director, lower lip trembling.

"But don't you see, I'm not *all* Invid," she replied. "I have—"

"You're all Invid as far as we're concerned," a woman officer sneered.

Marlene closed her eyes and shook her head. "If that's true, then how is it that one of your own kind loves me?" Her eyes found Scott, as did everyone else's in the room. "Tell them, Scott, please. Make them understand."

"Well, Colonel?" Vince said, averting his eyes. "Suppose you tell us."

Scott's hands clenched beneath the tabletop. He looked at Marlene as he slowly rose to his feet.

"I'm sorry, Commander," he began, "but I guess our trick didn't work." Again he locked eyes with Marlene. "It was a good idea to make it seem like you were releasing her in my custody, but I guess she just didn't buy it. I certainly did my part to convince her that I . . . loved her, sir. But she wouldn't tell me anything."

Scott swallowed hard and continued. "Hell, I would have told her anything she wanted to hear to get that information. I sure don't mind admitting now that this was the toughest charade I've ever had to play out. Pretending *love* for this . . . Invid. And all the while thinking about what they did to Earth, what they've probably done to our friends and comrades on the SDF-3." Scott snorted, averting his eyes from the table. "I think all I managed to do was help convince her she really *is* human, Commander. Imagine that, will you—this Invid, *human*."

Wide-eyed through Scott's confession, Marlene suddenly put her hands to her head and screamed.

The scream was a nonhuman one.

She aimed a finger across the table at Scott. "You *betrayed* me! You told me you *loved* me!"

Scott held his breath.

Marlene was about to continue, when her body was seized by a violent paroxysm. The two majors flanking her leapt from their seats as she began to fade from view.

"Don't touch her!" someone warned.

As if anyone was about to.

Scott thought he might pass out, but just then Marlene rematerialized, skin tinged green and expression vacant. Her right hand was still raised but pointed out the viewport. She regarded the table for a long moment, as though challenging anyone to speak. But it was Marlene herself who broke the spell her brief disappearance had cast.

"There," she said finally with utter contempt.

Scott joined the others at the table in following her finger.

"Ra-anaath's Star?" Obstat stammered. "Your queen is inside the black hole?"

"You asked to know," Marlene said flatly.

"Christ," Louis Nichols muttered. "Veidt wasn't kidding when he said the *Ark Angel* isn't built for the trip."

"I know how difficult that was for you, Scott," Vince said after Marlene had been taken from the room. "But we had to know. You understand, don't you?"

Scott looked up at him, face drained of blood. "And is she going to understand that I was lying just now?" He sighed heavily. "I've sentenced her to death, Commander. I've killed her."

Dr. Penn almost laid a hand on Scott's shoulder but withdrew it. "She had to remember who she was, son. The shock was necessary. You couldn't have prevented it, anyway. She belongs to her own kind, not here, divided, trapped in two separate worlds."

Scott uttered a sardonic laugh. "A lot of good it did us, Doctor." He motioned with his chin toward the viewport. "The SDF-3 is out of reach."

"Haydon doesn't seem to think so," Louie said into the silence. "Look," he explained as heads turned, "I realize that any directional coordinates we could coax from the Awareness would be useless now. But Haydon's obviously convinced that it's possible to follow the lead, no matter where it ends up."

Vince shook his head. "If you're thinking that I'll risk taking this ship into *that* . . ." he said, indicating Ranaath's Star.

Louie held up his hands. "I'm not. I was only going to suggest that instead of pilfering coordinates, we steal one of those *ships*."

Minmei was crying when she left the music room. But what she had first assumed to be a rapturous outpouring brought upon by the harmonies of the clones' psalms she now understood to be tears of sadness. The ancient songs had awakened an aged hurt inside her one she could not be certain was even *hers*, but it touched her as though it was and was connected somehow with Rem.

The tears were flowing patently by the time she rushed blindly onto the lift, where she ran straight into Lisa Hayes Hunter.

"Minmei," Lisa said, surprised. "What's wrong?"

The odd thing was that the sight of Minmei's tears actually helped to dam the flow of Lisa's own. Relieved by her exec only moments before, Lisa had nearly fled the bridge like a lovesick adolescent, crushed by the discovery that a romance meant to last an eternity was not even going to survive the football season! She was at a loss to explain just what had brought the nosedive on—some aftereffect of the argument with Rick, perhaps, or just plain concern for his well-being planetside—and she was headed for the nursery to press Roy to her breast with a vengeance.

"Do you want to talk about it, Minmei?" Lisa asked, feeling that the situation was awkward all of a sudden. Their friendship had been on a steady decline since Lisa and Rick's wedding day. The Sentinels campaign hadn't helped, nor had Minmei's fling with T. R. Edwards and her subsequent retirement from public life. But Lisa had heard that Minmei had been on the mend, thanks to Rem. And hadn't Rick mentioned something about her *singing* again?

Well, maybe it was one of those artistic mood swings, Lisa started to tell herself, when Minmei said, "It's Rem."

Lisa eyed the young woman who had slipped onto the lift behind Minmei and was off to one side now, pretending disinterest in the conversation. The woman had security written all over her.

"Come on," Lisa said, leading Minmei off the lift at the med deck. "Now tell me what happened," she added, a few steps down the quiet corridor.

Minmei sniffled and ran the back of her hand under each eye. "That's just it, Lisa, I don't *know* what happened. I just, it's just . . . I'm feeling like he *used* me. Just the way everyone else has done for my whole stupid life." She took a deep breath. "The singing hasn't *helped* me. It's made me feel *worse* about everything. He just wanted me to sing so he could take his little trip down memory lane."

Lisa waited for her to continue.

Minmei sniffled again. "It's for Zor," she said dismissively. "He thinks the old Tiresian songs will jar memories of Zor's early experiences on Tirol and Optera."

"Optera?" Lisa said, thinking suddenly of the planet below. A planet that had appeared out of nowhere.

"I just keep feeling he's betrayed me somehow," Minmei explained, sobbing. "He doesn't love me. He probably never loved me."

Lisa was not listening. Some half-formed realization had begun to vie for her attention, a thought she could not quite assemble. But before she knew it, she had taken Minmei by the upper arms and was shaking her. "Did Rem tell you why it's so important he recall Zor's memories?"

Minmei looked up, startled.

Lisa dropped her arms at her sides and exhaled.

"Minmei, listen to me. I'm on my way to the nursery right now because I feel like Rick's been lying to me about something. That he's really in love with that little idiot Sue Graham or someone. But I know that isn't true, even if he *has* been acting like a complete jerk." She looked into Minmei's eyes. "And I'm sure Rem hasn't betrayed you. It has something to do with this place, Minmei. Something we haven't considered yet." She gnawed at a finger, remembering Roy. "It's even begun to affect the children."

Minmei looked ashen. "Oh, please, don't tell me that," she said, turning to face the corridor wall. "You can't tell anyone, Lisa," she added, "but I'm carrying Rem's child."

CHAPTER
NINETEEN

Although Wilfred Gibley is most often credited with the discovery of machine mind and the development of cyber-interface technology (See Shi-Ling's "Sometimes Even a Yakuza Needs a Place to Hide"), Nichols was to become the movement's principal advocate and spokesperson. Evidence suggests that Nichols himself may have been working along similar lines as early as May of 2031, when he wrote: "It was Bowie [Grant] that started me thinking. He used to say that he thought of music, like mathematics, as this place somewhere out there that adepts could tune into. And that the key signatures and notes and scales were actually solid things you could approach in that realm. So I thought: Why couldn't it be the same for data? After all, what's mind but a union of music and math?"

Bruce Mirrorshades, *Machine Mind and Arthurian Legend*

HODEL, COMMANDER OF THE KARBARRAN FLOTILLA, counted down the seconds. He thought about Cano, the brother he had lost when the *N'trpriz* had been destroyed, and wondered how many others he would grieve for before the battle was through.

Haydon IV had yet to respond to the ultimatum, although the Tiresian, Cabell, claimed to have been in touch with a high-ranking official planetside who had affirmed that no prisoners would be released. The Haydonite had also warned against the use of force to achieve that end. In his capacity as amateur historian, Hodel was inclined to believe him. He was as conversant as any with the facts regarding the Mo'fiint Incident, in which 870 dreadnoughts at the command of a would-be empire builder had attempted to add Haydon IV to her long list of conquests. Eight hundred and seventy ships annihilated in a matter of minutes . . . But history was just that, or so the Karbarran High Authority had admonished Hodel when he had brought the Mo'fiint Incident to their attention. So, in his capacity as battle group commander, he was expected to disregard any Haydonite counterthreats communicated to the *Ark Angel* and accept on faith that history mattered only to the victors.

Moreover, it was obvious from the recordings made during the *N'trpriz*'s final moments that K'rrk had committed a series of tactical blunders. He had failed to break off communication with Haydon IV's artificial sentience and had thereby allowed the Awareness access to the ship's onboard Tiresian-manufactured AI—which in turn had been based on *Haydonite designs*!

This time in there would be no such contact. The Awareness had been given ample opportunity to respond; the deadline had not been met, and it was time therefore to actualize the threat. Haydon IV would be given no second chance.

And neither would the ships of the flotilla.

Hodel buried the thought behind a confident scowl and rose from his command chair as the zero-line display triggered battle-station sirens throughout the ship.

"Order all ships into attack formation," he growled to his communications officer. "Full ahead, on my command, Ntor."

"Aye, sir," Ntor responded from her station. "Sekiton drives at maximum power, all systems enabled."

The battle plan was a straightforward one now that the safety of the hostages was no longer considered a mission priority. Haydon IV was simply to be beaten into submission. The loss of the five hundred or so merchants and traders planetside would be regrettable but acceptable.

Colonel Mo'fiint had felt no need to justify her actions when she had given the order to attack Haydon IV. The goal, after all, had been conquest.

Much as today, Hodel thought.

"Planetary reconfiguration in process, Captain," the science officer advised. "Haydon IV is disengaging from the moon. Weapons' nacelles retracting. We are being scanned and targeted."

Hodel swiveled to study displays. The giant artifact was

rotating to face the flotilla, its matériel transfer tubes traversing local space like twin cannons. "Standard evasion, Ntor," he directed forward. "Close all communication frequencies."

"Repositioning of the labor droneships, Captain," the science officer updated. "They are being deployed to repel strikes directed against the surface."

Hodel growled to himself. "Order fighter teams away as soon as we're within range."

"Aye, sir."

Hodel watched the forward screens. "All right, Ntor, let's clear a path for them. On my mark . . ."

Aboard the *Ark Angel*, Louie Nichols and his crew of comic-crazed compjockeys were headlocked into that part of the ship's AI mainframe linked to the commo device Veidt had left in Excdore's care.

The data room was a yard sale of consoles, monitors, slave decks, sensory boosts, psi-amps, and enhancers; a tangled nest of F/O lines, power leads, and interface cables, with the team members positioned about like switches and relays— some sprawled on the floor beneath tables, cranial cyberports studded with titanium plugs and alloy adapters, others cross-legged atop tables and racks, fiddling with tuning knobs, keying input, fingering touchscreens, but loving every minute of it, thrilled to be back where they belonged, ghosts in the mind of the machine.

Vince Grant had just sent word that the Karbarrans were making their move and that Haydon IV was readying what promised to be a crippling response. It had been Louie's signal to commence an attack of his own devising, not directed against the planet, however, but against the psychodynamics of its ruling artificial intelligence. With luck, the Awareness would be too busy attending to matters of defense to notice Louie and his cowboys' subtle approach, too preoccupied carrying out the timeless dictates of its enigmatic programmers to realize that someone was toying with its emotions.

Louie, Gibley, Strucker, and the rest were not going in so much on-line as they were *on-wave*, in an attempt to grapple with the Awareness where it lived, loved, and loathed. Unified, the discorporate raiders aimed to plant the seeds of self-doubt, to stir a bit of regret, to suggest a path to redemption.

To inject a virus if all else failed.

Louie could feel the cyber surge as he punched into machine mind, the hands to which his thoughts were now only remotely connected hovering over the console's directional cross and touchpad, his hands-on-trigger-and-stick. The cyber-surge was the rush of a crimson-tipped stimulant, a kick clear out of the world. He could feel Stirson and Shi-Ling headlocked into the same vibe, telepathic twins flanking him like recklessness and daring, an upside Scylla and Charybdis.

Machine mind was dimly lit, boundless but crowded with the color-coded spires and sentry towers that guarded *Ark Angel*'s mainframe cores. Below was the network's familiar grid of pulsating lights, data highways for the grounded and uninspired. Louie laughed as he soared above bridges and constructs, executing flyboy rollovers between mainframe pillars and pyramids as he closed on the access link to Veidt's device.

Exedore's computer construct was over the horizon, stuck in the real stuff, blazing a trail for the team. Louie thought he could almost detect the Zentraedi's fingers hammering overhead like thunder in that weatherless domain.

Down the link into the device, a jump fueled by thought from ship to reconfigured world, into a much smaller space—a foyer of a kind, an antechamber defined by the dark maws of derezz gates, the looming shadows of security fences. Gibley's construct slid to a halt nearby, freaked by the sight, wavering like the filament in a shaken bulb. Exedore was giving it his all, hacking away with commands, but there were defensive commands beginning to line up behind the walls: retaliatory icons ordered in by executive decision.

Louie steeled himself, hands set for play in the *Ark Angel*'s dreamscape. Gibley, Strucker, Stirson, and Shi-Ling were eager trotters, panting at the start of the course.

An access window suddenly flashed transparent.

Exedore had punched through.

Gibley's construct took the point as the Awareness deployed its net.

Time to fry, Louie thought.

* * *

"I've found a way in!" Exedore announced, hands raised above the keyboard in surprise.

"Yeah, and I've found a way out," Dana told him from the front threshold as repeated blasts shook the room. The laser fence disabled, the Praxians had already gone through to lend support to the Karbarran revolt.

The ursinoids had streamed out of their cells only moments before at the sound of the first surface explosions, stacking bodies in the thresholds until the lasers were overworked, then flooding into the central confinement area armed with everything from furniture parts to sheets of alloy torn from the walls.

Most of level four was pure chaos. The Haydonite jailers had trained their forehead weapons on the mob and successfully decimated the Karbarran front line. But like the lasers, the hovering guards were soon overwhelmed and felled by body blocks and staggering paw-hand swipes.

Dana ventured that the Awareness itself was being overwhelmed by coordinated strikes launched by the ships of the Karbarran battle group. Haydon IV's big brain could not effectively oversee confinement zone security when it was busy fending off plasma bolts and safeguarding the spherical ships its factory had been spitting out. The laser fences had been the first to go, control of the jailers had been relinquished, and Exedore was telling everyone that he had secured a route into the heart of the central computer. It was a sure thing, then, that Louie's team would be able to follow Exedore in and loose their poisons.

In the meantime, Dana thought she might be able to assist both Louie and the Karbarran flotilla by opening up yet another front. At her insistence, Exedore had ferreted out the whereabouts of the power management terminals that controlled production of the sphere ships' stardrives. Readouts indicated that a few of those drives had already been installed, but most were still under construction. The way Dana saw it, Haydon and his hibernating brethren were not going to be thrilled to learn that someone had crept up the beanstalk and made off with the golden goose, or in this case, one of the ships built to whisk them off to their planned retirement community. But if she could arrange it so that the drives never reached the ships, the *Ark Angel* crew would be long gone before Haydon figured out what had happened.

Of course it would have been better still to incapacitate Haydon's alarm clock, or at least set the wake-up time forward a couple or three centuries, but Exedore had not had any success in zeroing in on that part of the Awareness, much less in divining just where Haydon was sleeping it off.

"So who's joining me?" Dana asked, wielding a table leg in one hand. "We got some labor droids to decommission."

"It's important that I remain here," Exedore said without taking his eyes from the monitor screen."

"You keep doing what you're good at, Exedore." She glanced at her parents, standing side by side behind the Zentraedi. "What about it? Mom? Dad?"

Aurora stepped forward while the Sterlings were casting uncertain looks at one another. "I'll go with you," she told Dana.

Dana adopted a dubious look. "That's good of you, kid, but I don't know."

"Remember the spores, Dana," Aurora said, reminding her of the mindlink they had once shared across a near arm's length of galaxy.

Dana nodded. "Glad to have you aboard, sis."

Max and Miriya adopted determined expressions. "All right, Dana, you win," Max said.

She quirked a smile at them. "Yeah," she said, "now I remember you guys."

"Fools," Vince said under his breath, "crazy fools. It's a suicide run."

Spherical bursts erupted in the darkness outside the bridge viewports. The *Ark Angel* had removed herself a safe distance from the battle, but even so it was apparent that the Karbarrans were sustaining heavy losses. Their strafing runs across Haydon IV's split hemispheres had succeeded only in riling the planet's defense arrays, which were responding mercilessly. Fortunately, the Karbarran commander had had sense enough to keep the factory-produced sphere ships between his own flotilla and the artifact's in-close plasma cannons. That at least had assured that the Awareness would fall into a push-pull dispute with its own programmed imperatives—

to protect the planet from attack while at the same time safe-guarding the ships it had assembled from the metallic stuff of its host/captive moon. As a result, Haydon IV had been forced to be uncharacteristically circumspect with its initial retaliatory salvos, and many of the Karbarran dreadnoughts had survived.

Close-up cameras revealed planet and flotilla in a savage dance around the production ships, each searching for openings. But the Karbarrans were having a difficult time maintaining formation in the face of such maneuverings. As an added irritant, the Awareness had directed most of its labor droneships against the flotilla's defensive fighter groups and was scoring heavily in all sectors.

"They should break off the attack while there's still time," Vince said to no one in particular. He felt Jean's warm hand on his shoulder.

"We've pinpointed the ship," she told him as he swung around from the view.

Vince glanced over her head at intel officers and techs grouped around the tactical board. In tight close-up on-screen was one of the interdimensional sphere ships, with few labor drones about.

"Is that the one?" Vince asked.

"Yes, sir," a lieutenant colonel replied. "We're certain it's the prototype. First off the line, first to be equipped with drive units." The young man swiveled to face Vince. "It's our best bet, General."

Vince answered him with a grim nod. "Any word from Nichols?"

"Just up, sir," a tech said, displaying a message on one of the sit board's peripherals. "Looks like they're inside the Awareness. We've also received reports of a full-scale hostage uprising planetside."

Vince studied the big board, then turned to the viewport, narrowing his eyes against an angry strobing of battle light.

"All right, gentlemen," he said after a moment. "Inform Colonel Bernard that his Veritech group has a green light. But make sure he understands they're to wait for Dr. Nichols's all-clear before attempting to board the prototype."

The tech activated the com-line. "Anything else, sir?"

Vince snorted. "Wish him Godspeed, Sergeant."

* * *

The Awareness was an argent temple that brought to mind Tiresia's pyramidal Royal Hall. Louie and his infiltration team approached it cautiously, evading program sentries when necessary, although most of those had been successfully lured away to implement Exedore's requests for system updates.

Once they were inside, the place turned out to be a labyrinth of command corridors and data reservoirs, as difficult to enter as it probably was to exit. But there was no time to be selective. Gibley surrendered the point, and Louie joysticked himself through a columned portal. Angling through a maze of lower function hallways, he began arming the virus charges the raiders had carried in. The idea was to home in on the source of the disruption signals that would result once they were detonated.

And in that, the charges did not disappoint.

The Awareness rallied, filling its instinctual level corridors with a veritable horde of antibiotic programs. But the teams' decision to engage early on had been predicated on the expectation of just such a primitive reaction, and by so doing, the Awareness not only lost momentary control of its logic circuits but allowed Louie's team to ascend rapidly through its command and control hierarchy.

Louie followed the path of most resistance, deploying ghosts to confuse trackers, and eventually entered a vaguely defined triangular chamber close to the pyramid's summit. Normally there would have been access codes to decrypt there, but the Awareness had apparently been engaged in entering them when the Karbarran attack had begun.

When Louie had brought the raiders to a halt, he sent three recon drones through the elaborate window at the chamber's apex.

The data they returned stilled his thoughts.

In the space above—the temple's golden triangle—were perhaps tens of thousands of discorporate intelligences.

Louie had discovered where Haydon and his race were hiding.

By the time he found the presence of mind to order the team out, the first of Haydon's antipersonnel security-force programs was already engulfing them.

CHAPTER
TWENTY

"Now, children," I heard one of the child-care staffers say into the mike, "stop being so damned destructive!" He turned to me red-faced and apologetic, but I was already thinking: Damned children, damned children . . . When and where had I heard that before?

Lisa Hayes, *Recollections: The Lost Journey*

REM DID NOT NEED THE CLONESONGS TO OPEN HIS mind to what had happened once Zor had left Optera with the Flower of Life specimens the Regis had given him. He knew from both the historical record and the cellular memories he had summoned while at work on Lang's facsimile matrix that the Regent had learned of his wife's infidelity, exposed the hoax Zor had perpetrated, and ordered the landing party to leave the planet.

Though the use of deception was still in vogue among the Tiresians of that period, the direction of physical force against other life-forms was not, and the landing party had assented to the outraged husband's demands and exited the Tzuptum system the following day. But instead of continuing with their planned tour of the Quadrant, they had returned almost immediately to Tirol, where Zor had described for the Elders the wonders to be found on Optera and had given them their first look at the mysterious Flower he had accepted on their behalf.

What had followed for Zor were years and years of tedious and most often solitary experimentation with the Flower. The

Elders had been pleased to accept his gift, but their disappointment was apparent. True, the Invid-Flower symbiosis seemed to be a process worthy of further investigation, but that was the end of it. The Elders lacked the necessary vision to see how the Flower might have any lasting import to human life. So Zor had endeavored to demonstrate just what could be accomplished by harnessing the Flower's bio-energy, and by employing the language the Regis had taught him, he introduced Protoculture to the Quadrant.

So began the brief but catastrophic era known as the Great Transition: the years of barbaric infighting that led to the formation of the Robotech Masters, the rapid redevelopment of terror weapons and spacefold drives, the bloody programs that anticipated the early clone experiments, and finally, the neural re-programming of the miner-giant Zentraedi.

Zor had long since lost control of his discovery and fallen victim to the Compulsion the Masters had placed upon him. And those same Masters would oversee his eventual return to Optera, no longer as trickster or would-be king but conqueror, thief, and destroyer of worlds . . .

Rem wept in his quarters aboard the SDF-3, recalling the hell Optera had been sentenced to by his clone-father and the millions-strong Zentraedi. The theft of the Flowers, the ravaging of that garden planet, the overnight devolvement of the Invid, the war that had raged across the face of countless worlds . . .

As little as two Earth-standard years ago, Rem had convinced himself that by reseeding Optera—New Praxis—he had actually redressed some of Zor's injustices. But he understood now that he had balanced only half the equation. The Flowers prospered, but only to serve the demands of the beings that sowed them—to yield up the Protoculture.

The Compulsion lived on. For in fabricating the matrix, Rem had helped deal yet another blow against the Flowers' true guardians.

He began to ask himself what Zor had hoped to accomplish by sending the original matrix to Earth. Zor's hand had been guided by something he had learned on Haydon IV, Rem knew that much. But what was it he had discovered there?

Some way to rescue the Invid, perhaps, to make amends to the Queen-Mother he had seduced.

Some way to balance the other side of the equation.

Rem realized that he would need Minmei's help one final time to dredge up nucleic memories of Zor's quiet rebellion against the Masters and of his critical encounter with Haydon IV's artificial sentience, the Awareness.

"I suppose we should be grateful they disassembled the thing," Emilio Segundo, the ship's pediatrician, suggested.

Lisa looked at him askance, " 'Disassembled,' Doctor? I'd say they *destroyed* it."

Kazianna Hesh issued a low, grunting sound that sent the nursery's Micronian balcony vibrating. "What can we expect," she said, "with world killers as their role models?"

Lisa could have almost believed she was conversing with one of the women in the childbirth class she and Rick had taken before Roy was born. Although Lisa, Dr. Segundo, and Kazianna Hesh were standing eye to eye, the balcony was some forty feet above the nursery floor.

But *killed* was certainly an apt description of what the human and Zentraedi young ones had done to the alloy and foam sphere they had expended such energy fashioning. The thing was literally in pieces, hemispheres cleaved, the complex transformable modules of their interiors scattered about. The nursery looked like a war zone, which was how the pediatrician had related it to Lisa over the intercom several minutes before.

"Did they give *any* explanation?" she asked him.

Segundo shook his head, one hand tugging at his salt-and-pepper goatee. "None whatsoever. One minute they had the sphere opened and transformed into something that looked to me like an outsize pair of binoculars, and the next they attacked it with every toy in the place."

"Complete with sound effects," Kazianna said. "Mecha flight sounds, explosions, death rattles, that sort of thing," she added, sensing Lisa's bafflement.

"So it was all an elaborate game—building this thing, then wrecking it?"

Segundo shrugged. "It would hardly explain the secrecy

they attached to it." He looked at Lisa. "And all this guarded behavior the staff claim they demonstrated."

"Oh, they did," Lisa affirmed, recalling her confrontation with Roy and Drannin. "Trust me on that one, Doctor."

Lisa stepped closer to the one-way glass to peer down into the playroom. The children, cross-legged—human and Zentraedi alike—had formed an inward-facing circle on the floor. "Let's have the audio again," she said after a moment.

Segunda activated a wall switch, and low-voiced chanting filled the balcony space. The chant sounded like some sort of monotone, three-syllable canine call: *Ur-rur-ra, ur-rur-ra, ur-rur-ra* . . .

"They've been at it for close to fifteen minutes now," Kazianna said.

Lisa was about to respond when the intercom sounded. Segundo made a volume adjustment on the nursery mikes and hit the com-line ready stud. Raul Forsythe's face appeared on-screen. "Go ahead, Raul," Lisa said, positioning herself in front of the camera.

"Message from below, Admiral," Forsythe began. "Two members of the scouting party have disappeared."

Lisa's hand went to her mouth. "Oh, no . . ."

"Seems scanners detected the presence of a life-form just prior to the disappearances—enormous by the sound of it. But the thing vanished before the team could fix its location."

"Any confirmation from our onboards?" Lisa asked.

"Not yet. But Admiral Hunter is requesting backup. They've got a lot of ground to cover, and it's slow going."

"Was he specific?"

"He wants two teams—one Sentinels, one Zentraedi."

Lisa turned to Kazianna to see if she was listening. The Zentraedi nodded, but Lisa noticed misgiving in her sad eyes.

"What is it, Kazianna?" Lisa said after she and Raul had signed off. "If you have any concerns about going planetside, now's the time to make them known."

Kazianna shook her head. "It's not that, Commander, it's the chant."

Lisa listened for a moment. The children seemed to have upped the tempo, if not the volume.

" 'Ur-rur-ra,' " Kazianna mimicked. "I think they're saying *Aurora*."

* * *

Toggled out of machine mind, Louie Nichols sat palsied at his console in the *Ark Angel*'s data room, his own internal systems scrambled by Haydon's security programs. That he had emerged with his personality intact was nothing less than miraculous, given what the Awareness had launched against the team. Gibley, however, had not been as fortunate. He was laid out like a rag doll on a table across the room, eyes wide but expression blank. Two med techs were working on him, but while they might succeed in keeping the body alive, Gibley was fried inside, a complete brainwipe.

"You okay?" Louie heard Strucker ask behind him. He turned and nodded.

"Command says Bernard's VTs are closing on the ship."

Louie took a deep breath. "Then we've gotta go back in. But this time we steer clear of that central shaft," he told his team. "Everybody got it? I think we bypassed command and control in the way up to Haydon's cyber-sleep chamber."

"On the left as we cleared that tall logic column," Stirson said.

"Right, I saw it," Shi-Ling agreed. "Green haze portal, like the one we developed back in Tokyo for Matushima."

Stirson grinned. "That's the one."

"First one in goes straight to drive programming," Louie instructed. "What we're looking for is an override command that'll allow Bernard's team to get aboard the prototype and steer it clear of the artifact." He thought briefly about Dana, moving against the factory's drive production center now. "If we can deactivate the drives of the rest of those prototypes, so much the better," he thought to add.

"Haydon's not going to like this one bit," Stirson said.

Louie had his fingers on the jump toggle. "Yeah, let's just hope we never have to answer to them face to face."

He toggled back into machine mind.

With crude shields and weapons raised, the four Sterlings emerged from the transport tube on level two, but all that greeted them was what remained of Glike's debris-strewn main boulevard.

"We must be on the surface," suggested one of the Praxians who followed them out.

The sky was a backlit haze, seemingly draped from the summits of Glike's ruined onion domes and spires. Though tinged with odors of dust and smoke, the air smelled like Haydon IV's saccharine-smelling own, but Max felt certain they were still subsurface. He thought it likely that the city had been lowered and moved inside during reconfiguration, that the overcast "sky" they were staring into concealed the ceiling of some cavernous hold.

It was irrelevant in either case, and in short order the hastily formed team had reconned the immediate area and set off for the drive production area Exedore had located, distant explosions and plasma cannon reports shaking the streets at random intervals. The farther they got from the transport tube egress, the more Max's hypothesis began to make sense. Glike's borrowed and indigenous architecture—which had always seemed purely aesthetic in both function and design—had been transformed and incorporated into the workings of a massive assembly line.

The robot masters in charge of production work barely acknowledged the humans as they followed Dana's lead across once-green parks that had become staging areas, along avenues converted to parts conveyers, past monuments and obelisks truncated and metamorphosed into stanchions and pylons, and through buildings that housed the busy machines themselves—lathes, presses, extruders, and such. Ultimately, Dana brought them to a building Max thought he recognized as the former headquarters of the Haydonite Elite. The adamantine arches and gilded roots of its almost pre-Global Civil War Arabic look were still in evidence among the ultratech computer devices that crowded the entryway.

"This is it," Dana announced loudly enough to be heard over the roar of the production line, "the brains of the operation." She was standing, arms akimbo, in that defiant superhero pose that had become something of a trademark.

Max, too, recognized it from the schematics Exedore had called up on the monitor.

Dana, scanning the power junction catwalks for Haydonites, snorted derisively. "Haydon wasn't expecting anybody to get this far." She aimed an index finger at a towering bank of apparently undefended data-control terminals. "We knock those out and production grinds to a halt in this entire section. Haydon'll have his ships, but they won't be able to take him anywhere.''

One of the Praxians stepped forward, a broad-shouldered white-maned Amazon a foot and a half taller than Max. ''We've come to silence this machine servant,'' she said in thickly accented Tiresian. ''Let's get on with it.''

Dana grinned and rubbed her hands together. She stooped to retrieve the table leg she had carried up from level four and said to Aurora, ''Watch closely, kid. We'll show you how it's done.''

Max received a gentle shove from Miriya and was about to join his daughter and the four Praxians when someone poured a bucketful of nitric acid into his head. That, at least, was how he decided it felt as he was dropping to his knees, hands pressed tightly to his ears. Dana and the rest were similarly felled, knees buckling, faces twisted up in pain.

Only Aurora appeared unaffected.

With effort, Max managed to lift his head and search the control room. Hovering fifteen feet above him was a group of four Haydonites, similar in aspect to the jailers who had patrolled level four's confinement areas, their *dzentile* glowing with charge.

Dana screamed and cursed, pounding the floor with a fist in an attempt to shake off the psychic force the Haydonites were directing against them. Through the mottled cloud her field of vision had become she spied Aurora and called to her in a pleading voice.

Aurora made no response. She stood stiffly above her fallen companions—arms at her sides, eyes unfocused—as the Haydonites began a slow descent.

But just when the four were reaching what would have been the Praxians' headtop level, Max heard a loud *swwooossh!* at the building's entrance and turned to see one of Glike's fabulous flying carpets come streaking into the room on edge. It was an exquisitely textured specimen, vaguely rectangular in shape, as large as a ball court, and it was headed directly for the hovering Haydonites.

They, too, swung around at the sound or presence of the thing and tried frantically to counterdirect it with last-moment sendings, but the carpet was already upon them, trapping them in a brilliantly executed broadside cigarette roll and propelling them clear across the control room.

Max struggled to his feet and ran to check on Miriya and Dana. The pain was gone, but trouble was still on the scene in the form of two additional Haydonites who had followed the carpet into the building, one with a coppery skin tone and bulging cranium.

Max was surprised to hear his name sent and shortly recognized the two as Veidt and Vowad.

"The Awareness has mitigated the strength of its directives," Veidt explained. "Several of us are now free to assist in your escape."

"We've got more than *escape* on our minds," Dana muttered, wiping her hands on her pants. The Praxians voiced agreement.

"Then it was you who sent the carpet," Miriya said.

The two Haydonites traded looks. "No," one of them started to send, when Aurora said, "I called the carpet."

Veidt nodded perceptibly. "I believe she did," he announced, nonplussed.

Dana looked at her younger sister and laughed. "Damn kids nowadays. Can't teach 'em a thing."

CHAPTER
TWENTY-
ONE

It has been claimed that all laws of science, our very ability to predict future events, will break down upon reaching the singularity. That the black hole's event horizon—trapped light's desperate spacetime path—is but a one-way membrane, we are about to find out. If only Dr. Hawking were here to join us.

Dr. Harold Penn, *The Brief but Timeless Voyage of the* Peter Pan

LIKE LASER LIGHT IN A SMOKE-FILLED ROOM, LOUIE'S cyber-self punched through the green haze security threshold leading to the Awareness's higher function core and arrowed straight into a cluster of telemetry commands in charge of programming dimensional data into the sphere ships' drives. The team was spread out in a V formation behind him, targeting ghosts against approaching strings of defense bytes.

Strucker had found that some of them could actually be absorbed and turned against their own kind.

Louie was a quarterback in that moment of stasis before the inevitable inrush of linemen and backs, searching through banks of data in a reckless effort to locate the prototype ship intel had indentified as nearly complete. The team was doing an incredible job of blocking the Awareness's poisoned advances, but the line was beginning to weaken.

Back aboard the *Ark Angel*, Louie's fingers tattooed hunches and possibilities to his discorporate mind; his fingers danced on the directional cross, maneuvering him clear of circuit frying, brainwipe booby traps.

Then, suddenly, he had it: an on-line ship designated by a perplexing series of emblematic icons and alphanumeric analogues. As expected, the ship had been safeguarded against entry, but no longer. Louie tapped the override program and keyed a new sequence of commands into the console.

Neuron probes, meanwhile, were nipping at the perimeter of the envelope in which he had secreted himself. There was no time left to search out the space drive production commands; Dana would have to see to it on her own.

"Toggle out!" Louie ordered as the first of the probes penetrated his defense net. "Toggle out!"

Scott Bernard maneuvered the Alpha through a storm of annihilation discs launched from Haydon IV's in-close plasma arrays. The planetoid's big guns were still trained on the few ships that remained of the Karbarran battle group. The ursinoids' fighter squadrons had been literally blown to pieces during counteroffensive impact runs by cloud after cloud of labor drones. Stray bits of those fighters drifted around the Alpha, touched by explosive glints, cyan and crimson.

But Haydon IV had been taking a pounding as well. It was a twin-eyed monstrosity below him now, hemispheric surfaces scorched and molten, factory tubes holed and venting gouts of alloy debris.

In the midground of the Alpha's curved canopy view floated a hundred or more of Haydon's sphere ships, temporarily abandoned in varying stages of readiness.

Scott had not flown a space combat op in well over a year and felt rusty. As rusty as the first day he had piloted a Veritech through Earth's atmosphere, a green VT Lunk had stashed away in an old barn. But no matter. The searing discs, the blue-green bolts, those swaths of agitated light were mild compared to his inner torment.

Marlene was dying.

Again!

And this time he had killed her.

"*Able leader,*" announced a female voice over the command net. "*Target ship's shields down and deactivated. You are go for boarding. You can take your team in, Colonel.*"

Scott acknowledged *Ark Angel* Command and went on the tac net to communicate with his wingmen. The squadron had lost only one mecha, a red Beta piloted by a Mars Base lieutenant Scott had known since childhood, who had gotten himself caught between Haydon IV's main guns and the Karbarrans' recently crippled flagship.

Atomized, Scott thought.

Released.

"Colonel," the command net voice squawked, *"why are you delaying? Target's shields are down, repeat, down."*

Scott shook his head clear of thought and addressed himself to the Alpha, thinking the mecha through to Battloid mode.

So reconfigured, the squadron began to follow him in.

The sphere ship enlarged before him until it obscured all else. The surface was ball-bearing smooth save for the faint outline of a hexagonal hatch low down on the curve of its starboard side.

There were no viewports, no visible weapons or scanner arrays. No way to see where they would be going and no way to protect themselves once they got there. But God willing, the hapless crew of the SDF-3 would be waiting for them.

And with them the Invid Queen-Mother.

Scott's hope and salvation.

"Just stay put," Vince Grant advised after he had expressed how good it was to hear Max's voice. "We'll get some Alphas down there to pick you up as soon as we can."

"I don't see that we have much choice, Vince," Sterling told him.

Outside the bridge viewports Haydon IV's primary batteries were inactive; they of course had been silent throughout the duration of the Karbarran attack, but now they were shut down as well. Early on the assumption was that the Awareness had quieted the planetoid's fire once the Karbarran flotilla had no longer been deemed a threat. But then Exedore had gotten word through to the *Ark Angel* that the entire superintelligence was temporarily shut down, probably as a result of the virus programs Nichols had infiltrated during the cyber-raid that had claimed the life of one of his team members.

The *Ark Angel* was closing on the battered planetoid after a brief reflex burn, most of its mecha squadrons deployed on search and rescue operations among the remnants of the Karbarran battle group. The pirated sphere ship—under remote control by the *Angel*'s AI—would be meeting them halfway with Scott Bernard's team safely inside.

"What are your survivor estimates, Max?" Vince asked.

"*Probably two hundred or so Karbarrans,*" Max responded after a moment. "*A lot of them in bad shape. About two dozen Praxians and three or four Spherisians. Then there's the seven of us.*"

"Seven?" Vince said.

"*Veidt and Vowad,*" Max explained. "*They helped us take out the production center, Vince. I've got no qualms about taking them along.*"

Vince mulled it over. "Guess they don't want to be around when Haydon wakes up, huh?"

"*Neither do I,*" Max affirmed. "*Honeymoon's over on this place.*"

A smile tugged the corners of Vince's wide mouth. "See you soon, Commander," he signed off.

In newspace, fifteen Zentraedi Battlepods launched from the SDF-3's forward mecha bay formed up on Kazianna's Officer's Pod and fell toward the vernal surface of an unknown world.

An unseen, unforeseen something had been detected there and had since disappeared with two members of Hunter's scouting party. The admiral—perhaps still unconvinced that the fortress had been flung far from familiar shores—had requested reinforcement from two XT teams, probably in the hope that someone—Karbarran, Garudan, or what have you—would be able to communicate with the unseen thing.

This unforeseen thing.

Kazianna found herself thinking of Drannin and the sphere the children had assembled and destroyed. Were they really chanting *Aurora*? she wondered. Sending a telepathic call to the youngest Sterling the way she had once sent one to her older sister across a sea of stars?

An SOS, Lisa had called it.

And what of this strange planet that had brought the fortress here? For that was how she considered it, despite what

Lang and the others were saying about intergalactic voids and patterning.

No, this was more than a world; she was certain of that much. It was perhaps even an intelligence unto itself; with something to teach them all.

The control consoles and acceleration couches, the general interior makeup of the sphere ship, had not been designed for human hands or eyes or posteriors, Scott had decided. Not, for that matter, with crystalline fingers, paw-mitts, or outsize limbs in mind.

The ship was merely a spherical chamber of light-emitting metal divided into several levels by featureless decking, unconnected by ladders, stairways, or lift tubes. On what seemed to be the command level was a continuous circumferential bench four feet from the floor without so much as a screen or a function key to mar its smooth surface.

It was only through Louie Nichols's remote manipulation of the external hatch that Scott's team had been permitted access to the ship at all, and only because of his deactivation of the ship's artificial gravity that they had been able to explore.

Then, just when Scott was thinking that no one outside of Haydon himself was ever going to be able to make use of the ship, the bench console came suddenly to life, banded in color like the planetary rings of some gaseous giant, and a huge projecbeam display of the *Ark Angel*'s bridge took shape in the center of the sphere.

"Doctor Nichols assures me that you can see me, Colonel," Vince Grant said, as though he were in the same ship. "Is that true?"

Wondering for a moment where to direct his words, Scott finally shrugged and said to the projecbeam image, "Not only you, General, but the entire *Angel* bridge. Doctor Nichols, Mrs. Grant, Doctor Penn, Cabell, Exedore, the Sterlings, all of you, sir." He thought about asking what the hell Veidt and Vowad were doing there but decided against it.

Louie Nichols nodded in the background. "We're going to begin ferrying some things over to you, Colonel," he began in an uncharacteristically subdued manner. "Components of the *Angel*'s onboard AI, which will ultimately become our interface hardware with that ship's power plant.''

"Then we *can* make use of it?'' Scott asked. "You can get us through the breach?''

Louie's face collapsed somewhat, and Scott recalled hearing about the teammate Nichols had lost.

"I'm certain we can do that much, Colonel. I'm just not as certain about getting us back out again.''

No one spoke to it.

Vince cleared his throat. "We'll commence transporting life support essentials, mecha, and personnel as soon as Doctor Nichols has his team in place.''

"Well, there's not much in the way of a welcome we can arrange,'' Scott told him. "We haven't found the liquor cabinet yet.''

Polite laughter greeted the remark, principally from Scott's own team members.

Vince gestured behind him. "Cabell and Exedore won't be joining us, Colonel. The *Ark Angel* will make for Tirol after disembarking her Karbarran passengers. And hopefully act as our beacon in this realm once we've, well, crossed over.''

Scott gulped, thinking of Ranaath's Star. "Who'll be crewing this ship, then, sir?''

"I've put it on a voluntary basis, Scott. Jean and I and Doctor Penn are coming over. And so far we've got three squadrons of mecha pilots and a sufficient number of technical assist crews.''

"I hope you've already counted me in, Commander,'' Scott said, sensing that Vince had left something dangling in the air.

Vince nodded. "I have.''

Scott folded his arms and stared at the floor. "There's just one more thing, sir . . . The, ah, Invid simulagent. I was, you know, thinking it would help having her along.''

"Marlene will accompany us, Scott.'' Vince traded brief looks with Louie. "There doesn't seem to be anything left for her in this realm.''

Or much left of her, Scott kept to himself.

The transfer of supplies and personnel took less than twelve hours, during which time Haydon IV did not so much as stir.

But finally the moment arrived for the *Ark Angel* and the pirated ship to part company.

Louie canceled the override and punched up the original commands the Awareness had programmed into the sphere's drives, and the ship's systems instantly came on-line.

While Cabell and the rest watched from the *Ark Angel* bridge, the sphere's massive drives flared once and hurled the ship toward the dark eye of Ranaath's Star. The sphere seemed to hang suspended at the edge of the whirlpool for the briefest of moments before it vanished from space and time.

Thousands of miles distant, the fey, aged crew of a second ship monitored the sphere ship's protracted plunge into the black hole and the subsequent departure of the *Ark Angel*. They then turned their attention to the reconfigured Haydon IV and waited.

PART III
AWAKENINGS

CHAPTER
TWENTY-
TWO

Survival recognizes and rewards anything that sustains life, and here was undeniable proof of that. No matter how noxious its central characteristic, it proved itself to have a stark value in what the Earthers call Darwinian terms—even a functional formidability.

The Scribe Triumvirate of Aholt, Ulla, and Tussas,
Nothing but Animus: A History of the Robotech Elders

DEATH, THEIR TIRELESS ENEMY, HAD THEM CORNERED at last.

It had pursued them for an age, ever since they'd cast off the bonds of a mortal life span and received unholy communion with the Protoculture a naïve Zor had fetched home to them from the stars. Death was the inevitable dark side of the bid they made, immediately, for eternal life. Not just longevity but *immortality*; anything less—prolonged years living in dread of the end—was nothing but a unique torment.

For the Robotech Elders, death had become the greatest of fears, in some ways a Singularity of fear.

Watching the sphere ship plunge into Ranaath's Star, somehow surviving the deadly swirl of the accretion disc, the utter annihilation of the event horizon, the Robotech Elders had shuddered at the risk its passengers and crew were running. Foolish little subcreatures, so reckless with their brief lives!

The Elders sat despondent, even their mindspeech silent, in their habitual circle. They arranged themselves in their triumvirate from habit—from reflex, by now. Between them was their darkened Protoculture cap, a mushroomlike console of instrumentality ten feet across, a hateful mockery of its former glorious self.

Once it had bent worlds to their will. In the years since the Elders had fled Tirol—upon the arrival of the SDF-3—it had kept them alive, barely, through its residue of power. With the disappearance of all Protoculture in the Elevation of the Invid race, the cap had died, become nothing more than a burnt-out artifact.

Their ship was a small prototype a Scientist triumvirate had been working on when the Invid onslaught had finally reached Tirol. The vessel was considerably smaller than the assault ships that had once carried the Robotech Masters' colossal Bioroids into combat, smaller than the tri-thrusters their Zentraedi giants had flown in battle in an age now vanished forever.

They had languished in it for years with little to behold but one another, each coming to hate the others and yet incapable of surviving without them.

Some of the craft's systems had been altered over the intervening years to run on more conventional power sources. Thus, it could still provide life support and had marginal maneuvering capability. But nothing could power the cap except Protoculture itself; after all this time the Elders were looking death in the face as they never had since that first, transmogrifying taste of the Essence of the Flower of Life, so long ago.

The SDF-3 had first shown up near Tirol to establish contact with them, to seek a peace, but the Elders had never really considered that idea seriously; they had presumed it was their onetime Zentraedi slave-warriors come home for final vengeance. Besides, when SDF-3 unfolded, the moon of Fantoma was already under genocidal attack by the forces of the Invid Regent.

Terrified as they were of abandoning their seat of power, lust as they might for the Protoculture the warring armies carried, the Elders had fled. There was too great a risk of death on Tirol, and their fear of oblivion outweighed any other impulse.

Learning the REF's true intentions, the Elders *still* shrank from any contact. Masters of deceit and treachery, they were incapable of trusting anyone else.

Their little prototype ship, with its superluminal drive, had made a few planetfalls over the years since (the Elders dared not show their faces near any of the advanced Local Group worlds they had once ground under their heel, of course). There were species sufficiently organized and domitable to be of some minor help—retrofitting the craft under the Elders' supervision, installing conventional power systems to minimize the drain on their Protoculture supply.

But the very act of dominating a population used up Protoculture at an agonizing rate, and the Elders feared detection by their former subjects, who were sallying out among the stars on their own. More than anything, however, the last Robotech Masters lusted for a return to their former power.

For that, they needed clones, warriors, the irresistible power of Robotechnology, but above all, they needed the secrets that had died with Zor. So they took to space again, feeding on bitterness and resentment of the universe. They were the unseen watchers of the Sentinels' struggles against the Invid, the hidden monitors of the conflict that had nearly consumed the Local Group like a black hole.

They looked for their advantage at every turn, but events defied them. Then the Invid transubstantiation swept away their last hoarded reserve of Protoculture like a whirlwind. Growing weaker, sickened like addicts gone cold turkey, they seemed wraithlike themselves. The Elders clung to life singlemindedly, feeding on their own rapacity—the stark craving to rule. They became their own worst tormentors.

Finally, as they spied on the drama played out around Haydon IV and Ranaath's Star, they felt the last of their life forces ebbing.

They had no idea how the planet had assumed its shape, or kept it, without the forces of gravity deforming and distorting it. The very idea of two half spheres the size of the opened Haydon IV was untenable by any physics the Elders knew.

But that was something for the lower orders—Scientist triumvirates and the like—to wonder about. The task of Masters was to rule.

Nimuul, the First among them, could barely lift his chin

from his breast as he sat sprawled in his thronelike chair. Still, when he managed to bring his head up a bit, his face wore the furious, blazing glare that was the Elders' only expression. It was an ax-keen, hawk-nosed face with sharp, angular cheekbones under which were scarlike creases of skin suggestive of tribal scars. His pate was bare, but fine, straight blue hair growing from the sides and back of his head fell to his shoulders.

Nimuul's fight to shape words was even harder than his effort to raise his head, but he chose the spoken word over thought-speech because only a trickle of their mental power remained. "We . . . must . . . reveal ourselves. To the . . . Awareness."

Hepsis, of the silver hair, stirred on his high-backed chair. His nailless, gracile fingers trembled feebly on its arm. But after a grunt he, too, brought forth sound. "No! The . . . risk . . ."

The third, Fallagar, was the most weakened by the prolonged ordeal. It seemed he could feel death before him, ready to blow his mind and personality away to nonexistence like a puff of dust. His terror gave him the strength to shape words aloud. "Our last chance."

He radiated waves of impotent rage and fear that even a nonsensitive could have felt. There was no telling what the Awareness of the planet would do in its battered, virus-altered state once they dropped their mental shields and revealed their presence—supposing that they could rouse it from its slumber. But there were no other options.

They were agreed. They dropped their shields warily, each making sure neither of the others betrayed him, left him exposed while ducking back behind psi-cover. With a heightened sense, they perceived the Awareness, hanging not far off in space, as a cold moonlet of mental energy.

Even at the zenith of their power the Elders had forborne to probe or seek to alter the Awareness of Haydon IV. They were averse to risk to themselves; the Awareness was tractable and presented no apparent threat. But always, in the recesses of their inner thought, Nimuul, Hepsis, and Fallagar had harbored misgivings about the titanic mindforce residing in the core of the artificial planet.

Certainly it had no reason to take pity on them; quite the reverse.

But Nimuul managed, "Let me . . . speak for us."

Where once it had shone forth like a nova, the triumvirate mental force of the Elders was a wan beam, like a ray from a dim nebula. But it carried Nimuul's message: *We are the last of the Robotech Masters. We can lead you to new Protoculture!*

With that, all three slumped, spent, in their chairs. Their breathing slowed, began rattling.

But within Haydon IV, something quickened.

The message activated a deeply nested subroutine, which enabled a function that had been totally inert, and so was missed, during Louie Nichols's epic cyber-burn. Mechamorphosis had always been a cardinal trait of Robotechnology, a reflection of Protoculture.

Cyber-systems could mechamorphose, too.

Deep in Haydon IV, new data highways shifted into existence, circumventing the blockages on the old. What pure information had done, physical change undid, at least in part. New topographic features—mountainous ones—grew out of reshuffled components.

The Awareness roused itself, took stock of the situation, acted. Control and other systems on the Elders' ship came to full available power. Its attitude thrusters fired, and it began a full-boost approach to Haydon IV even while its three occupants felt life slipping away.

The planet shifted massively as the Awareness ignored all the frightened queries from its inhabitants. The surviving Haydonites drew back, afraid to interfere.

Even as the ship closed on Haydon IV, a Brobdingnagian alloy tentacle took shape out of shifting machinery to emerge from one of the shot-up factory tubes. The Awareness guided the ship into the grasp of a specially fashioned claw. It was enfolded, and the enclosure was pressurized.

The lock cycled open in response to the Awareness's unspoken command. Remote units swarmed in around the Elders, propping them up on their thrones, inserting tubes, sensors, actuators. In seconds the Elders were encased in life support systems, their vital signs increasing.

The Awareness saw at once that the triumvirate could not

be kept alive that way for very long. It stepped up its efforts to revive them.

From a hidden storage nook deep, deep in its internal reaches, the planet fetched forth a half dozen or so eggplant-purple cylinders, round-bottomed and quiveringly gelid. They were the last of the particular manifestation of the fruit of the Flower of Life that the Invid Regent had grown in his hive on Haydon IV. That had been back during his occupation of the planet—before the Sentinels had unseated him in a cataclysmic battle—and now these few specimens were all that remained.

There was no Protoculture in them as such, true, but there was some vestige of the Flower's essence and substances akin to the ones on which the Elders fed. In moments, fluids drawn from the fruit were flowing into the bodies of the three.

They began to regain consciousness. The Awareness knew that this emergency measure would not sustain them for long; it introduced stimulants, heedless of the shock to their systems, and waited—*anxiously*—for some sign of life.

Nimuul's eyes blinked open. He did not feel well—indeed, he felt a bizarre disorientation—but he knew death had retreated, at least for the moment. He saw at once what had happened.

I will not deal with you, Nimuul mind-spoke to the Awareness. *I will bargain with your master only.*

By then Hepsis and Fallagar were awake, too, and the triumvirate integrated itself once more, still weak but less so than it had been in a long time.

We will speak only with Haydon.

There was a moment of utter silence all around them, through the ship and the life support systemry, in the air, and seemingly through the artificial planet itself. Then the Elders felt vibrations—physical, psychic, extradimensional—and Haydon IV began to move again.

The Haydonites saw, heard, and sensed the changes all around them. They began to assemble in designated places and make ready in answer to the instructions of the Awareness. The planet shifted and reconformed in its most important mechamorphosis.

The Elders, encased on their thrones, found themselves no longer in their ship; it had been dismantled around them. The

Protoculture cap was whisked away, straight up into the air, by some outsize waldo apparatus they glimpsed only for an instant.

The thrones were set in a line, facing the same way, on a circular platform containing the equipment that ran and controlled their life support. That disc sat in turn, now, in the middle of one of the Haydonite transport devices—what the humans had dubbed "flying carpets."

The claw must have drawn them back to the surface of Haydon IV itself. At least they found themselves atop a high tower, seemingly a mile and more in the air. How the planet retained its atmosphere and kept from freezing, they did not know. Below them the landscape heaved and crept, glittered and digested itself.

The carpet lifted off the tower and flew out over mechamorphosing terrain. The Elders, hair whipping in the wind, were held immobile by the life supports grappled in place. They could see other carpets, huge ones laden with thousands of Haydonites, converging.

Beams of light began to break from cracks in Haydon IV's surface, as if the Robotech landscape were a cracking coat of paint on a light bulb. There were deep reverberations from the planet's core. For the first time since their transmogrification to Elders, the three knew another emotion besides anger, fear, and the lust to conquer and rule. Even in them, spirits hollowed by centuries of slavery to the Protoculture, there was awe at the magnitude of what was taking place below.

Something climbed into prominence on the horizon—immense even at that distance and altitude. It had a curve to it, suggesting a cyclopean dome even bigger than the hives of the Invid. But the curve swept *in*, too, as if it were a sphere.

There were more flying carpets, the whole of the remaining Haydonite race coming together to watch their world carry out the purpose for which it had been given form so long ago. The Elders' carpet went into a descent, angling down toward the curve in the planet's surface.

It was not a dome but rather the open end of a curved, circular tube, as if an unimaginable horn of plenty had wound its way up from the heart of the world. There was an impenetrable darkness within it.

The Elders' carpet continued to descend while the carpets of the Haydonites ranked themselves in rows all around the gargantuan aperture below like angels assembling for a heavenly choir. The Elders strained against their confinement uselessly, then gave it up.

Their carpet was the only one to descend to the surface of the planet. It came to a stop before the yawning opening, but there was no telling how far; the scale of things threw off any normal sense of perspective.

A long silent moment went by, except for the wind fluttering the Robotech Masters' hair. Then, at the same instant, a light appeared far down the conduit from some source beyond its curve, and the Haydonites took up a single piercing, tentative note, a mental moan of ecstasy and holy dread.

The light grew brighter, and the note louder. Then all at once brilliance leapt forth from the maw of the great conduit, and the Haydonites' note became a full-throated telepathic cry. It was well that the Elders were connected and cathetered; they lost control of their bodily functions.

The light and sound grew until the planet shook. The winds tore across the Robotech plain, yet the Haydonites' carpets somehow held position.

And, deep in the soul of the light, something moved.

It came toward them slowly, unhurriedly—regally. Nimuul, Hepsis, and Fallagar, held fast, eyes threatening to start from their heads, watched spellbound.

The Haydonites' chorus swelled as if it would fill the universe as Haydon emerged from a sleep of eons.

"You can't be serious," Exedore said, though he had known Cabell long enough to be aware that no other possibility existed.

"See for yourself," the sage challenged, presenting the data caps with a flourish. "I've included the mathematics."

Ever since the two had returned to Tiresia, they had been busy around the clock, analyzing and collating their observations from events at Ranaath's Star. Now Exedore fed the caps into a projector; it took only a cursory scan to show that Cabell was right, at least in terms of the *implications*. The sphere ship's plunge into the black hole had revealed a new mathematical world, and one particular subfunction stood out glaringly.

I don't know why we didn't see this before, Exedore thought, a sure sign that the function he was looking at was valid.

Exedore looked back to Cabell but pointed to the equation in question. "This implies . . . *Anti-Protoculture!*"

Cabell was nodding almost tiredly. "You're correct, dear fellow; we should have realized it long ago. It's almost as if we'd been blinded to this side of the mathematics."

Of course it was old hat, scientifically, that each particle had its mirror image—an antiparticle carrying an opposite electrical charge—and that pairs would annihilate each other in a supreme release of energy whenever they encountered each other. But no one had ever supposed the yin/yang symmetry extended to this: a shadowy counterpart force to *Protoculture itself,* one whose first glimmerings implied apocalyptic mutual destruction should the two ever be brought together.

Exedore drew a breath and grabbed a calculator. "I suppose we'd better get to it, my friend. There is much to learn and not very long to do it."

Cabell was still nodding. "We must penetrate this frightening new secret before anyone else does."

CHAPTER
TWENTY-
THREE

I figured maybe the SDFs needed some new kind of unit patch—
say, a spacefold drive with a red diagonal through it.

Jack Baker, *Upwardly Mobile*

ONCE, DARTING DOWN INTO A DANGER ZONE IN HER
powered armor like a giant Robotech hornet, Kazianna Hesh
would have felt the urge to howl a Zentraedi battle cry.

Foeman, prepare to die! The Quadronos come!

But not here, not today—if "today" meant anything in
what the humans were calling *newspace*. She wasn't free to
throw her life away in splendid battle anymore, had obliga-
tions and priorities above even military glory—a child to protect.

Thus, she was a hundred times more dangerous than the
Kazianna of old.

With the fifteen Zentraedi mecha behind her, there was an
even division of eight powered armor suits and eight Battlepods. Eight males, eight females; even Exedore could not
say why the suit-configuration mecha responded so much better to women, the pods to men. It was simply so. They descended in frontal-assault formation to the planet that had
appeared from nowhere.

The humans and some of the others might rhapsodize over
the place and its forests and seas, but it was just another alien
world to her, with none of the perilous grandeur of Fantoma

or the austere dignity of Tirol. Perhaps there was something in newspace that liked the giants less than it did the rest.

If so, let that something beware; its foe was Kazianna Hesh, mate of mighty Breetai and mother of his son.

The Zentraedi squadron homed in on Rick Hunter's beacon, and Kazianna established contact over his tactical freq. At his direction, the giants dropped in for a landing on and around the high ground where the first party's Battloids had posted a guard.

Groundside, Kazianna and her spitfires remained sealed in their suits, but the pods opened to permit debarkation of the Sentinels' personnel: Baldan, Kami and Learna, Lron and Crysta, and several of the Praxian Amazons. None of them seemed any the worse for the ride.

Kazianna had taken a shine to the warrior women, had found a spiritual kinship with them, as soon as she met them. Indeed, the former Quadronos and the Praxians had done a little comradely drinking in SDF-3's split-level rec club.

Now, though, the Praxians were distraught, almost unsoldierly. Kazianna supposed it was understandable what with Gnea, their leader and one of the great heroines of the war, missing. When one was spoiling for a fight, it always made discipline secondary. No doubt they would settle down as soon as blood began to flow.

Now the only problem was to find someone to fight.

Down below, at the level of Kazianna's lower shins, Rick Hunter was finding out just how determined the Praxian furies could get.

"As you were!" He bellowed it with veins standing out in his temple and neck; it finally shut them up. "I didn't bring you down here so you could go charging off in all directions and end up missing, too! You're here to observe and advise, and anybody who can't follow orders is going back upstairs in a pod!"

That quieted them. Brudda, their section leader, drew a deep breath and saluted. "Understood, sir. We place ourselves at your command."

Rick forced himself to calm down, too. "Thank you. Lron, Baldan; over here, please." There was no point going over the whole business twice. "Kazianna, let me know if you can't hear me."

Zentraedi and Sentinels gathered before him; Jack, Karen, and the rest of the remaining recon party formed a semicircle behind. The mecha, weapons ready, took up a circle around the group, keeping watch in all directions.

"You know the main facts." Rick pointed out the route his recon party had followed. "We were advancing through a densely wooded area about a mile and one-half along that valley, with Sergeant Dante on point. Gnea moved up to walk the slack position, some six yards or so behind him.

"As we entered an open grassy area, both the sergeant and Gnea were enveloped by what appeared to be a somewhat different version of the luminous phenomena that—"

Jeez. Been talking bureaucratese in the TIC too long, Rick!

He started in again. "From what we could see, this hail-storm of light swirled down on them, and we lost them from sight. At the same time, sensors picked up an enormous life reading, but there were no large organisms in sight.

"The light was gone in a couple of seconds, and so were Angie and Gnea. We searched the area—no trapdoors, camouflaged openings, or other clues. We even blew open the ground and lasered down nearby trees; they were solid.

"I'm splitting you into search units. Battlepods and Quadronos will deploy on the ground; Battloids will fly recon and cover. I'm hoping the Garudans' extended senses, the Karbarrans' hunting and tracking skills, or the Praxians' scouting procedures turn up something we missed."

He looked to Baldan. "And I was thinking—maybe if there's some equivalent of the Crystal Highways here . . ."

Baldan nodded his gleaming head. "I'll do what I can do, Admiral."

Rick began calling off assignments. The mixed contingents sorted themselves out to move back into the target zone.

"Aw, *sca-rew*!"

Angelo Dante knelt with the stock of his rifle pressed to his cheek, swinging the muzzle this way and that in the milk-white mist. Not that there were any targets around; it was just something to do while he tried to sort things out. "Not again," he grated.

Like most of the younger Amazons, Gnea had developed a preference for modern, high-firepower weapons over the traditional arms of her Sisterhood. Now, though, for reasons she could not quite pin down, she reslung her submachine gun and took her halberd in hand, giving it a preparatory spin, the long curved blade leaving a silver trail in the air.

"You mean you've encountered this phenomenon before, Sergeant?" Like his, her voice brought no echoes. She wondered if they were outdoors.

"Naw. It's just—*weird* stuff like this, ma'am. It simply ain't *military*."

And it always sounded so goddamn lame in an after-action report. Like when Angie and the other ATACs went through all that crap in the Masters' spade-shaped mother ship. Living energy nexuses and mindmusic and alien horticulture. Try writing *those* up without having some G-staff chairborne commando laughing at you!

It was all too involved to explain to some dame from another planet.

Gnea pivoted, spinning her polearm to hold it at high port, and kept watch in the opposite direction. "What's the last thing you remember?"

"Uh . . . We were moving through that open area, and I felt something kinda strange, like the way electricity makes your hair stand up, only it was inside my head. So, that is—"

He hated to hurt a woman's feelings, but— "So I gave you the signal to pull back, only you didn't do it." He was making a circular motion with one hand.

She took a quick glance at it over her shoulder. "Oh, yes; your UEG field signal. It took me a moment to remember what it meant; in *our* army that's the gesture for close intervals."

That's what you get mixing different services together, he thought sourly, but kept it to himself. "So whatever that tinsel blizzard was, it got you, too." He began trying to raise somebody on the tactical freq.

Gnea sensed nothing nearby; visibility looked like it might be several dozen yards, but it was impossible to make an accurate estimate, lacking any point of reference. She set the spike butt of her halberd on the floor by her feet (at least, she assumed it was a floor; it was glossy and smooth, like a single white tile).

"Sergeant, I think it would've gotten us no matter what. And I don't think something's gone to all this trouble just to harm us."

Well, she was a cool one, he had to give her that. All frequencies were silent, and so Angelo came to his feet, rifle leveled at waist height, covering his field of fire. "Maybe not. Even though *some* aliens I've known like to collect specimens."

He slipped a pencil flare out of his belt pouch, struck it alight, and dropped it to the ground. "What we'll do is work out as far as we can, keepin' the flare in sight, and run a circular search pattern."

She frowned. "You mean split up?"

"*Hell* no! What d' ya think this is, a slasher movie?"

"Excellent." She whipped the halberd around again, bringing it *en garde*. Angie thought, *If this* is *a movie, at least the slasher's on* my *side.*

"Only," Gnea went on, wetting a forefinger and holding it up, "I seem to feel an air current coming from that direction. Shall we start there?"

"Good as any other."

They both moved to take the point at the same moment, then looked at each other. There was no telling who outranked whom. Gnea topped Angelo by half a head and more; from her looks and reputation and what he had seen of the Praxians already, he was prepared to believe she could handle herself. But still, she was carrying that frog dissector while he had a rifle with its selector switch flicked over to continuous fire. "Look, if y' don't mind?"

Gnea nodded with reserved grace. "By all means." She knew that some human males still harbored strange attitudes about females. But at least this one was quick to react, willing to shoulder a dangerous job. Perhaps he was even as competent as he seemed to think.

Angelo found himself staring into those inhuman eyes of hers, eyes that belonged in a bird of prey. He forced himself to look away from them. The two moved out with Gnea watching behind, going in a sort of sideways crab step. Their footfalls sounded lonely and small. In thirty paces (fewer for Gnea) the flare was getting dim behind them, but the current of air was stronger. "How long will it burn?" she asked.

"Fifteen minutes, anyway. Let's keep goin'."

"Yes, but drop another flare."

He did, not that there was much to go back to. Another thirty paces and the air had a distinct cold tinge to it.

"An exit, maybe," Angelo muttered, striking a third flare. Before he had to reach for a fourth, something loomed up in the mist before them. With scale so tough to judge, he thought at first that it was a city or at least a building.

They drew close enough to make out details. When they finally had a clear look at it, they stopped in their tracks.

Angie's jaw was hanging open. "Well, tug my gearshift and call me Five-Speed."

Gnea shouldered her halberd. "I think you might as well put your weapon up, Sergeant. Whatever did this, I doubt a laser means much to it, and we definitely don't want to offend it."

Angelo had never been very enthusiastic about taking orders from women except when they made overwhelming sense. Like now. He slung his piece, and they continued on, walking side by side.

"Y' know, this qualifies as theft of gov'ment property," it occurred to him to observe.

Gnea smiled unexpectedly. "And have you brought proof of ownership?"

That one gave him pause. "I don't think they put serial numbers on spacefold drives."

The Protoculture drives—or rather, the casing that held them, what the engineers called the housing—bulked before them, big as a building. Somehow, out in the open like that, they were less overpowering than in the SDF-3's drive section. Nevertheless, the two could not see the far end from where they stood.

Of course, the trillion-dollar question was how the hell the drives had *gotten* there—wherever "there" was—and who or what had done it. Angelo figured the answer to that one would go a long way toward explaining what had happened to the SDF-3 and what the newspace stuff was all about.

"They're ours, all right," Gnea said. "You see that multiphaser? Doctor Lang's work."

But for the first time since they had gone on-line, the fold drives were completely dark, inert. Like so many other Robotech devices, the housing had had all Protoculture drained from it. Only *un*like the rest, the physical structure had been stolen, too.

"Maybe there's another around here someplace," Angelo mused as he and Gnea began a slow tour around the huge drives housing. To him it resembled a great sealed city of domes, megablocks, and manifold roadways.

"Another fold drive array?"

He clicked his tongue. "Yeah. The one the old SDF-1 lost back in 'oh-nine, near Pluto. Maybe something around here collects 'em."

They completed a cautious circuit of the fold drives housing without finding anything else. Gnea pointed to a stairway leading to the service catwalks. "We might be able to see something from up there."

"Worth a try."

They made their way to the little mesa that was the top of the primary containment casing. But there was nothing to see; they could not even spot the flares. Angelo yelled into the wintry mist through cupped hands, and Gnea fired three spaced shots, but there was no response of any kind.

"I suppose we *could* reconnoiter further," Gnea ventured.

"*Huh* uh," Angie said firmly, seating himself tailor fashion with his rifle across his thighs. He dug for his canteen. "Now that we found 'em, I'm sittin' my butt right here on top of 'em till they take us home."

"Yes, I thought you might feel that way."

Oh, yes, la-de-da. Like she's got everything doped out. He stopped himself before taking the swig of water, though, automatically offering her the first drink. "Thirsty?"

Gnea canted her head at him. "I have water of my own, thank you." She swiveled her hip around to show him the canteen on her belt. It was an exquisite hip, in keeping with the rest of her. "Did you think a Praxian would be unequipped?"

"No. Who cares? Suit yourself." He slugged at the canteen in an evil temper.

She hunkered down, holding her halberd upright. Males were so difficult to understand, especially *human* males.

She recalled the infatuation between Jack Baker and herself. Of course, that had had a lot to do with the Compulsion

Tesla had worked on them both. But it had taught her something of the confusing, unsettling, and not always controllable nature of relationships between the sexes.

"If I've offended you somehow, Sergeant, I ask your forgiveness."

Sweet Baby Jesus cookies on Christmas! Now he *really* felt like dirt! "Naw, y' didn't do anything wrong ma'am—uh, Gnea."

She nodded sagely. "I'd heard you were heartsick over the officer Dana Sterling. Such things can be troublesome."

Angelo's face turned purple. "What'd they do, announce it over the PA?"

Actually, he *had* made some inroads with his former CO on the trip out from Earth. They had always had a sort of feuding friendship, and when Zor Prime died in the final explosion that released the Flower of Life across the planet, Dana and her senior NCO seemed to come together as naturally as magnets.

Then, of course, they had arrived at Tirol, and Dana had met Rem. Seeing what was between the clone and Minmei, Dana had forced herself to stay away from them. Things between her and Angie were never the same again, though. He figured that part of the reason she had stayed behind with her folks was because he—and Rem and Minmei, for that matter—were going on the SDF-3.

So, now that was general gossip, huh? Angelo considered Gnea, squatting there in that getup of hers—part armor, part uniform, mostly skin—and realized morosely what *truly* had him bristling at her.

"Hai!" she said, making it sound like a swear word. "Now I've done it again! I didn't mean to get you upset."

But he shook his head. "Drop it, okay? It's not important." He stood up just for something to do.

Gnea stood, too, and they were face to face. Almost touching. He could see the pulse beat in her throat and feel his own. She smelled exotic and exciting.

Looking into the avian eyes, he heard himself say, "I don't want to think about . . . about . . ."

She made a raptor's hissing sound and clutched the harness at his shoulder. Angelo reached his hand behind her neck and pulled her lips to his. He figured they probably looked funny, running their free hands all over each other, kissing and panting while holding on to their weapons and trying to keep lookout with one eye—in case the godless XT hordes came charging over the hill.

"Hey, before somebody gets killed," he got out of the side of his mouth, and carefully tossed his rifle aside. Her halberd landed on top of it.

They threw their arms around each other with a passion neither of them had ever felt before. It was all moans and fumblings, neither one familiar with the other's outfit.

They sank to the surface of the containment casing, still kissing and caressing. It was cold and, once they were out of their clothes, slippery. That made it more fun.

Angie had heard of transcendent experiences, but nothing like this. It seemed as though the whole world were getting brighter, going nova.

Waitaminute, waitaminute; it is!

"Angelo!" Gnea's nails dug into his shoulder; he rolled over and found himself staring up into the face of a deity.

Out of uniform in the presence of God. He wondered if it was a court-martial offense.

It was a visage formed from the white brume, a hairless, humanoid head, vaguely and yet unmistakably feminine. It seemed to take up the whole sky.

They heard its thought: *LIFE IS WASTED ON THE LIVING!*

CHAPTER
TWENTY-
FOUR

Not odd to note, perhaps, in view of the upheavals in that particular period of Aeon Lanack. But the truth is that in spite of the laborious, even stern, inquiries made by the Elders and their servants, no one ever seemed quite certain as to exactly where Zor came from. We know that, like so many others born during that era (for that matter, like many born before and after it and many born into other races on other planets), he was raised in a succession of government care facilities and the like from the time he was very young.

But no record of his birth or precise origin could be found. This frustrated the Elders, who wished to analyze and duplicate the secrets of his genius and extraordinary affinities, beyond words.

Cabell, *Zor and the Great Transition*

SHE HAD OFTEN CRASHED THROUGH ENEMY FORTIFI-cations or target cities, brushing aside buildings or shouldering her way between defensive works.

But now Kazianna Hesh moved easily and carefully through the venerable old trees on the planet that had appeared from nowhere. Her enemy had not chosen to reveal itself yet, and so caution was warranted.

Rick Hunter had assigned the Zentraedi to sweep paths accessible to their mechaed bulk; the humans and Sentinels were working their way through the denser growth, and a few Cyclone outriders advanced along the wider footpaths and streambeds. Periodically, she heard Jack Baker and Rick

Hunter trying to contact Sergeant Dante or Gnea on their tactical freq, but there was no answer.

Like Angelo, she tried to keep her mind on her job but found herself distracted. It seemed that her team was, too; she snapped at them to stay sharp.

What was it about the place? She had expected to have Drannin and the problems with the children on her mind, had recognized that she would have to make sure she kept full concentration. But she had not expected what she was feeling, what kept running through her mind.

Breetai, oh, my Breetai . . .

His face was there before her, his phantom arms around her; his kiss pressed on her lips.

Stop! You're a war leader of the Quadronos! But it did no good castigating herself. A moment later the memories were there before her again, as though she had not grieved and struggled to reclaim her life.

Breetai, my lord and my love . . .

What was it about the place?

Kazianna saw the sky reflected in her helmet facebowl and realized as if from afar that she had stopped advancing, was standing, swaying, in a grove of trees whose tips came even with the top of her powered suit. A leaf the shape of a kite came loose from a branch, fluttering down . . .

But it was only her body there. Kazianna Hesh was years and light-years away.

It was her first major action, an assault landing on a strategic Invid stronghold on icy Tawkhan, and everything had gone wrong: more Invid than anybody had projected, fleet deployment from fold jump hopelessly snarled, Lord Dolza's flagship missing and perhaps lost.

Kazianna was pinned down with what was left of her battalion—her battalion, because all senior officers had fallen before waves of Invid. Scout Shock, Trooper, and Pincer Ship, they seemed to spring from the ground, a horde for every individual the massed Zentraedi firepower burned down.

The resources of an entire sector had been marshaled. Out beyond the atmosphere a total of nearly a quarter million ships of all classes hammered away at one another. They

*were at virtual point-blank range for a space engagement;
Kazianna and the other ground troops could look for little
help from that quarter. Even on the daylight side of the planet,
the incandescent bursts flashed bright, far overhead.*

*The giants had never had music of their own; the Robotech
Masters had reserved the arts of the Muses and the Cosmic
Harp to themselves and their clone triumvirates, yet how the
blood sang in the veins of the Zentraedi that day! Fired by
the eons-old traditions and honor that Exedore had taught
them, they hurled themselves at the Invid with a will.*

*This was what the Zentraedi had been born for. They fol-
lowed their Imperative.*

*Oyster-shaped Invid troopships blotted out the sky. The en-
tire planet was a theater of war. Whole armies were thrown
against each other as if they were mere companies. Nearly
eight million Zentraedi eagerly locked in mortal combat with
over twenty million Invid.*

*Battlepod went muzzle to muzzle with Shock Trooper,
weapons vomiting forth death. Powered armor suits darted in
aerial combat, fought as infantry, and even rolled and tore
with the enemy hand to hand. There were massed charges of
entire corps, met by equal or greater numbers of teeming
Invid.*

*Combat heated the atmosphere of Tawkhan itself. Explo-
sions and energy volleys opened crevasses and shattered gla-
ciers; undersea onslaughts made the oceans boil; beams of
raw power melted ice fields and shook loose immense ava-
lanches. All across the planet the warfare raged in thick-
ening smoke and rain.*

*The stupendous barrages awoke the resentment of Tawkhan
itself, jarring its tectonics. Volcanoes blasted to life, and fis-
sures poured lava up through ice cap and seabed. Quakes
crushed or swallowed Invid and Zentraedi alike. Mud and
superheated water rained down. Floods swept mecha away
like bits of straw.*

*Through it all, Kazianna's unit made its way toward the
very heart of the foe's central hive, a daring thrust to end
the campaign with one telling blow. But it met with failure,
and what was left of her unit was about to be totally annihilated.*

Kazianna braced herself to grapple unarmed with a Shock

Trooper; her weapons were exhausted. Then the Trooper was gone, burned in half, the halves falling away in opposite directions. Dazed, Kazianna Hesh looked beyond where it had been. There stood the great Breetai, a metal war god in his personal battle panoply, a rifle as big as an Earthly artillery piece smoking in his gauntleted fists.

Behind him came a crack task force, ten divisions of elite troops, to strike at the very brain of the foe. Kazianna learned later that her own assault force had been a feint, drawing Invid attention away from Breetai's sword-stroke raid. In moments the special coalition of living computers that directed the Invid on Tawkhan—the piles of brain tissue lurking in their vats—would be destroyed in an apocalyptic contest with the invading foot soldiers and mecha.

In that second, though, all Kazianna Hesh saw was Breetai, striding his personal domain—the domain of battle—like an icon come to life. The most illustrious and successful of Dolza's field commanders and, after the Old One himself, the biggest and strongest of the entire Zentraedi race.

It was heresy to think this, but Kazianna did not care: He was like some higher being, some creature superior to other Zentraedi and even to the Robotech Masters.

But the worship was not mutual; Breetai was still directing his raid and barely gave her a glance. "You! Consolidate your unit and stand by!"

Then he was gone, and she was rushing to obey. Genders were usually strictly separated among the Zentraedi, where neither physical love nor natural birth were known; only the scope of the Tawkhan campaign had thrown them together so.

Thus, Kazianna Hesh could not understand what was happening to her—why did his voice and his look obsess her so? Was it madness?

She studied and admired him from afar, through an age of conflict and conquest. The closest she came to him was when he presided at an awards ceremony for Miriya Parino. Kazianna was only a few paces away, a company commander by then. Breetai did not even spare her a glance.

By that time he wore the alloy half cowl as a result of his terrible wounds, suffered when Zor was slain. But to her he was only that much more imperial looking. In those days the

Protoculture supply was dwindling, the galaxywide war running down like clockwork as both sides' resources and infrastructures declined. The central mission of the Robotech Masters, and thus the Zentraedi, was to find Zor's vanished super dimensional fortress and the last existing Protoculture matrix.

At long last came the end of an epoch, when the terrible beauty of Minmei's voice, along with human emotions, worked Armageddon upon the Zentraedi. The glories of their history turned out to be a tissue of lies concocted by the Robotech Masters. Kazianna and the rest were a pitiful handful of survivors.

But for her, something in the human emotions had stirred dormant feelings. For Kazianna, the example of Miriya Parino and her love for Max Sterling pointed the way to an even more audacious thought. If Zentraedi could love human, why could not Zentraedi love Zentraedi?

In the humble home on Fantoma where Breetai had dwelt as a simple miner an epoch ago, she went to him. And this time she did not permit him to ignore her.

When death took him from her in combat, she was nearby and saw him sacrifice his life to slay the Regent, end the war. There were fools who looked at the relative size of the combatants—Breetai nearly three times the Regent's height—and marveled that Breetai had not won outright. They understood nothing of the astounding power the Invid monarch had by then, the strength beyond mere size—or of the debilitating effects of Minmei's voice, transmitting her torment, forced upon Breetai by the malevolent Edwards.

Kazianna dismissed all fools. What Breetai had done with his dying breath, no one else who ever lived could have done. And he died in victorious combat, the highest Zentraedi fulfillment.

Watching him perish in an explosion like the birth of a star, she had wept for the single time in her life.

"Is anything wrong, Commander?"

Kazianna's executive officer's voice shook her out of the strange reverie, and she realized that barely an instant had gone by. The falling kite-shaped leaf whirled down past her facebowl.

"Negative. Resume sweep."

But something on the planet must have been probing her thoughts, scrutinizing her memories. If it was malign, she meant to destroy it, but for the moment she almost felt grateful to have had Breetai back again even for a few seconds.

Then the reverie was wiped away by a burst of static. "All units, all units! Hold position! *It's back!*"

"I specifically told the bridge officer not to inform you unless you inquired about the children," Segundo said. "I am aware that you're dealing with other crises."

"Understood, Doctor," Lisa acknowledged curtly. Even over the intercom screen he could see the strain on her face. "What is your assessment?"

The pediatrician stepped aside and let the pickups focus in on Roy, Drannin, and the other children. Once again they sat in their uneven circle, the Zentraedi children towering over the human.

But there was no doubt about their chant now. *"Au-ro-ra, Au-ro-ra, Au-ro-ra . . ."*

Aurora the psi-child, the accelerated-growth sprite, the one who reached across interstellar distances. Lisa had always been sure she would be able to keep jittery mommy stuff separate from ship's officer worries, but now she was less certain.

"I don't think this is a mental dysfunction or a behavioral aberration in the traditional sense," Segundo was saying. "I believe that they are rational but that they are responding in a way that we don't understand to a difficulty or necessity that we can't perceive."

On the bridge, Lisa heard people conferring behind her; the search operation—something was up. "Inform me of any changes, Doctor."

She turned to Raul Forsythe. "They've found Gnea and Dante," he said.

Somewhere far away, Minmei was singing, his head on her lap, her hand stroking his brow. Rem knew it, as he knew that her warm tears were splashing on his cheek, but that was in some other universe . . .

On Haydon IV, Zor saw no contradiction to what he had

already learned, though Vard had not yet reached the same level of enlightenment. Living matter, inorganic matter, machine, Protoculture—they were all united by certain basics. The fundamental building blocks of Creation had nothing to do with quantum foam any more than they did with plant sap.

The key understanding was that the universe was a result of the interaction of pure information. *Information organized in a way that was so subtle, all-pervading, and elegant that in the end all the wise men, mystics, and scientists had missed it.*

It was not a jarring note, then, to Zor, to see that fact manifested in the from of an artificial planet.

The expedition to Haydon IV had to be postponed twice while Zor gave his seeming obedience to the Masters and made secret preparations. By that time he was well along in his quiet rebellion.

The Masters, drunk on the power of Protoculture, were so arrogant, so sure of their hold over him. What better way to fight them than to feed those monstrous egos? They understood no more about Protoculture than a child knew of an energy gun it might find and brandish about.

But now at last he had come to Haydon IV in his super dimensional fortress, seeing that the preliminary surveys had not exaggerated its beauty, its magnificence. On his own urgings and from their hidden misgivings, the Robotech Masters spared the artifact world any visit from their Zentraedi giants; there was something about its storied Awareness *that made the Elders cautious. Haydon IV rendered tribute to them from its apparently endless wealth and went about its enigmatic affairs.*

The Invid, for their own reasons, never made the planet a military target. Maybe they saw it as too desirable a prize to damage. Or perhaps they had heard the daunting stories of how the planet dealt with invaders.

Zor was welcomed down by the inhabitants of Haydon IV with the kind of remote courtesy for which they were famous. And yet he felt their intense scrutiny. The confusions and mental fogs that plagued the survey team were no obstruction to Zor; where others had missed the looming presence and central importance of the Awareness, he had been attuned to it from the first.

As for actually gaining access to the Awareness, it was like some absurd parable. Where the Haydonites had turned back all inquiries and all travelers before, they simply watched him. Facing a stupendous hatch that blocked his route to the lower reaches of the planet, he reached by habit for a handful of dried Flower petals from the pouch he carried at his belt.

He chewed the petals and leaves frequently now—supposed his body was addicted to them, though the true craving stemmed from no physical need. As he tasted the little quid, he felt himself probed by sensor beams. A moment later the titanic door rolled aside.

The Haydonites who had flocked around him and kept him under surveillance since his arrival came no farther than the entrance, nor would he let even the faithful Vard accompany him. Zor passed into the lower depths alone.

He made his way down through the labyrinthine under-world, sustained by it and accepting the paths it opened for him. At last he walked calmly and unhurriedly out into the yawning techno-cavern where the Awareness waited.

It was a confusion of neon lines in strange patterns, a thing the size of a cruiser. By the time he came into its physical presence, he was quite well acquainted with it.

When he bespoke it now, though, the Awareness refused to answer. He had the feeling that it was waiting for some final proof, some bona fide, before it lowered its last defenses with him.

Zor reached into a pocket and drew forth an object he had prepared after long, hard pondering. It was an artificial jewel charged with Protoculture power, formulated from his studies of both the Haydonites' dzentile and—even more important— the organic gemstones manifested by the Regis when she had assumed humanoid form.

Zor lifted the jewel to his forehead in self-coronation. A bio-adhesive charge made it fast there. He willed a command, and a ray sprang forth to strike the resplendent cat's cradle of the Awareness.

There was a moment's gravid silence. Then a billion scintillating motes leapt from the Awareness, the material world seemed to fall away, and it opened its fateful dialogue with Zor.

CHAPTER
TWENTY-
FIVE

The will to power is disguised in a hundred thousand ways, on many worlds—as service to the public good, or defending the faith, or protecting the nest from outsiders. But at the core it is always the same; exposed to the light, its features are unchanging: a naked lust to dominate and control.

Not surprising, then, that on that fateful night in a hidden place, the Three who had sworn obedience to the will of the people piled hands in an unholy ritual. Sotted on Protoculture, they put all sham aside and anointed themselves as Masters.

The Scribe Triumvirate of Aholt, Ulla, and Tussas,
Nothing Save Animus: A History of the Robotech Elders

THE ROBOTECH ELDERS STOPPED STRAINING AT THE MED machines that held them fast. Behind their respirator masks, their furious howls ceased. Haydon was coming, and they understood that there was no escaping.

Like a mountain on the move, the figure in the gargantuan conduit approached them through the blinding light. With slitted eyes, the Elders watched it come. High above and all around, the Haydonites had ceased their mental hymn singing and fallen quiet.

With coronas of crackling energy radiating from him and lightning bolts crashing all around the heights of his head and shoulders, Haydon emerged.

Some of the intermittent transignal messages from their vassals—the Robotech Masters sent to ravage Earth—had told the Elders of the primitive religions of that blighted planet. Now a minor phrase came back to haunt Nimuul: *created in God's image*.

Small wonder the Haydonites were ready to swoon with adoration and ecstasy; before them was He in whose image they had been cast. The Elders used their resentment and irascibility to keep from yielding to the mesmeric spell the sight of Him cast.

Haydon wore—or had perhaps simply donned the illusion of—a billowing, high-collared cloak like the Haydonites'. From beneath it, feet extended, and yet they floated free of the planet's surface.

The stupendous head was smooth and hairless, reminding the Elders of their onetime warlord, Dolza, but Haydon's skull was higher-crowned and more finely shaped than that. His face was more defined than the Haydonites'; it was some countenance the Elders somehow half recognized but could not place. Where the Haydonites had been born without eyes, mouth, ears, nostrils, the face of Haydon gave the impression that it had once borne those features and they had atrophied from disuse.

Haydon bore no *dzentile*, though. In the middle of His forehead pulsed a gland or organ unlike anything the Elders knew of, ridged and scalloped like some shell thing's back, puckered closed like a sleeping blossom.

Haydon's blind cliff of a face panned His domain, drinking in the physical universe after His long hibernation. He became aware of the Elders—or perhaps He had been all along—and the cyclopean head tilted down. The mystic organ in His forehead bloomed open, and for an instant the Elders saw within—a shape and texture they could not discern that nevertheless paralyzed them with dread.

A beam of searing brilliance burst from the organ to play over the captives. *VERMIN, SPEAK!*

Nimuul answered with mindspeech: *Look to your proud fleet, Ancient One! Your grand design is in jeopardy!*

There was a concerted moan from the Haydonites, like a low wind. Haydon turned His blank face to the sky, and the beam from His forehead played out across the spherical ships drifting powerless in space over the world He had made.

The Haydonites and the Elders sensed swift communication between Haydon and His Awareness, like some deep-stratum perturbation. Plainly, Haydon understood then the enormity of what the Karbarrans, *Ark Angel*, and Louie Nichols's cybernauts had done.

From the organ on Haydon's forehead a black beacon shone forth, swallowing up all the light in its path. The Haydonites wailed wordlessly, and the planet shook.

Nimmul, Hepsis, and Fallagar united with even more desperation than they had in contacting the Awareness. *No, stay your wrath! We've come to offer you a bargain, and* Protoculture!

That gave Haydon pause. He stood erect once more, gazing out over His handiwork. A nimbus grew up around him, so effulgent that the Elders had to close their eyes. When they opened them again, Haydon had worked another miracle.

Where one had stood there was now a trio—a triumvirate, the Robotech Elders registered—shoulder to shoulder, facing outward in a circle. It was impossible to tell which, if any, was the original, but it was clear that while enormous, they were smaller than He who had levitated forth from the bowels of Haydon IV.

Without any talk, one went back down the conduit from which Haydon had emerged, another floated off across the machine landscape, the Haydonite carpets making way for him, and the third turned back to the Elders. *SAY ON*.

Nimuul responded: *We know where there is Protoculture, new Protoculture that the Regis did not steal! Enough to power all your ships. We will lead you to it gladly.*

Gladly. It was pivotal that Haydon be given the means to leave spacetime.

AND IN RETURN?

In return you will provide us with the means to exert our will over the Local Group star systems and their inhabitants. You will grant us your authority to rule the planets you touched so long ago.

DONE! The Awareness had already spoken to Haydon of the ships it had built and the single energy that must power them.

Agreement came so readily that the Elders were tempted to ask for more concessions, but they dared not. It was manifest that Haydon—or the *Haydons*—wanted nothing more from the physical universe except the means to pass beyond it.

Haydon raised one hand in a divine gesture. There was a psychic shuddering through the planet as the Awareness prepared to turn itself to new tasks; the Haydonites on their carpets came about in vast flocks to regroup and race away to all points of the compass, bent on missions Haydon had given them. First among those was completion of the unfinished sphere ships.

Haydon turned back to the Elders. *NAME OUR DESTINATION.*

Treacherous as they were, the Robotech Elders were loath to trust anyone. But before the might of Haydon they had no other choice, fearing that if they were uncooperative, he would snuff out their lives and go seeking Protoculture on his own.

The Elders joined their minds to speak, practically fondling the words with their thoughts. *Optera first—"New Praxis," it is called now. Then . . . Tirol!*

SO BE IT.

The planet shifted under them, already on the move. *FIRST, WE MUST GATHER UP OUR SPHERE SHIPS. THEN IT WILL BE NECESSARY TO DIVERT TO LASKAR.*

The Elders were puzzled even as they felt a certain lassitude stealing over them. *Your planet's primary? Why?*

FUEL IS NEEDED FOR SUCH A JOURNEY.

As they grasped the enormity of that, they felt themselves losing consciousness. A trick! *Stop! We demand—*

The Elders' thoughts faded as the med machines' sedation took hold. Haydon turned away from them disinterestedly as the carpet on which their thrones sat whisked them out of His presence.

Haydon had already given His command to the Awareness. Like a worshiping slave, it strained itself to carry out His directions to the fullest.

Haydon IV gathered in the sphere ships, finished and unfinished alike, holding them in readiness, then reabsorbed what it could of the factory tubes. Haydon saw that His discorporate hibernation had lasted longer than He had foreseen. That and the appearance of the Sentinels, plus the demands of producing the sphere ship fleet, had nearly exhausted the power reserves of the artificial planet.

Eventually, of course, power could be brought back to full by other means, but there was not time for that. While the Haydonites raced to carry out the labors He had assigned them, the planet left orbit and began its descent toward Laskar, dying lesser sun of the Ranaath system.

The star's place in the arc of the sky grew and grew as Haydon IV rushed toward it. The artifact world hurtled past the orbit of the system's innermost planet. At the same time a strange energy field polarized into existence, surrounding Haydon's handiwork to protect it—and more.

It was well within the reach of stellar prominences before it stopped. A preliminary beam licked out from Haydon IV, probing into the monstrous furnace of the star itself. Back poured a mammoth gush of naked power.

For several long minutes Haydon IV hung there, tethered to its star, drawing in energy as it had drawn in raw materials from the asteroid. Within, its reserves were restored, then filled to repletion, with all the power the planet would need.

The fiery stream of starfire stopped, dissipating, as Haydon IV moved away from Laskar again. As it went, Haydon had word from the Awareness of troubling findings.

At the edge of perceptible space there were aberrations and anomalies. The fabric of the continuum was losing integrity, and whole regions seemed to be disappearing.

Time was growing short, very short. Haydon IV's drive activated, its course charted for Optera. It went superluminal and vanished.

Still Rem drifted; still the nucleic dreams showed him the past.

Not even Haydon could predict how things would develop, while he slept, on the worlds he had touched personally.

Therefore, he left instructions with the Awareness that if any arrived with enlightenment, or even some portion of it, the Awareness would recognize that by certain signs.

And Zor had manifested such a sign; much (though not all) of the Awareness's data revealed itself. Zor mentioned the Texts of Haydon, of which he had learned, and they were opened to him. But not translated for him. *He had to dem-onstrate certain aptitudes or begone.*

The Texts of Haydon resembled no book or archive before them. They were a cyclorama of thought images and psi-memes. But Zor, with his Flower-altered mind, found them intelligible—barely. Had he not, the Awareness would have known and slain him on the spot.

He forgot about food and sleep, laboring to receive the disembodied knowledge until it seemed his brain would burst like a lightning-struck tree. But stopping was unthinkable, and he persisted, pausing only to ingest another petal or two of his shrinking Flower supply or, when he remembered to, drinking water from a font the Awareness had set by him.

In that manner Zor came to know the story of Haydon, first and greatest of the intellects spawned by the galaxy (the Texts had a bewildering way of referring to Haydon in the plural one minute and in the singular the next). In exploring and mastering the universe around Him, Haydon had gained im-mortality and probed the essential secrets of Creation.

But when His exploration of the universe seemed to hold no further mysteries, no further challenges, Haydon still had not found the answers that He longed for, the destiny for which, He was sure, He had been called into being.

Some of His investigations indicated to Him the existence of a level of being beyond those that could be seen or touched. Of a place outside His continuum where Haydon could at last find fulfillment, achieve a level of being that had become an undeniable need.

And Haydon found that He could not reach that other side. Every approach failed, every assay fell short, until at last Haydon faced the fact that He could not attain transcen-dence.

But that did not mean some other life-form could not.

And so began an age of grand experimentation, epic jour-neys, profound contemplation, and unprecedented megaproj-ects. The Garudans were endowed with their expanded senses and their psychotropic biosphere. On Spheris, crystal life-forms were given an evolutionary helping hand. An investi-gation into thought control went awry on Peryton, leading to the holocaust Moebius in which the planet became trapped.

Not least importantly, Haydon IV was given form, and its Awareness was brought to life.

Zor read on, feverish with the need to know. At last he came to the mention of Optera and the Invid. A curious race, Haydon found, with some promising characteristics, but apparently at an evolutionary dead end unless something new were added. And Haydon had that something in mind, an intriguing plant He had encountered.

The organisms on the plant's planet of origin did not seem to be exploiting the plant's potential, and so Haydon transplanted the entire species to Optera—leaving none behind. Zor stared long and hard at the image of the Flower's original home, such an unremarkable little place . . .

The introduction of Flower of Life to the Invid was like the recombining of long-sundered halves. Almost overnight the Invid's entire existence came to revolve around the Flower and something they seemed to perceive in it.

(A lab mutation of the plant, the ur-form called Sekiton, was introduced to Karbarra. But while the ursinoids there found many uses and demonstrated a peculiar affinity for it, the experiment was essentially a failure.)

The star-spanning experiments Haydon had begun were set in place, and Haydon began to prepare for His long sleep, weary of the tedium of immortality. The event of transubstantiation would cause His artificial world to awaken Him—more accurately, to return him from mere stored information to physical form.

The ticking off of the centuries began.

Zor lashed out, stopping the parade of thought records as a seething rage took hold of him. It had been bad enough to know that the Robotech Masters had perverted his discoveries and the Protoculture to evil ends—that the Zentraedi had laid waste to Optera.

Now, in addition, Zor understood that his meddling and the Masters' fiendishness had derailed a bold and unique attempt to push living intelligence through into an entirely new realm.

Zor threw back his head and roared up into the echoing spaces of Haydon IV's inner reaches, fists raised high, for the sheer iniquity of it all. The waste and suffering and loss, the death and devastation.

His fury combined with his contact with the Awareness gave Zor a moment of lucidity unlike any other he was ever to have. He suddenly had a vision, a Grand Design, of his own. He would atone for what had happened.

It was all there before him: a reseeding program; a mighty new starship incorporating everything he had learned about Protoculture with which to execute his plan; a renewal, especially of Optera and its idyllic way of life; and eventually, a return of the galaxy to the way it had been before the rise of the Robotech Masters.

And lastly, he thought, he would return the Flower to the world on which it had originated, for who could tell what role it had yet to play there? Yes, even Haydon had been shortsighted in that instance; the Flower deserved to grow once more in its appointed place, the unremarkable little blue-white world called Earth.

His exhaustion, his hyperstimulation through mental contact with the Awareness, his ingestion of the petals—perhaps it was just a combination of these. But the fact was, it was the image of Earth, the invocation of it, that brought on his seizure.

Zor cried out, thinking himself blinded, hands clamped to a skull that threatened to fly apart.

He saw a column of pure mind energy rising from the Earth, a pillar of dazzling force a hundred miles in diameter, crackling and swaying, swirling like a whirlwind, throwing out sheets of shimmering brilliance. It climbed higher and higher into space, all in a matter of moments.

Zor knew what the mind cyclone was, recognized it as the racial transmutation of the Invid. The pinnacle of the cyclone abruptly gave shape to a monumental bird, a phoenix of mental essence. The firebird of transfiguration spread wings wider than the planet and soared away, bound for another plane of existence, with a cry so magnificent and sad that his heart was wrenched by it and he was changed forever.

Zor shuddered, sobbed, and fell to the floor weeping, then lost consciousness.

In the sphere ship, Louie Nichols gathered the survivors of his team. Other personnel were distracted by the strange, swirling limbo through which the craft was passing on its way between continua; it was the cybernauts' chance to re-group.

They set up a prefab secure cubicle high up on an un-occupied platform. Louie was helped onto a robot med diagnostic table that deployed itself from a compact shipping case.

There were some gasps when he removed his tunic and they saw the marks the cyber-burn had left on his body.

He gritted his teeth. "All right, quit gawking. You know what we have to do."

They did. The headlockers began unpacking machines and remotes, fitting them together, and patching into power sources with protech proficiency.

Louie's mouth felt very dry, and when he tried to lick his lips, he could not work up any saliva.

Several remotes floated in at him. Behind them were the surgical waldos loaded with the implants and bionics he needed and wanted to receive.

Louie drew a deep breath and lay back down on the table.

Rem awoke. His head was still in Minmei's lap, but her tears had long since dried. His face was slick with moisture, however; he was crying as Zor had.

Minmei sang softly, sadly.

CHAPTER
TWENTY-
SIX

*When Nichols emerged from that lockbox cubicle his disciples
had set up, he was the same studiously irreverent young pain in
the neck who'd gone in—with some noticeable increase in vigor
and agility. But there was also an undertone of indefinable strain
to him.*

*I resolved to keep an eye on him; he played his part well except
for one occasion during transit, the one slip that hinted at the
change in him: He leaned to a scope that was controlled by a
sensor and of course accepted it matter-of-factly when the scope
swiveled to him and adjusted height, focus, etc.*

*What he didn't know was that the auto-adjust mechanism
wasn't working—had developed a glitch and been switched off.
But the scope's servos had obeyed his silent will, anyway.*

*It was no time to confront Nichols and his familiars, but there-
after I kept an even closer watch on them.*

> Dr. Harold Penn,
> *The Brief but Timeless Voyage of the* Peter Pan

FOR HER THE TRIBULATIONS OF THE PASSAGE WERE A
multiple torment, because she was not One but Two.

Marlene had heard the humans refer to the ghosts and visions, memories, and chimeras as space lace. She had heard
them talk of out-of-body episodes and afterlife experiences.
They were all but unintelligible concepts to her; being *in*
her present body was phantasmagoria enough, her *life* a
nightmare almost beyond coping.

By the time the hijacked sphere ship plunged into the gravitational abyss of Ranaath's Star, she seemed a ghost, a semitrans-

parent thing of ectoplasm fading fast. In a kind of terminal sleep, she was unaware that Scott Bernard kept a bedside vigil, though it made him nearly insane with guilt and heartache.

Marlene/Ariel's fold-jump dreams were a kind of mental multiscreen image deluge. She, too, experienced the birth/death trauma, understanding it in a way she never otherwise would have because in that moment *the nucleic memories and perspectives of the original Marlene Rush resurfaced.*

But, as well, she felt the cellular tide of the Invid like a moon-drawn ocean within her, swelling and falling. Ariel knew the all-encompassing sadness of the great Invid downfall and the loss of their paradise, recalled the unity of plasm that the Invid shared and what it was to be a race literally sprung from one flesh.

Marlene saw once again her youth, her coming of age on the REF expedition.

Ariel went through her strange birth, a shivering, naked simulagent delivered by a Protoculture-spawned egg.

Marlene: falling in love with the taciturn but idealistic Scott Bernard.

Ariel: the bewildering travels across a blasted Earth with the last Robotech fighters.

Marlene relived the moment, on the deck of a starship racing to do battle with the Invid conquerors, when Scott asked her to marry him and she said yes. Ariel witnessed the defeat of her race and the transfiguration of the Invid into a phoenix of psi-essence—and saw, too, where the phoenix flew.

Both were also silent watchers of each other's memories, like visitors to alien screening rooms. Their/her consciousness was wrenched this way and that by the unimaginable forces grappling at the sphere ship; between torment and joy they attenuated her . . .

Until there came a moment of profound trauma, the cessation of external influences—the ship's emergence into newspace. With an almost physical jolt, the two halves of her were snapped together, fully integrated for the first time.

She opened her eyes and saw Scott gaping at her. She looked down and saw that her body was completely materialized once more. She felt a tranquillity and quiet triumph. She was healed and whole.

He breathed, "Marlene."

Marlene. Yes, that *was* the name that fit her best, even though Marlene's memories and identity were only a component of what she was now. Ariel was a name the Regis had given her capriciously, and she was not Invid anymore.

She lay on a pallet spread directly on the ship's deck. Scott came to her side on one knee, hesitating to take her hand but wanting to. "You're alive. Thank God."

He was haggard and drawn, not from the passage to newspace, she knew, but from self-torture over what he'd done to her. With the disparate parts of her mind and psyche integrated, she understood what he had done and what external pressures it must have taken for him to do it.

His sense of duty, his fealty to his oath of service, his feelings of obligation to those on the SDF-3: those were human things, and Marlene understood them now.

"Yes, Scott. Alive." Her hand covered the last bit of distance to grasp his. His expression swung from astonishment and doubt to relief and the beginnings of rapture.

Before he could answer, though, a face appeared over his shoulder, long and pale with insect goggles, wearing an irrepressible smirk. "Back in action, huh, Marlene? Aces! Scott, didn't I tell ya this little jaunt would give her a new lease on life?"

There stood one of the main pressures that had forced Scott to treat Marlene as he had back on *Ark Angel*. Scott didn't know if Louie Nichols realized how lucky *he* was that all this had worked; had Marlene been put through all her anguish for nothing and perished, *somebody* would've paid.

Scott only grunted in answer to Louie's promptings and put his other hand on Marlene's. "Lie back, now; you've been through a rough time."

"Scott, I know what I'm saying. I've made a full recovery. Besides, I presume Doctor Nichols has some more questions for me."

She looked at Louie slyly. She still had that otherworldly strangeness to her, but there was a certain human knowledge behind it now. Louie found himself realizing what a dish she was. "You said it, gorgeous!"

Scott shot him a jealous glance, and Louie reined in a bit. Marlene rose to her feet without any difficulty, shaking back the waves of crimson hair.

"Um." Scott smiled awkwardly. "Welcome aboard the REF prize-of-war vessel *Peter Pan*." He shrugged.

Marlene stepped forward to look out over the inner globe of the ship. There was no shortage of space; a fairly healthy piece of legendary Macross could have been rebuilt inside the yawning sphere.

Improvised bridges, ladders, and catwalks connected the various levels and platforms, and human furnishings had been fastened to its decks with adhesives and strapping; the techs and engineers could find no way to drill or bend the stuff of the ship. " *'Peter Pan?'* "

"Yeah. 'Second star from the right, then straight on till morning', and all that," Louie supplied with one of his quirky shrugs.

Marlene watched people laboring over the interface equipment required to run the ship or setting up living facilities on unused platforms. It was odd to see portable sanitary booths side by side with modules of Haydonite technology and to smell heated rations there where Protoculture had been intended as the only sustenance.

There were parked mecha, too, and piles of weapons, ammunition, and ordnance; but no weapons had been mounted on the ship itself, since it was impossible to penetrate its hull for firing ports and anything mounted externally would have been annihilated in the passage.

"We're sure bombin' along now." Louie scratched his hennaed hedgehog of hair: "Thing is, we're not all that sure where we are. I hoped you could give us a clue, Marlene."

As she stood there gazing out, she wore the expression Scott had seen that day when she had first cast eyes on a mountain lake, not long after his team of irregulars had found her. Her beauty and her delight in nature's beauty had simply taken hold of him and never let go.

She smiled faintly, "What's the matter, Doctor? Afraid the others will think you're crazy if you tell them yourself?" She turned to Louie, who was for once speechless. Scott had the feeling that behind the goggles, byte buckaroo's eyes were starting from his head.

"You're in what some call newspace," she told them.

"Is the SDF-3 here?" Louie's levity had left him. "Is the Regis?"

Marlene turned to see what effect it would have on them

both. "Newspace *is* the Regis—is the entire Invid race, in a way. We're outside the province of spacetime. You might say we've entered the mind of the transubstantiated Regis herself."

Louie was quick to get in the next remark while Scott was still making choking noises and trying to shift mental gears. "Marl! Babe! Hey! *Work* with me, here! How do we *talk* to her?"

The corners of her mouth turned up ever so slightly. "I think you're about to learn."

The two men followed her gaze and saw what others were becoming aware of. On a platform near the center of the ship's interior, Aurora stood, a blue glimmer growing up around her. Max Sterling, standing near, had started toward his daughter, but Miriya was holding him back. As they watched, Jean Grant, too, put a restraining hand on him.

All through the ship people stopped working and turned to watch Aurora as they became aware of a chant impinging on the very fringes of their perception.

Au-ro-ra, Au-ro-ra, Au-ro-ra . . .

The rest of the ship's complement seemed to freeze, as if they were playing statues, listening to the cadence. Vince Grant, listening to some report; Shi-Ling, at the interface helm; Dana, poised on a maintenance job on her hovertank— all eyes went to Aurora.

All at once Aurora was not alone. Seated in a ring around her were what looked like transparent holograms of children large and small. They sat repeating their mantra, eyes lambent with eldritch fire.

Jean Grant breathed, "Roy!"

"Drannin!" Miriya added.

But neither they nor the others in their circle gave any sign of having heard. They were focused on Aurora, and she on them.

Louie, hypnotized by it, too, almost jumped in the air when Marlene spoke at his shoulder. " 'Straight on till morning,' Doctor."

Kazianna landed on streamers of fire, her weapons ready, as mecha and running ground troops closed in on the open field from every side.

It's back, the message had been, yet there was no sign of the sparkling rain that had spirited away Gnea and Dante.

But there *were* two figures in the middle of the field, scrambling around animatedly.

There were confused transmissions overlapping each other on the nets, but at last Rick got some order on the tactical freq. "Hold your fire, I say again, *hold your fire*! The swirling lights came back just as our point elements were entering the field, then disappeared. We have a visual on what appear to be Gnea and Angie. All elements stand fast and hold fire unless otherwise ordered."

With the field covered from all sides and other elements watching for a trap or sneak attack, Rick selected a recon team and elected to walk point. Jack Baker, Karen Penn, Lron, and Crysta checked their weapons, then spread out in a skirmish line, moving forward. Baldan came, too, carrying communications gear patched to the SDF-3's TIC and bridge.

No doubt about it, the sergeant and the Amazon were there once more. Rick was not sure what the flurry of activity had been when they had first reappeared, but it sure looked like some hasty clothes donning.

He and his team went carefully, testing the ground and watching the air around them, but there was no sign of a threat. Angelo and Gnea, squared away, were wandering around the spot where they had appeared, apparently searching for something. As Rick came up to them and Angelo came to attention, Gnea was carving a big X in the ground with her halberd, on the spot where they had popped back into sight, so that it could be found later if necessary.

Angelo pumped off a nervously crisp salute. "Um, Sergeant Dante reporting, sir. We, ah, that is—"

"Just take it slow, Angie. One thing at a time. Is there still a threat here?"

The big tanker swallowed. "There is, *everywhere* in these parts, sir. But no more here than anyplace else."

Gnea had joined them. Rick could not help noticing that she stood rather close to Dante, leaning on her halberd. "Give me the high points first," Rick told them.

Angelo's chest expanded as he drew a deep, resolute breath. But Gnea got the story in motion first. "We met the Invid Regis. This whole newspace is her realm. She's got the SDF-3's fold drives and won't give them back. She doesn't want us to leave."

Angelo still had his chest full of air. He let it out in one long sigh. "She says the *real* universe is ending, Admiral."

Rick looked at the X in the ground. "Does she know we're not finished with it yet?"

He said it to cover the fact that he was dumbfounded. What the hell was going on? The SDF-3 had been on its way home to fight the Regis. Was the war already lost?

Rick glanced from Gnea to Dante. "Looks like we're in for one helluva debriefing."

The communicator toned. The tiny screen showed not a TIC officer but Lisa's face. "Rick, we've had a new development here. Suggest you return to SDF-3 ASAP."

He ran a hand through his hair, wondering why it had not all gone white. "What's happened?"

He could tell it took some effort for her to stay calm. "The children—Roy and the others. They've made contact with Aurora Sterling. It seems there's a rescue ship on the way, but—the kids're in some kind of trance, and Segundo can't rouse them out of it."

There was a sudden ground-shaking eruption of flame and blast. Where Kazianna's powered armor had stood, there was only burning grass. High above, her armor darted for the SDF-3.

"No closer!"

Segundo looked ridiculously small blocking Kazianna's path to the circle of children, but he did not budge an inch when she seemed about to trample him flat.

Instead, she stopped. The humans knew more about young ones than she, and there was an undeniable ring of moral force in the Micronian's voice.

Still, it took a lot to keep her distance when Drannin sat bewitched with the others, droning Aurora's name. What made it all insane was that Aurora's image, or specter, floated in the center of their circle. Her eyes held the same macabre glow theirs did.

Lisa stood nearby, barely restraining herself from going to Roy. "Emilio, if this is a case of waking the sleepwalker, I'm willing to risk it rather than have their minds stolen."

She felt Rick's hand grip hers and give it a sustaining squeeze.

But Dr. Segundo was shaking his head. "It's not that. They

are still in their bodies, as it were, and I believe Aurora is, too. But this is not the sort of thing you can end simply by dashing water in someone's face.

"Some exchange of information is taking place; we can all feel that. Let it, for I suspect the children will not desist until it does."

Kazianna wavered like a tree swaying in a monsoon, then held her place. "For how long?"

Before the pediatrician could answer, someone shouted, "Look!"

Aurora was looking beyond the circle of children to where Lisa and the rest stood. She raised her hand to them in greeting or farewell—Lisa could not tell which—as the chanting grew louder.

Au-ro-RA!

Then the chanting stopped, and Aurora faded away. Roy and the others rose and faced their parents, their eyes still alight. Segundo had the sense to move aside this time; nothing was going to keep Kazianna from Drannin's side. Lisa and Rick ran to Roy, and other parents were right behind.

Lisa threw her arms around her son, possessed or not. She half expected him to feel clammy or wooden in her embrace, but he was just a little boy who might well do with a bath sometime soon.

As she knelt by him, though, he put one hand on Lisa's shoulder. "Mommy, 'Rora's gonna be here soon."

Rick hunched down by his son. "When? How, Roy?"

"Comin' in a big round ship. We told her how to find us. Mommy, we have to go."

"Yes, hon. We'll take you home right now."

Roy shook his head, eyes still flashing eerily. "Uh uh, I mean go from *here*. 'Rora said. Before it's too late."

"What did she mean?" Rick gripped Roy's shoulders and forced himself to look into the beacon eyes. "Too late how?"

"I can tell you," he heard somebody say.

Rick and Lisa rose, Lisa holding Roy. Before them stood Rem and Minmei, hand in hand.

"And the boy is right," Rem added. "There isn't much time."

CHAPTER TWENTY-SEVEN

*Why are Terrestrials so surprised there was no fossil evidence
or other indication of the Flower's origin left behind on Earth—
or the Pollinators' either? Hasn't it penetrated yet that we are
talking about Haydon?*

Cabell, *Zor and the Great Transition*

EVEN SET IN A ROW AS THEY WERE, LOCKED ON THEIR
thrones on the flying carpet like so many trophies on a man-
telpiece, the Robotech Elders made their acid resentment
known—by their eyes, their mental timbre, their very aura.

*Why are you not mustering your war machines? You must
crush the Amazons!*

Haydon was One again, standing afoot, as he rarely did,
far across the machine plain, tall as a peak. Nevertheless, he
caught their sour, almost pouting thought.

Haydon turned to them, rising from the alloy flatland and
drifting toward the fantastic tower on whose pinnacle they
rested. He was so huge that winds moaned and swirled in
turbulence at his passing. Even at that thin-aired height, his
head loomed above them.

*YOU ARE SUCH PETTY AND UNTHINKING ORGAN-
ISMS. NO WONDER YOU CAME TO THE PITIFUL STATE
IN WHICH I FOUND YOU.*

The Elders shot back, *You need the Flowers!*

*I HAVE ALREADY MADE THAT KNOWN TO THE PRAX-
IANS,* the great head sent forth its words.

What? No! You must take them by surprise, smash all re-sistance with your first blow! The artificial world must al-ready be depleted by construction of the sphere ships; surely it could not sustain a prolonged war.

Haydon drew back, light as a feather though he stirred immense air currents with his movement. *YOU KNOW NOTHING. THERE ARE OTHER WAYS TO ACCOMPLISH GOALS BESIDES MURDER AND DESTRUCTION.*

As he hung in the air, Haydon worked yet another change upon himself. This time the Elders were so shocked that even their crotchety sourness of spirit failed them.

Power systems had long since been installed on New Praxis, but tonight's ceremony decreed the light of torches.

The city had the look of traditional Amazonian architec-ture, which often reminded humans of a blend of classical Japanese and Dark Ages Nordic. Here, though, it was worked in local materials, the rough-cut stone being little different but the lumber taken from Flowers permitted to grow to mas-sive fruition. Though the feud wars of the Praxians had ended generations ago, their buildings still had the look of fortifi-cations.

The importance of the Second Generation Flowers went far beyond building supplies. As the only complex plant that would thrive in Opteran soil, it sustained much of the CO_2-oxygen cycle that made the planet inhabitable. Thus, much of the Praxians' effort at recolonization had been directed at a third seeding of the place.

Down the center way of their rebuilt city the Sisterhood came in a throng, marching somberly, torches held high. They were turned out in their best armor and accoutrements, weapons sharpened and polished, their fantastic war helms burnished.

At the end of the main avenue of their old cities was usu-ally the *Whaashi*, a birthing center or crèche. Though the women warriors knew nothing of courtship, sexuality, or pregnancy, at least until the Sentinels War, the monolithic *Whaashi* saw to it that their race endured. It had always been so, since the legend times of Haydon's appearance.

That was no *Whaashi*, though, at the end of the main thor-oughfare of the new Sisterhood capital of Zanshar. It was a big block of a place, reminiscent of the birthing places, but had been built with Tirolian and human help—because all the *Whaashi* had been lost when Praxis had been rent by planetary apocalypse.

Among the Sisters trooping along in silence with their fluttering firebrands, a few smaller figures could be seen—a child sheltered under the flow of a mother's embroidered cape or walking alongside, trotting to keep up.

They were children—all female. Some were from the Praxians' contact with humans or, in a handful of cases, clones of Tirol. But they were few, and while they were loved, they were not the offspring of the *Whaashi*, and the rites and gifts of the *Whaashi* were ingrained in the Amazon psyche.

The building at the end of the avenue was another kind of lifeplace, where the sciences of Tirol could bring forth clones of Sisters who longed for progeny. These children, too, were cherished and made welcome, but they were not the blessing of the *Whaashi*, either, and most Sisters yearned for the mental communion with the *Whaashi* that brought forth a *new* and *destined* infant.

Waiting at the top of the steps at the cloning center was Bela, a rank of guardswomen below her also bearing torches. As the crowd entered the plaza before her and spread out to fill it, Bela threw back her campaign greatcloak to expose her sword hilt, its grip wound in golden wire, its pommel a flashing blue gem held in a claw of black iron. From the other side of her belt hung a big, use-worn Badger pistol.

She rested her gauntleted hand on the sword hilt. Out of the sky darted a bright shape of silver-blurring double wing sets. Hagane, Bela's *malthi*, perched on her shoulder and gave a piercing warning cry. When the Sisters had poured into the plaza and there was silence, Bela spoke.

"I have had the dreams, even as all of you have. I have seen the reports of how the stars are disappearing from the sky. What these things mean, I do not know. Yet, as we were called to this place and time by voices within us, so we have come.

"Has Haydon truly spoken to us? I cannot say, and all the reports and messages from other worlds are in conflict and confusion. But the dream I dreamed showed me a rebuilt *Whaashi*, even as it did you, and—"

She stopped, feeling a presence behind her. Hagane uttered a jarring whistle but then fell uncharacteristically silent. The throng gasped, and Bela turned to see Haydon. It took her a moment to find her tongue.

"Greetings, O Mother," Bela cried, and kowtowed. The rest of the Praxians genuflected.

Over them hung the image of the changed Haydon, a Haydon of the Yin aspect. The conformations of the blank skull, the contours of the vast body under its cloak, the very emanations the figure gave off—these left nothing in doubt. Haydon was as Haydon had been in a bygone age.

The final proof lay in the tone of the mindvoice, unmistakably feminine. *AS I SAID I WOULD SO LONG AGO, I HAVE COME BACK TO THE SISTERHOOD OF PRAXIS.*

The figure had come from nowhere and might as easily have been some transignal image or holograph. But the Praxians' inner senses knew differently.

"We thank you," the thousands of voices murmured together.

It was the great secret the Praxians had hidden from all others, even their Sentinel allies: the distaff side of Haydon's godhead that had made itself manifest nowhere else in the universe.

I WILL RESTORE THE WHAASHI. *AND IN RETURN YOU WILL DO THAT WHICH I REQUIRE OF YOU.*

Bela had always considered herself devout, and the very thought of a new *Whaashi* was enough to make her heart leap. But something had happened to her in her service with the Sentinels, experiences that had taught her that a leader could not afford the simple, open faith that others clung to.

Thus, when the glad shouts of the Amazons died away, Bela raised her formidable voice. "We thank you and praise you for this benevolence, Haydon, First Mother! Yet what is the nature of the task you require of us?"

There were some angry mutterings from her subjects over her impertinence.

GO FORTH NOW AND GATHER IN ALL OF THE FLOWERS OF LIFE THAT HAVE NOT REACHED FRUITION. THOSE THAT HAVE BORNE FRUIT OR WILL BEAR IT, LET BE. ALL OTHERS ARE NOW CONSECRATED TO ME.

Immature Flowers? "Protoculture," Bela breathed to herself, not daring to say it aloud. Then, as loudly as she could, she demanded, "Why does the First Mother want Protoculture? We, who have fought in wars caused by it, must know for what purpose it is intended!"

The objections and chastisements of the crowd were louder. "What does it matter?" "You blaspheme!" "Anything! Anything for the *Whaashi!*"

The former Sentinel allies had engaged in open combat, and the political brew of the Local Group was turning toxic. The concerns and dangers of other planets were no longer the Praxians' affair, especially since defying Haydon would jeopardize the granting of the *Whaashi*. Such was the popular sentiment in the plaza.

The singular organ in the center of Haydon's forehead burgeoned open and lit like a star. Her wrathful voice filled their minds. *THAT IS NOT FOR YOU TO QUESTION! DO AS I BID YOU OR FEEL MY DISPLEASURE!*

Even more terrifyingly, Optera/New Praxis ground like illfitting bones under their feet. The Amazons, who had already lost one homeworld to upheaval, moaned their dismay.

There were hundreds of voices crying out to surrender the Flowers. Bela drew her weighty, two-handed shortsword from its scabbard so that the blade flashed with light from the torches and from glimmering Haydon.

"I forbid it! Not until we know the purpose behind this commandment."

She had received word of the SDF-3's disappearance, of course, and the events at Haydon IV—conflicting reports that only added to her misgivings about setting free more Protoculture. The apparition Haydon might even somehow be the trick of an unknown enemy.

But the crowd was not with her. Their fear of Haydon's anger and planetary catastrophe and their need for the *Whaashi* were too great. With a unified roar, they swept up the steps.

Bela's personal bodyguard wavered, some of them more attuned to the crowd's position than to the queen's. But it hardly mattered; hesitating to hack or open fire on their own Sisters, they went down under the wave of tall fighting women.

Bela herself stood straddle-legged on the steps, sword in

one fist, assault pistol in the other, to meet them. But when she saw faces she loved, comrades she'd served with, mothers of children she'd held coming for her, she knew she could not do them harm.

The crowd had stopped short before her, daunted by her even in the extremity of their passion.

Bela holstered her pistol, sheathed her sword, and stood with arms hanging limply at her sides. The crowd turned back the way it had come. Already Amazons were organizing harvesting operations. Haydon, looking down, found Her handiwork good.

"And so the final phase of my—Zor's—plan was set in motion," Rem said.

He lifted his hand to Rick and Lisa Hunter. "And the cycle of the story comes around to Earth once more. The last planet Zor seeded, or rather, in Earth's case, *re*seeded with the Flower. With the SDF-1."

"And Zentraedi help," Kazianna murmured while she was mulling over all the things he had told them.

"Yes, the first to fall prey to the lure of song," Rem told her soberly. He reached out his arm to encircle Minmei's shoulders. "I suppose every child of Tirol is susceptible to it, really.

"The Protoculture gave me insights into the power of the Cosmic Harp and how music could throw down even the Robotech Masters' mental domination."

Dolza found that out, Lisa thought, but kept it to herself so as not to switch the conversational track.

They were assembled in the big bilevel conference area—most of the leaders and certain others whose testimony was pertinent. Caffie and other refreshments had been brought. Screens kept a constant vigil on the children and their chanting, but nothing seemed to have changed except that Aurora's form phased in and out from time to time. She would not or could not respond to any of the grown-ups, but everyone got the feeling there was a lot of information being exchanged between her and the SDF-3's children.

"With music, Zor—*reprogrammed*, I guess you could say, a few of the Zentraedi most loyal to him," Rem said. "Although I prefer to think of it as liberating them. It never occurred to the Masters that the Zentraedi could find a cause higher than obedience.''

"Lucky for Earth they didn't learn their lesson," Rick whispered to Lisa.

The thought troubled her for a moment. What if the Robotech Masters had somehow eliminated their Achilles' heel? Surely Earth would have been devastated far worse than ever Optera was.

But it had not happened; it was not *meant* to. She dismissed the thought; it was not time to be morbid.

And yet she felt sure the thoughts and feelings of all aboard were being probed and in some cases manipulated.

Lisa hurried to get a word in before Lang could; the scientist looked half-ecstatic, half-deranged with all that new insight. "Rem, we *must* stick to the point. What is the nature of newspace, is there really a relief ship on the way, and are all personnel safe at the moment?"

She meant the children, and no one begrudged her the preoccupation. Rem replied, "Just so. I believe the story told by Gnea and Sergeant Dante is entirely true. I believe that all that has happened is tied in with the master plan of Haydon.

"The Regis told you both that she, which is the same as to say her entire race, now desires a return to the Invid's pre-Zor state on Optera, isn't that right?"

Angelo responded, "Yes, sir," and Gnea inclined her head, making her *malthi*-winged helmet glitter.

"Very well. Ladies and gentlemen, Zor's dream has come to pass," Rem said. "The fleet you sent to Earth must have driven her from it in a supreme mating with the Protoculture itself. But for whatever reason—I suspect because the Regis was forced into it by violence—this transcendence has not worked out as intended.

"We find ourselves in a situation of danger not only to ourselves but to the entire universe. I believe that unless some solution is found, by the nature of Protoculture, all of the Creation that we know will vanish as if it never existed.''

At his end of the table Lang watched and listened to Rem with a fascination and a sense of dismay that had been growing for months.

The clone had been scarcely more than a boy when the REF had first encountered him. Now, grown and filled out, he was very much the image of Zor, albeit with some slight genetic alteration. But even more tellingly, in the wake of his clonesong dreams, he spoke with the voice of Zor—with an utter certainty about the nature of Protoculture and the fate of spacetime.

Lang studied Rem's face. It was the same countenance Lang had first viewed decades ago on the other side of the galaxy, ageless and graceful. Then it had stared out of a screen and had spoken incomprehensible words. Now it lived before him.

Lang listened carefully to what Rem was saying, but within the scientist there was a pall, a feeling of total defeat.

Despite all his assumptions and all his efforts, it was not Lang that newspace was trying to contact, to use and deal with. The mantle of ultimate Protoculture destiny had fallen on Rem.

All Lang's hopes were dashed. It had been his creed that the Protoculture had sought him out, that he was at the center of the Shapings. Now he saw the cruelty of it, that he was no more a luminary of the Shapings than one of the children or Sentinel fighters, perhaps no more than that overmuscled tank sergeant, Dante.

It couldn't be! He'd come too far. He *refused* to be done out of his place in the Shapings. But how to avoid it?

Lang was a past master at concealing his feelings. Nothing showed on his face, but inside he felt an icy thrill of hope and dread.

The Shapings had come full circle, and in some ways the pattern was ripe for repeating. Or if not, at least Lang's place in the great cycle would be secure.

CHAPTER
TWENTY-
EIGHT

*Those critics contending that the personnel of SDF-3 were un-
forgivably blind—in not seeing the implications of their own behavior in terms of the "birth trauma" nature of their transit
into newspace—are nothing but (God forgive me) lard-bottomed
armchair generals.*

*Given the stresses of what they were going through, the emo-
tional wringer pressing out every one of them, and the demands
of constant strife and danger, the SDFers' confusion was almost
inevitable.*

*Only children, fools, and those who have never known hard-
ship could argue otherwise.*

Pastor Basil Yanamamo,
Pipeline: Experiences in Birth and Death

"**K**AREN, WAIT!"

He had finished postflighting his Alpha and had rushed so
that he wouldn't miss her, but somehow she had completed
her task even quicker and left the flight deck.

As he caught up with her in the passageway, Karen spun
on her boot heel, tapping her toe, arms crossed, features
composed in heavy weather warnings. "Make it brief, Jack."

He trotted to a stop, feeling something that would have
been akin to *déjà vu* if he had not known *exactly* where he'd
felt it before: every time they had squabbled, disagreed,
clashed, or vied for the upper hand.

"Aah, it's no big thing. Just thought we could hit the mess
if you want some company for dinner."

She was not looking any kindlier. "Don't you want to find out what's going on at the meeting?"

"You mean what *went* on; I heard it's just breaking up. But by the time we grab a bite, there'll probably be an intel summary we can get a peek at."

Her eyes narrowed. "Then maybe stop for one or two at the officers' club? Possibly a dance?"

Actually, that was just what he had in mind. He answered warily, "Why, is there something wrong with that?"

"Hah! Honestly, Baker, there're cockpit canopies harder to see through than you are!"

"Whoa—ho—wha—" was all he got in.

"This is so typical," Karen said through clenched teeth. "We're stuck in newspace or wherever it is, possibly forever, and suddenly it hits you that we should be seeing more of each other."

"Well, yeah, that just happens to be the case," he said lamely. Then he heard laughter and realized that there were some enlisted ratings standing back by the hatch, ordnance men and women taking a break before going back to rearming the mecha.

"Haven't you goddamn BB stackers got anything better to do?" he railed at them. When he looked back, Karen was gone.

This time he had to grab her sleeve to stop her, and he thought for a moment she was going to sock him. At least they were out of anyone else's earshot.

"Have it your way, Karen! Let's go back to the cats-and-dogs routine."

"*My* way? I want you to think about that, Jack. Remember back when we were stranded on Praxis and you got so domestic? Even though you put on a front when there was anyone else around. *You* were the one who was all set to plow the north forty, lasso goats, and raise us'ns up a crop of rug runners. Right?

"Then we get off the planet and back into the war, and your priorities revert. That's your pattern. When you were laid up after Burak gored you, you were actually acting human for a while, but once you were up and around, *ugh*!"

Jack had his mouth open to object, but Karen had been saving this one up for a long time, and he didn't stand a chance. "And *now* we're beached here in newspace and you're making an approach run. Well, spare us both the thrill, Baker!"

"You knew I was insecure and thoughtless when you got me to fall in love with you!" he hollered.

Karen uttered a wordless *ki-yi* and tried to take his nose off with a snap kick. Jack just managed to fall back but tripped over a stanchion and whapped the back of his head on a viewport rim, going down.

He sat there seeing stars. "King's X! What're you, working for the Invid?"

She was torn between concern and the urge to do mayhem. "Oh, Baker, damn your eyes!" She knelt by him. "Here, let's see."

"No! *Ouch!* You're just trying to finish the job."

"Stuff it, you big baby. You didn't even break the skin." She released him and let him get up by himself.

"You made your point, Karen. You don't want me to talk to you unless I've already talked to you several times earlier that same day."

"Stop trying to twist things, Jack."

"Yeah, all right. I bet you think that effing *Sean Phillips* is more considerate, right?"

He rubbed his head gingerly, gazing out the viewport. There were more stars than there had been a while ago. "D' you suppose she's bringing in biota?"

"What?"

"You heard what Dante said about the Regis. All these stars she's making appear here in newspace— Are there life-forms on them? Maybe even intelligent ones? Is she ripping them off from someplace else or just thinking them up?"

"You're asking the wrong woman."

"Mmm. Okay, look, how about dinner a week from Friday?"

"I don't think they have Fridays in newspace, Jack." She turned toward the officers' mess, more slowly this time.

He fell in beside her. "How about breakfast tomorrow? In my bunk?"

Bowie, the Muses, Sean, and Marie had stayed well back during the meeting. There were plenty of astonishing revelations but not really much anybody could say or *do* about anything—certainly not the ex-UEG fighters or the siren Muses.

As the meeting began to break up, Sean yanked Bowie's sleeve and pointed with a sneaky smile and half-lidded eyes. Angelo Dante had wandered over to the hatch just about the time Gnea, her attention seemingly elsewhere, had eased back out of the crowd.

A look passed between the two. Gnea left, and Dante hung back, scanning the compartment to see if anyone had noticed them.

"Don't let him see you watching!" Sean hissed. The ATACs and Marie quickly glanced elsewhere. Musica and Allegra gazed at them uncomprehendingly, then at each other, so the effect was the same. A moment later Angie was gone.

"Angelo Dante?" Bowie boggled. "No, must've been something that wants us to *think* it's Angelo Dante."

Musica had caught on, and she was smiling, too, slipping her arm through Bowie's. But Allegra said slowly, "You mean you think he's not human?"

Marie Crystal laughed. "*Oh*, no; he's human, all right, no matter how he tries to hide it. I bet he and Gnea are gonna Indian wrestle to see who carries whom across the threshold."

Sean sighed and made lewd, fishy kissing noises at her until he realized that two senior staff officers were glaring at him. Marie added, "Now that I think about it, though, there's been a *lot* of slap and tickle going on since we entered newspace."

"If I understood it right, that's what Lang was driving at," Bowie put in thoughtfully. "Maybe creating a newspace macroverse is like writing a song. You can't just haul off and do it cold; you haveta draw on inspiration."

That had them all silent and thinking. The loves and attractions of the SDF-3's complement were only *part* of the mental and emotional baggage they carried.

"It occurs to me that maybe we all want to be *real* careful about what we think and say and do around here," Marie pondered aloud.

Perhaps I saw this day coming all along, Lang mused, keying the armored vault module with his spoken password,

DNA code, and brain scan. *Why else would I have made this shrine to it?*

The vault module had been aboard the SDF-3 all along, transferred there from storage on Earth. The Robotech equipment it held had been removed from the just-crashed SDF-1 within days of Lang's first encounter with it in '99. The equipment sat before him now, silent and patient, looking little different from the way it had in the instant when Lang had first seen Zor's face on its screen.

He ran his hand along it, the console that had been the nucleus of the SDF-1's living Robotechnology. It had been replaced by human interface equipment, which had then been set up in a conventional bridge arrangement where Henry Gloval set his strong hand on the tiller of galactic history.

But the original systemry was here, preserved, inert. Touching it, Lang felt his skin tingle, recalling the unspeakable shock when pure Protoculture, amassed and controlled by Zor's least comprehensible devices, had flooded through him. It was an event that belonged if not on the ceiling of the Sistine Chapel, then perhaps on a matrix containment casing, Lang thought ruefully.

He had kept to himself as much as possible the profound changes the Protoculture had worked in him and his new affinity for it. He was absolutely indispensable to the new Robotech Age, and so his strangeness was overlooked. People hailed him as genius, as savior, yet he'd been confronted every day, from the first crash exploration in '99 to this moment, with his own shortcomings and fear.

By long habit he glanced back to make sure the vault module was totally secure. He reached out and tapped a code into a touchpad.

Zor's master console came to life.

Not to full power, of course; there was little Protoculture now, and it all had the unavoidable Second Generation impurities and unsuitability. But the infusion let the alien indicators and displays show that they still waited. He could flood the devices with Second Gen power whenever he chose.

Up until a short while before, he could have taken a second boost—could have done that at almost any moment over the decades. His powers would quite probably be increased geometrically; the math and research data were promising on that point, just as they led to the inescapable fact that he would die very shortly thereafter.

Zand had been willing to risk it after that first *voluntary* exposure to the Protoculture he had taken against Lang's orders and behind his back. Though neither of them mentioned it later, Lang had been quite prepared to shoot his colleague down in cold blood rather than see him take that next step toward the godhead.

Most of that stemmed from fear of what the second boost might make of Zand, who was none too stable as it was, of course. But wasn't there more to it? Jealousy and a refusal to let Zand have something that he, Lang, feared to claim as his own?

No matter. Zand had had his transcendence, all right. And to hear Dana Sterling tell it, it was all in line with the fear of the Shapings that was almost a religious fervor within Lang now.

Here in newspace, though, the Shapings had gone awry or petered out or . . . Lang was not sure what.

His polestar faith, the Shapings, led him no more. The politicians and the military would go on pretending there was something they could do, but he knew differently. There was only one possible way to save the lives onboard the SDF-3 and, more important, the universe threatened by newspace.

That route lay in a direct encounter with the Shapings. And the only way anyone would do that would be to raise oneself beyond the limits of mortal power, at least for a single moment.

Only no one was going to do that with Zor's equipment, not with Second Gen Protoculture at any rate.

At least . . . *not as the console was configured now*.

Lang drew his stool closer and sat absorbed in the console. After long minutes he reached for a sensor and hooked it into one of the system's peripherals. He took up a touchpad and began keying equations into his mainframe, scarcely aware that he was doing it.

He paused to run his hand along the console in thought, recalling its Protoculture thunderbolt, and almost threw down the touchpad. It was madness!

There was a sudden flux in the equipment—not unusual;

he'd had to jury-rig a lot of the modifications that let it use Second Gen Protoculture. He forgot his frustration and fear, watching rainbow waves of distortion chasing each other across the ten-foot screen.

Lang did not even need to wonder what he'd see next; he had viewed the recording so many times that he knew the pattern of the static that preceded it.

He was staring at the ageless, elfin face again, with its wide, almond eyes, framed by a mane of bright, starlight hair. He'd long since memorized the sounds of Zor's speech of greeting and warning.

Zor's recording. Kicked up at random by a meaningless Protoculture hiccup, some might say.

But Lang took his touchpad back in hand and sat down, staring unblinkingly at Zor. When the recording had run its course, he went back to his calculations.

All across New Praxis the surface-effect and aerospace vehicles were on the move.

The Amazons had come there with little agrarian experience; they'd hunted, herded, and gathered the untended bounty their homeworld offered up naturally. But they had met their new planet's demands with their innate adaptability and their hard-nosed refusal to give up.

They raised some of their food in vats, greenhouses, and aeroponic domes, but the key to their survival had been rendering parts of the stalk and roots of the Flower of Life edible (the fruit being deadly to them). They had learned to farm.

And now they were learning to reap in a way they had never conceived of.

From every point of the compass the ground wagons, air lorries, and skyboats converged. Military, private, common carrier—every vehicle on the planet had been mobilized by women working to exhaustion and beyond. None had slept since Haydon's appearance.

In the main plaza of Zanshar, before the cloning center, the pile of Flowers grew. Every specimen had been carefully scanned to make sure it was unpollinated. All had been bagged in clearseal to ensure that they stayed that way.

And that raised a troubling point. For some reason the

mysterious little Pollinators, whose nature it was to tend the Flowers and who had ranged freely across New Praxis, had disappeared. Some thought that an evil portent, but no one dared voice the opinion.

The pile of bagged Flowers grew and grew, higher and higher, until it had attained the top step and spilled against the high front doors of the cloning center.

Bela watched from the opposite end of the main thoroughfare, from the uppermost parapet of her castle. The Amazons' big orbital freight shuttle was nearly ready to receive the bounty of New Praxis. Cargo pods were already being wheeled into place to transport the Flowers.

Bela had sent her guards and advisers from her. Silently she watched through the night as Flowers were trundled off toward the shuttle pad. The shuttle lifted off like a morning star for its flight into high orbit and a rendezvous with Haydon IV (how the artificial world had drawn so close without colliding with New Praxis or, at the very least, causing catastrophic damage, no one knew). It would return with the sealed, prefabricated modules that would be activated to form a new *Whaashi*.

But in the meantime, what dark harvest have we reaped? The thought came like a sword cut, over and over.

CHAPTER
TWENTY-
NINE

"Peter Pan, huh?" I said to him. "Hope we packed plenty of pixie dust, Tink."

Louie Nichols, remark to General Vincent Grant, quoted in Nichols's *Tripping the Light Fantastic* (fourth edition)

IN SPITE OF HIMSELF, HE WAS NEARLY NODDING OFF WHEN he felt his wife's fingers dig into his arm. "Max! Look!"

The fingers sank in with enough strength to make him wince; becoming a mother had not robbed Miriya of any of her Zentraedi sinew and vigor. Max was instantly wide awake, sitting up straight on the sleeping pad he and Miriya had thrown down on the bare deck to keep a vigil by their daughter.

He saw what she meant at once: Aurora was blinking as if coming out of a dream, and the apparitions that were the SDF-3 children had vanished.

Miriya was first to her daughter's side, feeling her forehead with one hand, checking her pulse with the other. On the other deck levels, people were taking note of the change.

Aurora put up with the fussing but insisted, "I'm all right, Mother. Father." She put an arm around each of them and hugged.

Max offered up a prayer of thanks. Aurora was so ethereal, so seemingly unsuited for hardship and strife—it broke his heart whenever he thought of her coming to harm.

Jean Grant had arrived to gently nudge Miriya aside and

run a diagnostic scanner over Aurora. Louie Nichols was there, too, practically jumping up and down, dying to ply Aurora with questions. Max laid a restraining arm on him. "Give her a minute, Doctor."

"Jean, I'm perfectly fine," Aurora insisted gently, pushing the scanner away. "And we really haven't any more time to waste."

"What happened to the children?" Louie burst out, unable to contain himself anymore. "Why'd they break contact?"

"I'm still in fourth-level contact with them," Aurora corrected. "But second-level, which you saw earlier, is somewhat draining. And it's no longer necessary; I know our course now."

She stepped through the circle of people around her to a makeshift ramp that led toward the control area. Jean protested, "Wait, sugar; you need to rest a bit."

"There's no time, Jean." But before Aurora could set foot on the ramp, Max blocked her way. "Hold on a second, hon. You *have* to tell us what's going on."

She smiled at him sweetly. *A smile like a springtime sunrise,* he thought; her shoulders felt so frail in his hands.

"Well, I have to take control of the interfaces, to direct the *Peter Pan* on the last leg of the trip," she told him. "Basically, we're navigating through a—a mind continuum, you might say. As Marlene told you, it's what the SDFers call newspace. Different from the physical universe and even from Doctor Nichols's cyber-dimensions. So I have to take the helm to guide us."

Her face changed then, becoming sober, and Max felt her delicate hands close on his. "And there's something else. Newspace *reacts* to what's in us, our thoughts and emotions and experiences. It has no true form of its own, and so it draws from what it finds. The children say be very careful what we say and do and think."

"Yes," someone agreed, and Max saw Marlene standing nearby. A somber, intent Scott Bernard hung back a step behind her. "We must all be careful now," Marlene went on.

"Mm-hm," Aurora said, hair bobbing as she nodded her head. Then she drew his head down so that she could whisper in Max's ear. "But especially you, Father."

* * *

"And the Praxians don't respond?" Exedore frowned.

Cabell raised his hands hopelessly, then dropped them again. Before them, the big transignal communicator was silent. "The installation we left on New Praxis was working," Cabell insisted. "The last message from Bela talked about disturbing dream aberrations, and our remote instruments indicated that Haydon IV was approaching the planet. As you can see, our link with the Amazons is now silent. The obvious conclusion is that Haydon is awake. I fear the worst."

"The Flowers," Exedore rasped, running a hand through the bright disarray of his hair.

Cabell inclined his head slowly. "The Flowers, of course. And after that, inevitably, the matrix."

They turned as one to look out the window of the lab at the immense rebuilt pyramid that was the Royal Hall, where the only Second Gen matrix—the "facsimile," as Lang called it—had been stirred to fitful, difficult-to-control life.

"What if we simply surrender it to Haydon?" Exedore mulled.

Cabell answered, "It may come to that in the end, but I would see our subsequent chances of survival as very slim."

And by "our" he meant every single living thing in the universe and possibly, knowing Cabell, its inanimate material as well.

"We could create another matrix," Exedore said.

Cabell put into words what they both knew. "Yes, but that would take time, perhaps months, and Haydon will not endure such a wait. No, He means to supercharge the matrix with the Flowers from New Praxis and start at long last on His final journey."

There was a rapping at the open door: Lantas, Cabell's new student and research assistant since her return aboard the ship comandeered by Dana Sterling and the 15th ATACs. She was the last surviving member of a Scientist triumvirate, a bright and energetic young woman, her hair a mass of pink ringlets. She had adopted a protective, almost proprietary attitude toward Cabell and Exedore, making them the missing members of a new triumvirate.

Now, though, Lantas looked young and frightened. She said, "The captains of the Local Group are here."

They trooped into the room—Karbarran and Spherisian, Garudan and Perytonian. Strange to see them striding along together, when in the near past there had been so much friction among them.

The captains drew to a halt before the three. Hodel, the burly Karbarran, spoke for them; the flotilla was mostly Karbarran, after all. "We have had word of Haydon's approach. Tirol has given us reason to hate it over the centuries, but in the Sentinels War, you here became our allies. More to the point, we think your researches into using the matrix to halt the shrinkage of the cosmos are our only hope of survival. We therefore cannot surrender the matrix to Haydon, no matter what.

"*Tracialle* will lead the fleet into battle. Your Tiresian techs have agreed to man the *Valivarre*." His main regret was that the powerful *Ark Angel* had, after delivering the scientists to Tirol, departed for return to Earth; it would have added tremendously to the flotilla's firepower.

Exedore had heard something about the Tiresians' crewing *Valivarre* for battle. With all the Zentraedi gone save only himself, the ship had to be refitted for use by Micronians, of course. But how surprising that the clones, after centuries of docility, should leap to defend their planet and the matrix with all the stoic determination of Zentraedi in a suicide charge. It was a time of horrors but, truly, a time of wonders as well.

"I tell you again that I doubt you have any chance of victory," Cabell was saying. "But I know that won't dissuade you. What, then, do you wish of us?"

A Perytonian, Purg, spoke up, tossing his needle-sharp horns as he did. "Tell us of the Awareness, the seat of its consciousness, where its vulnerabilities lie. It is weak now; if we destroy it, Haydon will be unable to wage war."

Cabell was shaking his head measuredly. "Firstly, the planet has gone through such radical mechamorphosis that there is no telling where the Awareness is now. Nor is there any reliable way of detecting it.

"But more importantly, destroying the Awareness will not guarantee that Haydon is powerless; far from it. I implore you all to hold back. Exedore and I are trying to develop some kind of defense to keep the artificial planet at bay."

What he did not tell them was that if worse came to worst, he and the micronized Zentraedi meant to destroy the matrix utterly. The residents of the Local Group looked to it as their only hope of salvation.

Captain Prah, the Spherisian, answered. Her ship, the *Quartzstar*, was the newest, smallest, and most beautiful of all the Local Group vessels. Spheris was perhaps the least warlike of the allies, and so Cabell hoped for some word of moderation from her.

But she said in a voice that had a high crystal ring to it, "We cannot risk Haydon's gaining the ultimate power of the matrix, nor can we gamble the lives of Tirol's people. Therefore, unless this weapon of yours is forthcoming, the flotilla will advance and engage Haydon IV as soon as it appears in this system."

"I am Zentracdi," Exedore said, hands clasped behind his back. "I understand your feelings. Nonetheless, I beg you to reconsider."

The captains' silence was as emphatic as any spoken refusal.

"Go, then," Cabell told the captains. "Exedore and I will see if Protoculture has any secrets left to teach us."

Over and over, during the headlong days of the Flower harvest, her hand went to her sidearm and she drew a breath to summon those guardswomen who were still faithful to her, to go out and stop the collection, prevent the delivery to orbit, or die trying.

But each time, Bela's hand unwillingly released the gun's grip. To do that would mean fighting and killing her Sisters and make her worse than Haydon, worse than an Invid. What was to happen now was beyond her power to control.

In time the cargo ship lifted off, climbing to orbit on its antiproton-power trail. It was gone for more than ten hours, off-loading its Flower cargo and taking aboard the promised modules. When it made planetfall again, it seemed as though every childless woman on the planet was waiting to greet it, to help in assembling the modules.

Haydon and Her works remained an enigma; the modules, once activated, shifted position and assembled themselves, the Amazons not daring to interfere or try to probe the secrets of Her devices.

Still Bela sat in her aerie, glaring down the central boulevard of Zanshar. Dawn rose on a plaza from which the cloning facility had vanished, replaced by a *Whaashi*. A lottery was being held in the open square for a fair and orderly allocation of access to the place of miracles.

When the first woman entered the *Whaashi*, Bela rose from her place and went to her palace's command center. There she watched on a projecbeam screen as Haydon IV got under way again.

She expected to see a planet restored to high-sheen, flawless max-function, but it was not so. It looked as if there had been some repairs, and certainly the artificial world was maneuvering powerfully and quickly, but signs of damage were still to be seen.

Then Haydon IV was gone, superluminal. Bela commanded her techs to make yet another attempt to establish contact with Tirol despite the interference that had been frustrating them thus far.

Curse the Shapings!

With Aurora's hand on the tiller—or rather, her mind guiding the *Peter Pan* through a modified "thinking cap" (she refused to have anything to do with Louie's cyber-sockets, and Max and Miriya would not have permitted it, anyway)— the sphere ship emerged into newspace.

It was as if an encasing bubble had popped; all around them were stars and nebulas, and nearby the Super Dimensional Fortress swung in orbit over a world swathed in the white clouds indicative of a living planet.

"We took longer to get here than the SDF-3," she explained, "because our drive is so different, and so was our route through Ranaath's Star." Dr. Penn, Louie, and the rest did not get to find out why, because Lisa Hunter's face appeared on the main projecbeam imager and her voice rang from the speakers.

"Attention, unknown vessel. Attention—Aurora! *Vince!* Max, Miriya—lord, it's good to see you all!"

A lot of people on the *Peter Pan* were trying to talk at the same time, Aurora being a notable exception. Vince silenced them with one stern command. "At ease!"

Lisa went on. "The children said you were coming. Vince, I have to warn you: There's no guarantee you won't be stranded here, too, unless you get out of newspace *now*, this moment."

Louie Nichols had crowded up next to Vince, recognizing Lisa from old newscasts, tapes, and having seen her once in person during the SDF-3 launch ceremonies. "I think we've got a handle on that, Admiral."

Vince frowned at Louie but tolerated the intrusion. "Lisa, d' you have maneuvering power?"

"Barely, Vince."

"No problem. If you'll hold your present orbit, I'll match up with you." Harry Penn was studying his instruments and giving Vince a can-do nod.

"Very good. I'll convene an emergency conference. We can begin transferring personnel to your ship right away."

Vince drew a deep breath but decided not to contradict her quite so publicly. It might cause serious morale problems—maybe even a breakdown in discipline—to announce that nobody was going anywhere for a while.

The main delay in docking ships was necessitated by *Peter Pan*'s techs having to fit external securing gear on the outer hull. But two hours later the mated air locks opened, and despite the strain of the crisis, there was a reunion that made the bulkheads rattle.

Lisa had left Forsythe in command of the bridge. She waited on the SDF-3's side of the lock, since it was roomier. Vince stepped through from *Peter Pan*, they saluted each other, and then he swept her up in a laughing hug. Rick did not bother with salutes, throwing his arms around Jean and bussing her soundly.

Restraint and order broke down, with more hugging, joy, and laughter than any of them could recall in a long time. Vince was in no position to object, since he no sooner released Lisa than he was confronted by his son. Bowie held out a hand shyly. "Hello, Dad."

Vince took it and shook it, but Jean threw her arms around Bowie and kissed him over and over, laughing even though there were tears streaming from her eyes. Musica and Allegra watched from one side, fascinated. Then Jean embraced *them*.

The two groups met and mingled in individual encounters that varied greatly. Dana managed to clutch both Sean and Marie to her and at the same time kiss a strangely blushing Angelo Dante, while Gnea looked on dubiously. Harry Penn embraced his daughter and spared a handclasp, albeit a cool one, for Jack Baker. Scott Bernard led Marlene over by the hand to meet Lang, who seemed subdued, even shy, out in public like that. Kazianna sat to one side, not wanting to trample anybody, but knelt to exchange kisses, like humans, with her old comrade-in-arms Miriya. Angie saw Dana's face go blank and distant as she caught sight of Rem.

Minutes went by before Miriya realized that Aurora was not anywhere to be seen. She mouthed the name to Max, and he shrugged helplessly while Rick Hunter pumped his hand and pounded him on the back. Then Miriya realized that there was a spreading pool of silence over by *Peter Pan's* lock and another on the opposite side of the compartment. The crowd went silent by degrees, becoming aware that Aurora waited on one side, Roy and Drannin and the SDF-3 children on the other.

Some had not seen the children's glowing, otherworldly eyes before; there were murmurings and uneasy shiftings in the crowd. People instinctively made way until the children and Aurora were staring at each other over a gap of empty deck. Aurora and Roy moved at the same time, drawing close like kids in a pretend wedding.

When they came together, they took each other's hands, and a crackle of blue radiance startled the grown-ups. Aurora informed her parents, "The others and I must talk."

Roy led her over into the circle of lamp-eyed youngsters, and the group headed for the lock. Lisa wanted to haul them back, but Jean put a restraining hand on her arm. "We need to talk, too, Lisa."

With some difficulty, Lisa cut the core leadership people out of the herd and got them across the passageway to the conference compartment. Vince and his essential people came, too, while the rest of the celebrants repaired to a nearby rec hall to carry on with the reunion.

"We've run some calculations," Lisa began before everyone was seated. "I want to get all personnel evacuated in one hop if you have sufficient deck space. Even if that means we'll be sitting on each other and take only the clothes on our backs."

Rick had been watching the troubled look on Vince's face and braced himself as the general spoke. "Lisa, I'm not sure we have any place to go back *to*. Whatever it is that happened when you were drawn here, it's affecting the universe. Louie, maybe you'd better take over."

Louie rose, adjusting his black goggles, his grin coming and going in tics. He launched into a recap of what had happened, the SDFers interrupting with intermittent questions but for the most part listening.

The transcendence of the Regis and her race, the appearance of *Ark Angel* in Earthspace, the search expedition for the SDF-3 and the battle at Ranaath's Star—Louie recounted it all succinctly, although Lisa noticed that he described the strange psi-contact between the SDF-3's children and Aurora in oddly neutral terms, apparently not wanting to offer much theory about that just yet.

Lang watched Nichols, that Robotech up-and-comer. The scientist, having studied some of Louie's brilliantly insightful work, became convinced nonetheless that Louie saw the solving of the mysteries of Protoculture not as a holy pursuit and the search for the Grail but rather as some immense and rather elite game.

So: there was Rem the reborn template, and Nichols the secular adept, along with all the others—half-breeds, *Wyrdlings*, mind-savants, and the rest—gathered in one place at last. But none of them could occupy the place in the Shapings that Lang could.

If only he had the strength to seize it.

CHAPTER
THIRTY

In that happy-yet-sad reunion with the people from Peter Pan, *I felt one special pang but kept it to myself.*

It was clear how much Scott Bernard's mixed feelings about Marlene had put him through, but in some ways I couldn't help envying him. As much as I loved Rick and Roy, I couldn't help thinking about other human DNA remains, in other wreckage— at Sara Base, on Mars. How would I feel if Karl Riber reappeared?

At one point I discovered I'd been sitting there for five minutes, staring out the bridge viewpane, lost in that thought. And realizing newspace's apparent affinity for our memories and emotions, I knew we really had to get out of there.

Lisa Hayes-Hunter, *Recollections: The Lost Journey*

THE ROBOTECH ELDERS' TEMPERS FLARED, EVEN THOUGH the rage was impotent. *You fancy yourself a god? Then act like one!*

Haydon ignored them as usual. That was far more infuriating than if he had caused them pain or silenced their mental rantings.

The Second Gen Flowers from New Praxis had been taken below the surface of the artifact planet, and faraway sounds and tremors indicated that they were being processed, or perhaps digested, in some fashion. And yet, aside from Haydon IV's superluminal passage to the Valivarre system, nothing seemed to have been accomplished.

If the Awareness and your facilities cannot produce any warcraft or combat mecha, then arm the sphere ships and send forth your Haydonites to do battle! You cannot venture into combat this way; OUR lives are at risk as well as yours!

Haydon was as imperturbable as he was vast. He watched as the planet went subluminal and swung toward majestic, green Fantoma. His planet's sensors told him that His arrival had been noticed and that a flotilla of ships was deploying even now to intercept.

He ignored their hails. Once He would have swept them aside like so many gnats or drowned them under an ocean of His own war simulacra. But the damage done to Haydon IV by space attack and cyber-burn had limited His options.

That only meant that His victory would be somewhat uneconomical, a bit inelegant. In another way, though, it would show those absurd little creatures what an *intelligent* mind could do with Robotechnology.

The Elders felt the world shifting and quaking around them again. *What are you doing? We demand to know!*

Haydon made no response as long moments slid by and the artificial planet seemed on the verge of tearing itself apart. The Elders raged and vituperated, but at last, their fury spent and their apprehensions waxing, they spoke the words they had not used since the days of their mortality.

We . . . beg you to tell us what is happening.

Haydon's blank face gazed down at them indifferently. *YOU PRESUMED TO CALL YOURSELVES ROBOTECH MASTERS? I WILL SHOW YOU WHAT MASTERY IS.*

With that, light burst from the organ in His forehead, and Haydon levitated into the air. At the same time, the carpet carrying the Elders' imprisoning thrones rose, joining Him as an immense bubble appeared from somewhere to enclose Haydon.

The planet below was going through profound mechamorphosis. It was only as the bubble climbed high above the atmosphere that the Elders began to understand the mind-numbing scale of it.

Having had little time to train together, the pickup flotilla of the Local Group was fortunate that it had experienced no collisions, much less that it had somehow gotten into a passable formation.

Tracialle led the way, with *Valivarre* prominent on the right wing of the formation. The armed merchantmen of the Karbarran fleet were the flotilla's backbone, with the other planets' vessels interspersed all through the three-dimensional deployment scheme.

Hodel watched as long-range sensors fed him information about the intruder world's approach, noting the appearance of the bubble high over it but more concerned with the throes of the gargantuan artifact itself. It seemed that Haydon IV was trying to self-destruct, fly apart in uncountable pieces or grind itself to dust.

"We're detecting anomalies," a clone from the *Valivarre* reported.

"Indeed?" Hodel scoffed in a moist rumble. "Don't you think they're apparent?"

"I am referring to new topographical features on the target world," the answer came back. "Their existence defies gravitational influence. Immense amounts of power are being expended. We have analyzed our findings and believe that an unprecedented kind of *mechamorphosis* is taking place, and its speed is accelerating."

Hodel's barrel-chested laughter stopped suddenly as his own techs snarled at their positions. "The clone is right," someone growled.

"See! See!" another cried.

A visual magnification was flashed on the main screen. In it, Haydon IV could be seen quickening its transformation. Apparently the modular alterations had been accomplished earlier—perhaps in flight—and this was the final rearrangement.

Hodel was a captain, not a scientist, but he had more than enough technical background to know that no physical materials, no conventional power source, could possibly achieve what he was witnessing. Haydon IV should have been annihilating itself with those upheavals.

It was not, however. It was taking on a new shape. Its astonishing division at Ranaath's Star was nothing compared with what it was doing now.

"Mechamorphosis, in truth," Hodel heard Prah say from the *Quartzstar*.

Hodel roared and slashed at the air with his claws. "How long before we can close with them?" Perhaps Haydon IV was as yet defenseless.

"Thirty-two minutes until they're in maximum range," a

bridge crewwoman called out. "But the speed of the mecha-morphosis is increasing. Estimated time to completion, twenty-eight minutes."

"We will attack and obliterate them before they can catch their breath and prepare for battle," Hodel howled. "Full speed ahead! All ships, watch your deployment and intervals and prepare to attack!"

Before them, Haydon IV grew. It contorted and re-formed, land features sliding, rising, falling—extending and reconfiguring in ways Local Group science would have pronounced impossible.

The substance of the planet was redistributed, prominences growing and lengthening, the center shrinking. Even the Karbarrans knew a cold fear, their snarls and rumblings more muted as they watched the artificial planet take on the form of a megacosm Robotech warrior.

Max was glad Lisa forcibly broke up the meeting when she did; in another few minutes, Nichols and Lang might have attempted some kind of voodoo dance to summon up the Regis, while Rem and Marlene performed a little lounge-act mind reading and Dana told a fortune or two.

Emotions had run high as theories and assertions clashed. It seemed that all the mystics knew pieces of what was happening but that nobody had the big picture. A lot of people at the meeting were still at the trying-to-believe-it stage.

Perhaps the major distraction, however, was the conviction many of the adults had that the *real* action was going on down in the child-care center. Aurora and the SDF-3 kids were being exactingly recorded, but Obstat and the others were not likely to learn much from the motionless, silently communing séance the rug rats were holding.

The real question, of course, was where the Regis was and how to get in touch with her. Lots of people had ideas, but none of them sounded very convincing to Max.

Vince, Lisa, and Rick were off to cope with whatever tangible problems they could find and handle—integrating working teams, transferring supplies to the *Peter Pan* just in case there was no choice but to run for it, resuming patrols of the planet.

Max, like Miriya, had left his seat after the adjournment

and gone to comfort Dana. Encountering Rem seemed to have knocked her feet out from under her; they were not used to seeing their gutsy older daughter so despondent.

Miriya had one arm around Dana, who was nearly her height, before Max got there and led her off into an empty adjoining compartment. Dana's head leaned on Miriya's shoulder. The look his wife shot him told Max that he ought to hang back for the time being.

Lisa and Rick had made some vague reference to Max's going to work coordinating the combined fighting elements of the joined ships, but Max did not feel much like talking war right at the moment.

He turned instead to find his way aft and see if Aurora's kiddie coven had broken up yet. He wandered along, thinking of her whispered message to him. Why was he, especially, to be on guard there in newspace—to be careful of his thoughts? Aurora either could not or would not clarify.

Distracted, he realized he was lost. It had been a long time since he had wandered the passageways of the SDF-3. There was no one around, but he got his bearings and began moving aft again. He went slowly, meditating.

Peace had seemed at hand when the Sentinels War ended. He and Miriya had played less and less of a role in the fighting, and he would have been perfectly happy to go on the inactive rolls for good.

Once, he'd been the terror of the Robotech battlefield, a dogfight wizard with a mother lode of the right stuff, an unparalleled feel for his mecha, and unrivaled combat instincts. Slight, pale, and bespectacled, he seldom attracted a second glance from a stranger, but he had no equal among humans, Zentraedi, Invid, or any other species.

Max passed into a big, empty observation area, its sweep of viewport showing a broad expanse of newspace and the appearing stars.

Funny how that Robotech *gift* of his had just gradually slipped into the background as being a husband and father became more and more central in his life. As if whatever had given him his matchless skills had been rechanneled.

He stopped, instincts telling him that he was being watched. With absolute certainty, he pivoted suddenly toward the viewport.

Something hung there in the night of the SDF-3's shadow, looking back at him. It was a shape blocking out the stars, the unreflective black of soot or that jersey dress Miriya had. He could not make out its shape, but it moved slowly like a marionette drifting in water. It was difficult to estimate, but he got the impression it was only about a hundred yards or so from the hull . . . and it was big.

Without taking his eyes from it, Max edged over to an intercom on the bulkhead and signaled the bridge. "This is Sterling—Max Sterling on Foxtrot Deck, compartment, uh, H-2108 starboard. I have a visual on possible bogey." Something about the indistinct shape made his stomach twist, and sweat had started at his forehead.

A brisk voice—Mr. Toler, Max thought it was—answered. "Our sensors show nothing, Commander."

"Then they're malfunctioning! Gimme some hull lights down here, *now*!"

High-candlepower external lights sprang to life out on the hull. The harsh illumination they threw forth splashed against a shape that made Max's mouth fall open.

It was not like any mecha he'd ever heard of, though he'd been pretty sure he knew them all. It incorporated features of Invid Inorganic, RDF Beta Battloid, and Robotech Master Bioroid. But the bulbous torso with its plastron cannon and the reverse-articulated legs immediately made him think of Zentraedi pods. And its single-lensed turret of a head sported long, gleaming saber-tooth fangs like those of a Hellcat.

It floated out there, looking straight at him with its yellow and red lens, while Max whispered a soft, almost admiring obscenity. Seconds ticked by while the two stared at each other.

He heard running feet and glanced over automatically to see Colonel Xien dash into the compartment with some staffers bringing up the rear—a mere flicker of the eyes. And yet, when Max looked back, the black mecha was gone.

"Commander Sterling, we have nothing on scopes or visual," the voice from the bridge said a bit primly, perhaps peeved at Max for implying that those on watch would let something sneak up on the ship. "Whatever it is, we don't see it."

Max stared at empty space for a few moments before keying the intercom to reply. "That figures. It wasn't here to see *you*, either."

It was a race against time that had the Elders frothing behind their respirator masks. The mechamorphosis of Haydon IV into a Robotech warrior was an astonishing achievement, violating laws of engineering and strengths of materials by means of higher powers Haydon reserved unto Himself.

But still the transformation was too slow to suit the Elders.

The rabble are too close! Nimuul protested, following developments via the planet's mental data dissemination nets. *Where are your weapons? Why do you not fire?*

Haydon was smaller than they had yet seen Him, appearing from the west like a moving crag. *I WEARY OF YOUR STUPIDITY.*

There was a multiplicity to the voice, as if more than one were speaking. The Elders became aware of other moving shapes. *BEHOLD AND LEARN.*

From east, north, and south came other embodiments of Haydon returning from unguessable missions. As the four merged, there were outpourings of radiance too intense to bear; when the Elders could look again, Haydon was a single figure, back to his original size.

Once more he flew off over the terrain of His synthetic world, which had in effect become a mecha, and the Elders' carpet lifted off to follow.

They were not far from the right arm's juncture to the body, but from their viewpoint it was more like a curve in the world, vanishing away, with another even greater bulge rising out of sight far beyond. They were too small to have any sense of the planet's new shape.

A yawning opening appeared in the surface of the planet, and Haydon entered in serene, floating fashion. The carpet trailed obediently after. Haydon IV reverberated to the shocks of the final reconfigurations. As it did, the first maximum-range salvos began to blossom around it.

The war machine waited in space as the flotilla of Local Group ships rushed to the attack.

PART IV
FINALE
AND
OVERTURE

CHAPTER
THIRTY-
ONE

It's been said that we're all three people: the one we see our-
selves as being, the one others see us as being, and the one we
really are.

The Regis seemed determined to explore all of those, and I
don't know which frightened me most.

Dr. Harold Penn,
The Brief but Timeless Voyage of the Peter Pan

BECAUSE DANTE AND GNEA HAD BEEN ACCOSTED
there by the Regis's strange luminous effects, it was decided
that the attempt to establish contact with her should be initiated on the planet, which some scholar in the SDF-3 crew
had dubbed Omphalos.

Most of the command people were all for it, since it was
seemingly the only course of action open to them. Rick and
Lisa were more hesitant, since the experts felt the only plau-
sible method of communicating with the vanished racial en-
tity/queen lay in Roy and the other children; everything that
had happened regarding newspace thus far indicated that it
was a domain with a special affinity for psi-phenomena. Certainly the Regis had not responded to any conventional attempts at communication.

Calculations showed that the breach draining the substance
of the universe into newspace was widening, though. There
was a growing faction among the theorists, lining up behind
Lang, who believed that real spacetime would be altogether
sucked into the adjunct province of newspace and find itself

under the dominion of the Regis. Thus, the children's lives were *already* horribly at risk, and the perils of contact with the Regis must be borne.

A lot of people in G2 and G3 wanted to make a landing in force to secure the area against any possible hostile action by the Regis—post Battlepods, hovertanks, Veritechs, and the rest in a layered defense. But cooler heads prevailed; mecha firepower probably would not amount to much against the entity that controlled newspace.

So, two shuttles flanked by one Alpha and one Beta descended as if on a diplomatic mission, slow and steady, followed by two pods and two suits of powered armor. Once down on Omphalos, the party formed up on the ground and moved out for the field where Angelo and Gnea had disappeared.

They could have dropped in for a landing directly in the field, of course, but it was felt that going in on foot would help re-create the circumstances of the first encounter and look much less belligerent. The Alpha was sent back aloft to patrol, and the ground party started walking.

Rick and Lisa led the way. Roy was farther back, with the children and most of the other parents. Scott Bernard was following close behind the Hunters. Marlene came after him, a part of the group at her own insistence and over his objections. The Hunters and the rest welcomed her presence; she was the closest thing the expedition had to an expert on the Regis.

The landing party was armed, but it did little to assuage Rick's nervousness. He did not really think guns would do much good against the dangers that menaced his ship, friends, and family.

Lisa cast a glance back to make sure the kids were all right and to see if the other parents were coping emotionally. All of them were under stress, but she was particularly worried about Max. If the Veritechs' top gun was starting to see things that weren't there, *anybody* could lose his grip.

In the last few hours others had begun falling prey to the insidious effects of the new continuum. Word had it that the Karbarrans' morose augury chants had brought them Wagnerian visions of doom. The Garudans' *hin* sendings had the lupine XTs fatalistic and despairing. Baldan had had ghostly encounters on the Crystal Highways of Omphalos and at length had been ejected by them.

Even the music of the Muses and the Cosmic Harp had taken on a doleful sound they seemed helpless to rise above.

The libidinous climate of the past few days had changed, and the only possible explanation was that something about the Regis had changed.

And what if Her Highness doesn't feel like granting us an audience? Rick was asking himself at the same moment. *Do we sacrifice a few oxen, blow on a ram's horn, or what?*

But as he pushed through the last screen of bush, he saw that there was reason to hope for an audience with the Regis, after all: The field had changed, even though nobody from the SDF-3 or the recon flights had seen it.

Where the swaying grasses had grown to midcalf height, there was a structure that brought a sinister grunt from Scott. "Invid hive. Huh. Looks like a miniature Reflex Point."

It did indeed, but it was far smaller than the sprawling stronghold/nerve center that had been the Regis's seat of power on Terra. It was a dome with the same organic look, the same glowings in orange and red and yellow, like a super-high-speed photograph of a thermonuclear explosion. Around it was the strange foam of bubblelike objects suggesting concentric waves coming in at the dome, as at Reflex Point; there were the same smaller peripheral nodes, much like the central structure, all of them interlinked by a network of conduits or accessways as brilliant as tubes of flowing lava.

"Maybe we should send in a recon team," Lisa said.

"I don't even see a way in. Scott?"

But before the Invid invasion veteran could answer, there was a commotion from farther back in the line. It was Drannin and the other Zentraedi children, followed by Roy and the humans, pushing to get through and head for the miniature hive.

"Roy, wait!" Lisa dodged around Payton, another Zentraedi giant-youngster, to try to stop her son. Just then, knocking small trees aside, Kazianna and a Zentraedi male caught up to head off their kids.

Roy did not push Lisa away, but he writhed in her grasp. "Mommy, please! She's waiting to talk to us. But we haveta hurry!"

Lang had left his place in line, too, with Louie Nichols and his cyber-whiz disciples in his wake. "I understand your reticence, Admiral, but the lad is right. Right now our chief jeopardy lies in delay.''

''But how do we get—'' Rick swallowed the question when he turned back to the mini-hive. There was a dark semicircular opening directly in front of them.

His lips became two thin lines, and he turned back to his little command. "Listen up! We're going in. Remember your orders, and I want all weapons on safety and either holstered or slung.''

The door was high enough even for Zentraedi. The party filed into the uncomfortably warm darkness under the dome, smelling again the strange aromas and alien odors—some pleasant, others not—of an Invid hive.

It was like being inside a cathedral of dark stained glass. Most of the space enclosed under the dome was occupied by a veined bronze sphere that shone dimly. There was room for even the tallest Zentraedi to stand erect. The contingent from the SDF-3 ranged themselves along the wall, waiting to see what would come next.

Rick felt sweat trickling down his uniform collar and soaking his shirt. He had faced Zentraedi and the Regent, but he had never felt the misgiving he felt there in the shrine of an entity that was close enough to a deity as to make no difference.

The children looked at one another with their lambent eyes, then stepped closer to the sphere, joining hands—the Zentraedi sitting in lotus position so that the humans could reach them. Aurora stood in the middle of their line, a nimbus of whirling scintillas welling up from her.

Without warning, a zigzag bolt of incandescence broke from somewhere overhead to smite the bronze globe, turning it into a ball of deep amber light. Shadows moved within it, and then they saw the face of the Regis, exalted and endowed with a terrible beauty, gazing back at them.

They heard her voice in their minds: *AT LAST, THROUGH YOUR EVOLVED CHILDREN, YOU HAVE TOUCHED THE PLANE UPON WHICH WE CAN COMMUNICATE. KNOW THEN THAT THE CUSP IS NEARING IN WHICH ALL THAT EXISTS WILL COME TOGETHER IN THIS, MY CREATION, MY NEWSPACE.*

Rick realized that he had been waiting for Aurora to speak; after all, the children were the ones in contact with the higher mental realms where the Regis moved. He saw his mistake: The children might have powers of communication and perception, but they lacked their elders' experience and training, their grasp of the situation and ability to deal with it. Despite the kids' astounding powers, the outcome of the crisis would still hinge on the adults' actions.

He was the leader of the ground unit, and it was his place to speak up, but before he could, Lang's voice broke the silence.

"Mother of the Invid race! Why have you brought us here? Why is the universe we know being drawn into this one? Haven't the Shapings been fulfilled?"

Rick saw that Lang was not addressing what was to him a critical point: getting the fold drives back and getting the SDF-3 and *Peter Pan* out of newspace. But before he could interject that matter, the Regis answered.

KNOW THEN THAT I WHO AM THE REGIS AND ALL OF THE INVID RACE IN ONE ENTITY BROUGHT YOUR VESSEL HERE IN MY TRANSUBSTANTIATION BY MY DOMINION OVER THE PROTOCULTURE. YOUR SDF-3 WAS SELECTED BECAUSE ITS ENGINES WERE BEST SUITED TO SUCH A CONTINUUM FOLD. YOU MADE THE FIRST TINY PUNCTURE THAT HAS BECOME A MIGHTY RIFT IN THE BARRIERS BETWEEN THE REAL UNIVERSE AND NEWSPACE. BUT MORE IMPORTANTLY YOU ARE HERE BECAUSE YOU NUMBER AMONG YOU SO MANY WHO LED THE WAR ON THE INVID AND WHO HAVE STRONG TIES TO THE PROTOCULTURE AND THE SHAPINGS—THE GREAT, INELUCTABLE CYCLE OF COSMIC EVENTS.

Looking about her, Lisa thought how true that was. Oh, a few like Exedore and Cabell were absent, but of the survivors of the Robotech Wars, most of the principals had been snatched in the dimensional fortress or drawn hither in *Peter Pan*.

And if the Regis could assert her will so thoroughly over events, what hope could mortals have of prevailing against her?

AS ONCE UPON EARTH I SOUGHT TO FIND, THROUGH EXPERIMENTS IN MY GENESIS PITS, THE IDEAL FORM THAT MY RACE WOULD ASSUME FOR ITS EXISTENCE ON THAT PLANET, SO I HAVE BROUGHT YOU HERE FOR MY STUDY. BY SIFTING THROUGH

YOUR PSYCHES AND WHAT SOME OF YOU CALL YOUR SOULS, I WILL DECIDE THE NEW MENTAL AND EMOTIONAL CLIMATE OF THIS CREATION OF MINE, THIS MALLEABLE DOMAIN, THIS NEWSPACE.

Lang seemed to have assumed the role of speaker, and he showed a pronounced vexation when Louie Nichols butted in.

"Hey, retro back a second! You mated with the Protoculture, you went through your transcendence. What more d' you want?"

TRANSUBSTANTIATION IS A MOCKERY, A PRISON! I WAS DRIVEN TO SEEK IT BY YOU HUMANS! THE SHAPINGS ARE A HOLLOW JOKE, A CELL WITH NO EXIT.

The Karbarrans were growling as if they might utter some defiant roar, and so Rick hastened to say, "But what *do* you want?"

A harsh beam of light sprang from some unseen source to pin Rem squarely. It was not a weapon, and yet he cried out, throwing an arm across his face.

I WISH ONLY A RETURN TO THAT STATE MY INVID AND I ENJOYED WHEN ZOR CAME LIKE A THIEF IN THE NIGHT. I WISH OPTERA TO BE AS IT WAS AGAIN AND FOR THE INVID TO REVERT TO THE FORM WE KNEW THEN.

"Then why don't you *do* it?" Louie shouted. "You have total control over newspace."

BUT NOT CONTROL OF THE SHAPINGS! AND BECAUSE THE INVID LEFT THEIR FORMER STATE BEHIND TO WAGE WAR AND STRIVE AGAINST THE SHAPINGS, CLOSING CERTAIN CONFIGURATIONS BEHIND THEM, A REVERSION TO OUR ORIGINAL STATE IS THE ONE THING I CANNOT DO, EVEN HERE.

NEITHER DO I WISH TO LIVE IN THE CHAOTIC NOT-LAWS THAT ARE THE NATURAL STATE OF NEWSPACE. THEREFORE, I WILL PERMIT THE REAL UNIVERSE TO BLEED INTO THIS SPACETIME, AND WHEN ALL MY RAW MATERIALS ARE AT HAND, I SHALL REFASHION ALL THE COSMOS IN THE IMAGE I DEEM FIT.

"No!" With help from Minmei, Rem was struggling to rise. "It's not their fault! You can't banish away their entire existence!"

AND WAS IT MY FAULT WHEN THE FIRST OF YOUR BLOOD, ZOR, CAME LIKE A POISONOUS VIPER TO OPTERA? WAS IT MY FAULT THAT YOUR ROBOTECH MASTERS DECREED THE RAZING OF OPTERA? THE UNIVERSE CARES NOTHING FOR JUSTICE . . . NOR DO THE SHAPINGS.

It was Learna, mate to Kami and at one with the *hin*, who spoke then. She stood erect, and even though she was of smaller stature than anyone else there but the children, her foxlike appearance gave her a certain nobility that struck the others with an undeniable poignancy.

"Then why spare us? Why not obliterate us and make a clean beginning?"

No one else had been brave enough to call out the question. The Regis hesitated long seconds before replying.

BECAUSE I NEED TO STUDY YOU. I MUST DECIDE WHETHER THERE SHALL BE IN THIS NEWSPACE THE ONLY THING YOU MORTAL RACES HAVE DEVELOPED THAT IS OF ANY SIGNIFICANCE: LOVE.

"In spite of what it did to her," Lisa heard Rick murmur; she had been thinking the same thing.

Louie Nichols's voice cracked. " 'Only'?" he cried. "What about intelligence?"

A MERE COPING MECHANISM. AN INEVITABLE OUTGROWTH OF EVOLUTION.

"Art, literature," Rick heard Dr. Penn say.

CONCEITS, DEVISED TO FILL THE WAIT BETWEEN SUCCESSIVE FEEDINGS AND SLEEPS.

"Music—" Bowie started to protest, but the word was drowned out.

ENOUGH! YOU ARE NOT HERE TO IMPORTUNE ME!

"Yeah, here it comes," Dana heard Louie Nichols mutter. Louder, he added, "Why'd you have the kids bring us here?"

MY EXPANDED SENSES INFORM ME THAT THE REAWAKENED HAYDON, IN COLLABORATION WITH THE ROBOTECH ELDERS, EVEN NOW LAUNCHES AN ATTACK ON TIROL IN AN EFFORT TO RECOVER THE FACSIMILE PROTOCULTURE MATRIX. SHOULD HAYDON WIN, HE WILL ENTER NEWSPACE BY MEANS OF THE SHIPS BUILT BY HIS ARTIFICIAL PLANET AND HIS ARTIFICIAL RACE.

WITH THE POWER OF THE MATRIX AT HIS DISPOSAL, HE MAY BE IMPOSSIBLE TO STOP. HE WOULD CONTROL THIS PLACE THEN, AND HAYDON WILL HAVE LITTLE TOLERANCE FOR THE CONVENTIONAL SPACETIME BODIES, LAWS, AND ENTITIES THAT HE HAS BEEN TRYING SO LONG TO PUT BEHIND HIM.

"Why are you telling us this?" Lisa demanded.

TO PREPARE YOU FOR WHAT IS TO COME. IF AND WHEN I MUST COME TO GRIPS WITH HAYDON, IT WILL BE A BATTLE OF MENTAL FORCE AND PSI-ENERGIES— OF IMAGES AND POSSIBILITIES. SINCE I HAVE BEEN MONITORING YOUR PSYCHES, THE THINGS I HAVE SEEN WITHIN YOU WILL BE IMPORTANT WEAPONS. YOU ARE ABOUT TO BE CAUGHT UP IN AN APOCALYPSE.

"No!" That was Minmei, tears in her voice, she and Rem supporting each other and looking as if they were at the end of their strength.

"You can't! We—we have innocent children with us. At least spare them!"

WAR SPARES NO ONE; YOU KNOW THAT AS WELL AS I.

There were roars from the Karbarrans, baying from the Garudans, Gnea's angry Valkyrie war cry, and more, all mixed in a general howl of outrage. The Regis took no notice, however.

Her voice thundered in their heads. *PREPARE YOURSELVES.*

Within the blazing sphere, her countenance faded out, replaced by brighter and brighter glory. Once more they had to shield their eyes.

. . . RESIGN YOURSELVES.

When they opened their eyes again, the hive was gone and they were standing in a field of waving grass under the calm sky of Omphalos.

CHAPTER
THIRTY-
TWO

You humans should cavil less about our tempers. I have observed your own behavior. With better fangs and claws, you might go far.

Lron, as quoted in Noki Rammas's *Karbarra*

THE LOCAL GROUP CAPTAINS, FOLLOWING HODEL'S EXample, had spoken boldly and resolutely in exhorting their crews. When they initiated their attack on the hulking worldlet-size Robotech warrior, though, it was with considerable caution.

The first strike brought improvised strategic missiles to bear: subluminal spacecraft packed with thermonuclear explosives set to run by remote control. Drones and robot probes went in ahead of them, firing with hastily installed weapons, to draw fire and test the megacosm-mecha's defenses.

The remotes' visual pickups gave their controllers a strange view of a reconfigured Haydon IV, which looked less and less like a humanoid figure as the kamikaze sortie closed on it. Hodel found himself expecting the action to start once the remotes flew in between the extended arms; physically impossible as it was for structures that size to move with any speed, he could not help feeling that one of them would lash out at any moment to swipe the jury-rigged ships out of existence.

That did not happen, though, and Hodel dismissed the notion as the natural expectation of the Karbarrans, whose bear-ish fighting style relied so much on their awesomely powerful arms. He bent closer to peer over a remote operator's shoulder and follow the attack.

That particular ship was a Tirolian courier craft, small but very fast and agile. It dove in at Haydon IV as the planet's plasma guns started firing at extreme range. As the intel staffs had projected, there was no repeat of the Awareness's taking over of automated systemry. Because of damage suffered in Louie Nichols's cyber-burn or the battle near Ranaath's Star, or perhaps even as a result of this final mechamorphosis, Haydon IV's guiding AI seemed no longer capable of that sort of hostile action.

The courier was preceded by probes that had been mounted with additional booster thrusters for the suicide mission. The long-range flaring of the plasma batteries hosed annihilation discs across the night of space, their accuracy not very impressive at that range.

The probes and drones bore in, their onboard computers and sensors augmenting the guidance from their shipboard operators.

"Clumsy," Hodel said in a low guttural voice, meaning Haydon IV's defensive fire. "Slow."

He looked over to Ntor. "It's been weakened. We've got them now."

She growled loyally. "Aye, sir. But—" Her sense of duty made her add, "I still detect subsurface activity. There appear to be immense servos, energized and functional."

"Do they have mechamorphosis capability?"

Ntor wuffed to herself, studying her instruments. "Negative, from what I can see."

Hodel flipped a fearsome paw. "Then servos will do them no good. I'm more concerned about those sphere ships; keep a careful watch."

But the remotes plunged down toward the immense torso of Haydon IV without meeting opposing vessels. "They couldn't get 'em powered up," Hodel concluded.

Prah, Spherisian captain of the *Quartzstar*, came up on the command net. "Captain, may I suggest that we preserve some of our lead element drones for recon."

"Agreed," Hodel said. He had not really expected the

decoys to survive the approach, but things were going better than he had hoped.

A half score of the decoys, most of them bulkier mining probes, had been lost to the close-in plasma guns. As many more swooped in to take up strafing attacks on the defensive batteries in twisting, dodging flak-supression runs.

The artifact planet's guns now divided between the attacking drones and the oncoming remote-controlled vessels, along with the additional drones escorting them. The courier ship began its dive into the guns' close range. The target zone was crisscrossed by geysers of annihilation discs, one right on top of the next, at such a high rate of fire that they were practically touching.

The probes' firepower was not sufficient to penetrate the armor of the massive gun turrets, but their attacks helped spoil the plasma cannons' aim and did do at least some damage to the targeting sensors. Nevertheless, one by one the drones and probes were potted out of the air by the sheer volume of firepower down near the planet's surface.

But by then the courier was juking its way down through the AA fire, homing in on a large fire-control complex in the general vicinity of the megacosm-mecha's solar plexus.

On the bridge, Ntor reported, "Sir, we're detecting a power influx to those servos again."

Hodel tore himself away from the main action long enough to snap, "Any movement?"

"Not yet, sir."

"Keep me informed."

Then he was back watching the main screen as the courier swooped like a hawk at Haydon IV. There was a moment of utter disappointment as a glancing hit by a disc damaged one of the steering thrusters, but the operator had sufficient auxiliaries to compensate.

Spread out back in the courier's wake, more kamikazes took up their approaches.

Ntor spoke up again. "Sir? Servos activated. The arm booms are moving."

Hodel checked the readouts. The arms were moving so slowly that they presented no credible threat. Still, moving like that—they reminded him of something, some Robotech legend . . .

"Missile one: thirty seconds to impact," someone remarked, and Hodel broke off his musings.

"Make sure surviving drones are clear of ground zero," Hodel ordered. "Get—*uurrrr!*—numbers five, seven, eight, and ten on recon sweeps of the far side."

"Fifteen seconds."

The courier craft had slipped down under the AA guns' lowermost angle of fire, too low for most defenses to target. Streaming smoke and flame, it wobbled and rattled across the last miles, the fire-control complex looming up like a Robotech scarp.

"What was that?" Difficult to make out either on visuals or, thanks to the alchemist's mix of energies down below, by sensor, *something* seemed to go flashing across the corpusterrain of Haydon IV. Like a skimming blue shadow, it flickered straight for the target area.

The courier's visual pickup cut out at impact, of course, but other instruments showed the abrupt outwelling of the explosion: the nearly magical appearance of a superfireball that put many watching it in mind of the big bang.

"Damage report!" Hodel was grunting excitedly even while the fireball expanded. If there was anything left of the complex, he would target a second mop-up missile ship at it; if not, he would accelerate the other kamikazes to their assigned targets. The proof that the attack weapons could strike home on Haydon IV had him exulting.

But then came Prah's voice from *Quartzstar*. "Attention, *Tracialle*! Our instruments show failure to impact. Something shielded the target area from the blast."

"Impossible!" Hodel bellowed so loudly that even his fellow Karbarrans winced.

Ntor spoke up. "Negative, sir. Look." She had split the main screen. Next to the real-time image of the expanding nuke strike, she was projecting the flicker that had raced across the surface of the megacosm-mecha.

It was a large blue circle, like the image of a spotlight on the surface of Haydon IV. It streaked straight for the impact point, a dot of light some hundred miles across and yet small in comparison to the gargantuan torso.

The *Tracialle*'s techs were confirming what *Quartzstar*'s had found: The nuke hit had been deflected. "And see, two more of those strange energy loci,'' Ntor added. Hodel yowled angrily at the three blue circles, drifting here and there across the modules of the reconfigured planet like buzzing insects.

Without warning, Exedore appeared on the main screen. ''Captain Hodel, I have seen this phenomenon before. It's a pinpoint barrier system, though how Haydon learned of it, I don't know. There's no time to explain; you *must* withdraw your fleet.''

Hodel's paw smashed his command chair's arm. ''There are only three of those miserable little dots. We'll hit them with everything we have, all at once—and wipe them out!''

Waysee, commanding the two-ship Garudan contingent, came up on the net. ''There's no guarantee we'll be able to concentrate our strike precisely enough.''

Hodel shot back, ''There is if you all listen to orders! Now, link your operators to my controllers, who will coordinate all strikes. We'll soften them up with the suicide ships, then blow them away!''

''More readings from the forearm booms,'' Ntor said to him.

Hodel whirled. ''Any sign of offensive capability?''

''No, Captain, just power buildup.''

Hodel barked a laugh. ''Much good it will do them when ten ships punch in at once. Controllers! Prepare for a unified strike operation—simultaneous hits all across that empty suit of tin out there.''

As the fleet re-formed and moved in again, all decoys and kamikaze ships leaping ahead for the coordinated attack, Exedore checked and collated data back in the Royal Hall.

''I don't know how they did it, Cabell. Perhaps the Haydonites learned something when they were holding us captive, or perhaps it's something uncovered back when the Regent had the Sentinels captive on Haydon IV.''

''It may be much simpler, something implicit in Robotechnology that Haydon discovered just as the Micronians did.''

Exedore shrugged helplessly. ''Just so. In any case it proves that we don't know what we're up against. We *must* get Hodel and the others to break off the attack.''

"Retreat: something Karbarrans have never been good at," Cabell observed.

At least Hodel had the caution to stay well back while launching his attack wave.

Fire from the plasma batteries was less effective now that the drones were down and strafing the planet's surface; those that had been dispatched to scout the far side were brought back and hurled into the assault. As Hodel had observed, the racing pinpoint barrier shield circles could not be everywhere at once.

But just as it had served SDF-1 so well decades before, the defense cut into the attackers' advantage dramatically. Nevertheless, the decoy craft wreaked havoc all over the near side of Haydon IV.

Of the ten nuke-primed ships sent ahead to smash resistance, two were destroyed by fire while still far above the artificial world, and another two on approach, even though by then the decoys had put many gun emplacements out of action.

Hodel, howling in battle lust, ignored Exedore's attempts to reach him by commo. Ntor watched the buildup of the energy in the booms but dared not bring them up again.

The surviving ships streaked down to strike as planned, dispersed across Haydon IV. Three were met by pinpoint barriers, but the other three struck in the chest, neck, and lower abdomen of the Robotech figure that was the artifact world. This time the planet shook from superbombs so massive that even a continent of armor was not proof against them.

Haydon IV was ripped open in three places, energy and vaporized systemry fountaining from it. Secondary explosions rattled the megacosm-figure and vented themselves in the vicinity of the right shoulder, blasting it open. The streams of annihilation discs died away.

The Karbarrans on the *Tracialle*'s bridge, growling their war chants, led the way in to the attack. The rest of the Local Group ships raced after, some of the other races even taking up the Karbarrans' chant.

Haydon IV loomed near, and the fleet primed its weapons for a last decisive assault. At last Exedore managed to override the fleet's communications and put his image on their screens.

"Reverse course, you fools! Retreat! *The booms—the booms are weapons too!*"

The precise nature of the threat had worked at his mind even as it eluded him, until he chanced to glance over at a schematic in the communications center there in the Royal Hall. On it, the figure of Haydon IV was represented as a sort of crude outline, and he saw things for what they were.

Instead of the articulated Robotech waldos and forearms, the planet's limbs might have been clubs, or the arms of a horseshoe magnet, or a tuning fork . . .

Or the bows of the SDF-1.

"Get out, get out before it's too late!" Exedore screamed, but few were listening.

One was Prah in the *Quartzstar*. "Attention, Hodel! Urgently advise you break off attack until considering Exedore's advice. Energy buildup along forearm booms has intensified."

Hodel wasn't having any, and neither was anybody else aboard the *Tracialle*. Around the booms, bubbles of snapping, coruscating energy were forming and bursting in brilliant effervescence, but that did not deter the rest of the fleet for a moment. Prah, however, began to deviate from course, shearing away from the attack run and demanding that Hodel and the rest do the same, heeding Exedore, before it was too late. The *Valivarre* emulated her, largely because of the Tirolian clones' respect for Exedore and Cabell. The bulky mining vessel fell in behind the glittering, glassy bauble that was *Quartzstar* even as Hobel growled his contempt for them and returned to his assault.

Haydon IV was being shaken by massive internal quakes and eruptions. The pinpoint loci were gone. The fleet's sensors marked a hundred great exposed, defenseless targets and too many smaller ones to count. In its eagerness, the *Tracialle* outran the rest of the Local Group ships, hot to draw blood.

Tongues of orange starflame were slithering and looping around the booms and writhing up and down them, seemingly eager to be set free. Hodel thought the booms not worth bothering about but fired a bow sweep of missiles at them as he neared, just to be sure.

Flashing along at attack speed, the Karbarran was nearly past the booms when his missiles struck, and doomsday fell.

All at once the energies in the booms surged, unleashed, just as the SDF-1's bows had configured into a main gun and fired on her launch day so many years ago. Hodel's missiles were vaporized.

A cloud of swirling energy appeared between the booms, and a raving torrent of utter destruction shot out from it. The superbolt, miles in diameter, lanced out and washed across the oncoming Local Group ships; where it had played, nothing was left behind but elementary particles.

Valivarre and *Quartzstar*, both damaged by the mere peripheral wash of the volley, braced for another. But none came. Indeed, the booms were blackened and leaking power fluxes. The volley had damaged Haydon IV as well as wiping out most of the flotilla.

"We—we'll pull back and wait," Prah said in a subdued voice; the clones on the converted Zentraedi ore ship concurred.

The *Tracialle*, damaged by the abrupt appearance of the power storm between the booms behind it, somehow escaped annihilation by a split second. Shuddering and breached, its commo systems fried and others threatening to fail, it dived for the planet.

"I don't think any of the others made it, sir," Ntor reported. "At least, I have no visuals on them. Most other sensors were knocked out."

"Then it's up to us," Hodel said calmly. "Aim for the heart."

They all saw what he meant, an exposed control nexus as big as a floodplain on the mecha figure's upper right chest. What little data they had indicated that it was a vulnerable point.

They also knew that there was no going back, even if the booms were inoperative. The *Tracialle*'s engines were going fast—they would overload in moments. Like most of the others, Hodel and Ntor felt that they had already witnessed this death once, in their augury chants.

The few cannonades of discs the plasma guns could manage were a pale imitation of their former selves, hopelessly low-power and inaccurate. The far greater danger was that the Sekiton-fueled ship would shake apart, but somehow it held together.

By some fluke of technology or caprice of the Shapings, the Karbarrans' commo began functioning again just at the end, and the survivors heard their roars as the *Tracialle*'s crew went to sink their fangs into their enemy's heart.

Down and down their ship plummeted, into the breast of Haydon IV like an avenging comet. The detonations it set off sent the artifact worldlet into lethal convulsions.

Quartzstar and *Valivarre*, carrying out repairs to restore life support and some measure of maneuvering power, were lit by the distant nova of Haydon IV's death blow. Prah watched sadly and was about to turn away, when someone said, "I'm scanning spacecraft—many of them!"

Prah rapped, "Origin?"

"They are sphere ships; I believe they emerged from the far side, just before the end."

For a moment Prah thought that it was to be the end of her vessel, after all. But the swarm of sphere ships, a hundred and more, formed up and set off without paying *Quartzstar* or *Valivarre* any heed.

Their course pointed straight for Tirol.

CHAPTER
THIRTY-
THREE

This cadet-graduate will make either a passable officer or a very troublesome convict.

Final evaluation from the file of
Southern Cross Lieutenant Dana Sterling

THERE WAS NOTHING FOR THE GROUND PARTY TO DO BUT return to the landing zone; the Regis ignored their demands that she come back, listen to reason, answer their questions, show some mercy.

The quietest among them were the children, who seemed distracted and uncommunicative. Scott noticed that Marlene was very much like them. He realized he had been holding his breath, dreading the moment when arcane forces would suck her soul and body into the oneness of the Invid race that was the Regis.

But apparently the trauma she had undergone had insulated her from that for good. She really was *herself*. He was grateful for that but furious at the trick of fate that had put them back together at last only to schedule Armageddon a few days or hours away.

Still, when he reached tentatively for her hand and she smiled bittersweetly, taking his hand fondly, there was a lightness to his soul that had not been there since the death of Marlene Rush on a day long gone.

There wasn't much vigilance to their withdrawal in spite of

Rick and Lisa's dispirited promptings. What good to keep your guard up when all of newspace might well attack at any moment?

Rick thought twice before approaching Louie Nichols; the Regis might be listening in. But then, the same could be said about the deepest security vault on the SDF-3.

"Louie? What about the *Peter Pan*? Can we make a run for it if we have to?"

Louie worked his shoulders, adjusted his goggles, and went through some more of his repertoire as they walked along. "I doubt it. It turns out that the sphere ships aren't exactly like I thought they were. Not really built with a return trip in mind.

"Think of 'em as bobsleds, created for a single voyage along a particular flow of force—down a snowy hill, if you see what I mean. The *Peter P.* might be forced up the hill, but I wouldn't bet on it."

He looked so downcast that Rick figured Louie was regretting that he had ever gotten involved in the rescue attempt. He patted one skinny shoulder. "I don't know if I ever said thanks, Louie. I'm grateful for your being here to help, grateful as an officer and grateful as a man with a family in danger."

That seemed to take Louie by surprise, but he mumbled some acknowledgment. Then he picked up his pace, head bent in thought.

Max Sterling had to restrain himself from grabbing Aurora and clasping her to him, shielding her with his body. That way, the Black Knight mecha—or whatever it was that his combat skills had brought into existence in newspace—would have to come through him to get her. But she was so fragile, so ethereal that he didn't want to frighten her. And so he hung near her like a shadow, peering and glaring in all directions, sweat running down his face.

He was a fighter jock, a mecha warrior; his talents lay elsewhere, and he always felt insufficient to cope with the expanded powers and perceptions of his youngest. And now she had sensed some terrible peril, become its focus, and there was little, perhaps nothing, he could do to help.

Nothing but protect my daughter with my life.

At least one person in the group had kept her training in mind and was maintaining a high level of alertness as she went, though. Dana was carrying a Wolverine rifle at the ready, more than willing to open up if a target presented itself, *wishing* for one, if the truth be known.

She had fallen far back to walk rear guard, relieving Lron. The sight of Minmei and Rem leaning on each other had abraded her nerve endings and left her in an empty, murderous mood. Even in the worst of those days after her parents had left on the SDF-3—times when she had found herself in some agency-sponsored home or care institution—she hadn't felt quite so resentful and drained.

That was because she hadn't met Zor Prime yet, no doubt. And once in a while she got a visit from a friend who loved her unconditionally.

She heard the chirping yip faintly. The person ahead of her—Dr. Penn, his mind apparently a million parsecs away—did not seem to notice it. But Dana recognized it at once.

"*Polly!*" She said it softly, not wanting the others to come barging back to her. The Pollinator was *her* pet, *her* lifelong friend.

Only, how had Polly gotten there? He had disappeared—*let's see*—back on Tirol, just before she'd lifted for Haydon IV. Well, if walls and doors were no barrier to him or his kin, why should space be?

Manifestly, it wasn't, because there he sat, like an animated mophead, thirty feet back the way she had just come. His head was tilted to one side, and he gazed at her bemusedly, as if *she* were the one who'd disappeared without warning and *he* was the aggrieved party.

SOP said that she should signal for a halt and request permission and backup before fetching him, but by that time Polly might take it into that cute knob-horned head of his to vanish again. Dana glanced to make sure Harry Penn hadn't noticed—he was still going his way deep in thought—and turned back to make the pickup on the Pollinator.

"Don't give me that innocent look, you little deserter!" She knelt by him, shifting her rifle so that she had a free hand to scoop him up. "Maybe I oughta tie a bell to your collar. Or better yet, get a spacefold *leash*—he-eeyy!"

Wait a minute! Polly had somehow gotten himself not just across space but into *newspace*. That must mean there was some way back *out*!

"Oh, baby! Wait'll Louie and Lang hear this—umph! You been puttin' on weight, or what?"

The Pollinator dragged at her arm, nearly pulling her to her knees, the sheer mass of him unbelievable. "What's wrong—*holy f-fff*—"

Polly, back on his little muffin feet, was no longer the adorable teleporting pet she loved. His feet sprouted black claws, and his sheepdog face took on an evil leer. What really sent shivers down her spine, though, was that he was *growing* like an inflating life raft, only faster.

Dana gave a yell and stumbled back, bringing her rifle up, wondering if the Pollinator had fallen prey to some weird newspace rabies. Her finger was on the trigger, but she hesitated; this was one of her few true friends, after all, and friends meant everything to her.

Polly's hide showed through the molting white pelt as the creature grew: black, smooth, and hard-looking. Polly heightened and broadened, bigger than Dana already, rearing back on two lengthening hind legs.

Dana had hesitated to give the alarm, fearing that someone would shoot her dog, but that ceased to matter. The Pollinator let out an eerie inorganic sound, like a processed challenge roar.

"Polly, stop! Stay back!" She had the Wolverine up, centered, backing away herself. The thing in front of her took a step toward her, though, and when its massive black foot touched down, there was a distinct metallic sound.

It leaned toward her, and from its sheepdog face there appeared a single red-yellow lens.

Dana howled fiercely for a universe that would turn a dear pet and friend into a deadly foe. She brought the Wolverine up and fired a sustained burst at the thing that had been the Pollinator.

Farther up the line, everybody froze. Harry Penn blinked, coming out of his distraction, getting his bearings. "It's Dana!" he yelled to those ahead of him, and turned back, drawing his Badger.

Max, farther toward the front of the column, caught the news as it was passed along. People were yelling conflicting questions, answers, and orders.

Max moaned aloud. "Dana!" He pressed Aurora into Miriya's arms. "Hang on to her!" Rick and Lisa had come hurrying back down the column, berating people to set up security and guard against a surprise attack from another quarter. Lisa was calling in air cover; Rick was trying to find out what was going on at the rear.

People formed up to defend the children, Kazianna towering among them and unlimbering her oversized weapons. Max shoved his wife and daughter toward them. "Vince! Don't let anything happen to them!"

Then he was off to the rear, leaving Louie and his cyberteam where they had set up rifle positions, dodging Scott Bernard, who had Marlene clasped to him protectively.

Max broke through the final screen of foliage to see something immense and black standing with its back to him, the sun of Omphalos doing little to relieve its intense darkness.

Those who had already gotten to the scene—Harry Penn, Bowie, Lron, and a few others—wavered, holding their fire, not sure what was going on. The black mecha had bent to pick something up. It turned toward them, straightening to its full height, with Dana in its armored fist.

Lron raised the squad laser weapon that he carried like a rifle and would have fired into the black mecha's leg in hopes of bringing it down; Max knocked the laser's thick barrel down. "Hold your fire, all of you!"

The thing clutching Dana raised its free hand, pointing at Max. She was struggling determinedly but weakly to break out of its grip; the effort was hopeless, and she did not seem to have the breath to yell to those below. Huge, humped, and misshapen as a giant troll, the black mecha leaned toward Max as if about to speak.

But before it could, thrusters shook the ground and one of the escort Veritechs arrived, a Beta in Guardian mode. It landed like an eagle ready to do battle, its balled armor fists cocked.

Its pilot couldn't open up, though, since Dana was in the line of fire. The pilot began to shift his VT through mechamorphosis, going to Battloid, but before he could, the black mecha leapt at him and with one swing of its fearsome fist smashed the VT down.

The Guardian/Battloid crashed to the ground, broken and

smoking. Even as people raced toward it to rescue the pilot, the black mecha hit its foot thrusters and shot away into the sky, still clasping Dana.

In the middle of the confusion another escort VT, an Alpha, appeared, called back from its CAP flight, requesting instructions. As boss of the SDF-3's fighter command, Max got on the net.

"Get down here right now."

"But Commander Sterling, shouldn't I—"

"I said land!"

With a dozen different matters vying for his attention—guarding against further attack, counting heads to see if anyone else had been taken, checking whether the Beta pilot was still alive, raising the dimensional fortress for reinforcements and to arrange a safe pullback—Rick didn't realize what Max was doing until it was too late.

Max was gone, the second-generation Alpha shrieking away in Fighter mode, going supersonic in its ballistic climb, its sonic booms shaking the ground of Omphalos. The VT's pilot was standing there bareheaded—Max having appropriated his thinking cap helmet—staring after his departing craft.

He saw Rick. "Sir, he didn't even stop to call for reinforcements."

"I know; it's being done."

Of course, it would be precious minutes before more VTs could get there from the low-orbiting SDF-3. The fighter jock nodded. "No way was he gonna wait, sir."

Rick, watching the spot where Max had disappeared in the distance, agreed. "No, the gauntlet's been thrown, Lieutenant."

The Alpha was one of the best in the SDF-3 inventory, a souped-up new armored Alpha version of a second-generation VT—that was why Max had assigned it to fly security for the ground party—but it was all he could do to keep the Black Knight in view.

"Black Knight" was the way he had come to think of his antagonist. Supposedly, that made him the White Knight, but he felt a poor excuse for one.

And a despicable failure as a father.

He had worried about Miriya from the first, always apprehensive because she had gone through the sizing chamber, had been subjected to so many dangers, had nearly died in battle and childbirth alike—he himself had nearly killed her! And for Aurora, otherworldly entity from the very start, with her mind powers and unnatural maturation rate, Max had had constant concern.

But Dana, Dana . . . what malign brilliance for the being that ruled newspace to test him this way! He had left Dana behind on Earth against his own better judgment when the SDF-3 set forth. No one but Miriya—except perhaps Aurora—knew how bitterly he'd condemned himself when he'd heard about the suffering and hardship she had had to bear.

Never knowing a true home, growing up in war, her heart wounded terribly by Zor Prime and her very essence nearly raped by the madman Zand—Max could barely bring himself to think of those things, for when he did, he wished he had never been born.

His love of his family and the sense of calm Miriya and Aurora gave him were the things that had made Earth's greatest Robotech fighter gradually put aside combat over the years. So of course, what better way to draw him back into war in all earnest than this? And again it was Dana, poor Dana, suffering because of Max.

What pitiless genius! The Regis would have her fight.

Max realized he'd been rasping an endless string of soft, monotonic obscenities and stopped. He monitored the fighter ops and tac nets only to discover that none of the other VTs could get a fix on the Black Knight. Nor could the SDF-3, even though the bandit was making a paint as big as a house on *his* scopes.

He was not surprised.

With his burners wide open, he gained slowly on the grotesque mecha. It was not going at multimach—which it certainly seemed capable of doing—and it was staying at low altitude. He prayed that that meant Dana was still unharmed.

The Black Knight went all the way down to the deck, and Max lost it in terrain obstructions and ground scatter. He brought up a detailed topo display from the SDF-3's orbital mapping memory but couldn't guess what the kidnapper's next move would be.

He was so intent on it that he almost died; the night-dark

mecha came howling out of a mountain rift, firing a spread of missiles at him from the bulbous pods under its strangely articulated arms.

Max reacted instantly, plying the Hotas but, more important, imaging through his thinking cap. The uncanny instincts and nearly instantaneous reflexes that had made him a living legend were as sharp, as apt, as ever. The Alpha rolled vertical, two missiles boiling by just beneath his overturned canopy, then rolled again into a power dive, narrowly avoiding another spike-snouted killer.

Max banked, nearly tearing the VT's wings off, as the enemy came charging straight for him. The fist that had held Dana was enclosed now, a smooth armored globe; there was no way to tell whether she was alive or dead in there.

The Veritech dodged the Black Knight, then Max went ballistic and poured on full emergency military power as his antagonist launched another spread at him. He twisted and jinked, cutting in his jamming and countermeasures gear as missiles seared by and left their fiery corkscrews all around him.

Swathed in their trails, he mechamorphosed on the fly, went to Battloid, turning and coming to bay with his rifle/cannon in his mecha's alloy fist as the enemy came howling up after him.

Max was about to open up with the heavy pulsed laser battery but stopped himself at the sight of the globed fist. The famed top ace reflexes failed him, and he froze, unable to use his weapons.

The Black Knight opened up with a mecha hand weapon of its own, an affair shaped like a dory, from which purple lightning broke. Max feinted, jetted the other way, and nearly eluded the shot. But a snapping tongue of discharge caught the Battloid's left leg, blasting a rent in the armor there.

But in the interim, the distance between the two had closed. Max gathered himself and kicked in all thrusters, pouncing on the enemy rather than avoiding it. The Black Knight caught him with terrifying strength.

The two mecha fell through the sky, locked together in mortal combat.

THIRTY-
FOUR

*And so these equations expose a long-hidden truth: We now
know the nature of the heretofore unimaginable energies that
existed in the first, irreducible instant after the creation of the
universe. That the last vestige of them is to be found in the
distilled essence of a Flower is something to ponder, were there
time.*

But there is none.

From Exedore's notes, written in the Royal Hall
during the approach of Haydon IV

BY THE TIME CABELL RETURNED TO THE OBSERVA-
tion/command post high atop the Royal Hall pyramid, the
drives of the departing evac ships were mere sparks—there
were a dozen or so of them, containing a few thousand clones,
human holdouts, a handful of XTs, and a pet or two.

Exedore noted the smudges and stains on the old savant's
robes. "There was violence."

Cabell nodded wearily. "I did what I could, but yes. Less,
though, than I'd feared, given the fact that there was only
room for a relative few to escape. All dread the sphere ships'
coming."

Exedore grunted. *Valivarre* lay dead in space undergoing
repairs; the ore ship might have lifted the entire populace of
Tiresia to safety. But then, there had been no time to organize
a large-scale evacuation; those who had escaped on the few
ships at the spaceport were essentially those who had been

there or nearby when the disastrous battle demolished the Local Group fleet.

"At least the wait will not be long," he added. The flock of a hundred-odd ominous metallic bubbles was even then entering the upper atmosphere. "The rest will go underground to shelters, I suppose, or perhaps break into the bistros for a final toast to life."

"That's more than the Haydonites got, or the Local Group fleet crews, either," Cabell observed. There was no sign of Haydonite life aboard the sphere ships, and it was presumed that the artificial race had perished when Haydon IV had been destroyed. Neither was there any sign of the Awareness's survival, and that was of some comfort to the two savants; the Awareness had been perhaps Haydon's greatest weapon.

"Come," Cabell bade. "We've not much time."

Not having caught his breath, he was huffing again within a few steps. Exedore caught up and lent a supporting arm; he was physically younger, though he was the older of the two.

They went to the pinnacle of the Royal Hall, which they'd polarized to transparency, so that it seemed open to the sky. In it was the facsimile Protoculture matrix.

They had both seen the original and now considered this Second Generation manifestation. Lang had once observed how it resembled an old-time representation of an atom: a complex interlinking of ring orbits some two hundred feet across, suspended in midair by its own internal forces.

However, where the original matrix glistened in rainbow colors, this fabrication was harsh white and gold, and the musical sound coming from its gleaming nucleus seemed more strident, more ominous, than that produced by Zor's original creation.

Now, though, the two observed in the matrix certain anomalies and instabilities that hadn't been there a short time before. Their research told them that, indeed, the Shapings were reaching some climactic point, a cusp or crux in events even more important than the conversion of the original matrix years ago in the mound where the SDF-l lay buried.

"Come," Cabell bade Exedore. "We haven't much time."

They went to where a new piece of apparatus had been set up. It suggested a kind of elaborate laser drill or boring unit, heavy with magnetic bottling fields and insulator rings.

"The buildup of Anti-Protoculture energy is still below what the job may require," Cabell said, "but it will have to suffice."

Exedore drew a deep breath, running both hands through his unruly red thatch. "Are you sure we're doing the right thing?" Once it was done, there would be no backing out, not to mention the danger to Tiresia and perhaps to all of Tirol.

"The matrix mustn't fall into Haydon's hands!" Cabell insisted. "Otherwise, he'll reduce all that remains of the universe to mere fuel and raw materials for his mad ambitions."

Exedore sighed. Cabell was right; it was just that the first matrix had been the Holy Grail for so long, and the second had required such extraordinary striving and genius. To destroy this last vestige of the power of Protoculture seemed to run counter to everything the long wars and researches had been about.

"You're correct, of course." Exedore clapped Cabell on the back tiredly. Strange and sad that things should end this way.

And an end it would be, since neither of them could survive this last-ditch effort to thwart Haydon's scheme. Exedore thought of the Micronian stories: Sampson in the temple, Horatio at the bridge. Exedore and Cabell at the Second Gen matrix would outdo all of those.

Cabell had brought forth two protective faceplates, handing one to Exedore. "Here you are, my dear fellow."

Exedore accepted his, slipping it on. "You know, Cabell, I still maintain that one of us can in all likelihood carry out this, er, procedure. There is thus no reason for you to make this sacrifice."

"Now, now. We've been all over this, old friend. There's no guarantee that one operator could balance the induction field and simultaneously calibrate the integration mixture. And it's far too late to automate the process. No, that just won't do—otherwise I'd have insisted *you* leave."

Exedore shook his head, settling the faceplate into place. Strange how, so late in his long years, he had become friends with such an odd assortment of beings: Micronians, Sentinels, even a clone of Zor himself. And Cabell, who was a companion and kindred soul, rather than the master his position would once have required him to be.

Both of them were working as fast as they could even while

they were musing. Surveillance satellites gave word that the sphere ships were making planetary approach at much higher speed than had been foreseen.

Still, Exedore saw calmly, he and Cabell would have time to carry out their last act. The special magnetic bottling fields began to come into existence, and in another few minutes Protoculture and Anti-Protoculture would mix in mutual annihilation.

There was another warning tone from the surveillance satellites. "An energy plexus of unknown type has been detected, originating from the sphere fleet, moving in the direction of Tiresia."

The two companions stopped their work and looked at the speaker. "Describe its nature."

"It is nonmaterial," came the reply, "a webwork of mental energy in some ways resembling the Awareness and yet unlike it."

Cabell was horrified. "That is because it is no longer linked to the instrumentality of Haydon IV. We've been caught unawares!"

He leapt to his controls, Exedore doing the same, and they prepared to fire the Anti-Protoculture infusion device, ready or not. But even as they did, the computer voice from the satellite net announced, "Calculations show that there is no time to complete your current endeavor. The Awareness has raced ahead of the sphere ships and now encompasses the Royal Hall."

But by then Cabell and Exedore didn't need the computer to tell them something was wrong. A sparkling network, like a highway system of strobing luminescence in the sky, had sprung into being all around the hall—not the Awareness itself but a side effect of the Awareness's presence, an exertion of its artificial mind powers.

The inside of the grand pyramidal chamber holding the matrix became like an aquarium filled with strange, insubstantial waters, shimmering air showing colors to which neither Exedore nor Cabell could put a name. It made the facsimile matrix's music turn ominous and caused it to glimmer in a new and sinister fashion.

Cabell, suffused with light, felt his consciousness slipping away. "Fire! Do not wait!" He held his grip on his senses for an extra moment, contriving to fall against the control panel and hook one arm over the ignition release, dragging the lever down with him.

Exedore, seeing what he had done, stabbed with the last of his strength for the firing button, even though he thought the charge was too low to accomplish the full destruction of the matrix. As his finger descended, he saw that the firing unit was aglow with the Awareness's light.

It all made such chilling sense; the Awareness had been removed from its instrumentality—Haydon IV itself—and yet maintained in a coherent state. *So Haydon has disembodied his AI construct and sent it here to fuse with the matrix—its new instrumentality.*

The firing unit failed to function, of course. The device built by Exedore and Cabell to destroy the matrix began to die, its fields falling silent, its Anti-Protoculture beginning to decompose at once, returning to the quantum foam from which it had been extracted with such enormous effort.

The light effects of the Awareness's merging with the matrix showed some of the cat's-cradle patterning that had been observed within Haydon IV. Exedore slumped in his place at the controls.

All across Tiresia, those who were brave, curious, or fatalistic enough to want to bear witness to the end peeked forth from their concealment. Out of the Royal Hall's peak rose a swirling nebula, showing some characteristics of the Awareness, some of the facsimile matrix, and some that were totally unfamiliar.

The nebula lit the city as it ascended higher into the night toward the waiting sphere ships. Tiresia was spared a last and utter destruction. Exedore and Cabell roused themselves from the paralysis of the Awareness's visit and watched the nebula of force rise up into the blackness to rejoin Haydon.

Max had hoped to score a quick victory in hand-to-hand combat with the black mecha, but the enemy machine was tremendously strong and agile, at least a match for his Alpha and maybe more.

He held his own against it, though, his own lightning reflexes being relayed through the "thinking cap" and a lifetime's training in unarmed combat coming to his aid.

Above all, he clung to the thing's globular right fist, terrified that if he released it for even an instant, the black mecha would harm or kill Dana, perhaps even by smashing it against Max's own Battloid.

The two war machines wrestled and struck at each other as they fell from the sky, neither one's thrusters able to stop it or give it the upper hand. Max tried to force the foe's right arm around to gain leverage with his Battloid's legs and rip loose the all-important right arm. But the enemy was fiendishly clever and nearly managed to kick his Battloid's head off.

In all the confusion, though, the two managed to get their foot thrusters under them and cushion their fall somewhat. They crashed into the top tier of a three-layer forest canopy, breaking off limbs and sending wildlife flapping and skittering.

They hung up in the second tier layer, entangled in more branches and networks of heavy vines. Max thought he saw a chance to pin his antagonist where one of the great trunks divided, immobilizing the black mecha and giving him the chance he needed to rescue Dana.

But the foe seemed to read his mind and struck at the Battloid's head with the globe at the end of its right arm. Max dodged desperately to avoid harming his daughter and lost his balance. The Black Knight brought its huge left fist down on the Alpha where a human's collarbone would be.

The Battloid reeled, falling . . .

Rick dashed to catch up with Louie, who in turn was hotfooting it so as not to fall behind Lang. "Halt, goddammit!"

If anybody could shed some light on what was happening, it was the two Protoculture hotshots, but neither seemed inclined to stop. Finally Louie, younger and fleeter of foot, caught up with Lang and hauled him around by one shoulder. "Doctor! Listen to me!"

"Let *go*!" Lang shoved Louie with that strange strength Rick had seen him exhibit on one or two rare occasions. But though Louie was hurled back with extreme force, taking an impact against a tree that made Rick wince, he bounced back for more, taking up the chase again.

"Rick!" It was Lisa; perhaps no other voice could have made him stop and turn around just then. She was coming along at a run, too, with Scott Bernard and Marlene. The children and most of the others were following more slowly in good order, but Rick noticed that Kazianna was nowhere to be seen.

He got on the tac net to the guards posted back at the landing zone. "Hold Doctors Lang and Nichols under close arrest until I get there—and *keep 'em away from each other*!"

He had time to repeat the message for clarity's sake, with the guard detail commander acknowledging, before Lisa caught up.

"Rick, Marlene says everything's starting to unglue or melt down. Something's trying to change even the Regis's plans."

Marlene was nodding. "I can feel it, even though my connection with the Protoculture isn't as strong anymore. I believe that the Regis and something else are about to lock in some tremendous struggle."

"Haydon?"

Lisa nodded, "It sounds like a good bet. I wanted to hear what Aurora had to say, but she's gone, too—she and Miriya and Kazianna."

She pointed to a disappearing Quadrono armored suit, vanishing in the direction Max and the Black Knight had taken. "Something about that black mecha, and none of them would take the time to explain."

Rick wanted to wait until they were all back aboard the SDF-3 to clear things up, but he understood that there might not even be *that* much time. "What do Roy and the other kids say?"

"They're too upset to make a lot of sense, but they obviously think something very dangerous is about to happen."

"That's it, then; we get everybody back to the ship before we do anything else." As he said it, they heard the sound of heavy engines, and one of the two shuttles lifted off. Rick got the group moving as fast as he thought they could stand. Luckily, Kazianna had left her Zentraedi behind to help maintain security.

Just before the party reached the landing zone there was another roar, and an Alpha went leaping away after the shuttle.

When the group got to the remaining shuttle, they found dazed security people dealing with their own wounded. "I—I'm not sure how it happened, sir," a rattled commander told Rick. "We had Doctor Lang and Doctor Nichols in custody—and then suddenly Lang had knocked out three of my best people, and the shuttle hatch opened all by itself to let him in.

"Everybody piled on Nichols to make sure he didn't get away. We had 'im held down pretty good until one of the Battloids just knelt down, without anybody even at the controls, to get him loose. Then he boarded and flew off after Lang."

"The new age of miracles," Vince muttered.

Rick didn't answer. Lisa had already sent someone to see if the remaining shuttle was working; it was, as were the mecha.

"Various people have had their mental powers expanded in one fashion or another," Jean Grant observed. "It seems that, at least in some cases, those expanded powers are now growing."

Rick heard a thoughtful note in her voice and turned to her to see her looking at the SDF-3 children. Lisa blurted, "Jean, what are you saying?"

For a moment Rick feared the same thing his wife did: that Jean's point was that the children were now to be considered a threat, that it had at last come down to war within families.

But instead, Jean Grant showed the first hint of a smile they had seen from her in a long time. "What I'm saying is, the children think it'd be a good idea to get *out* of newspace— and the Regis is somewhat occupied all of a sudden—*and* somewhere *not too far away, our spacefold drives are sitting there waiting for us*."

In the moment's silence that followed Rick heard the strange cries and stridulations of Omphalos's wildlife. Vince threw an arm around his wife and kissed her. "You're one of a kind, kid."

Rick was already giving hand signals. "Okay, get ready to board. We'll all have to squeeze onto one shuttle."

"Are we going home, Daddy?"

He reached down and gathered up his son. "Yes, we are."

CHAPTER
THIRTY-
FIVE

How hot a pilot was Max Sterling? Perhaps this simple obser-
vation makes the point best: Among the VT fighter jocks, his
modest, upbeat middle-American manner of speech replaced the
Chuck Yeager drawl that had dominated among pilots for de-
cades and sifted down among other fliers as well.

If you don't understand how very much that meant, go ask any
old stick-and-rudder hand.

Theresa Duvall,
Wingmates: The Story of Max and Miriya Sterling

ALL HIS TRAINING, EXPERIENCE, AND REMARKABLE
skills came to nothing in that critical moment after Max was
struck by the Black Knight.

But blind chance stepped in to fill the gap, if only for a
half instant. A springy hawser of vine had become looped
around his Battloid's foot, and it served the dual purpose of
swinging him around to where he could get a grip on the
immense tree trunk from which he was suspended and allowing him to lash out with his foot.

But most importantly, it bobbed him out of the line of fire
of his foe's dory-shaped hand weapon. The purple lightning
snapped and discharged, blowing a distant limb to vapor;
before the enemy could correct its aim, the massive metal
battering ram that was the Battloid's foot connected. The
Battloid-scale hand weapon went flying.

At the same time, Max was firing thrusters, righting himself. He rose on full back and leg blasts to grapple with his

292

enemy, pounding the weapon out of its fist. Locked together, they fell to bend down a stout branch that, even though it cracked somewhat, sprang back like a diving board to flip them into empty air. They left behind a trail of smoldering foliage and a few fires, but the vegetation was too wet to burn easily.

Again they fell, but this time Max had both hands fast at the Black Knight's right wrist. Both fired thrusters, heaving this way and that, kicking and flailing. Max saw the ground coming at him and twisted to cushion his landing with blaring power bursts. The black mecha wasn't as alert, and he managed to land on top of it.

They had come down in a large clearing, branches and leaves and lengths of vine raining down after them, along with burning bits of debris.

The enemy lay there stunned and partially staved in, shorted power leads crackling and throwing off sparks. Max seized a hold, planted his feet, twisted, and pulled with all the might he could focus through the thinking cap. With a shower of sparks and the tearing loose of strangely designed linkages, the right arm came off.

While the foe thrashed and bounced about the clearing in spasms, Max jumped clear to lay the globe aside carefully. He wanted more than anything to make sure Dana was all right, but there was no time. The living demon that was the black mecha might come at him again at any moment.

There wasn't even time to answer as, amazingly, he heard Kazianna Hesh's voice come over the net, though he thought his com equipment had been knocked out. "Max! Where are you?"

Even more strangely, he thought he heard Miriya's voice, too, and strangest of all, Aurora's—for Aurora seemed to be speaking directly into his mind.

Father, no! No!

It was no time to give in to hallucinatory voices, though; the Black Knight was back on its feet, coming his way in a tottering run that covered a dozen yards at a time. Max imaged, and his rifle/cannon slid into his grip; the thought that his daughter might even now be lying there dead made it that much easier to draw a bead.

"Max! *Freeze!*"

He had no idea why Kazianna would be yelling that in his ear, and so in the end it was confusion rather than discipline that made him hesitate for the telling split second. In that moment the Quadrono powered armor suit came barreling through a curtain of thick-leaved branches and interwoven vegetation, throwing itself on the Black Knight from the left.

Max held his fire and watched, astounded, as Kazianna sought not to terminate the enemy but to subdue it without harming the occupant *and to shield it from Max's fire.*

The Black Knight fought wildly, but Miriya had come into battle fresh and uninjured, armor operating at peak levels, with the advantage of surprise. Moreover, the viragos of the elite powered armor units in effect fought exclusively in what the REF would term Battloid mode; the contest was on Kazianna's chosen turf.

Kazianna called into play all the tricks of close-in mecha brawling that she had picked up in a long Quadrono career. Though the interloper was clever and savage, in the end Kazianna held it immobilized and forced it to one knee, standing behind and maintaining a complicated arm-bar hold on it.

Max expected her to deliver the *coup de grace* or at least disable the thing utterly. But to his shock, Kazianna freed one hand for a moment, made a quick move, and dropped a hand weapon of her own onto the forest floor, almost within reach.

Max made a decision and raised the rifle/cannon again, hoping he could avoid hitting Kazianna but determined to blow away the black mecha. His Battloid's finger was squeezing the trigger when Miriya's voice came to him again. "Max, don't shoot!"

And Aurora's voice spoke in his mind: *We have to break the spell, Father! Don't you see what's happened?* She sent a vivid image into his mind, the clearest mental link he was ever to have with his confounding younger daughter.

"Oh, my God," he whispered.

His Battloid's hand lowered, the rifle/cannon falling from its lax grip. He waited as Kazianna slowly released her hold on the Black Knight. The thing reached out slowly, almost unwillingly, taking up the gun Kazianna had thrown down, and began to come to its feet.

The war queen of the Quadronos waited, tensed, to pounce on the strange mecha again if it seemed about to fire on Max, but such a contest might come out either way. The thing was moving uncertainly, as if in a trance.

Max could feel Aurora's thoughts pouring toward it. Miriya's voice came over the com net to it. "This isn't what you want. Come back to us."

Max stood looking into the weapon's muzzle, arms hung at his sides, in the profoundest torment he had ever known. "Whatever happens, *please*—always, always know that . . . that I love you. We've always loved you with our whole hearts." Then he stood up straight, the gun barrel centered on him, waiting.

The Black Knight's aim wavered, and after what seemed like a lifetime it dropped the weapon with a cry of utter misery in a voice they all knew. The mecha staggered, and Kazianna caught it, already working at the unfamiliar lockdowns to crack it open.

Max dashed to them, reconfiguring as he went so that he sprang down from a kneeling Guardian whose huge metallic hands helped keep the supine Black Knight steady. As he got down, Aurora and Miriya were emerging from Kazianna's open helmet, Miriya helping Aurora lower herself to the ground. They had ridden in the powered suit, which had been retrofitted back during the monopole mining operations on Fantoma to carry Micronian observers.

Kazianna had gotten the soot-black, alien-contoured chest plate open. Max, Miriya, and Aurora scrambled up and raced to gather around the pilot's seat, Max fumbling to remove from her a thinking cap that looked more like an instrument of torture.

Dana, coming out of whatever spell it was the Regis had used to throw open her dark side, blinked up at them. "Dad, I—*uhhh!* Don't hate me; I didn't want to—"

"Shh! We know; everything's all right."

"Dana, we love you; oh, sister . . ."

Then all four Sterlings were weeping, trying to talk at once, hugging and kissing each other. At the same time they struggled to get Dana out of the pilot's seat/iron maiden into which she had been transferred somehow from the globular prison out at the end of the Black Knight's arm. Aurora's emanations of grief and joy bathed them all, Kazianna included.

Kazianna eased back a bit once Dana was down on solid ground again to give the four some room and privacy. She thought of the strange interludes that had come upon the newspace castaways, and some abrupt instinct made her look straight up into the sky.

Framed by the hole the descending mecha had made in the forest canopy, a single gargantuan eye that Kazianna knew now for the Regis's gazed back.

The giantess murmured, "You never learned *this* from Zor, did you? No, nor from the Great Work, or your Genesis Pits, or even the transcendence itself."

But the Regis made no answer, and there was no sign what the new data would mean to her race/self.

Then that last, separated part of her attention was gone, reunited with the rest of her, as the Regis addressed herself to the threat she sensed from Haydon.

People were used to deferring to Lang, to obeying without question the driving force of the SDFs, RDF, and REF. Even when he landed in a shuttle whose jamming gear was fouling up communications with the planet below, even when he emerged alone and gave orders to seal all flight decks and air locks, even when he walked away without a word of explanation or authorization, they automatically moved to obey. Even Xien knew his authority lay, in reality, somewhere far below Lang's.

Perhaps every human's did.

Niles Obstat attempted to get into the shuttle, to shut down the countermeasures and jamming gear so that the SDF-3 could contact the ground party, but the shuttle refused to open no matter what he tried.

Lang was already racing to his sanctum sanctorum back near Engineering when he heard the PA chatter about an unauthorized air lock opening and the arrival of an Alpha. He was too busy thinking about other things to curse, but his lips curved a bit in a cold smile. Nichols the cyber-master; what an unexpectedly worthy opponent!

Louie emerged from the VT to find the people waiting for him looking like the victims of some psychic plague: dazed and unfocussed, not sure who or what to trust, least of all their own senses. At least Xien and Niles Obstat summoned up the resolve to confront Louie and try to intervene.

Louie swept them with his black, bug-goggled gaze. "I can't explain; follow me if you like. Lang has to be stopped."

Xien stepped in his way. "Admiral Hunter hasn't given any orders."

"The Hunters and the rest are all right, I think. Ask them yourself."

Louie had glanced to where Lang's abandoned shuttle was carelessly parked. Crew members were swinging a heavy-duty cutting unit into place for forced entry. At Louie's glance, various nearby sensors registered a change, and somebody from the TIC reported that the jamming had stopped.

Xien's mouth became a thin, resolute line, and he pulled his sidearm, training it on Louie. "You stand fast until the admiral says differently."

He had just turned to muster a security detail to bring Lang to ground, when they all heard the grinding of mecha.

All over the hangar deck war machines were moving, mechamorphosing, rousing up like wakened fairy-tale monsters. Xien was brushed back by a Guardian's careful hand, unhurt but helpless to interfere. The would-be security detail found themselves boxed in by a Battloid and the single functioning second-generation Destroid aboard. Similarly, other personnel moved out of Louie's way or were moved from it.

Louie showed a bit of harried delight as three figures stood forth from the shadows to regard him. Strucker, Shi-Ling, and Stirson had to maintain their concentration with so many mecha to remote-control.

"Keep them all here," Louie ordered his men. "Same goes for the Hunters and the rest."

"Listen, you need us with you," Shi-Ling began.

"Uh uh; I've got Lang's number, but he'd just burn you out."

The unplugged people present heard the toccatas and rondos of data only as dim sounds from control panels and computer units. To Louie and his disciples it was a symphony and light show that surrounded them and validated Louie's assertion with hard proof: Only he, with his augmentations, could hope to survive a clash with Lang. Stirson conceded, "We understand. Wipe 'im, man."

Louie ran on his way. He never knew if he found the passages empty by some doing of Lang or as a result of the Regis or sheer coincidence. He got to Lang's sanctum sanctorum to find the heavy hatch of the armored vault module hanging open.

Emil Lang was poised on a stool within, contemplating the apparatus taken so long ago from Zor's quarters. Now it was radiant with Protoculture.

Lang spoke casually, without looking at him. "I think you'll find this interesting, Doctor. Do come in."

Louie shrugged out of his jacket. Where his black turtle-neck was torn, the bionics and chip technology that had become parts of his body could be seen, along with the cyberport at the back of his neck.

Lang glanced at him. "Don't be frightened; it's too late for you to do me any harm, so I've no need to harm you."

Louie was not ready to put money on that yet, but it was certain that Lang was on his own playing field. Oh, maybe there was something Louie could do about the door servos or the conventional light fixtures, but everything of any significance was Protoculture, and Lang had already proved who was top dog in that particular arena.

Louie gulped but entered. What else was there to do? "Doctor, look: I know what you're thinking, but you *can't* control the Shapings. Remember what happened to Zand?"

Lang's voice cut like razor wire. "You impertinent little cyborg Pinocchio! Do you think you've risen so high that you can look down on *me* in that fashion?"

"That wasn't what I meant."

Lang eyed him and grudgingly believed him. "*Doctor* Nichols, if what we are observing were allowed to come to pass—if real spacetime were drawn into newspace and the whole re-formed along lines chosen by the Regis—I believe that your somewhat unorthodox intellect and talents would make *you* the new template for the nature of Protoculture.

"And I do not find that an easy thing to concede."

Louie swallowed. "I just—"

"Please. Allow me to finish. As glorious a thing as that

new universe would be—that fresh start, that shining *correction*, perhaps, of all that's gone wrong with our old one—there is much that would inevitably pass away. Maybe most, or virtually all, of everything we have known.

"I don't celebrate evil or pain, oh, no! But all that's happened *means* something, perhaps gives some irreducible validity to existence itself. Or maybe the struggle of evolution against entropy, of ferment against mere sameness.

"And I find that I cannot let the past die, for all its shortcomings. There are too many precious things in our spacetime, preserved in amber, as it were. I won't let them perish."

Louie wondered if he had the strength to wrench that long control around on its hinge, swing it against Lang's head, get in the first shot. "You can't do any of that by trying to control the Shapings, Doctor. Zand proved that."

Lang shifted to turn a dial. The console shone brighter and sang more gloriously. "I know that. What I'll do is merge with them. For they, too, are reaching the end of a vast cycle.

"Not that I'm of any significance, but perhaps I can be like an insignificant snowflake that determines which way the avalanche shall fall. In any case, I won't know, for Emil Lang won't exist anymore."

Louie had taken Lang's shift of position into account and now gathered himself. But Lang threw him off by rising, and Louie noticed for the first time that something truly new had been added to Zor's apparatus: a pair of brass handgrips set perhaps a yard apart on the console.

Lang smiled suddenly, his black, all-pupil eyes gleaming limpidly. "There's no one else eligible for the job, so I have to try, at the very least. Won't you wish me well . . . Louie?"

Louie froze and found himself answering, "I do, Emil. I wish you well."

He moved with all the speed he could muster but stopped just before he got within reach. The control bar was forgotten, the fight forgotten. Louie Nichols found himself guided by a simple intuition—nothing to do with Shapings or psi but only a feeling that the man had spoken the truth.

"I wish you well."

"Thank you, Louie. Good-bye."

Lang rose unhurriedly and seized both handgrips. A light like the beginning of the universe filled the vault module, and Louie felt as if all the winds of time were blowing through his brain, something so symphonic and grand and terrible that he shrank from perceiving them.

He was hurled back through the air, through the door of the vault, as the light expanded.

CHAPTER
THIRTY-
SIX

*What with all the new psi-powers—and other faculties—we
saw manifested along the way, maybe this whole kick-out's just
been the universe's way to give evolution a leg up.*

Bruce Mirrorshades, *Machine Mind and Arthurian Legend*

DOWN NEAR RANAATH'S STAR THE SPHERE SHIPS SPI-
raled along the accretion disc, orienting themselves for the
final transit.

The mingled energies of Second Gen Protoculture and the
Awareness cloaked them, so that they were like a string of
mirror-perfect pearls, to shield them against the tidal forces
and the more menacing phenomena beyond.

Within the ships, all platforms but one were occupied by
simulacra of the One Haydon, giants but still minute now
that they were parts: tens of thousands of them watching silently over the ships' systemry as the moment approached.

On that other single platform stood the Robotech Elders,
watching gleefully. The infusion of Protoculture had freed
them of the need for their life-support thrones; they were
swelled and vibrant with the vitality the Second Gen essence
had given them.

They waited near a sphere of their own, a small vessel
fashioned and put there by Haydon. In it they would journey
back from the moment of intersection with all the power of
Protoculture at their command. That power would bring the

Local Group under their dominion, just the springboard they needed to put the universe at their feet.

The Elders, looking like scavenger birds on a storm wind, gazed into the scanner hungrily.

The Event Horizon loomed up before them.

"I just get the feeling that the people in this whole long historical contest are starting to fall together like pieces of a puzzle," Jean Grant pondered. "I mean, from Zor to Roy II—"

"It's as likely as any other explanation," Lisa admitted.

Just then Rick turned to them in the crowded shuttle, lowering the com unit he had been using to follow what was going on between the SDF-3 and the shuttle's com officer. He was still holding Roy II in his lap, but it didn't look out of place with humans and XTs and Zentraedi children and so forth all crammed into one ship.

"Somebody shut down the commo jamming, but I don't think we're gonna be able to make any sense of anything until we get back to the SDF-3. Louie and Lang are having some kind of showdown or something. But at least Vince has Engineering alerted and getting set for the big push."

Lisa reached out to smooth Roy's raven hair. Even with the proof that the children had preternatural powers, even accepting the fact that they were the newspace strandees' only hope of survival, she had trouble from moment to moment keeping herself from denouncing the plan Rick had formulated.

She reminded herself of the Sterlings' encounter with the Black Knight, though. What hope was there for Roy if he became part of the Regis's lab experiments? Or if Haydon took over?

The shuttle and accompanying VT and Zentraedi arrived on the hangar deck to find Louie's cybernaught team under close arrest—having surrendered, apparently, because outside interference in the confrontation between Louie and Lang was impossible now—and most other people trying to sort themselves out.

"We've got a team by the main hatch to the compartment where Lang and Nichols are," Xien reported a bit shakily, "but as yet they can't get it open. Some kind of cyber-stunt."

He glared at Louie's fellow grid-gallopers, who did not appear to notice.

"Never mind that for now," Vince said. "We've got to detour around that compartment and get back to the drive section. Are the new patch-ins rigged?"

An engineering officer who looked like she was not old enough to vote reported, "The teams are almost ready, sir. I've had my people leave a lot of leeway in the leads and cables, because nobody seems sure just where the drives'll be situated when they, um, appear."

IF they appear, Vince amended, but kept it to himself. There was also the possibility that the SDF-3's spacefold drives would show up upside down or something, but there was not much point worrying about that. "Very good."

The Sterlings were still clinging to one another, but Aurora tugged to free herself. "I have to go aft with the others. But I wish you'd come."

Rick and Lisa knelt by Roy. Lisa ran her fingertips through the boy's fine hair. Rick told his son, "Don't be afraid; we're gonna be right there with you."

He was already tugging at their hands. "We haveta hurry!"

Rick had already directed Colonel Vallenskiy to remain in command in the TIC; Lisa had left Raul Forsythe conning the bridge. They both stood, each taking one of the boy's hands, and hugged each other quickly and very urgently.

Just then there was a message over the PA. Karen Penn, who with Jack Baker was leading the security team that was covering the compartment containing Lang and Louie Nichols, reported, "Admiral, something's happening in there. I'm not sure what."

The rest of it was lost in the sudden soaring of sound, the rising vibrations-that-were-not-vibrations, that shook the ship. Light seemed to come from everywhere, and someone screamed. Wind squalls swept the vessel. All at once there were radiant vortices everywhere, shooting back and forth at high speed like living things, going through solid bulkheads without any perceptible resistance.

Vince bellowed, "All right, stations everybody! Stand to! Let's do it, people!"

The flux-storm, or whatever it was, abated a bit, and people rushed off to their stations. Scott and Marlene went with the party headed for the drive section, as did a lot of the XT Sentinels and Zentraedi. Even Veidt and Vowad went along. Rem, Minmei's hand in his, was following step by slow step when another light-storm struck.

This one was different, a cloud of lumens that closed in around them alone, and none of the others seemed to notice. Minmei screamed, cringing to her knees, arms closed protectively around her middle. Rem knelt next to her, eyes slitted against the onslaught.

The cloud became a face that Rem recognized. The Regis looked down emotionlessly at the two.

NO, YOU WON'T BE SAVED. ALL YOUR PLANS WILL COME TO NOTHING. THIS IS THE MOMENT OF MY TRI-UMPH AND YOUR EXTINCTION.

"No!" Rem howled. He hauled Minmei to her feet to seek shelter, but when he started off, she pulled in another direction. "That way! That way!"

They left the cloud behind, though there were still swirls of fury around them. Minmei led the way down one passageway and then another until they came to a quarters hatch. Rem hit the release and on the other side found a pistol leveled at him.

Bowie stared down the barrel. Rem felt his pulse pound, waiting for the blast. After a long hesitation, though, Bowie bit out, "Close it. Seal it behind you."

Rem saw then that Musica was trying to comfort Allegra, both Muses huddled together in the lower bunk. Bowie reholstered the sidearm, saying, "I don't know what's happening, but I know I want the Singers and me together when it does. No more soldiering for me."

His eyes flicked to Minmei. "What brought you back?"

She was sobbing, shaking her head, chest racked, unable to tell him. Maybe she could not have even if she hadn't been crying. Rem took her into his arms.

Bowie went to where his compact synthesizer keyboards were set up next to the glowing Cosmic Harp. "Well, maybe you just wanted to be played out with some song. Good a way to go as any."

His fingers touched keys, evoking full, uplifting chords. "It's what I was planning on."

Minmei swiped back the limp hair from her eyes, lifting her head. "Yes. Music."

Rem helped her over to where she could slump into a seat near Bowie and sat stroking her shoulder, back, and face. Bowie played a melody she knew, and she lifted her voice. At least she could give her unborn baby that much.

Minmei lost herself in the words for a few bars, shutting out the rest of the world, until she realized that Musica had sat to stroke notes from the fine lines of resplendence that were the strings of the Cosmic Harp.

Musica sang, too, and in a few more moments Allegra joined in. The SDF-3 shook and jolted, distant shrieks and wails rang from far-off bulkheads, doomsday light anomalies impinged again and again at the edges of their song. But within it, for the moment, the music somehow kept them safe from the terminal spasming of the Shapings; from the probings of the Regis or, perhaps, only from her malice; from the rift-energies as newspace drew in realtime's structure; and from the desperation and despair claiming so many others aboard the SDF-3.

In the drive section, techs were being ordered back to stand along the bulkheads and everybody was donning headgear. There was no time for much else in the way of safety precautions—like getting all hands into spacesuits—and no telling what sort would be needed.

Pinwheels of ghostly pastel flame swooped and buzzed through the cavernous compartment like startled birds; the mental sounds and the jarring of the SDF-3 were increasing.

The children had formed their circle of power once again, this time with Aurora as a link between Roy and Drannin. They were situated off in one corner of the compartment in the hope that they would be out of the way of danger. The parents moved back, Lisa releasing Roy's shoulder only after Rick put his arm around her.

Rick tried to get Jack or Karen on the intercom to find out what was happening at Lang's sanctum, but all communications seemed to be down.

The children had taken up a new chant, the eerie glow of their eyes brightening. Rick could not hear it over the astral storm that blew and crashed around them, then, leaning closer, did hear.

Ro-bo-tech, Ro-bo-tech, Ro-bo-tech . . .

The children had picked their mantra, their source of power and unity, their psychic spell word and focus; something about it made the parents, the techs, and the rest stand a bit straighter, hold their chins a little higher. Lisa felt Rick squeeze her hand and saw that his eyes were glistening with tears.

The chant became louder than the astral storm not in sheer decibels but in the minds of those gathered. Their physical surroundings—the drive ancillaries, the bulkheads—fell away in a panorama of boiling psi-stuff, and the children forced back the curtain with their unity, searching.

Ro-bo-tech! Ro-bo-tech! Ro-bo-tech!

The perceptual mist fell away and they saw the SDF-3's drive housing, like a phantom, translucent and insubstantial, there where it had once been.

Angelo Dante sent up a cheer, feeling a personal stake in the matter of the drives, and was the first one to grab a connector cable as thick as his own upper arm, ready to hook up.

But Gnea held him back, just as Vince Grant and some of the others called out for everybody to keep their distance. The drives were still insubstantial; the children had not fully materialized them yet.

The chant became more intense, and the drives took on solidity. They became opaque, then substantial.

And then the sky opened up.

The Regis looked down, anger somehow showing forth from her blank mask of a face.

I HAVE BROUGHT YOU HERE, AND HERE YOU WILL REMAIN, RAW MATERIALS FOR MY TRANSFORMED NEWSPACE!

Long cyclonic whips of otherworldly force lashed in at the drives from everywhere, striking at their housing. The children's chant wavered, became unsure. The drives lost substance once more and faded; the ectoplasmic storm closed in.

But the Regis's face remained above those gathered below.

I WILL BROOK NO MORE INTERFERENCE!

Around each child a dark corona grew as the Regis sought

to waft them away into her own zone of existence. The chant faltered, the children fighting her will, but the coronas became darker and darker still.

Like dozens of others, Rick and Lisa leapt forward to save the children but rebounded from a barrier of force that encompassed the circle. Lisa watched, helplessly sprawled on the deck, as Roy and the rest faded from view into night.

In the compartment holding Lang's vault module, Louie Nichols zeroized his goggles' transparency and threw his forearm across them for good measure.

The brightness was too intense for sight to have any coherence, anyway. At the ground zero of Lang's ultimate Protoculture act, Louie found himself perceiving things with new and different senses.

He beheld the end of Lang by immersion in the Protoculture. In the end, the man's expanded intellect, colossal as it was, was overshadowed by his boundless *delight* in the elegance, subtlety, and mystery of the universe and of life itself.

As Jovian as those things were, though, Lang had been right; somehow, Louie sensed that Lang's essence was no more than a single snowflake against the endless winter vista of the Shapings. The single particle that had been Lang floated away to become part of the Shapings, the man himself lost and gone forever.

Because the nature of Haydon had not been intended for the transition to newspace, the sphere ships exerted unique adaptive energies to the transit.

Negotiating perilous intercontinua commissures, they endured and wended toward their destination but accumulated more and more excess psi-quanta in their force envelopes. It was not unlike a skier building up more momentum than was desired and finding himself unable to shed it.

The sphere ships would either reach the bottom of their hill with incalculable mental energy potential or perish in a failure that would destroy everything, everywhere, everywhen.

Lisa watched her son pulled from sight without even the hope that she could sacrifice herself to save him, without even the hope that she would have his body to mourn over.

Then something changed the world of ectostorm and mind-blast there in the violence of the drive compartment, something that called the unleashed fury to heel for an instant and calmed the cataclysm for a beat. Lisa knew what it was, but it took her a moment, in her stunned state to fix words to it.

> *Life is only what we choose to make it*
> *Let us take it*
> *Let us be free!*

Lisa heard Rick croak, *"Minmei!"*

By the time Lisa had levered herself up and looked around, there were indescribably sweet notes backing Minmei's silvery voice and other voices chiming in.

Minmei stood near the hatch, looking scared and weary and haggard, but she clung to Rem, who bore her up, and she became a pure instrument for her song.

> *We can find the glory we all dream of,*
> *And with our love,*
> *We can win!*

Musica and Allegra wove their spell behind hers. The Cosmic Harp danced like a starry spiderweb under Musica's fingers. Giving it all a kind of human interface was Bowie, eyes closed, drawing lofty chords from the synth-keyboard slung over his shoulders.

Scarcely aware of it, Lisa also took in Jack and Karen and Harry Penn, all of them apparently out of breath and hunkered down near the harp. Of course; it hadn't just levitated itself there.

But her thoughts were all for Roy and the kids; Lisa looked back to see the dark coronas fade a bit, the children still sitting in their places.

As Minmei let her song take flight, the chant came up beneath it, somehow merged with it—
Ro-bo-tech! Ro-bo-tech! Ro-bo-tech!

CHAPTER THIRTY-SEVEN

The quick and the dead—we're both!

Remark attributed to
Rick Hunter at the
Intersection

RICK THREW HIMSELF AT HIS SON, DREADING THE BARrier that would hurl him back again.

But this time he made it, passing through a sort of resistance area, a membrane. He went down on one knee next to his son. "Roy, try again. Try for the spacefold drives again!"

Roy left off the chant, though the others kept it up, to look at his father with glowing eyes. "We're trying, Daddy. But that lady, the Regis—she put them someplace that we can't find them."

"Keep looking; they have to be *somewhere.*"

God, what was he doing, giving psi-search pointers to his superkid? But he couldn't help it; he had to do something, had to keep them in the fight.

"The drives might be anyplace, Roy, anyplace in, um, space or time! Look everyplace."

Then he quailed a bit as tentacles of astral malignance curled and quested overhead, the Regis trying to reach the children again. But Minmei's song kept them at bay.

Rick realized that his son was tugging at his arm. "Daddy, we found them. We looked across time, 'n' we looked across space."

"What? Buddy, you're beautiful!" Rick didn't know if he was laughing or crying. "Can you bring 'em back?"

As an answer, Roy pointed. Outlines were appearing, an enormous containment casing coming into existence. Cheers began around the compartment.

Rick came to his feet, ready to start lending a hand hooking up the fold drives. He was going to give a cheer himself until he realized that something was not right.

Others were beginning to see it, too, especially engineering types. The casing took on more and more substance, and one by one people in the drive section understood what they were looking at. Rick had never actually seen the object he now beheld, but he had certainly seen enough holographs, schematics, tapes, and such.

"Christ," he whispered.

"We got them, Daddy!" Roy squealed delightedly.

"Y-you sure did, old-timer." And solved—and created— one of the great mysteries of the Robotech Age.

We will win!

Minmei's song hit a crescendo and stopped.

The original fold drives from SDF-1 sat there, big as ten diesel locomotives and just as solid. Lisa was staring at them, speechless, as techs approached them tentatively. Then she blurted, "Careful! They may still be hot."

She meant thermal energy, not hard radiation, but the heat was quite minimal. Not bad, she decided, seeing that as far as the drives *themselves* were concerned, they had just finished taking the SDF-1 on a jump from Earthspace to the orbit of Pluto.

They'd been snatched from that instant directly to this one, though decades had passed in the interim.

"Oke—" Vince Grant finished gulping, and tried again. "Okay! A fold drive's a fold drive. Let's get 'em hot-wired." People hopped to it.

Pursued by the Zentraedi, the SDF-1 had attempted a fold jump to hide in the lee of Earth's moon. A miscalculation— or so it was said—had sent the ship to the edge of the Sol system, where the drives immediately vanished, leaving behind only a few winking luminous particles. Then SDF-1 had begun her years-long odyssey homeward.

Lisa wondered what Henry Gloval would think of all this. Maybe he already knew.

The design of the SDF-3's drives was based on that of the original Super Dimensional Fortress. There was no time for niceties, and there was every possibility the ship would be blown to nothingness, but the drives were connected. There was a residue of First Generation Protoculture left in them in the wake of the Pluto jump, but the instruments showed that trace vanishing—melding with the Regis and newspace, apparently—even as techs were charging into action.

The psi-fog the Regis had manifested, along with its squall effects, had retreated, though the children had broken their circle and Minmei was no longer singing. "But that don't mean the dame is gonna leave us alone for long," Angie said, frowning.

"*Has* she gone?" Miriya asked Aurora.

Aurora's brows met. "Something else is placing demands on her attention."

"Haydon," someone said, and they realized that Louie Nichols was standing there, looking like he had been through hell.

There wasn't even time to comment on his exposed bionics. "Are you sure?" Vince demanded.

His team, who had stayed in the background through the Regis's appearance, closed ranks behind Louie. "Ask Marlene."

She nodded her head unwillingly. "My instincts tell me the same thing."

"And what's going to happen here in newspace has nothing to do with us anymore," Louie added.

"All the more reason to haul anchor," Angie snorted.

Indeed, there was nothing the contingent from realtime could do in a collision between such entities. But while the preparations for the jump were rushed to completion—with Louie and his team quickly becoming key players—Lisa turned to something else she had to do.

Minmei still stood with Rem's arm around her. Lisa went to her and took both Minmei's hands in hers. "Thank you for what you did. Thank you for saving my son, Minmei."

Minmei stood away from Rem. She and Lisa held each other, Lisa patting Minmei's shoulder. "I heard the children's voices, and I knew my place was here." Rick and others, mostly parents, closed in to thank Musica and Allegra; the Muses smiled timidly. Bowie was already in a clinch with his parents,

"Ahem. Isn't anybody gonna thank the furniture movers?" Jack Baker hinted.

The idea to get the siren music to the drive section had been Minmei's, of course, but if he and the Penns had not happened upon her and the Muses and Bowie—drawn by Minmei's a capella singing—as they struggled along with the harp, things would have gone very differently.

Karen gave Jack an elbow in the ribs. "You're not really going to be happy until you're an eighth-*dan* schmuck, are you?"

But Harry Penn, having gotten his breath back, gave Jack a clap on the back. "I'll say this much for you, Baker: You hold up your end." That made Karen's eyes go large; she had assumed that her father's loathing of Jack was set in permacrete. Jack looked dumbstruck.

"This is no time for a whoopee," Vince Grant reminded everybody loudly. He turned to Lisa. "Replacement fold drives on-line, Admiral."

Pull pin and throw, Rick thought.

Lisa keyed an intercom. There was still static, as there were still muted sound and light phenomena loose in the ship. Raul Forsythe responded from the bridge. "Navigation has worked out algorithms that *should* be what we need to find our way out," he reported, "but there's no way to check 'em."

"There's one," Lisa replied. "Exec—"

All of newspace seemed to go through a paroxysm, an expand-and-contact feeling that made everyone cry out, as if the warp and weft of it were caught in some unthinkable contest of forces.

"—ute fold jump, Captain!" Lisa finished.

Everything around them seemed to be dissolving into distortion. Rick heard screams and orders, reports and moans. He whirled and yelled his son's name, but all sane perception seemed to have fallen away to nothingness.

Then the fold drives hummed, building power, and coherent reality rezzed up again. Rick took no chances but snatched Roy up into his arms again, other parents following suit—including the Zentraedi, which was quite a sight. Lisa faced the fact that she could not command her ship by intercom and let Raul concentrate on running the bridge.

Vince had been holding his breath, not knowing how the SDF-1's drives would take to Second Gen Protoculture—hell, he hadn't even known how the SDF-3's would. Now he found out, as the smooth fold sequence stuttered, the sound of the drives falling off.

"Run start-up sequence again," he'd just said, when everything around him dissipated into perceptual chaos again, making him feel he was going mad.

In a place with no real existence in space or time, the onrushing Haydon, with all the accumulated energies of his crossing, rushed headlong at the Regis, who was determined to defend this, her last domain.

The rift between the domain of newspace and realspace widened, all things flowing together at the cusp. The very end of the Shapings had come.

With the residue of the expanded senses he had been given by exposure to Lang's discorporation, Louie Nichols perceived the settling of that single snowflake on the endless winter landscape of the Shapings. It took its place, losing itself in the whole. But its very arrival generated the movement of those beneath it, and they imparted infinitesimal shifting to those farther down. There was mass movement.

Aboard the SDF-3, the start-up sequence ran again and the fold drives raved to life. This time the process caught, and everyone aboard could feel the generation of the fold jump field as it sprang out from the ship. Once more they were passing into the unknowable.

For Haydon there could be no going back; for the Regis there was no retreat. Collision was inevitable, and only one entity could survive.

Both beings registered the jump of SDF-3, though the Regis could spare no attention for it and Haydon saw no reason to; the cosmos for which it was bound would soon be destroyed, anyway. They charged upon each other to do ultimate combat.

Then both near deities let out silent emanations of shock, wonder, fear, and awe.

The Shapings were shifting in a way unique in all their long history.

In that intersection, Haydon suddenly had access to a wider mental vista, a fuller historical perspective, than he had ever had. The Regis, meanwhile, was opened to a total vision of all that had taken place and all that would. Both knew humbling and unprecedented sensations of acceptance, resignation—and peace.

It was as if all continua and all probabilities were rotating on infinite axes beneath them. Once again the Regis was transformed into a phoenix of racial essence, about to take flight for a final destination. But Haydon turned, in the eternal instant when the rift in spacetime still yawned wide, and reached into the SDF-3, searching.

At the moment of Intersection, as a side effect miracle, the perceptual blindfolds fell away from the eyes of the SDFers, and they gazed across time.

Kazianna Hesh clutched Drannin while the Super Dimensional Fortress plunged into the eye of the continua hurricane. If death rose up to claim her at last, she knew how to greet it; she was Zentraedi.

But instead, what she thought at first to be a hallucination manifested itself before her. She saw mighty Breetai as she had first seen him, unscarred and unbeatable, leading the legions of the Zentraedi to victory.

As she saw and heard her love again, watched him leave his mark, huge and unique, on galactic history, Kazianna came to realize that it was no dream or specter. Somehow she was seeing across the conventional boundaries to points on the timestream where he still existed.

She witnessed again the terrible battle in which Zor died, the great slaughter of Dolza's fleet, Breetai's triumphs in the Malcontent Uprisings and the Sentinels War.

She saw herself again, too, as she went to him on Fantoma and awakened love in him as he already unknowingly had in her. She saw how he had become truly happy for the first time then.

There was no hard and fast linearity to the scenes. She was seeing *many* times and places where Breetai was in effect alive still and would always be so—as Lang had intended, though Kazianna knew nothing of that at the moment.

She saw him presiding like some war god at the postbattle revels of the Zentraedi, proud of his conquests and yet weighted, always, by the burden of his leadership. Nevertheless, Kazianna knew a fierce joy that some part of him would preside forever in the halls of victory.

And she saw him brooding, about to enter his final contest against the Invid Regent, and knowing that this time the Shapings had a different outcome in store for him.

She felt Drannin stir in her arms. "Is that man my father?"

Is. That was the right word. She understood now that he was no more lost to her than if he were on some far shore. She was *still* with him in many times and places and knew a certainty that she would be again.

"Yes. That is Great Breetai."

The child was silent for a long moment, then his voice rang out across the barrier between them. "Hail, Breetai!"

At that moment Breetai's head rose from his preoccupations, and one of his very rare smiles touched his lips. He had known, going to his death, that his wife carried his son. Now Kazianna had no doubt that somehow he had heard the boy's voice across time.

She held herself very erect. "Yes, hail, Breetai." But she said it with a lover's softness.

For Lisa, it was Karl Riber: the love of an older man—all of nineteen!—for an introverted sixteen-year-old. She was the daughter of a military family, he a gentle thinker and dreamer.

She saw that his lonely life at Sara Base on Mars was not as horrible as serving in the RDF would have been. When he met death in the Sara Base raid, she did not turn her eyes from it, and she saw a vast calm in him then. Karl had never feared dying; he understood life too well. He had only shrunk from killing, and in the end the life he'd left behind was the kind of monument to peace that would have pleased him.

For Lisa, other faces and scenes rose up from the time-stream, too: the mother she'd remembered dimly but now saw afresh and more fully; her father, in his good moments and bad, making her even more grateful that she and he had become friends once more, at the end.

She had lost many friends and now saw glimpses of those who'd been closest to her.

Sammie, Kim, and Vanessa made her smile with their bewildering mixture of high spirits and dead-calm combat savvy. She let the tears come as she saw Claudia Grant once more, in all her best friend's moods and moments, and blessed whatever agency it was that gave her this interlude of insight and remembrance.

And of course Lisa beheld Captain Henry J. Gloval across the gulf of years—in his assorted tempers and aspects, the emphatic humanity he hid under a gruff exterior. She had long ago recognized that *he* was her father in the truest sense; she considered herself fortunate that that had been so.

Lisa saw the bridge crew formed up on the day when she had been promoted to captain, rendering their salute. She saluted them back, happy that that day was still alive and eternal somewhere.

All through the ship, the SDFers cast their gazes across space and time. Human and XT alike, Vowad and Veidt no less than the rest, growing even closer in their contemplation of Sarna. The Muses glimpsed their sister Octavia and heard for the last time their original, perfect harmony.

Bowie's soul played a haunting martial blues for General Rolf Emerson. Scott Bernard saw outtakes of Marlene Rush meld with those of the simulagent Ariel/Marlene, the two now being one; he blinked mentally in surprise, compelled to think through the implications of that.

As for Marlene, she saw the timescenes of Marlene Rush as well as those of Ariel, and that completed her long self-healing.

Dana was overjoyed to see the three Zentraedi spies— Konda, Bron, and Rico—once more, though she had kept them so alive in her heart all along that she never doubted for a moment that they existed somewhere. She, too, looked upon Rolf Emerson with fond acknowledgment. But then the image of Zor Prime came to her.

She tried to drive it out at first, thought of the images of Intersection as a kind of torture. She found that she had to watch, though, and the more she saw of Zor Prime's tormented life, the more she understood.

Dana cried out as she saw the things to which the Robotech Masters had subjected him, the ways in which his personality, his will, his very soul were mauled and marred—the way in which he fought a ceaseless struggle against the memories of his past incarnations.

At a certain moment, overcoming her own resistance, she felt herself send out an unspoken forgiveness. That deliberate act somehow shook her loose from the worst of the bitterness that had racked and entrapped her since the explosion of the Masters' ship that day high over the Mounds. In the end it was a cleansing, not easy to endure but one that saved her.

Rick was glad he had Roy in his arms. For some reason, like Kazianna, he and his child communed in the glimpses across time. "That's my father, your granddad, and our flying circus." Roy giggled and *ooh*ed at the aerobatics but took in the old man's crusty, smiling face and barnstorming joie de vivre silently, with great attention.

Rick, too, knew enormous gratitude that this experience, whatever it was, had come his way.

Ben Dixon came into the timescenes later, not the first time Rick had seen his image since the big VT flier had tuned out, but it was always good to see him. Claudia Grant and the Bridge Bunnies, Gloval, and the rest made him feel he had led a very charmed life indeed.

And a long time later, so it seemed, he told his son, "That man there is Roy Fokker, and your mother and I named you after him."

Roy II put his head on his father's shoulder and took it all in wordlessly, saw his father as a much younger man, too. At length he said, "Was he really your big brother, Daddy?"

"No. He was a lot more than a brother."

"Will you teach me to fly?"

"Yes. I will."

For Minmei, as for many others, there was a certain relief

in the faces she did *not* see in the timestream. Her parents and cousin were absent, and so she felt she could hope they were still well back on Earth. She feared at first that she would be forced to review the terrible things she'd seen, people and creatures she'd encountered, but this side effect of Lang's final act was not connected to that sort of thing. Of Edwards there was no sign. Surely the evil moments endured in time, too, but the point seemed to her to be that, abandoned to themselves, they lost much or all of their power.

Mad Khyron and Azonia, the Regent, and all of that stamp—let them stay encysted, shunned, and unvisited in their various pigeonholes of time. She turned her eyes elsewhere.

It hurt to look at the painful parts of Lynn-Kyle's life, but she also saw the fine parts, the heroic and idealistic side. She saw again that he had died trying to save her and end the war; the love for him that she had suppressed was free to find its rightful place in her now, with no power to do her harm.

She renewed her affection for Janice Em. Android or no, Lang-agent or no, Jan had perhaps been her truest friend and best song-soulmate.

Looking in on the SDF-3, Haydon found what he had been searching for.

Minmei had no idea how long she had been watching the flow of scenes when another voice reached her, and somehow she knew it was not a part of her Intersection-generated views of time. It was Rem.

She turned, somehow breaking the trance, to see that he was being swallowed up in white translucent banners of force.

She tried to move, rooted to the spot. "No!" He began to fade from her sight.

She cried the word like a plaintive song—"No-ooo!"—and somehow its power, the power her voice had always had, overcame whatever was immobilizing her.

Minmei threw herself at Rem, feeling the energy discharges around her, clinging to him, and together they vanished from the starship.

CHAPTER
THIRTY-
EIGHT

The music plays, and everyone must dance.

Twentieth-century song lyric

AT THE INTERSECTION THE ROBOTECH ELDERS, IN their smaller-model sphere ship, shrieked their outrage and despair.

We had an agreement!

Haydon answered, *THAT MEANS NOTHING TO ME.*

Free us with the Protoculture as you abandon your sphere ships!

What they said was true; the individual simulacra of Haydon were vanishing from sight. Somewhere beyond, they sensed, the One Haydon was coming into being again. He had no further use for the ships or the Protoculture—indeed, He released them to meet their own discorporation.

But the Elders' sphere He kept under his mental control. *YOU, I WILL BRING WITH ME INTO MY NEW DOMAIN, AS I SHALL BRING ONE OTHER CONTAINER FROM SPACETIME.*

You struck a bargain with us!

DID YOU THINK I COULDN'T SEE BEYOND YOUR WORDS? INTO YOUR THOUGHTS?

Then the Robotech Elders wailed in truest fear; they'd planned to betray Haydon at the earliest juncture if the opportunity arose. Instead, they saw, He had brought them along until he could exact a satisfactory revenge.

He was immortal but mortal enough to feel that urge.

The venue known as newspace was empty, the stuff of conventional spacetime banished back to the place from which it had come. Haydon wanted no part of it; that was the entire *point* of His great effort.

Instead, He discharged into newspace all the accumulated energies of His crossing, giving Himself unending raw material with which to work. Haydon willed new and utterly alien physical laws into being and set out to explore and shape His new domain.

Except, that is, for two bubbles of normality. The first among those was the prison of the Robotech Elders. He imprisoned them once more in the hated thrones, in the bondage of systems that would ensure their survival. They perceived that some of the substance forming their bubble was the stuff of their Protoculture cap itself—depleted, reshaped, used in irony by Haydon.

Then Haydon accelerated the flow of time within the sphere—to ensure its passage there.

Tens of thousands of years might pass while Haydon's attention was elsewhere for an instant, but every so often Haydon would look in on them and see how His little experiment was going.

The Robotech Elders, imprisoned in the hated circle in which they had started, had their Immortality at last.

Perhaps the best summation of subsequent events is found in *Recollections: Peacetime* by Admiral Lisa Hayes-Hunter.

So those glorious old drives brought us home at last in grand style. Some people griped that it was a near thing, pointing out that the drives were about to blow when we came crashing out into Earthspace, but take it from me, they'd have done whatever they needed to, to get the job done.

Of course by "home," I mean conventional spacetime; the Sol system wasn't exactly the old neighborhood for the XT Sentinels, the Zentraedi, and so forth.

That didn't matter much at the time.

The pure joy of getting back to Earthspace was dampened, of course, when we realized that Minmei and Rem had disappeared. This, even though the pilots originally "kidnapped" from Red and Blue teams were miraculously put back aboard SDF-3, Veritechs and all, at the Intersection. As of this writing, there is no indication whatsoever of what happened to them, and all efforts to locate them or establish their fate have been fruitless.

The second great shock of our arrival was the calculation (by astronomical AIs, from the positions of planets in the Sol system) of the elapsed time since the departure of Peter Pan. Foldspace had played another joke on us.

More than ten years had passed.

But that wasn't enough to dampen our morale, not after what we'd been through. I think that those on board SDF-3 during that moment of Intersection will always be different. *We were given a new perspective on life and death and our place in the scheme of things; that left its mark on us.*

And so SDF-3 started for Earth one last time, driven by auxiliary power. Somehow the transit from newspace had drained away all our Second Gen Protoculture, even what was left in the various mecha. We shall not see its like again, as the saying goes.

There's no denying the sheer joy of homecoming, though. The Earth below us was the first and best surprise: pristine and beautiful, her surface restored, her ecosystems flourishing with a vitality they hadn't known in a century and a half and more.

Maybe it was some kind of payback.

We arrived to find that Earth had muddled through the multiple crises that had beset her, largely with the help of exotic new technology developed from information brought home by the Angel.

But largely, it was a matter of humanity's being sick of war. I've heard of old soldiers retiring from the carnage to create and retreat into a beautiful garden somewhere. I guess that's more or less what happened to the entire species Homo sapiens.

Water ice had been brought in from offworld, pollution damage cleaned up through bio-remedialism and other newly devised techniques. The drifting space junk from the Robotech wars had all been removed, or burned itself up in atmospheric entry. The planet started getting better simply because people stopped placing impossible demands on it and began giving something back. Too, the population had been drastically, catastrophically reduced.

Besides, there was aid from the Local Group worlds that had, by that time, reached Earth via the new, non-Protoculture Pseudojaunt drive. (What beautiful starships the new technologies make possible! Earth looked like she had magical treasures in orbit around her when we arrived.) The old government had been swept away; what had replaced it was benign, democratic, and very *participatory.*

We weren't surprised that Louie Nichols and his byte-punchers, in particular, saddled up and threw themselves right into that new ferment.

I got a sense of how much things had changed when we [the Hunters] went with Scott Bernard and Marlene to catch up with old friends down in one of the Restoration Bureau's South American reserves. Young Stone Face had by then broken down and faced the fact that he loved Marlene (later, Scott even asked and got a reconciliation with Marlene Rush's parents, who'd survived on Tirol) and proposed *to her.*

But he still felt he needed a little moral support for this mission, I guess.

His old comrade Lunk had buried his bitterness, however, even though he turned his face away and was shaken by sobs when he saw Marlene. But Lunk gave Scott a sincere handshake and Marlene a heartbreakingly chaste kiss on the cheek. I'd seen old pictures of him, and Lunk had changed a lot, stomach expanded, hair thinned to a gray fringe around his bald head. He looked like a sad old simian.

Rand and Rook Bartley showed up with little Maria; there was a lot of ribbing about the success of Rand's Notes on the Run, *Rook doubting he could cut it as a Forager anymore. He did seem a little chagrined, especially since his wife still looked like she'd kept her biker edge.*

Still, it was plain that they loved each other, even if Rook wasn't happy about little Maria's preoccupation with her word processor.

Just as things became less formal, we were almost run over by a dinosaur. From what I'd heard of Annie LaBelle, I shouldn't have been surprised that she was a reckless behemoth driver.

Rick and I were looking around for guns that we weren't carrying—since nobody has any on Earth anymore—but Roy II thought that thunder lizard was just the greatest thing since crayons.

And sitting on a saddle up behind its head was Annie. It was a seismosaurus, she told us later, biggest of the herbiverous heavyweights; it sure impressed me.

With Annie was her husband, Magruder, the two of them looking—and dressed—like a new-tech Tarzan and Jane. Scott made some comment about how nicely she'd sprouted up and filled out, and Magruder seemed to accept that with great pride.

At the local Bureau HQ, Annie and Lunk filled us in on all the strides genetic engineering had made since contact with the Local Group—and especially, of course, with the Tirolians.

Even fossilized genetic models could be revived, and existing ones cloned and varied, differentiation being so important to species survival. Not only were pandas, snow leopards, and whales thriving, so were passenger pigeons, giant sloths, and woolly mammoths.

And of course, the biggest debate at that time was whether it would be immoral to bring Neanderthals back from extinction (or, to put it another way, leave them extinct). Annie and Magruder—both of whom had advanced degrees in neogenetics—were passionate about opposite sides of the argument, as ready to punch it out as they were to kiss and make up.

At any rate, Scott and Marlene's strike-force reunion turned out well, but I had my first real exposure to the fact that an aging SDF skipper wasn't exactly in demand anymore in this brave new world. I was out of phase, bereft of background data.

There were more shocks waiting for all of us.

What hit Scott and Marlene hardest, I think, was news of the death of the freedom fighter named Lancer, also known as Yellow Dancer. But something bore them up when they heard how he died flying a disaster relief mission. I think it was the insights of the Intersection, where we all saw the big picture a little more clearly.

That, plus the fact that his music lives on after him, as popular now as Minmei's. People started to talk about slipping in ringers of the two—re-creation artists—for "The Concert That Never Was." The idea was almost universally ignored. Perhaps *the slimy-souled people who came up with it would feel differently if they'd gone through the Intersection.*

The effects of that passage and its insights were pointed up electrifyingly when a few of us were flown out for a tour of a big reforestation program in Alaska. It was an especially affecting trip for Rick and me, since we weren't so far from where the Grand Cannon installation once was.

We were shown to where people worked, patiently reseeding the restored and prepared slopes with tiny firs. I didn't notice anything in particular, walking past a bent figure that seemed to be giving all its attention lovingly to what was being done. It was Dana, a few paces behind, who let out a yell.

Rick and I turned to see the Sterlings and our guide looking on in horror as Dana, hauling at the worker's faded coverall, prepared to deal him a blow to the side of the temple with the heel of her cocked-back hand. No question about it, she was out to kill.

Part of our astonishment, too, was the appearance of the worker. I have never seen such a gnarled, pitifully scarred, frightened creature in my life. He'd dropped his little tray of seedlings, and all he could do was cringe and whimper. Yet Dana, eyes bugging from her head, wasn't deterred a bit.

Rick and I were revving up, trying to get to her to stop, like cartoon characters having trouble getting into motion. Max and Miriya, who'd been looking the other way, were kind of tangled up with each other.

But there was someone else to intervene. Not that Dana was overpowered—a tough proposition at any time. Still, when Aurora's gentle hand came to rest on Dana's tensed, heel-shot one, the action froze.

"You don't want to do that. Sister—"

And with that, Aurora went up on tiptoes to whisper something into Dana's ear. The rest of us had stood rooted, and we saw Dana's hand relax as she released the man cowering in her grip. Dana looked around the reseeded slopes, the life that was coming back to a devastated wasteland, and turned away.

As Dana walked back toward our shuttle, one of the program supervisors gently got the man back to work, saying reassuring things, calling him "Alf."

I ran a check and found out about the assassination of

Milicent Edgewick and the disappearance of her familiar.
Dana's instincts were correct, and the brainwiped, hollow
wretch she'd been about to kill was Farnham, once known as
Senator Alfonse Napoleon Russo, though now he only answered to the name Alf. How he found his way into a custo-
dial rehab program for marginally functional war casualty
types, no one was able to say.

Heaven knows, Dana had good cause to execute him; all
of us did. But seeing what he'd come to in the end, we dropped
the matter. I've never presumed to ask Aurora what it was
she whispered into her sister's ear, but I imagine it was to
the effect that there'd been enough death; part of the revivi-
fying process we and the planet are undergoing has to do
with putting certain things behind us.

SDF-3's returnees scattered to all corners of the world in
those weeks. Louie Nichols and his team were quick to start
snooping into the Post-Protoculture technologies, and they
were welcomed with open arms by the Earth's top research-
ers, then castigated for their heretical approach to things.
Nothing new there.

Nevertheless, Louie & Co. became the driving force toward
this new grail called Instru-Mentality. Implants that will give every
intelligent being powers of teleportation, psychokinesis, telepathy,
and the rest would be the next logical step—a new dawn, to be
sure—but I can't help wondering if we're ready for it.

But as Cabell pointed out, no one was ready for Robotech,
either, when you come right down to it.

Anyway, the Robotech Age, with its mechamorphosis and
Protoculture, has passed away forever, and something else
must now come onstage.

The experiences of various others have been set down elsewhere, by themselves and third parties. Of the rollicking
group (Dana, Sean, Marie, Jack, Karen, and several more)
who became the Crazy Eights Exploration and Development
Co., Unlimited, much has already been written—a good deal
of it on indictments. And why they took on Lunk as their head
wrench wrangler and mojo hand, I cannot guess—but it's
probably one of their few sources of good karma.

Still, they're young and carefree, and they keep claiming they've got the galaxy by the bustle.

If you've been lucky enough to get a seat at Bowie Grant's Blue Harp Lounge to hear Musica and Allegra sing and play along with him or have caught them on tour, you know how well they're doing and why.

One of the tenser moments occurred as Angelo Dante set off to introduce Gnea to his parents. He was so nervous that she offered to change into more conservative Earth garb (and a lot of us were all set to pitch in), but Angie said no; quite an independent move for him. We all heaved a sigh of relief when they fell in love with her.

The visit was rather hasty, though, since Gnea was being rushed back to New Praxis (Optera) by special courier ship—including the penalty weight of the fruitcake from Angie's folks—to brief Bela on all that had happened—

—and, of course, to help take care of all those little Invid they've got running around once more.

Jean Grant once spoke of pieces of the puzzle fitting together, and there's probably no more prominent example of that than New Praxis.

For some reason the Regis didn't suffer the delay in time that we did, and when the altered Shapings permitted her/his Race to return to spacetime, I suppose it's no surprise, they came full circle—and, from what we can tell, took on the original state in which Zor found them.

The Second Gen Flowers of Life bloom there now, with hordes of little Pollinators to make sure they bloom. (Dana keeps insisting that one in particular is hers and hers alone, and the critter seems to feel the same way.) Anyhow, everybody's happy the Pollinators are sacred beasts on New Praxis these days, protected by the brawny arms of warrior women, because the galaxy has had enough of Protoculture.

Riding herd on all this is a graying Bela, with Gnea taking up the reins bit by bit. And their fighters, women who've lost a world, now posting guard over creatures whose only desire is to be left alone: there's a higher symmetry to that.

Because, surely, this is the fate we all felt the Regis cry out for back there at the Intersection. We don't probe into the

Invid hive life, but I suspect She lives there someplace inside Optera, more happily now than at any time since Zor came.

I do not ask, though, for anyone to pursue these questions.

And yet there come reports, fourth- and fifthhand, that a new entity is being brought to life down there in the hive. From what little the intel officers—kept conscientiously at bay on the surface—can tell, it is a male who will have the capacity to erase or perhaps refurbish certain chemical/energy memory systems.

A new and better Regent?

On another front, Gnea promised to build quarters in Zanshar just for Angie's parents so that they can visit whenever they please. And feel guilty about not being there. I suspect Gnea's figuring on a few daughters to keep Angie busy and perhaps give him a new perspective on women.

The Sentinels see each other infrequently now, not because we're sedentary but rather because so much more is happening everywhere. The Zentraedi, of course, are based on Fantoma but can be found anywhere heavy-g operations are going on, especially in monopole ore mining. Their numbers increase at a far, far slower rate than in the days of cloning, but from what I hear, they still favor their new—timeless—method of reproducing.

The survivors are just starting to live—all of us.

Drannin is looking more and more like Breetai every day. He still shows those glowing eyes, though, as do all the SDF-3 children. Their psi-abilities and other exceptional attributes of strength, speed, and dexterity continue to increase. They can still giggle, but at other times they seem to have their glowing eyes fixed on some far horizon the rest of us can't see.

Does the name "Darwin" strike a bell?

The human race—and others—are ready for a new and different kind of leap across the stars, a peaceful one this time, and these glow-eyed children of ours are proof.

That was part of the reason we went forth, wasn't it? To find out what we could ultimately become? In any case, Roy II forgets to brush his teeth if Rick or I don't remind him, even if he can argue spacetime algorithms with Louie Nich-

ols. And bedtime is still bedtime; the kid gets a swat on the landing gear if he's being too muley.

Keeps us all humble.

I suppose I was looking the other way, but it seemed like I was the only one surprised when Aurora ran for Interworld Council and became the youngest representative-elect ever. She's not maturing at her accelerated rate anymore, but no one appears to care.

Max and Miriya are Earth's ambassadors to Tirol/Fantoma, of course, so they get to see Aurora all the time.

Which sounds good to an old lady whose son and husband seem to spend most of their hours in that damned old Fokker. Somehow, the little Dr. 1 triplane made it through the whole newspace dustup, stowed away down there in a hold in SDF-3. Roy-my-darling-boy handed Rick the wrenches and whatnot, and Rick put some kind of power plant into that kite that makes it do things Manfred von Richthofen could only dream about.

They're up in it most of their waking hours, as Roy feasts on the wonders of Earth. I'm invited along whenever I want to go (and intrude upon the male bonding? Thanks, Rick!), but my editor keeps yelling about this deadline.

We didn't come home to paradise; there are still crises and suffering and conflict, but it's a very different world, a different galaxy, from the one we left when we entered newspace.

Louie Nichols once confided to me that he thought the Shapings had come to an end, that a certain cycle of downfall, redemption, and renewal had played out to its finish, leaving us to make our own Shapings from now on.

I like the sound of it.

Looking back over this manuscript, I see there's no way I can fit in every detail.

Such as: that boisterous exploratory tour Exedore and Cabell took, the pink-haired Lantas mother-henning them, here on Earth, and Cabell's newfound dotty passion for classic rock music (who can explain the Presley fixation?).

Or the story of how the Haydonites—those saved from the wreckage of their world—have become a sort of wandering

interstellar Peace Corps. Much of their effort went into help-
ing Earth and New Praxis rebuild.

The people at New Random House are just going to have
to understand that I can't write CLOSE-FILE to this one;
among other things, work on SDF-4 is nearing completion.

Vince Grant, Crysta, and Baldan will be here any minute
to take me upstairs for another inspection tour. Soon we'll
know whether the saga of Protoculture made itself felt in the
Andromeda Galaxy or if things there are a new story entirely.

When I joined the service, no woman had ever commanded
a spacecraft-of-the-line. Through luck and the turn of events
and a bit of merit, I've commanded the greatest vessels Earth
ever put into space. Having achieved that, I'm not ready to
hand it over yet.

Check back with me in another ten years or so.

Rick made me watch Roy Fokker's favorite old-time movie,
Things to Come, *and that "Which shall it be?" speech at
the end never fails to make the two of us tear up a bit. But
at least now we know the answer to the question posed by
Raymond Massey, and it is one worthy of the human race.*

Still, I can't get it out of my mind that one part of this
story hasn't been finished and, it seems, never will be. At
least not in my lifetime.

. . . but her songs play on after her. And the universe lis-
tens . . .

The Flowers grew best up on the hill near where the
SDF-3 fold drive casing sat.

Minmei liked going up there to sit and think and to sing
into the dark spaces cast by the casing's mighty shadow, especially now that her time was drawing near.

The second bubble in newspace, shielded from the in-
Human forces of Haydon's new natural laws, was very different from that in which the Elders passed their eons.
Perhaps some of the materials came from the sphere ships;
in any event, Minmei and Rem reigned now over a worldlet
encompassing a small island and a tiny sea.

They wandered it at their pleasure. Even though the life-
forms there were alien, there was nothing to hamper them on

the land or menace them in the sea; the new dominion was benign.

Why Haydon had chosen to leave the drives there on the hilltop, they were not sure; some godly whim, perhaps.

They had no reason to complain, though, as they had no reason to complain of the gentle climate or the passage of the warm sun across the seemingly infinite sky. At night the stars, nebulas, comets, and frequent meteors entertained them, though they suspected that the show was all illusion.

Rem examined the Flowers of Life that grew around the silent drives and pronounced them harmless, pollinated; soon they would bear fruit.

Every now and then, at night, they could hear the yips of Pollinators playing around on the hillsides, but the little beasts took fright and fled when they heard Rem and Minmei coming. She took no offense and knew no despair; she had all the time in the world to win their confidence.

Rem was sitting in thought, off at the end of the point, watching waves break on the reef. He often did that, and she let him.

He had built a simple, complete, comfortable life for them both, using their world's resources and the tools and materials that the invisible Haydon had provided—had left waiting against their first moment of reawakening. She loved Rem's company but did not begrudge him his solitude.

And she valued her own. Minmei sang to the little life in her womb, sang all the songs she knew. The songs would become a part of the being within.

The songs would become a part of everything he did or fashioned.

And in the end Minmei's songs and voice would become a part of the Protoculture itself—the *key* to it.

Her glimpse of the Intersection and the inevitable nature of the Shapings' cycle had imbued in Minmei a sense of acceptance.

Even heredity conspired. Rem's genetic structure had been altered from that of the original Zor, but now, in joining with hers, it would produce the man who would change the universe. Not a duplicate or clone but Zor himself.

Minmei did not understand by what process her baby would become that man, but Rem seemed certain of it and the inevitability of it. *Haydon*, he would say, and then he would go down to the sea to be by himself for a while.

Minmei turned to the long shadow cast by the drives and sang a note. Something moved iridescently in the shadows far out beyond her worldlet's atmosphere. It was enormous, something felt rather than seen.

Minmei knew what Rem was thinking: of the suffering and strife that would begin when Zor grew to manhood. But she herself was not so sure. The Shapings had fallen away, and perhaps that meant that Reshapings could bring things to a better resolution.

As she sat plucking idly at the petals of a Flower of Life, a sudden thought struck her. *A woman can have more than one child.*

She heard a distant hail; Rem was trotting along far below, coming up the beach to help her down the steep hillside trail.

Minmei uttered another note into the darkness; there seemed to sit, for an instant, an Optera undefiled by Masters' wars or Sentinels' counterattacks. And beyond it was a galaxy at peace with itself.

Waiting for her child. Bit by bit, she was getting them perfect. Out in the vastness, working as an artisan to shape her vision, the Awareness of Haydon, left behind by Him to carry out this specific function, waited patiently to form a new and more perfect Creation, in harmony with her song.

She did not know yet whether this cosmos she was shaping would replace the one she had known or stand as an alternative. She did not know if it would be the one into which her son would enter.

But a woman can have more than one child.

Minmei let the note die away, and the darkness came forward again, to conceal her work.

She went to sit on a rock, cooled by the sea breeze, and wait. As she sat, she sang.

THE END

Published by New Random House
2156 (Earth actual)

ROBOTECH CHRONOLOGICAL SUMMARY

1171 Aeon Lanack	Zor is born on Tirol.
1256–1490 A.L.	Quadrant exploration by the Tiresian technovoyager ship *Azstraph*—the "Venture."
1520 A.L.	The *Azstraph* enters the Tzuptum system and inserts itself into orbit around Optera. Zor encounters the Flower of Life, makes contact with the Invid, and seduces the secrets of the Flower from the Queen-Mother, the Regis.
1697 A.L.	The *Azstraph* returns to Tirol. Zor begins to experiment with the Flower specimens he has brought with him from Optera.
1755–1836 A.L.	Zor conjures Protoculture from the Flower and eventually falls victim to the Compulsion placed upon him by the Tiresian Council of Elders. Origin of the Cult of the Three-in-One and ascendancy of the Robotech Masters. Fall of the Royal Hall, as the period known as the Great Transition commences.
1920 A.L.	–16 Aeon "Robotech" Development of the spacefold drive. Creation of Tirol's clone population and neural reprogramming of the Zentraedi miner giants.
88 A.R.	The razing of Optera by the Zentraedi.

157–500 A.R.	Consolidation of the empire of the Robotech Masters. The Invid, after a burst of monocellular reproduction, declare war on the Robotech Masters.
566 A.R.	Zor's voyages deliver him to Haydon IV, where he has a profound encounter with the planetoid's artificial sentience, the Awareness.
	Zor designs and builds the starship that will come to be called SDF-1, and—backed by a group of loyal Zentraedi—begins his "quiet rebellion" against the Masters.
	Zentraedi commander in chief Dolza forms an uneasy alliance with Zor, who has by now become hopelessly addicted to the dried leaves of the Flower.
580–640 A.R.	Zor's clandestine seeding attempts take him to Peryton, Karbarra, Praxis, Garuda, and Spheris.
671 A.R.	Zor steals the single extant Protoculture matrix from Tiresia and conceals it within the spacefold drives of the SDF-1. The fortress, with its skeleton crew of loyal Zentraedi, is folded from Tirol's corner of the galaxy.
1999 (Earth actual)	An alien spaceship crash-lands on Earth, effectively ending almost a decade of Global Civil War. Originally called "The Visitor," the ship is dubbed Super Dimensional Fortress I—the SDF-1.
	Dr. Emil Lang, after an initial recon of the ship (in the company of Roy Fokker, Henry Gloval, T. R. Edwards, and others), begins to unravel the secrets of the extraterrestrial science known as Robotech.

Macross Island becomes the focal point of Robotechnology, and restoration commences on the SDF-1.

In another part of the galaxy, Zor is killed by Invid soldiers during a Flower of Life seeding attempt. The Zentraedi Breetai is wounded during the same raid. Commander in chief Dolza orders Commander Reno to return Zor's body to the Robotech Masters on Tirol.

Instellar war with the Invid, whose homeworld, Optera, has been defoliated by the Zentraedi, continues to chip away at the fringes of the Masters' galactic empire.

2002   Destruction of Mars Base Sara. Lisa Hayes's fiancé, Karl Riber, is killed. Lisa turns 17.

Development of the reconfigurable Veritech Fighter.

On Tirol, Cabell "creates" Rem by cloning tissue from Zor. The Masters, too, have their way with Zor's body, cloning tissue for their own purposes and extracting from the scientist's residual cellular memories a vision of Earth—destination of the fortress and Protoculture matrix he has stolen and spirited from their grasp.

2003–08   Rise of the United Earth Defense Council under the leadership of Senator Russo, Admiral Hayes, T. R. Edwards, and others.

Roy Fokker and Claudia Grant become fast friends.

Lisa Hayes is assigned to the SDF-1 project on Macross, under the command of Captain Henry Gloval.

Tommy Luan is elected mayor of Macross City.

2009   On the SDF-1's launch day, the Zentraedi (after a ten-year search for Zor's fortress and the missing Protoculture matrix) appear and lay siege to Macross Island. The fortress makes an accidental hyperspace jump to Pluto, carrying the island and its population of 75,000 along with it. 15-year-old Lynn-Minmei and 19-year-old Rick Hunter are caught up in the space-fold.

Lisa Hayes turns 24.

2009–11   The SDF-1 battles its way back to Earth with Macross City rebuilt inside its massive holds.

Rick Hunter joins the RDF and earns the rank of lieutenant, with Ben Dixon and Max Sterling assigned to his VT squadron.

The Battle at Saturn's Rings.

Lynn-Minmei is voted "Miss Macross."

Breetai calls up the Botoru Battalion, led by the notorious Khyron the Backstabber.

The Battle at Mars Base Sara.

Rick, Lisa, Max, and Ben are captured by Breetai and interrogated by the Zentraedi commander in chief, Dolza.

The Earth forces learn of the term "Protoculture" for the first time.

Three "micronized" Zentraedi spies—Rico, Konda, and Bron—are successfully inserted into the SDF-1.

The SDF-1 lands on Earth.

2012   Lynn-Minmei is reunited with her cousin, Lynn-Kyle.

Rick Hunter is seriously wounded during a Zentraedi attack on the fortress.

Roy Fokker is killed during a raid led by Khyron.

After almost six months on Earth, the SDF-1 is ordered to leave by the leaders of the UEDC.

Ben Dixon is killed.

Little White Dragon is aired.

The Minmei Cult has its beginnings aboard the flagship of the Zentraedi fleet.

Lynn-Kyle founds a peace movement aboard the SDF-1.

Asylum is granted to the three Zentraedi spies.

Max Sterling weds former Zentraedi Quadrono ace Miriya Parino.

Exedore arrives aboard the SDF-1 for peace talks.

The Zentraedi armada appears in Earth-space and lays waste to much of the planet.

At Alaska Base, the Grand Cannon is destroyed and Admiral Hayes is killed. T. R. Edwards survives and vows to avenge himself on Rick and Lisa.

The SDF-1, with an assist from Lynn-Minmei's voice, defeats Dolza's armada of five million ships and returns to a ravaged Earth.

A period of reconstruction begins, with humans and Zentraedi working side by side.

The Robotech Masters lose confidence in their race of warrior clones and begin a mass pilgrimage through interstellar space to Earth to recapture Zor's Protoculture matrix. Zor Prime comes of age.

2013   Dana Sterling and Bowie Grant (son of Claudia Grant's brother, Vince) are born.

The factory satellite is captured from Commander Reno and folded to Earthspace.

Dr. Lang and Professor Lazlo Zand begin work on a secret project involving artificial intelligence. Zand takes particular interest in the infant Dana after undergoing a Protoculture mindboost.

2014   Khyron makes a surprise appearance and takes Minmei and Lynn-Kyle hostage.

The destruction of New Macross, the SDFs 1 and 2, along with Khyron's forces. Henry Gloval, Claudia Grant, Sammie Porter, Vanessa Leeds, and Kim Young are among the many casualties. The remains of the three ships are buried under tons of earthen debris dredged up from Lake Gloval.

2015–17   Zentraedi Malcontent Uprisings in the Southlands Control Zone (South America). Jonathan Wolff comes to the attention of Commander Max Sterling.

The Robotech Expeditionary Force is formed for the express purpose of journeying to Tirol to sue for peace with the Robotech Masters. Aboard the factory satellite, work commences on the SDF-3.

Rise of Monument City and Anatole Leonard's Army of the Southern Cross.

Lynn-Minmei takes on a singing partner, the android Janice Em, at Emil Lang's urging.

The Invid complete their conquest of Garuda, Praxis, Karbarra, and Spheris.

2020

Rick Hunter and Lisa Hayes wed aboard the factory satellite. Dana and Bowie are given over to the care of Rolf and Laura Emerson.

The SDF-3 is launched. Minmei and Janice Em are caught up in the spacefold.

Rick turns 29; Lisa, 34; Dana and Bowie, 7. Scott Bernard, Lang's godson from the recently completed Mars Base, turns 11.

2025
(Earth actual)

The Invid Regent takes Tirol. Sickened by his blood lust, the Regis leaves Optera for Praxis to carry on her Genesis Pit experiments.

The Robotech Expeditionary Force arrives in Fantomaspace and engages the Invid; the fortress's spacefold generators are damaged. (The REF is unaware that the fold has taken five Earth-years and believes the date to be 2020.) T. R. Edwards and his Ghost Squadron capture the living computer the Regent has left behind in Tiresia's Royal Hall. Tiresians Cabell and Rem inform the Plenipotentiary Council that the Robotech Masters are on their way to Earth.

The Zentraedi contingent of the REF agree to be returned to full size so that they can mine Fantoma for monopole ore to fuel a new fleet of warships.

The Sentinels—composed of Praxians, Garudans, Karbarrans, Haydonites, Spherisians, and Perytonians—are formed to liberate planets recently conquered and occupied by the Invid horde. The Hunters, Grants, Sterlings, and others leave Fantomaspace aboard the *Farrago*.

On Earth, Senator Wyatt "Patty" Moran and the apparat of the Army of the Southern Cross consolidate their power and take control of the Supreme Council.

Dana and Bowie grow up under the care of the Emersons.

2026
(Earth actual)

Karbarra is liberated. Tesla and Burak form a curious partnership. The Sentinels' ship is destroyed, and the Ground Military Unit is stranded on Praxis shortly after the Regis's leavetaking for Haydon IV. Praxis explodes. Death of Baldan I.

T. R. Edwards holds secret talks with the Regent and begins a personal campaign to capture Lynn-Minmei.

Wolff and Janice Em return to Tirol. The Invid Tesla murders a simulagent sent to Tirol by the Regent.

T. R. Edwards begins to hold sway over the REF's Plenipotentiary Council. Wolff is accused of murder and piracy. Control of the Fantoma mining operations passes to Edwards.

Garuda is liberated. Rick, Lisa, Rem, and Karen Penn suffer the nearly fatal effects of the planet's atmosphere.

Baldan II is "shaped" by Teal.

The Zentraedi leave Tirolspace with the monopole ore needed for the fleet's warships.

2027
(Earth actual)

The Sentinels arrive on Haydon IV shortly after the Regis's departure and "surrender" themselves to the occupying Invid troops. Rem learns that he is actually a clone of Zor. Janice Em reveals herself to be an android. Sarna is killed.

The enigmatic Haydon becomes a source of interest to Lang and others.

A prototype ship under the command of Major Carpenter leaves Tirol for Earth.

Edwards loses his grip on the Council after troops sent out to hunt down the Zentraedi side with them instead. Wolff, Breetai, and Grant return to Tirol and clear the Sentinels of all charges.

Haydon IV and Spheris are liberated. Tesla leaves the *Ark Angel* for Optera to have it out with the Regent.

Aurora is born to Miriya Sterling on Haydon IV.

Edwards and his Ghost Riders flee Tirol for Optera, taking Lynn-Minmei and the awakened Invid living computer from Tiresia with them.

2028
(Earth actual)

Jonathan Wolff leaves for Earth.

Edwards arrives on Optera. Tesla is chased off; Breetai and the Regent die together.

Exedore arrives on Haydon IV with the Council's peace proposal for the Regent.

The Sentinels move against Peryton. Tesla and Burak sacrifice themselves to end the planet's curse.

2029
(Earth actual)

The battle for Optera. Edwards, Arla-non, Teal, and Janice Em die.

Dr. Lang makes a series of shattering discoveries about the spacefold generators his teams have used in Carpenter and Wolff's ships.

Exedore makes a startling discovery involving Zor and the historical Haydon.

Ark Angel begins a slow return to Tirol.

Breetai's son, Drannin, is born to the Zentraedi Kazianna Hesh.

2030
(Earth actual)

Roy Hunter is born in Tiresia. The REF and Karbarrans begin work on the main fleet ships. Lang's Robotech teams perfect an integrated system of body armor and reconfigurable cycles known as Cyclones.

2031
(Earth actual)

Dana Sterling and Bowie Grant turn 18, graduate from the Academy, and are assigned to the 15th Alpha Tactical Armored Corps, which includes Sean Phillips, Angelo Dante, and Louie Nichols.

The Robotech Masters arrive in Earthspace, and the Second Robotech War begins.

Major Carpenter's ship returns from Tirol.

Zor Prime is introduced to the 15th ATAC.

2032
(Earth actual)

End of the Second Robotech War. Zor Prime's attempt at destroying the Masters' flagship results in the loosing of the Flowers of Life from the Protoculture matrix concealed within the spacefold drives of the buried SDF-1; spores cover the planet, and the Flower takes root, alerting the Regis's sensor nebula.

The Invid "disappear" from Tirol's corner of the galaxy. It is assumed that the Regis has begun her move against Earth.

The Mars Group leaves Tirol with 18-year-old Scott Bernard aboard.

Lazlo Zand dies.

Jonathan Wolff's ship returns to Earth. An anti-Invid underground is established before the Regis arrives. Dana commandeers Wolff's ship after the drives are retrofitted with a device perfected by former 15th ATAC whiz kid Louie Nichols.

The Robotech factory satellite returns to Earthspace.

Optera is fully seeded with the Flowers of Life and given over to the homeless Praxians, who rename the planet New Praxis. The Flowers become the crop for a new Protoculture matrix created by Rem, who has managed to tap some of his progenitor's—Zor's—memories.

Max, Miriya, and Aurora Sterling arrive on Tirol from Haydon IV.

2033 (Earth actual)	The Invid Regis arrives on Earth. Her newly hatched army of soldiers and mecha destroys the factory satellite and easily defeats Earth's depleted defenses. Hives and farms are set up worldwide, and some Terran captives are forced to work in labor camps, harvesting Flowers and processing nutrient for use in the Regis's terror weapons and battlecraft.
	Arrival of Dana Sterling on Tirol. With her are Bowie Grant, Sean Phillips, Angelo Dante, Musica and Allegra, and many of the Masters' clones.
	Shadow Fighters and neutron "S" missiles are developed by the REF for use in the assault against Earth. Nearly instantaneous spacefold becomes a reality for the main-fleet ships.
2034 (Earth actual)	Arrival and defeat of the Mars Attack Group sent by the REF.

Scott Bernard and his ragtag band of freedom fighters—Rook, Rand, Lancer, Lunk, and Annie—begin a journey toward the Regis's central hive complex, known as Reflex Point.

Marlene, Sera, and Corg are birthed by the Regis.

2035
(Earth actual)

The Jupiter attack wing arrives in Earthspace. Photojournalist Sue Graham dies on Earth.

The REF main-fleet ships are folded from Tirol to Earth. The Regis and her children take leave of the planet in the form of a phoenix of mindstuff, annihilating the returning ships in the process and ending the Third Robotech War.

On Haydon IV, Veidt and Exedore are present at the reawakening of the planet's artificial sentience, the Awareness. (Max and his family are also on-planet. Cabell is on Tirol.)

The SDF-3 fails to remanifest in Earthspace. Rick turns 40 (or 45 by chronological reckoning); Lisa turns 45 (or 50).

Aboard the *Ark Angel*, which has been spared the fate of the rest of the main-fleet ships, Scott Bernard and Vince and Jean Grant commence a search for the missing fortress.

ABOUT THE AUTHOR

Jack McKinney has been a psychiatric aide, fusion-rock guitarist and session man, worldwide wilderness guide, and "consultant" to the U.S. Military in Southeast Asia (although they had to draft him for that).

His numerous other works of mainstream and science fiction—novels, radio, and television scripts—have been written under various pseudonyms.

He resides in Ubud, on the Indonesian island of Bali.

Portions of *The End of the Circle* were written in Lamu, Kenya, and Katmandu.

(PUBLISHER'S NOTE: While the above biography is accurate, it is actually a composite bio of two authors who agreed to merge minds and identities, and reflect the influence of various friends and advisers for the Robotech series. Now, with the completion of the saga, they are separate entities once more. This is not, however, to suggest that Jack McKinney will disappear. In fact, a new project is already in the works.)